Dancing Priest

By Glynn Young

www.dunrobin.us

Permission to quote in critical reviews with citation:
Dancing Priest
By Glynn Young

ISBN 978-0-9832363-5-1

Printed in the United States by Dunrobin Publishing

www.dunrobin.us

For Janet

Acknowledgements

I don't know if it takes a whole village to publish a book, but a lot of people helped make it happen.

Mark Sutherland walked up to me one day and said, "When are you going to let me publish your book?"

Adam Blumer (http://blumereditorial.com/) did an extraordinary job of editing – thorough, meticulous, and thoughtful (and he taught me to put the second comma back in a series of three – book style versus Associated Press style that had been branded on my brain for four decades).

Claire Burge took several photographs, any one of which could have been the cover.

Jeremiah Langner did a wonderful job designing the cover.

My friends at The High Calling, led by Marcus Goodyear and L.L. Barkat, offered encouragement, prayer and conversation.

Cody, our Cavalier King Charles Spaniel who died at 14 last year, slept on my feet through numerous writings, drafts and rewritings.

My family – Travis and Stephanie, Andrew and grandson Cameron (and grandchild on the way) – are an ongoing blessing.

And this never would have happened without Janet, the trophy wife I married when I was 21 and the trophy wife I'm still married to.

Glynn Young

Dancing Priest

Part I

Edinburgh

DANCING PRIEST

Chapter 1

"You know what'll happen? We'll get an American."

"Tommy."

"That's precisely what'll happen. An American doing a study abroad so he can go back and tell his friends how odd the Scots are. Or worse, he'll call us British."

"Tommy, their dormitory burned down. Almost four hundred students have no place to live. Perhaps one hundred are American."

"The university can sort it out. They don't need us. And we need quiet. I've got major projects due this term. And you've got a thesis, if I recall."

Michael grinned. "You know you're going to give in."

The fire had occurred right as the new term was starting, and the chancellor had made a plea for help with temporary housing. Friends since childhood, Michael and Tommy shared a room in a senior dorm. Tommy McFarland, five foot ten with curly, red hair, had a swimmer's build, while Michael Kent, five foot eleven, had black hair and the build of a cyclist—slender but with distinctively muscled calves. To each other, they were "Tomahawk" and "English."

The room was large, in one of the university's recently renovated dormitories. Designed as a three-person flat with its own bath, the rooms were whitewashed plaster and stone with paneled wainscoting and door frames. They could easily accommodate a third roommate.

The chancellor's plea had been posted on walls and notice boards, slipped under doors, and e-mailed to student accounts.

"Or we'll get one of those people who like to cook their meals in their room, and dogs and cats start disappearing, and everything smells like some foreign spice."

Michael laughed. "You're a case. I'm telling the housemaster that we'll take one on."

"You don't see if I'm right. You'll regret this, English. Trust me."

The next morning, Michael caught up with Tommy at ExpressoYourself, the Scot-owned coffee shop Tommy insisted was better than Starbucks. Michael preferred Starbucks because, he pointed out with ample justification, the coffee tasted better.

"We have a roommate," Michael said.

"American, right?"

"Yes, he's American. Starting his third year. And he's in a study-abroad program. The housemaster told me a few minutes ago."

"I knew it," Tommy groaned, putting his head in his hands. "We'll get nothing but complaints about the weather and that there are only four choices for television." His head shot up. "Come on. He's likely to have already moved his things into my area." He hurried to the door.

"He's not likely to have many things to move in, Tomahawk," Michael called in his wake. "They burned up, remember?"

After the fire, what David Hughes possessed was exactly one backpack, a laptop, and books for three of his five classes. Sandy haired, standing about five foot nine, he looked like an American, or at least how Europeans expected Americans to look. Both Michael and Tommy could see the apprehension in his eyes.

"It's great of you guys to take me in. I know this is a big hassle."

"We're glad we had the room, David," Michael said.

"You don't cook, do you?" said Tommy.

"No," David said. "Is that important?"

"Only to a Neanderthal like the Tomahawk here," Michael said. "Don't worry about it. And we call him Tomahawk because it describes his personality perfectly."

Tommy glared at Michael. "And we call him English because that's where he came from, and you never trust anyone from down there."

"First, some introductions," Michael said. "I'm Michael Kent. Fifth and final year theology. University Cycling Team."

"He's omitted a point or two," said Tommy, "like all of his fatal character flaws, of which there are a considerable number—it's genetic with the English. And that he's training right now in the hopes he gets a shot at the British Olympic Cycling Team for the Games next summer, which is doubtful given how parochial and narrow minded the English are."

"And that," Michael said, pointing to Tommy, "is one Thomas McFarland, professional cretin. Fifth and final year architecture. Swim team. Engaged to one Ellen Grant, senior in education, with official plans to marry after graduation in May. She's incredibly decent and remarkably good-looking, and we've no idea what she possibly sees in the Tomahawk here."

"She knows Scot quality," Tommy snorted, "and she knows you never trust the English."

"You guys seem to have known each other a long time," David said.

"We grew up together," Michael said.

"I came to his rescue when he was being bullied in grammar school," Tommy added.

"Some rescue," Michael said. "We both ended up with black eyes. But we've been best friends ever since, much to my occasional amusement and perpetual embarrassment. Tommy's right, I must have a fatal character flaw to have put up with him for so long. So, David, how did you end up at Edinburgh?"

"David Hughes," he said. "Native of Denver, Colorado. Now living in California. University of California at Los Angeles. Brother to a twin sister with an older brother who's just finished his medical residency in Denver. Major is British history, specifically eighteenth century Scotland. My sister, Sarah, is here, too, although I'm not quite sure why. She's an art major. She wants to be an artist, maybe do something with art direction in movies. She also attends UCLA. I'd been planning this since last year, and she threw her application in at the last minute. We both got accepted."

"First, California," said Tommy, "there is no British history. There is, however, a history of English tyranny, which to Scotland's great shame continues up to the present moment."

"Tomahawk here is a Scot nationalist, which I'm sure is a huge surprise," Michael said. "And he swims better than most fish. So, David, what are you doing for clothes?"

"Wearing what I have on," he answered. "Everything burned in the fire. When the fire alarms sounded, I threw on some clothes, grabbed my backpack, and ran. I've got classes this afternoon and a dinner with my sister and a faculty member tonight. Do you know where I can find a clothing store?"

"Here," Tommy said, walking to his closet. "You're about my size. You can wear one of my shirts."

"We'll help you find a shop tomorrow," Michael said. "And help yourself to my ties. Although you might prefer to look at Tomahawk's tie collection. He's known for being something of a fashion dandy."

"Which," said Tommy, "is infinitely preferable to the spandex and polyester that comprise some ninety-four percent of English's wardrobe and which he tends to wear twenty-four hours a day, including as pajamas? He claims it's because of the cycling team, but I suspect there's something perverted going on."

Chapter 2

And spandex cycling pants and a polyester jersey were exactly what Michael wore that afternoon to his class, Medieval Church Art. Bike practice was right after, with barely enough time after practice to change clothes for his job as a waiter at the faculty club.

The secular academicians of the university found the fact hard to fathom, but Medieval Church Art was one of the most popular courses at Edinburgh, taught by an eccentric Irishman (Tommy claimed *eccentric* and *Irishman* were redundant when used in the same sentence). Dr. Seamus Fitzhugh breathed fire and passion into what should have been deadly dull, even for art majors. But even business and science majors juggled schedules to take the class, all for the opportunity to experience grand teaching. For Michael, the course was an approved elective, but for his MA divinity (honours) degree, with a focus on evangelism and world missions, it was still something of a stretch. But he was looking forward to the course; this was the first class of the term.

He parked his bike at the back of the crowded lecture room and found a seat. All seventy-five places in the class had been filled. At the end of his row, a teaching assistant was handing out what looked like a syllabus ("also available online," a voice at the front was saying). As Michael passed the stack to the student next to him, he saw her.

She was sitting two rows down the amphitheater-like lecture hall and four seats to his right. Soft brown hair with blond highlights, tied in a ponytail. A white, starched blouse like a man's dress shirt. Jeans. Slender almost to the point of thinness. High cheekbones. Light makeup.

She's beautiful. Who is she? She must be new; I've never seen her before. His heart pounded. He felt his ears become hot. He looked at the syllabus in front of him but couldn't see anything. He looked up again. She was still there. This wasn't his imagination. She was real, the most beautiful creature he'd ever seen. No one else seemed aware of her. Everyone, including her, was focused on Dr. Fitzhugh.

He knew, almost as if a voice had spoken to him, that this young woman had been created for him, and he for her. He realized this with utter comprehension and clarity.

The certainty in his mind startled him. Michael had no doubt as to the truth of the thought. He looked around, but no one else was reacting. His throat was dry, his heart still pounding.

She is the one.

He didn't hear one word of what the famous Dr. Fitzhugh said that day.

As class ended, he grabbed his bike, looking round to catch sight of her. He bumped his way through the crowd in the class hallway, oblivious to the choice responses to his rudeness.

He caught up with her outside.

"Excuse me," he said.

"Yes?" she said, turning toward him.

Her voice is music. "I saw you in class," he said.

"Yes?"

"I wanted to introduce myself."

She waited.

"I'm a fifth-year theology student, and I was, well, wondering if you might like to have a coffee sometime." *She's American.*

"No."

"No?" he asked.

She shook her head. "No. Although the theology angle is original."

"Original?" Michael felt like he was missing something.

"Yes. As a pickup line. It's my fourth one today, and it's certainly the most unusual."

"Wait, it's not, a — "

"Look, I'm sure you're very nice. Everyone here is very nice. And every male here seems to think he's God's gift to women, especially American women. I don't know what you think we are, but I'm not interested. Not now. Not ever. So buzz off." She turned and walked away.

Except she didn't say *buzz*. She yelled the more graphic Anglo-Saxon word. Michael blushed.

Hearing scattered applause, he looked around and realized they had drawn a small crowd. "I think her meaning's pretty plain, mate," one student said. Several laughed.

Red faced, Michael got on his bike and headed for practice, perplexed but still certain.

She stopped. She knew she'd been colossally rude. But this was the fourth time today. *They assume that American girls are easy hits.*

But she *had* gone too far. She turned to look for him but caught only a glimpse as he pedaled away. *I'll apologize when class meets on Tuesday, even if it means I have to have coffee with him.* But she felt uncomfortable, knowing she'd done something wrong and would have to wait days to set it right.

At least this one was good-looking.

David met his sister at her dorm, and they walked together to dinner with a faculty member, a friend of their father's.

"Tommy and Michael are great, Sarah," he said, "except Michael calls Tommy 'Tomahawk' because of his personality, and Tommy calls Michael 'English' because Michael's from England, although he sounds like a Scot to me. Tommy's already named me California."

"I'm just glad this worked out," Sarah said.

"Talk about a relief. And they didn't have to take in a roommate because they're both fifth year and upperclassmen are exempt from a lot of the rules and programs. But they have a three-man room, and there's plenty of space. Another night on the floor of the Student Center would've been a pain. I can't wait for you to meet them. Tommy's on the swim team and Michael's a cyclist.

He's training to try to get on the Olympic team for the Games next summer. Isn't that wild?"

"They sound great—and it sounds like you landed on your feet, as usual. You probably could've ended up with all sorts of strange roommates."

Quentin Manning, professor of economics, enjoyed teaching at university. He taught subjects that interested him, he did research, and he'd authored three books on innovative ways to employ venture capital that fascinated American executives.

Which is how he came to be a consultant for Seth Hughes of Los Angeles. Hughes, a venture capitalist, avoided information technology start-ups ("Got burned badly, Manning, in that bubble of the late '90s") and had a marked preference for biotechnology firms.

Hughes, with vague disappointment but general acceptance as if this had been a battle fought many times, had told him last year that his son, David, was planning to spend a study year abroad in Edinburgh. Hughes seemed to be apologizing for David, who was studying Celtic and Scottish history, and wondered, could Manning look out for him?

Which Manning was certainly glad to do, especially for a client who paid as well and regularly as Seth Hughes. The only wrinkle had come in early May, when Hughes called for his help to shoehorn Hughes's daughter into the university and into Seamus Fitzhugh's class on Medieval Church Art. And Manning had managed to pull off the request. It had been relatively easy to get her late application reviewed and accepted but considerably more difficult to get her into the class. Yet Manning had done it.

So here he was, sitting in the faculty club with David and Sarah Hughes this Thursday evening, planning to be welcoming, kind, and genial. They were attractive young people, like so many American students. But he was surprised in just the short conversation so far to find that young David was, as Manning instantly recognized, a classic academic. His father had probably been hoping for a business entrepreneur and got a Celtic historian instead. *And Sarah Hughes is a most attractive young woman with a very strong character. No nonsense here, from either of them. They both have more of their father in them than Seth Hughes probably realizes.*

The two young people sat across from him. Their waiter came up, and Manning saw Sarah's face flush.

David jumped up. "Michael! I didn't know you worked here. This is Dr. Manning, a friend of my father's. And this is my sister, Sarah."

Manning smiled. "Michael. How good to see you. How are Iain and Iris? I haven't seen them in two months or more."

Michael was mortified. He'd seen them walk in, felt his heart start pounding when he recognized Sarah, and then, seeing David, realized the connection. He'd begged the club manager to assign someone else to the table but was told to do his job.

Michael gave a small nod to Sarah and smiled at David as he answered Manning. "They're fine, sir. Ma's been spending a lot of time with her gardening clients down south. And Da, well, Da is as busy as ever at the racecourses, although the season ends soon."

Manning turned to David and Sarah. "Michael's father is a good friend. I spend too much time following my racehorse investments, and he's one of the best equine veterinarians in the British Isles, although he steadfastly refuses to give out any stable tips. And his mother is a highly regarded garden designer."

"Michael and his roommate, Tomahawk, have taken me in after the fire," David said.

"That," Manning said, "would be Thomas McFarland?"

"Yes," David said. "Do you know him?"

"Yes," said Manning, "I had the pleasure of Toma— uh, Mr. McFarland—in my economics class."

"They've been great," said David. "And I'm wearing Tommy's shirt and Michael's tie—I haven't had time to replace my clothes yet."

"David, I believe your sister and I have a class together," Michael said. "It's very nice to meet you, Sarah. You can tell we've already started acclimating David to living with crazy people."

Sarah smiled weakly. *He's going to let me off the hook.*

"Now," Michael said, "let me tell you what's not on the menu. We have two specials tonight, braised beef in wine sauce and a tilapia with hollandaise. They let us have a bite in the kitchen, and they're both excellent, but I think I'd favor the fish."

Sarah stared at her menu. *He's definitely let me off the hook.* "I don't know if I'm hungry," she choked out.

"Are you all right, Sarah?" David asked. "Are you feeling okay?"

"Yes, yes, I'm fine. I'm just not hungry."

Standing next to her, Michael leaned forward and pointed to the salad selections. "There's a seafood salad that's actually quite light. And I could put the dressing on the side."

His hand is beautiful. I should draw his hand, she thought. *Delicate yet masculine. The wrist is narrow. A strong hand but a gentle one. Beautiful fingers. Hands you could feel safe in. Why am I thinking these things?* "Yes, that would be fine." Still embarrassed, she couldn't look at him.

Michael took their orders to the kitchen, returning shortly with wine for Dr. Manning and water for David and Sarah.

"He's a delightful young man," Manning said after Michael had left to wait on another table. "You're very fortunate, David, to end up with him and McFarland, although be prepared for McFarland's pranks. Michael is an interesting boy but rather perplexing. So much promise, but he's getting his degree in theology of all things."

"Theology?" Sarah asked. This was getting worse all the time. He *was* a theology student. She had told a theology student to . . . buzz . . . off.

"Oh, yes," David said, "he's in his final year for his MA. He's specializing in evangelism and missions."

"Like I said," said Manning, "theology of all things. You would've thought that young people would know better today. A waste, really. But his parents are that way, too. His father was telling me the last time I saw him that Michael was in Botswana, I think—some place like that in Africa, or it might have been Malawi, some exotic place—on a mission trip this summer. Something to do with building a church. I didn't think young people bothered with things like that these days. My dear," he said, turning to Sarah, "are you quite all right? You look positively ashen."

"Oh, yes, I'm sorry. I'm just a little tired."

"You might want to try the wine. It's quite good. Michael may become a priest one day, but he knows a good wine."

Sarah somehow managed through the rest of dinner.

Chapter 3

On Friday morning after classes, Michael biked to the cycling team's rooms at the gymnasium. The university biking season generally ran from February to June, but this visit wasn't about the regular season. In several weeks time, he and two other Edinburgh team members would hear whether they'd been selected for the Olympic Cycling Team.

After yesterday's experience with the beautiful Sarah Hughes, he thought a long ride would help.

The Olympic team was a long shot. After the rules had been changed a few years back, amateurs—including university cyclists—had been crowded out by the professionals. *And with some justification. The pros rode all the time—this is their pay packet.*

But Michael thought he might have a chance. He'd done well at the individual time trials and the distance tests, and he'd finished second in the mass sprint in the road racing and time trial heats in early August. Although he'd grown up with a mountain bike, he preferred road racing.

The only negative had been the formal interviews. Some interviewers were amused that a theology student could ride a bike—and even more amused that anyone would seriously study theology. Which had very little to do with the Olympics but a lot to do with the increasing antagonism directed at anything religious, especially Christian but often extending to Muslims and others as well.

Michael understood. The church in Britain was on life support, with more Anglican parishes in England closed than open. Many properties had been sold for recreational halls, mosques, and meeting halls for the evangelical groups that were small but sprouting up everywhere. They and the Muslims were on the upswing, but neither could make up for the massive decline in attendance at Church of England churches. And it was suspicion of both the evangelicals and the Muslims that was moving British society toward something less than tolerance. *Interesting that in the name of tolerance British society is growing far less tolerant,* Michael thought. *Not the best time to choose the priesthood for a career.* And there was zero chance of being assigned to a parish in Britain.

Ma and Da hadn't pushed him in this direction. They were Presbyterian, strong believers in their own church's evangelical wing. They'd been as surprised as anyone when he told them he was planning for full-time ministry— as an Anglican priest.

But not the Anglican priest commonly perceived or misperceived. Michael had a different idea in mind. In a few places the number of Anglicans was increasing and priests were needed—like Africa and Latin America. The growth of Anglicans in North America was also impressive but largely due to conservative congregations fleeing the increasingly liberal and rapidly declining denominational churches in the US and Canada. Without his realizing it, Michael's Anglicanism had been profoundly shaped by his parents' evangelical, Presbyterian faith, to the point that his theology was evangelical in content though surrounded by an Anglican liturgical form.

Philip Johnston, archbishop of York, had singled out Michael and three others in the divinity program at Edinburgh. He had captivated them at a missions conference with a speech on Africa. Second in the C of E hierarchy, Johnston was a native Nigerian and a key link in the chain to the archbishop of Canterbury, who was desperately trying to hold the worldwide Anglican community together, a community heading toward schism over the liberal theology embraced by the North Americans and most of the English hierarchy. The liberals were in the ascendant, controlling almost everything except the parishioners, who were leaving in droves.

And now there was this beautiful vision in his head, the one who had flung the two-word imperative at him and then shown up at the faculty club, looking more flustered than Michael felt. *The sister of my new roommate.*

When he saw her in the class, he didn't know she was American. Her nationality didn't matter. She'd taken instant control of his imagination.

A long ride was definitely in order.

Two hours later, pouring sweat, he pedaled to the dormitory. Tommy had taken David shopping for clothes and then to stay the night with him at Tommy's parents'. Tommy had had his fiancée, Ellen, fix David up with her best friend, Betsy Binn, for MedFest tomorrow, and they were getting together tonight for some of the prefestival celebrations and for David and Betsy to get to know each other.

Michael smiled. *For all of Tommy's deprecations against Americans, he's going out of his way to help our American replace his wardrobe and find a date. Typical Tomahawk, violently opinionated and terribly generous, often at the same time.* Michael knew the opinions were mostly for entertainment purposes. *Mostly.*

MedFest was small-time in festival-loving Edinburgh. University-sponsored, it was held the first weekend in September, the start of fall term. All decorations, entertainment, and food booths were required to be Mediterranean—Spanish, Provencal French, Italian, Greek, Turkish, Lebanese, Israeli, Egyptian, or North African. Two years before, the student governing council had embroiled itself in a major controversy over whether Portuguese fare qualified, since Portugal didn't border the Mediterranean. But good humor had prevailed and Portuguese allowed in.

Michael had made no plans for a date, although Evelyn McLin had dropped enough hints. Tommy and Michael had known Evelyn for years. She'd set her sights on Michael, which Tommy found endlessly amusing. Tommy had anointed her Evil McLin, which Michael had to admit wasn't altogether off the mark. She'd belittled Michael's chosen profession, determined to put him on a more financially rewarding path. Michael generally avoided her.

Not asked to be Michael's date, she would be, Tommy predicted, on the prowl tomorrow, looking to meet him "accidentally" at MedFest.

As Michael came into the dorm lobby with his bike and backpack, the housemaster stopped him. "Mr. Kent, you've got a visitor. She's been waiting a good two hours." He pointed toward the visitor's lounge. Thinking about Evelyn, he turned warily.

It was Sarah Hughes.

She stood, clutching a large artist portfolio from her last class of the day. He stood still, gripping the bike, as she walked to him.

"I came to tell you how sorry I am," she said. "After my, my outburst yesterday, I felt terrible and tried to apologize, but you were gone. And at dinner last night, I died. I said terrible things, and there was no excuse, and there you were. This isn't just because you helped my brother—please believe that. I was going to apologize on Tuesday if I saw you. And if you can't forgive me, I understand. I just want to die. I felt so badly I couldn't sleep last night, thinking about how I could apologize—" Tears rolled down her cheeks. A few students stopped to watch, and the housemaster was definitely captivated.

"Would you like a coffee?" Michael asked.

"What?"

"Starbucks is around the corner. I love Starbucks."

She looked around, seeing the small but intensely curious crowd. "Yes, that'd be fine."

Michael handed over his backpack and bike to the housemaster. "Watch these for me, will you, Charles? I'll be back in a bit." He took Sarah's portfolio and guided her out the door.

Neither spoke until they reached the coffee shop. As they walked in, the baristas shouted their hellos to Michael, who introduced Sarah and then ordered their coffees.

"You don't have to be so nice."

"I know," he said, "but it's a bad habit I picked up from my parents."

"You didn't say anything at dinner last night. You could've let me have it right there."

"True."

"You could have passed it off as a joke."

"True again, but—"

"But?"

"But you'd have turned me down flat when I asked you out."

16

She laughed. "You're probably right. Anyway, thank you. You were perfectly kind after I had been . . . something less than kind."

"So tell me about yourself," Michael said as they sat down with their coffees. "David only told us that your decision to come to Edinburgh was last-minute and that you're studying art."

"Something past last-minute. My father had to pull some strings." She sipped her coffee. "David's the serious student. He's planned this for some time. He knew before he started college that he would spend a year abroad, preferably here, and he knew what he wanted to study and what he wanted to be. He has this great passion for Scotland's history and culture. He's followed the plan relentlessly. As for me, well, I'm more the family's free spirit, which is maybe why I'm in art. There was no reason for me to come to Edinburgh. I should've stayed at UCLA, but when I realized David was definitely going, I panicked."

"Why?" he asked.

"We grew up together. We've done everything together. He's my anchor. I wasn't ready for the separation. Not a very imaginative reason, I suppose."

"It sounds like there's more to it."

Sarah looked at him and nodded. "We were born and raised in Colorado, and during our senior year in high school my mother left us. Just walked out. It was devastating. My father took it badly. We'd had no clue, and neither did my father. Although maybe we should've known or at least suspected. Our older brother, Scott—he's just finished his residency at a hospital in Denver—he's going to be a wonderful doctor. Well, Scott had an inkling of something being wrong. He said Mother was sounding more and more distant whenever he talked to her, like she was disappearing or fading away."

"What happened?"

"She left with Dad's business partner. Apparently they'd been having an affair for a long time. He and Dad had been partners since college. So for Dad it was both a personal blow and a business blow. He pulled up roots, left Colorado, and moved to Los Angeles. Anywhere was better than Denver after that, and my grandmother lives in Santa Barbara. David had already been planning on UCLA, and I followed in his wake. I think we clung to each other to deal with what happened."

She paused. "I sound like I follow everyone else's lead."

"No," Michael said. "Well, yes. But that's not what it is, I think."

"You're easy to talk with."

"Another bad habit I learned from my parents." He paused and then plunged. "By the way, this is poor timing on my part, but would you be interested in doing MedFest with me tomorrow? I mean, if you haven't already been asked or have other plans. And I'm not trying to play on your guilt about yesterday unless it will make you say yes." He smiled.

"I was going to stay in my room and study. So yes, I'd love to go with you. And not out of guilt." She stared at his eyes. *They're captivating. That color — it's like the color of . . . well, like sky. You could get lost in that color.*

Michael beamed. "Wonderful. I'll meet you at your dorm at nine thirty?"

"That'll work." *He seems completely unaware of the effect he has on me or any other female.* She'd seen the heads turn when they walked in.

After walking Sarah to her dorm, he returned to his own to retrieve his backpack and bicycle from his housemaster.

"Mr. Kent," Charles said, "I'd offer a bit of sartorial advice."

"Yes?"

"Asking a young lady out, even for a coffee, seems to demand something more than spandex."

Michael looked down. *I'm still wearing my cycling rig. I didn't even think.* He blushed.

"And a bath might not hurt as well."

Chapter 4

Scotland's weather was always iffy, but Saturday was sunny and mild. *Radiant, in fact*, thought Michael as he and Sarah walked toward George Square, the festival's center. They chatted about Dr. Fitzhugh and medieval art (not that Michael remembered anything from the first lecture) and Sarah's other classes. They were just starting to talk about Michael's summer trip to Malawi when they reached the square.

Several hundred people were milling about. A band was warming up to play.

Michael looked round. "Tommy and David are about or will be soon. We'll hook up with them shortly, I think."

"David'll be surprised to see us together. I didn't talk to him last night," said Sarah.

"He was at Tommy's parents' to meet Betsy. And be ready for a diatribe from Tomahawk about the English and Americans always conspiring together."

She looked at him, puzzled. "But you sound like a Scot. Oh, wait, David said you were born in England." Michael started to explain, but then they heard the music.

The band beginning to play was from Greece. It was a crossover group that mixed classical and rock, popular and even operatic. As it started to play music tantalizingly close to a tango, the singer began wowing the crowd with his beautiful tenor voice.

Michael looked expectantly at Sarah and held out his hand. She took it. He put his arm around her waist; she placed her hand on his shoulder. They began to dance.

Other dancers soon stopped to watch them.

She moves in every way like I move, Michael thought. *It's as if we've been dancing forever. And perhaps we have.*

The crowd remained silent, watching.

Ellen and Tommy, with David and Betsy behind them, pushed their way to the front of the crowd. "What's going on?" Ellen whispered to Tommy.

"It's our Michael," Tommy said. "But who's the girl?"

"It's my sister, Sarah," said David in a surprised voice. "They just met the other night. I can't believe how good they are."

"They're incredible together," said Ellen. "She's anticipating his every move, exactly when she should."

"It's one of the most sensuous things I've even seen," whispered Tommy. "Who'd have expected something like this from our English?"

The band's singer, inspired by the beauty of the dancing, poured himself into the song, his voice enhanced by the silence of the crowd.

As the song neared its end, Michael and Sarah slowed with the music. The entire crowd leaned forward, waiting to see the finish. Ellen clutched Tommy's hand. Betsy put her hand on David's arm.

They watched as Michael's arm went around Sarah's shoulder, as she leaned back but tilted her head forward. Michael leaned toward her.

The music ended.

The crowd held its collective breath.

Michael's lips lightly, tenderly touched Sarah's, and then lingered.

After a moment of silence, the crowd erupted in cheers.

Michael and Sarah looked around and then blushed, realizing for the first time they'd been the only dancers. Tommy and the others rushed to them.

"Michael!" Tommy said. "I'm stunned speechless!"

"The first time that's ever happened," laughed Ellen.

"I've got it!" said Tommy, ignoring her. "The name for a new event at MedFest. The L.T.E.! The Last Tango in Edinburgh!"

A photographer for the *Scotsman*, haunting the festival for a photo, captured the final moment. With the cheering crowd and the buildings of George Square as the background, the picture of Michael kissing Sarah was published in the Sunday newspaper and distributed on wire services. It wasn't particularly newsworthy, but it was an interesting picture for copy editors to use after a slow

20

news day. Seth Hughes saw the photo in the *Los Angeles Times* on Sunday, wondering what his daughter was up to. His mother, Helen, saw it in the Santa Barbara paper. Scott and Barbara Hughes, David and Sarah's brother and sister-in-law, saw it in the *Denver Post*. Iain and Iris McLaren, Michael's guardians, saw it in the *Scotsman*. The archbishops of York and Canterbury saw it as well, as did the coach for the Olympic Men's Cycling Team and King James III in Buckingham Palace.

Evelyn McLin didn't need to see the photograph in the newspaper. Standing in George Square, she'd seen the actual kiss.

Late that afternoon, Michael walked Sarah to her dorm.

"It was a great day," Michael said.

"It was a wonderful day, Mike. Thank you for asking me."

"You're a fabulous dancer."

"Matched only by my date," she smiled.

"About the kiss," he said hesitantly.

"It was part of the dance."

"I didn't expect . . ."

"I know. Neither did I. But it fit, didn't it? It fit. It was a gift."

"It *was* a gift. And fit it did. It seemed part of the dance."

"So, Mr. Kent," said Sarah, "tell me why your accent is different. It's Scot, but it's softer. And you don't look like a Scot. Or English either, for that matter. But David says you're from England originally?"

"It's why Tommy calls me English. I was born in England but raised here."

"Your family moved here?"

"No. My birth parents were killed in a car crash. Ma and Da are my guardians."

"I'm sorry."

"It was a long time ago," he said. "I was young, six years old. I don't remember much. My mother was from Italy, and I apparently favored her."

They walked along the sidewalk. She looked at him.

"So why theology?"

"Ma and Da raised me to believe in God. It wasn't something unusual; it was something that just was. They were Presbyterians, though. I threw them a curve with the Anglican bit."

"And how did that happen?"

"I rode my bike past an old Anglican church twice a day to and from school. One day I stopped and went in. It was as if the church was calling to me. The building was really old, but the priest wasn't. He was fairly young. Still there, in fact. Father Andrew Brimley. When I was thirteen, I started attending Sunday services, which Ma and Da weren't totally comfortable with, but they met with Father Andy and decided it was okay. I even got Tommy to go. He's a believer, too, although he prefers the John Knox brand of belief."

"John Knox?"

"A Reformed firebrand who gave Mary Queen of Scots a great deal of grief with his scolding tongue. The perfect role model for Tomahawk."

"And Malawi?"

"I'm passionate about Malawi, so fair warning. Four of us from theology school spent six weeks there this summer, inspired by the archbishop of York. We worked under the Anglican Church of South Africa and helped build a church—physically build it, I mean. Working with the church elders and some young people. It was some of the hardest work I've done in my life. And in my free time I got to teach kids about Jesus. And how to ride a bike. In fact, a project I'm working on this term is finding used bikes to ship there."

"I hear the passion."

"They're wonderful people. They've so little compared to us, and yet they give so much. This little congregation has all the problems of Africa— disease, hunger, and poverty—and yet they always give thanks to God. I realized that I was part of something far larger than anything I'd ever known, as if God had given me a glimpse of his kingdom, and it was more beautiful than I could've expected."

They reached Sarah's dorm. "I'm sorry," he said. "I get carried away."

"Don't apologize, Mike. It's part of who you are."

"You ask a lot of questions." Michael smiled.

"I'm interested. You're an unusual guy."

"I don't mind answering them. You're an unusual girl."

They stood silently.

"So, Sarah, if I called you, would you consider perhaps going out again? I mean, you won't hurt my feelings if you say no. But, well, I'd probably be crushed, but I think I'd understand. Except I wouldn't. I'm mucking this up."

"No, you're not." She smiled. "I'd really like to go out again, Mike."

"Super. Can I have your phone number?"

She gave him her cell number, which he entered into his own.

Her phone rang. "Excuse me, Mike. Hello?"

Michael spoke into his phone. "Sarah, this is Michael Kent. I was wondering if you might be free Tuesday for dinner. There's a good pasta place close to here. It's short notice, but I thought we both have to eat, and I'm hoping you're free."

She laughed. "You're an idiot. Say seven thirty?"

"It's a date."

They both hung up. She kissed him on the cheek and turned toward the dorm.

I could fall in love with him, she thought. *Easily. I have to be careful. I'm not ready for a relationship, not after Terry.* She stopped and looked back toward him. He was still standing where she had left him, his hand touching his cheek where she had kissed him. She smiled and waved. *And I'm not ready for his religion. It's really too much. He's too passionate about it. And I'm just not that way. But he's not anything I pictured a religious person to be. He's great fun. And what a dancer.*

But it was the memory of his kiss at the end of the dance that stayed with her.

And his eyes . . . like the color of sky.

Chapter 5

As the weeks passed, Michael and Sarah developed what friends began to call a "relationship."

One night in the dorm room, Tommy observed that this English-American thing was becoming serious, earning a grin but no verbal response from Michael.

"Well," David said, "other than the fact that I don't see my sister anymore unless I find Michael first, why would you say that?"

"She calls him Mike," Tommy said. "Nobody calls him Mike. He's always insisted on Michael. But she calls him Mike, and he doesn't mind a bit. Now, if Evil McLin called him Mike, there'd be a scene that'd make the BBC."

Michael focused on the paper he was typing.

"So if this fair American maiden has a special dispensation from the gods to call him Mike, she needs a nickname as well. Since Mike is pretending to ignore us, what can you tell us about Sarah that would aid our quest for the perfect nickname?"

Tommy and David bantered back and forth, while Michael remained silent but occasionally smiled.

"When we arrived at the airport here, she couldn't find one of her shoes," David offered. "She went through customs with one shoe off."

Tommy slapped his pencil down. "That's it! It's perfect! We'll call her Shoes! We'll tell her it's because her name is S. Hughes, and then we'll find the perfect moment to reveal the real pedigree."

Michael laughed. "You're one evil miscreant, Tomahawk. If you spent half as much time on your courses, you'd graduate with highest honors."

Mike and Shoes became a familiar sight around the university. Michael would sit in the back of Sarah's Master Drawing Class and pretend to study while he watched her and the other students work. Sarah would show up at cycling practices and attend the team's practice races. Although he invited her several times, the one invitation she always declined was to accompany him to church.

"I'm just not ready for it, Mike," she said. "I know David's going with you, but I'm not there, okay?"

After one cycling practice, Michael walked from the locker room to where Sarah and friends of other cyclists were waiting in the gym. He dropped his backpack and flopped down next to her.

"Tired?" she asked.

"Utterly exhausted but suddenly revived by a vision of absolute loveliness."

"I like the theology student pickup line better. So, I have a favor to ask."

"Anything."

"I'd like to draw your leg."

Michael sat up. "Pardon?"

"I'd like to draw your leg," she repeated. "It's an assignment for Master Drawing. We have to draw a part of the human body from life. And it can't be of me."

"So you want me to bare my shapely leg?"

"Yes. And not the whole leg. Just the calf."

"You want to draw my calf then."

"It's okay, Mike?"

"Of course, but only for Shoes," he said. "So when do we do this?"

"How about now? I could do the preliminary sketches now, in fact."

"I take it this assignment is due tomorrow."

She blushed. "Guilty as charged. I've been spending too much time watching someone at cycling practices and put this off to the last minute."

He sighed. "So it's my fault. Do you want my right or my left?"

"Your choice," she said as she pulled out her drawing pad and pencils.

"Then left it is, the closest to the artist, and I won't have to move." He pulled up his pants leg.

"Can you take off your shoe and sock?"

Michael rolled his eyes. "Where is this going to stop?"

She grinned. "With your sock."

He removed his loafer and sock.

"Perfect. Just stay still. It helps that you shave your legs."

"It's what prevents me from pursuing a professional racing career," he said. "You have to shave your legs because of the road rash if you fall or crash. The healing goes faster. But it's a monumental pain to shave."

"You're expecting sympathy from me?" She became absorbed in her drawing.

He watched her, fascinated, because he'd seen how she blocked out the world when she was drawing or painting. He watched her soft, golden-brown eyes move from his calf to the pad and then back again. She'd furrow her brow and frown, then her face would clear, and she'd work the pencil again.

He knew she'd hear very little of what he might say, so he remained quiet and simply enjoyed watching her. *She's incredible.* And then he felt a shadow, a cold shadow, pass between them.

She leaned forward and touched his calf, startling him. Her hand touched him, almost caressing the muscles.

"Can you tense it?" she asked.

Speechless, he complied. He felt her hand touch the rock hardness of his calf, her palm and fingers pressing and probing.

He was thankful she wasn't looking at his face. He was red. His mouth was dry. No one had ever touched him like this before. Her fingers moved gently, verifying what her eyes were seeing. She'd return to drawing and then reach back, touching his calf again.

Michael had dated girls throughout school and occasionally developed a crush, but nothing lasted. He'd worried about it and then decided to just enjoy going out. But no relationship had lasted as long as this one, even if it'd been just shy of three months since he first saw her in class. He'd held her hand, he'd put his arm around her, and he'd kissed her—several times, in fact—but this gentle touching and probing of his calf unnerved him.

Finally she said, "I think it's done," and showed him the drawing pad.

He saw an almost perfect representation of his calf. He could still feel her hand, but he could also still sense the shadow.

"Great," she said as she turned the drawing back toward herself. "You're super to let me do this. Do you have time for a coffee? My treat."

He smiled and nodded, still too shaken to speak. *Thank you, Lord, that she didn't want to draw my chest.*

Chapter 6

Michael would look back on the fall and winter as a golden time when everything seemed to go right—with his studies, with Sarah, and with cycling. Tommy and Ellen continued to plan their wedding after graduation. And David and Betsy had hit it off. The six of them became a common sight around the university.

Three months after MedFest, Michael received the phone call from the British Olympic Committee. He sat for a moment, almost too stunned to move, then biked to ExpressoYourself, expecting to find Tommy and David and most likely Sarah.

They were laughing at something Tommy was saying when Sarah saw him. Michael smiled at her and nodded.

She jumped up so quickly her chair fell over. "Mike!"

Tommy looked at her, then saw Michael.

"You made it," Tommy said.

Michael nodded. "I'm in for the road team."

"And that means exactly what?" Sarah asked.

"I qualified for the individual and team time trials and the four-day stage race. Doug Brant and Bob Semple are in, too, Doug for BMX and Bob for mountain biking."

"You made the Olympic team!" Tommy yelled. "We're going to Athens!"

Michael, Doug, and Robert were headlines in Edinburgh and all over Britain. Three university students from Edinburgh—along with some forty professional cyclists, all from England or Wales—had been selected for the British Olympic Men's Cycling Teams. Edinburgh celebrated. Banners appeared at the Student Center and divinity school.

Archbishop Johnston called from York. "Congratulations, Michael. We're all very proud. It's a great honor, and we celebrate with you. It's also not a bad thing for the church—one of our own will go to the Olympics."

"Thank you, sir," Michael said. "By the way, our first team meeting's this weekend, and it's in York. Might you put up three penniless students from university?"

The archbishop laughed.

While Michael was on his way to York on Friday, David and Sarah were scouting places to eat for lunch. David wanted to talk with her, he'd said, just the two of them.

"How serious is this with you and Michael?" David asked as they sat at a table.

"I like him a lot, David. A whole lot."

"Sarah, I figured that out. You've been seeing only each other for over three months now."

"What does Mike say about us?"

"He doesn't. You're a side of him that he keeps very private, like he's holding you close. And Michael doesn't need to say anything, not with Tommy there. Tommy says he's never seen Michael like this before. Not with any girl."

She concentrated on her sandwich.

"What about Terry?" David asked.

She looked surprised. "What do you mean, what about Terry?"

"Sarah, you know, the guy in Los Angeles who thinks he's engaged to you? The one who works for Dad. The one you were dating before we came to Scotland."

"We're not engaged."

"He assumes a lot, I know, and I'm sure part of the attraction for him is that he works for Dad and marrying you would be a great step in the right career direction. But isn't there some understanding?"

"I've never encouraged him, David."

"Sarah, you didn't answer my question. Didn't the two of you have some understanding?"

"Terry's a lot of fun, David, but I'm not marrying him. There's no ring, no engagement, no nothing." She hesitated. "And Terry's no Mike."

"I know that. But you haven't exactly broken it off with him, have you? Terry may think he still has a big role in your life. Have you heard from him since we came to Scotland?"

Sarah looked down and shrugged. "A few e-mails."

"A few e-mails," David repeated. "Knowing Terry, probably more than a few. Why haven't you cut it off, if you're dating Michael?"

"Why is this so important right now? Can't we just go out and enjoy each other and the friends we've made here?"

"Sarah, Michael's so in love with you it almost hurts to watch."

She looked out the window of the sandwich shop. "I know," she said quietly. She looked at her brother. "David, I've fallen in love with him as well. I want to be with him all the time. I love listening to him talk about everything, even his religion. I've even started drawing him to the point where I don't think I want to draw anything else. But I just can't see how this can work. He's going to be a priest. Can you see me doing the vicarage thing? Tending the garden and smiling at all the old ladies? Or going to Africa? Me? I just can't picture it. I just can't believe like he does. It's too unreal. Surely you can understand that."

David hesitated. "No, I can't. Not anymore. Sarah, I've become a Christian."

Sarah stared at her brother. "What?"

"Tommy and Michael—and especially Tommy—well, we've had long talks. I could talk to them. I could ask questions and express doubts about everything, and they would listen."

She folded her arms. "You've been brainwashed."

"That's not what happened."

"They gave you attention, and you were grateful for it."

"They gave me attention, Sarah, but it was more than that." He leaned forward, his face intense. "They gave me acceptance; they helped me see that God accepts me the way I am. I prayed, and it all made sense."

"I can't believe this," she said, her voice rising. "I can't believe you bought into this nonsense."

"The point here isn't about me. It's about you and Michael."

"Michael who helped brainwash you?"

"Stop it! You don't understand the first thing about it, and you just sit there, judging me and Michael and Tommy and Ellen and Betsy—"

"Oh, so Ellen and Betsy are in on this, too? Where do I fit into the picture? What am I? Everyone's little missionary project? Who's going to be the first to save Sarah's soul?"

"Jesus already did that." David stood, red splotches on his cheeks. "I'm not asking you to like it or even accept it. But I'm telling you two things. First, you look bad when you talk about things you don't understand. And second, if you're not careful, you're going to really hurt Michael. And yourself. I don't want to see that happen. To either of you."

"You know what I think, David? That Christmas break won't come too soon. Maybe we should just go back to UCLA and forget all of this."

He stood. "You can do whatever you want to do, Sarah. I'm going home for break to see the family. Then I'm coming back. And staying. Permanently."

He walked out of the shop.

She sat there, trembling. She knew she was being foolish, knew that David was right, especially about Terry. But she was angry. She thought they were all friends, and they were, with each other. *I'm the outsider, different from even my own brother.*

The worst part was Michael. She was furious with him and Tommy. *They took advantage of David's vulnerability.*

As angry as she was with him, she also missed him. Terribly. And he'd been gone to York only since this morning. She missed his eyes and his smile and his easy laugh. She missed his taking her hand, tentatively at first and then with confidence. She missed the playful way he cocked his head at her.

She was disgusted with herself. *It's ridiculous, just a phase. David'll get over it. And we'll go on like before.*

She threw the rest of her lunch into the waste bin and walked out.

At the next table, Evelyn McLin watched her leave.

After breakfast with the archbishop, Michael, Doug, and Robert met with their team, coaches, and several sponsors. The women's team, also in York, met separately.

In the locker room of the York Velodrome, they sat in three team groups in a semicircle. Arthur White, the road team coach and chief for all the men's cycling teams, stood at the front of the room and went straight to the task at hand, the Olympics.

"Gentlemen," White said, "take a look around you. These are your teammates, the cyclists who'll depend upon you, and you upon them. Cycling is a team sport, or most of it is anyway. And we are a team. We're not a group of cyclists hungering for individual glory.

"We have fewer than eight months before Athens. You've day jobs, other cycling responsibilities, university course work"—looking at the three students—"or some combination thereof. There's going to be an enormous amount of training ahead, both with the team and by yourselves.

"You have the training schedule. You'll notice the need to clear your calendars from June first through the end of July. That's not a request. If you simply cannot miss the Tour de France, then the time to leave is now."

No one moved.

"You'll be up against some of the most accomplished cyclists in the history of the sport. I don't have to tell you about the Belgians, the Italians, and the French. The Australians are a threat. So are the Americans, especially in mountain biking, but they're strong in road racing. There are even the Norwegians and Ukrainians, who could easily take a medal.

"Nobody expects much from the British." He paused. "We're going to surprise people.

"We'll watch a lot of DVDs and old videotapes. And that's during the winter when the weather outside makes cycling impossible, which won't be often. When it's bad, we'll ride stationary bikes." There were smiles.

"We'll learn our competition, what makes them good and what makes them great and why they win races. We'll learn their weaknesses, and every rider has a weakness, including every man in this room. We'll learn to compensate for that and help each other. You'll also train on your own, apart from team meetings. And we'll help you map your individual training and a small group program."

This is going to be one of the most intense training experiences I've ever had, thought Michael. *I can hardly wait.*

"We'll have three teams in Athens—road, BMX, and mountain," Coach White continued. "The road race includes the individual time trial, the team time trial, and the four-day stage race that has both individual and team components and rankings.

"We intend to win a share for Britain. Across the board."

White looked around at the young faces. "A few of you can win the gold. That doesn't mean you will, of course, because it takes more than ability and skill. But you have the talent and experience.

"We start this afternoon. I trust you each brought your bicycle. Eventually we'll get our training bikes and then the bikes for Athens. This afternoon, I'm breaking you up into groups of three to do basic sprints and time trials. Regardless of the team you're assigned to, we'll be training together. So suit up."

Michael was grouped with two professionals. Roger Pitts was a twenty-six-year-old cyclist from London who had won three stages of the Tour of Britain and just missed out on winning third on the podium for the overall general classification by sixteen seconds. Frank Reynolds, twenty-five, was a native of Suffolk who'd won several regional races.

"So," said Pitts, "you're the priest from Scotland." The three mounted their bicycles.

34

"Word travels fast." Michael smiled. "Not yet. Next year."

"Catch me, priest, if you can!" Pitts yelled as he quickly accelerated. Michael began to crank.

Reynolds, amused, watched the two. *Pitts is in top form, but the university guy isn't half bad. In fact, he's unbelievably good, and I think he's just about to catch and pass Pitts by. Wow!*

The group was quiet during the Sunday night drive home.

"I hurt everywhere," said Doug Brant, who was driving. Their bicycles were mounted on the car roof and at the rear.

"But it's great, isn't it?" said Michael. "The pros aren't so bad, although I think they've naturally banded together to keep the three amateurs in their place."

"I noticed some coolness," Doug said.

"It's the sport itself," Michael said. "It's like the different perceptions they have in America and Europe about cycling. America sees it as a very European, classy thing to do, and so it's attracted the middle and upper-middle class. In Europe, cycling was born and grew up in the working classes. We have a bit of that here. We're the three university snots, and just about everyone else went straight into cycling from school—university being a hindrance to a cycling career."

"We'll just have to show them how we do it in Scotland," Bob Semple said. "They'll be on our turf in two weeks, and they'll find out what it's like to ride the Highlands. But you're right, Michael—they're a good group, if a bit standoffish, that Pitts character being the worst. He was not happy with you. But if you're going to show off and challenge someone, you should know ahead of time whether you can beat them."

Michael called Sarah as soon as Doug dropped him off at the dormitory.

"We're back."

"How was it?"

"Grueling. But good. It's a good team. We'll just have to learn how to work together. I missed you."

She hesitated. "I missed you, too."

"Are you okay? Is something wrong?"

"No. David and I had an argument. I'll get over it."

Michael looked over to where David was studying. "He looks fine from here. Buried in a book."

"So I'll see you tomorrow?"

"Absolutely. I'll catch you up on the whole training. Plus an interesting breakfast with the archbishop. I'm not sure what Doug and Bob made of it." He paused. "It'll be good to see you. It's been only three days, but it seems like months. I don't know what I'm going to do when you fly home for Christmas."

"You'll be so busy training you won't even know I'm gone."

"You are flat-out wrong."

"See you tomorrow, Mike." He could hear the smile in her voice now.

Putting down the phone, he looked over at David. "So, our David, how was the weekend?"

"Quiet. Tommy and Ellen were doing wedding stuff. I saw Bets Friday and Saturday."

"And Sarah?"

"Sarah and I had a fight. I think it was about God."

Michael knew David would likely be short on details. "Do you think she's open to talking about faith?"

David shook his head. "No, just the opposite, I'd say."

"Would you be surprised if I told you that I'd love to hear more and you're saying infuriatingly little?"

"No, that wouldn't surprise me," David said, "but I think I'll let you two sort it out." He dodged the pillow Michael threw.

36

Chapter 7

In the two weeks before Christmas break, Michael knew Sarah was preoccupied, but she wasn't saying much. Whatever it was didn't seem to have anything to do with faith, the one subject that could create long silences between them. David finally told Michael that Sarah had reacted badly to his conversation with her about faith. Michael knew this was the major issue facing them, all the while confident she'd come around eventually. *She has to*. In fact, as Sarah suspected, they were all praying for her. The only problem was that the harder they prayed, the more resistant she became.

David had been preoccupied as well. He'd been having long cell phone conversations with his brother, now living and working in San Francisco.

Michael hadn't yet brought Sarah home. He'd made a few vague references about her, but Iris suspected something was afoot and wondered if at the bottom of it was a female, possibly *the* female in the newspaper photograph.

"Seems like there's a woman involved here somewhere," Iain said to Iris at lunch over sandwiches and ale.

"And why do you think that, Iain McLaren?" Iris asked, surprised he'd guessed her thoughts.

"I've been there," he said. "I know what it's like. He's acting the same way."

By the Monday before Christmas break, Sarah and David had their tickets for their Wednesday flight scheduled, the day before Christmas Eve. Michael was borrowing Doug's car to take them to the airport. He was glad to have the growing intensity of his training schedule to keep him occupied while Sarah was gone for almost a month. They'd already planned phone calls during the holiday.

On Monday, as usual, the week started off at ExpressoYourself.

David had left the dorm early, and Tommy was sleeping in. Michael's lectures were over for the term, and he had only one short paper to complete. So he slept in as well.

At nine, he walked into the coffee shop. Glancing at Sarah and David as he ordered his coffee, he could see something was wrong.

"What's wrong?" he asked, sliding next to Sarah.

Sarah said nothing, and David looked away.

"Should I come back? Is it a brother-sister thing?"

Sarah shook her head but still didn't speak. *She's been crying.*

"It's about going home," David said finally.

"And?"

"It's complicated."

"I'm sorry," Michael said. "I'm prying."

"It's okay," David replied. "We probably need to tell someone. We didn't know everything until last night."

"Is someone sick?"

"No," David said. "It's Dad."

Michael decided that waiting was the best response.

"At Thanksgiving," David said, "Dad went up to see Scott and his family in San Francisco."

Michael nodded.

"The hospital was having a blood drive, and Scott talked Dad into giving blood. When Scott asked him his blood type, he said it was AB. Well, Scott told Dad that he couldn't be AB because Scott is type O."

"I don't understand," Michael said.

"A parent who's type AB can't have offspring who are type O."

"Couldn't your mother have been type O?"

"It doesn't matter," David said. "If either parent is AB, it doesn't matter what type the other one is—you can only have children who are type A or type B."

"Oh," Michael said, understanding dawning. "So that means that if your father is type AB . . . "

David nodded. "Then Scott couldn't be his son."

"Oh," Michael said.

"We're also type O," said Sarah. "David and I."

The silence lasted. Michael looked from Sarah to David and then back to Sarah. "So what happened?" he asked.

"Scott had blood tests done for both himself and Dad, to make sure," David said. "And sure enough, Scott was O and Dad was AB. Dad took it badly. Scott was upset himself. Dad insisted Scott check with us to find out our blood types."

"So," Michael said, "your father finds out he's raised three children who aren't his biological offspring."

"Right," said David.

"How's he dealing with that?"

"He's not," Sarah said. "He's told Scott that he doesn't have a family. And now he understands why Mother left. He says she betrayed him for thirty-two years, and he never had an inkling. So it's good-bye. He's cut the three of us off. And his grandson, Scott's son, Scottie. Scottie idolizes my father. Mike, he's seven years old. How do you explain this to a seven-year-old?"

Michael put his arm around Sarah's shoulder. "You can't, not in a way that makes any sense. It's like telling him he doesn't matter anymore. And it doesn't make any sense to a twenty-year-old either." Sarah leaned her head on his shoulder.

He turned to David. "So what happens now?"

"Dad—if I can still call him that—put money in an account to cover us for the rest of college," David said bitterly. "He left Scott in charge of it. And he told Scott good-bye. He said we're not his children, and he could figure out who our father is."

"The former business partner?"

David nodded. "Scott and I look so much like each other that we never stopped to think that we didn't look like our parents. Now we know. From Dad's perspective, his marriage for more than thirty years was a sham, and he's just now finding out. And he's just walked away." David looked down, unable to continue.

"Scott says that Gran—that's our grandmother—is furious with Dad," Sarah said. "But he won't budge."

"Scott's invited us to his in-laws in Phoenix for Christmas, but we'd be really out of place," David said. "We could stay with Gran, but who wants to go home right now? So we're talking about going to London, doing something different, seeing the city."

"Nonsense," said Michael. "You don't want to spend Christmas in London by yourselves. You'll come home with me."

"Mike," said Sarah, "your parents don't know us. They don't need this mess with strangers at Christmastime."

"They'll love having you. And they have a lot of experience with orphans. I turned out okay, mostly anyway, in spite of Tomahawk. I'll call now, and I promise that if there's the least hesitation on their part, I'll call it off."

David looked at Sarah. "What do you think?"

Sarah looked from David back to Michael. Michael pulled out his phone with a smile. He made the call and was grinning by the time he was finished.

"That's that then," Michael said, ending the call. "It's a plan. I'll bike home Thursday morning and get the car and then pick you up."

"Are you sure this is all right?" Sarah asked.

"It's fine. It's infinitely better than spending Christmas in a London hotel."

Chapter 8

Michael picked Sarah up on Thursday morning; David was already in the car. He'd told them to pack for two weeks and then decide whether they wanted to go on to London, back to the dorms, or stay on at the McLarens'.

They merged into the growing holiday traffic for the drive to the McLaren farm.

"I love the farm," said Michael. "It's a magical place, especially if you look at it through the eyes of a child. Da rebuilt the stable, where the horses that need attending board. There's about eighty acres now. It was smaller when I was a boy, but Da has added to it as properties became available.

"What Ma has done with the gardens is incredible, but you won't be able to get the full effect until May and June. You'll see their structure, though, and it'll give you the idea. It's all structured around woodlands and the pond, about twenty-five or thirty acres in all. You have to walk through it to see the smaller gardens that are embedded within the woodlands. She has a perennial garden, a rose garden, and a boxwood garden. And she's been putting in a wildflower garden." He peered through the windshield at the sky. "We may get some snow. That'd be perfect. Oh, another thing. On Christmas Eve, me and Da do our Christmas shopping. It's been like that since my first Christmas with them. It's really more an excuse that Ma and Da worked out years ago to get us out of her way while she prepares dinner. Tommy comes along, and we'll see a lot of him and Ellen during the holiday." Glancing at David in the mirror, he added, "And we'll likely prevail upon them to bring Betsy as well."

"Perfect," said David, "I'm already enjoying this. Nothing to study, sleeping in, wandering around a farm, seeing Betsy. It may not get better than this."

"So, Sarah, you can come with us tonight, or you can stay with Ma. She'll be doing the cooking and baking, I expect."

Sarah smiled. "Mike, you sound like a little kid."

"I love Christmas, don't you? Ma and Da always make it special. We've a dog, too. I hope you're not allergic. He's actually the son of the dog we had when I first arrived. That was Duff, and we were inseparable when I was growing up. He died a few years back, and Ham is his son."

"Duff for Macduff and Ham for Hamlet?" David asked.

"Da's a Shakespeare fan."

As they left the outer suburbs, the countryside grew more rugged.

"You biked all this way this morning? In the cold?" asked Sarah.

"It's easier than it looks," said Michael. "You'll see the hills up behind the farm, where I first did serious mountain biking. And grade school was three miles away, so I learned to bike that. It just grew. In high school, I started on the road bike. It seemed natural to join the cycling club at university."

"And now it's the Olympics," David said. "Your parents must be proud."

"They are, but I think they're gladder for me. Da is this big bear of a man; in fact, that's what I thought he was when I first came to the farm. A big, red bear. And Ma is beautiful. I fell in love with her from my first morning at the farm when she fixed griddle cakes. Although the first time I saw her, I remember being scared to death.

"We're here," Michael said as he turned into the McLarens'.

"Wow!" said David.

"Oh, Mike, it's beautiful," said Sarah.

And it was, even in the stark overcast gray of winter with no snow yet. Set well back from the road, the farmhouse was whitewashed with a gray slate roof, and while it couldn't be called a country estate, it was clearly comfortable. Behind it was a forested area moving up the side of the hills with bare hills above the trees.

"That's where you mountain bike?" asked David.

Michael laughed. "It looks worse than it actually is. There's a maneuverable switchback trail to the top. And the view is dazzling. You can even see some of Edinburgh. We can hike it if you'd rather do that than bike up."

They entered through the front door. "Ma! Da! We're here!"

Iris walked in from the kitchen. "Welcome to you both. We're so glad to have you."

Michael saw Ma's knowing eyes move from Sarah to him.

Sarah spoke. "Mrs. McLaren, we don't know how to thank you for putting us up for the holiday."

Michael grinned. "Or putting up with David."

Iris glanced at her son. *Yes, he's nervous. He wants our approval, but he's so far gone that it won't really matter.*

"Hey!" said David.

"Michael," said Iris, "why don't you show our guests to their rooms, and I'll find your father. He's out in the stable tending to a mare that wants to foal too soon."

"This way," Michael said, heading up the stairs. "I'll give you the one-pound tour and then take you outside. David, throw your stuff here in my room—we're bunking together. Sarah, you've got the guest room down the hall here."

After hanging up her clothes, Sarah joined Michael and David in Michael's room.

David was walking around, looking out the windows at the view of the hills behind the house. Sarah looked around the room and inspected the photographs, biking ribbons and trophies, and pictures of Michael and the McLarens; Michael and Tommy as youngsters; Tommy and Ellen as older teenagers; several of Michael as a small boy with a white-and-russet spaniel; Michael as a teenager, usually with a bicycle.

"That's Duff," Michael said, "the dog who took me in hand—or took me in paw, I should say—when I came. Ham's probably out in the stable with Da."

Sarah looked from the photos to Michael and back to the photos. "It's fascinating to see how you've changed and how you've stayed the same. It's a wonderful room."

"And take a look at the view," David said, pointing to the window. "It's fantastic."

"I love this place," Michael said. "It's a great place for a kid, but I still love it. But it's more than a place. It's what it is because of Ma and Da. Come meet Da."

They headed downstairs to find Iain and Iris in the kitchen.

Michael's right, Sarah thought when she saw Michael's father. *He's like a great big bear.*

Iain stood six four in his socks. Redhaired and barrelchested with a ruddy complexion, he was showing a few signs of gray but still exuded energy. *This is a man who gets things done.*

"Welcome, young people," said Iain. "Welcome to the McLarens'. Michael has told us a bit about you but not too much, so you're going to have to fill in some gaps. Iris has lunch almost ready, so why don't I show you the stable. And Michael—you can help your mother."

"I learned early to follow orders," Michael said.

Iain and his two guests walked out the back door.

"So, son," Iris said, "you can set the table while you tell me about Sarah."

"And David," Michael added.

"But Sarah first. I've eyes, you know."

Michael laughed. "Either I'm sensationally obvious, or you just know me too well."

"Both," Iris said. "So tell me."

"She didn't plan to come to Scotland. David did. He's the organizer and has his school career mapped out. I think I told you he's studying Scottish history; she's studying art. She's a first-class painter, Ma."

"I saw she'd some art things with her when she arrived."

"She did, but I think it's more for if the muse strikes her."

"So you met her through her brother when he came to room with you and Tommy?"

"No, actually I met her in class. We had Fitzhugh's lecture on Medieval Church Art together." Michael decided to omit certain details of their first meeting. "I asked her to MedFest. She's a great dancer, too; she took a class in ballroom dancing like I did."

Iris smiled. "I saw the photo in the *Scotsman*."

Michael blushed. "And, well," he paused as he looked at Iris, "we've been going out a bit."

"More than a bit from the looks of it. You almost glow when you look at her."

"I do? Well, she's wonderful, Ma. They've had a spot of family trouble, which is why they're spending the holiday with us."

"Nothing serious, I hope."

"It's pretty serious, yes. There wasn't a place for them to go, although they had their tickets for California."

"So what is she like, son?"

"Ma, she's wonderful. She's soft and strong at the same time. She's the most beautiful thing I've ever seen—that's obvious—but it's more than that. She knows me. And I know her. I want to be with her all the time."

"What does she think of your chosen career?"

Michael's face clouded. "It's a problem. Ma, she's not a believer."

Iris was silent.

"I mean," Michael said quickly, "I think she's open. And David's become a believer. But she's not there yet."

"Is that a problem?"

45

Michael paused before answering. "Yes, Ma, it's a problem. I can't ask her to be part of my life, to be a minister's wife, if she doesn't share that. So I've put off thinking about it. But she knows this, too. So I've been praying, and maybe you can pray as well?"

"It'll all come right," Iris said as she touched his cheek. "And I'll pray for you both. Now, finish with the table and pour the water."

In the stable Iain was enchanted with the two Americans. Ham seemed to adopt David, who was pleased with the dog's attention.

David was full of questions about the horses and what Iain did. Sarah occasionally interjected her own question or comment but mostly just listened. And watched. Iain sensed she was watching for clues about Michael.

As soon as they'd entered the kitchen, he'd seen that Michael was smitten. Completely. And he could see why. Sarah Hughes was a very attractive young woman. *But it'd take more than that for Michael. So she must have a depth to her as well.* And was she equally smitten with Michael? *Now there's a question that doesn't have an obvious answer.* So Iain decided to find out what there was about this young woman that had so captivated his son.

"What do you think of Scotland?" Iain asked.

Sarah smiled. "I didn't expect it to be what it is," she said. "I mean, I hadn't been here before, so I didn't know what to expect, other than the tourist stereotypes—you know, the clans, the kilts, the bagpipes, Rosslyn Chapel, and all. David was the expert, and he knew everything. What I've learned in the short time we've been here is that it's different from the States, but people are a lot the same. They care about the same things, they want the same things. The buildings are older, but even the university is not so different from UCLA."

Iain nodded. "I think you're right. I've only been to the States twice, and what I saw had more to do with horseracing than anything else, but a racetrack is the same no matter where you are. Politics is a bit stranger here, though, and the church hasn't yet figured out how to halt the decline it's been in."

David followed Ham to the rear of the barn, where the dog seemed to be investigating an unexpected smell.

"Were you surprised when Mike decided to study theology?" she asked.

He lets her call him Mike. This must be serious. "Well, yes and no," Iain said. "For a bit all he talked about was professional bike racing. That was a worry; it's not an easy life. Not that Michael was looking for an easy life, but he'd be spending the next ten years living from season to season and race to race. Gradually, with the influence of the local Anglican priest, Father Andrew, that began to change. Michael believes, and he believes strongly."

"I know," Sarah said, "we've talked about it."

Iain sensed tension. "So Michael says you're studying art. Do you plan to teach or curate?"

"Actually, neither. I want to draw, and to paint." He saw her shyness in talking about it.

"It's an act of creation," Iain said. "And it's a God-given gift, I tell Iris. There's something in the creating of things, whether it be writing or painting or even designing a garden, that takes us toward the mind of God." He looked to see the girl's reaction.

She was listening intently. "I don't really understand it," she said. "Whatever the source, it seems to come to me at its own time and choosing."

Diplomatic response, but she's just answered my real question by not answering it.

David wandered back toward them with Ham. "Lunch should be about ready," Iain said. "Did Michael tell you about Christmas Eve?"

David nodded. "The men head for the shops in Edinburgh, and the women relax, I believe he said."

"You can put it that way, and I might agree with you"—Iain laughed— "but don't let Iris know. Sarah, you're welcome to come with us."

"Actually, Mr. McLaren, I think I'd like to stay here with Mrs. McLaren."

He smiled. "Iris'll be glad for some female company; all she gets around here are me, Michael, and Ham. She doesn't count the horses."

Chapter 9

After lunch, which lasted longer than the McLarens' norm, the men left to get Tommy and head to the city after a warning from Iris to watch for snow.

"They'll be gone for hours," Iris said to Sarah. "They pretend they like to wait until the last moment to buy gifts, but it's more to get out of my hair while I work on Christmas dinner. And thank you, dear, for staying. Just watch out that I don't put you to work."

"I'm glad to help," Sarah said.

"Michael's very fond of you."

"I've never met anyone like him."

"Neither had I. Nor Iain. Michael's blessed us in more ways than I can count."

"Mrs. McLaren?"

"Call me Iris."

"Iris"—Sarah smiled—"how did Mike come to be here? He hasn't really said much, other than to say his birth parents had been killed in a car accident and you and Mr. McLaren were his guardians."

She calls him Mike. I'd better look closely at this young woman. "That's all true, Sarah. But the story's more complicated. While it's Michael's story to tell, there's some of it that he doesn't remember, except for what we've told him. And we'd only pieces from the lawyer and the chauffeur. Everything happened so quickly, we were all a bit bewildered."

Iris handed the pile of bread dough to Sarah, telling her to "give it a bit of knead."

Sarah worked it as she waited for Iris to continue.

"Iain and I never had children. Not for any biological reason. We just seemed not to have any."

"Where did you meet?"

"At a dance. I was from a small town near Glasgow. I was visiting a cousin in Edinburgh, and we went to a dance at her school. And there he was. He was tall even then, and he asked me to dance, and as big as he was, he was the most graceful boy I'd ever danced with. He'd just started university—he was just a year ahead of me—and we dated until he graduated. We married when he started veterinary college.

"Those were crazy days. You only do those things when you're young because you don't know any better and you don't understand how much life is stacked against you. You believe you can do anything. So Iain finished his vet studies, and because he'd specialized in horses, he'd four job offers. He accepted one here in Edinburgh; he wanted to stay in Scotland, and the others were in England. And he did well. For a while I tried my hand at a few things—managing an office, a restaurant manager, some odd things—and then I took some classes in garden design. I'd always liked gardening, and there was a good instructor at the university, a local nurseryman. He had us look at gardens all over Scotland and the north of England. He loved roses, but he really emphasized native plants, and I loved that.

"So life went on. Iain was becoming known for his flair with horses, and his list of clients grew to the point where he set up his own veterinary practice. And it kept growing. That's probably enough kneading, dear. Why don't you wash your hands, and I'll have you work on the crust for the mince pie while we let the dough rise. Good.

"But the children never came, though we tried often enough. We never hit the mark and finally resigned ourselves to having none."

"Until Mike," Sarah said.

"Until Mike," Iris agreed. "I'll never forget that night. It was a Friday. Iain had been gone the week, and we decided to just go out that evening and enjoy ourselves. We ate at this French restaurant in New Town. Pricey, but this was to be a treat. We went to a play, some light comedy. We got home around midnight; we might've stayed out later, but Iain had a horse or two to look after. He always has a horse or two to look after.

"The phone was ringing as we walked in the door. I knew it had to be for Iain; only vet emergencies called that late, so he answered it while I fixed tea.

50

Here, dear, use the pastry cutter to trim around the edges. That looks perfect. I'll let it sit in the fridge while the oven heats. The mince is ready to go. There."

Iris continued. "I could hear him talking, and something was wrong. I caught only a snatch or two about a boy. I came into the den just as he hung up. And he told me about Michael coming. It was quite a shock.

"Michael's father was Iain's biggest client. It was the family attorney who called, to tell Iain that Michael's parents had been killed in a car crash and that his father had named us as guardians.

"I didn't know Michael's parents. Iain has said this was a second marriage for both, that they'd met at a cancer hospital near Brighton when their spouses were dying. She was from Italy. Well, they got married. Michael's father was older than his mother—a good fifteen years or so—and his family saw her as something of a gold digger, I'm afraid. He'd a son from his first marriage; the boy was really a young man at school in London, I believe. He hadn't spoken to his father in several years because the second marriage had happened so quickly after his mother's death, just a month or two. He came down from London with his cousin; from what the chauffeur told us, they descended like vandals. They ordered Michael out of the house. A six-year-old whose parents had just died. I can't imagine what possessed them. You can blame a lot on grief, but this was pure meanness. The attorney was frantic to reach us, and we'd gone into town for our date.

"So he sent Michael with the chauffeur. Just like that. They'd barely time to pack a suitcase. The chauffeur drove through the night to get here, and he'd somehow managed Michael's bike into the car boot. The oven's hot enough now, dear. Just slide the pie right in there. Perfect. And set the time for thirty-five minutes, would you? The timer's on the counter next to the oven. And that's how he came. They were supposed to send his clothes and things, but they never did. So Michael came to us with his bike, a change of clothes, and a jacket.

"We didn't know what to do. We didn't even know if we could give him the proper care. But when he arrived, we both fell in love with him at once. It wasn't because he was a beautiful child, although he was that. Black, curly hair and those incredibly blue eyes. But he'd a way about him from the beginning. It made you want to love him. I'll never understand what the brother was thinking.

"Michael was terrified, but what he remembers most about that first night was Duff, our spaniel. Iain had gotten Duff from an elderly client who'd sold his horses and was going into a nursing home. He was the sweetest dog. Duff must've sensed what Michael needed and stuck to him like glue. He even slept with Michael in bed that night, and it wasn't long before his bed was permanently in Michael's room. They were inseparable.

"I'll never forget what happened when Iain put Michael to bed. He'd been up there a while, so I thought they were talking. But I found Iain sitting on the stairs, crying. I don't know if I'd seen him cry before, but he was sitting on the stairs, just crying his eyes out.

"When I asked what was wrong, he couldn't speak. Then he calmed a bit, and he said Michael had asked him what a 'dirty little dago bastard' was. It was what the cousin had said—'Get the dirty little dago bastard out of here.'"

"Oh, Iris, how awful."

"Awful wasn't the half of it. It got worse within a couple of months. Iain's practice began to fall off. Clients stopped calling, saying they'd made other plans. He was having trouble finding work. He even started seeing small animals, dogs, and cats—which horse vets generally don't do. We thought we might have to sell the farm."

"What happened?"

"One of the jockeys later said that it was the cousin, whose father was, well, a very influential person. And for whatever reason, they started leaning on people not to use Iain. We even considered emigrating to Australia or New Zealand, starting over. And that may have been the intention all along—to get Michael out of the country permanently. But then a new client showed up, and he didn't care what people said. He wanted the best vet he could find for his horses, and that led him to Iain.

"The client was a businessman from the States, which may explain Iain's fondness for Americans. Not to mention me, who likes food on the table and a roof over her head, especially with a little boy running about."

"Mr. McLaren told me earlier that he had been to America once or twice."

Iris nodded. "That was the client. He was wonderful. He helped Iain get other clients, and slowly, one by one, the old clients started coming back. Some I'd have shown the door, but Iain's not one to hold a grudge."

"Why would the cousin do that? Wouldn't he and the brother have been glad for you to have Mike?"

"I don't know, Sarah, but I suspect it was because they were both embarrassed. Or the cousin was just flat-out vicious. But I really don't know.

"What I *do* know is Michael changed our lives. When I saw Iain sitting on the stairs, weeping for the boy, I fell in love with the man all over again. Michael worked like a tonic on us. And he was a good child. He'd his ways like they all do, and he got into occasional trouble, especially once Tommy McFarland showed up. But it was the good kind of trouble. No one hurt and no damages—or maybe just some minor damage now and then. Normal high-spirited boy kinds of things. And Tommy was good for Michael. He hadn't been around other children in England. I know Michael was good for Tommy, at least keeping the worst of the mischief under control."

"Do you have any concerns about Mike becoming an Anglican minister?"

Iris looked at her closely. "I did, Sarah. Iain and I are Presbyterians, good strong Calvinists. We didn't have any instructions on how to raise Michael. His father was C of E, and his mother was Catholic. We didn't know what Michael would study at university, and we were thankful that it was something besides racing bikes. But he's a good head on him, and he knows his mind. Father Andrew's been a good influence, and we didn't have a problem as long as we knew he'd continue to grow as a Christian. So I'll ask you the same question. Do you have any concerns?"

"Mike and I haven't talked about it very much, but David and I have. David's become a Christian. Tommy and Mike both had a lot of influence—and Tommy probably more than Michael. He's been around David more because of Mike's training schedule and, well, other things, I suppose."

"Like being preoccupied with pretty Americans."

Sarah blushed. "But I haven't answered your question, and the answer is yes. I do have concerns but not about Mike. My concerns are about me. Iris, I don't have Mike's faith. I suppose that God must be there, somewhere, but I can't say He's interested in me specifically. Mike's completely confident in his faith."

"Michael has assurance. He knows, that's all. It's that simple. And for Michael, that assurance is a song in his heart. It's a blessing to have it."

"It must be. But I care for him deeply, and I want to believe—I really do. But it just doesn't come."

"Give yourself some time, Sarah. Don't let Michael rush you into a decision you're not ready to make. It's easy to get carried away with him because he thinks he has enough faith for any number of people. And he probably does. But you need to know your own mind about things."

"This isn't the conversation I thought I'd be having, Iris."

"Nor me. But Sarah, I love that boy. While he's too old for me to tell him what to do, I still want to. And if we keep having this conversation, we're going to burn the pie. Here, can you open the oven while I take it out?"

After setting the pie to cool, Iris fixed tea. "So, I've answered your question about Michael. Why don't you tell me about Sarah and David?"

"We've always been close," Sarah said. "He's two minutes older than I am, and David probably planned it that way. We grew up in Denver with our older brother, Scott, who's twelve years older, so he was almost like another family. Scott's now a doctor in San Francisco. He and his wife, Barbara, have a seven-year-old boy named Scottie. I don't know how much Mike may have told you."

"He's a male," Iris said. "Assume he told me nothing. Well, that's not true. He told me you were American and studying art, and your brother is studying history. And of course we knew about the dorm fire."

"In our senior year of high school," Sarah said, "my mother left my father for his business partner. And while we weren't young children anymore, she left us as well. In fact, we haven't heard from her since that day we came home from school and found her note. 'Dear David and Sarah, I'm leaving your father. I'm sorry. Good-bye. Love, Mother. P.S. Meat loaf's in the fridge.' That was it. She left it on David's desk. We looked in their bedroom, and she'd cleared everything out—clothes, shoes, everything.

"We called Dad, and his secretary got him out of a meeting. David read him the note, and he came home. Two days later, he heard from his business partner. They'd worked together since college."

"He must've been crushed," Iris said.

"He was. It was bad. So we graduated a few months later, and since we were going to UCLA, Dad decided to move his business there. He was from Santa Barbara originally, and our grandmother still lives there, so it wasn't alien territory for him."

"He's still there?" Iris asked.

"We haven't talked with him in a while," Sarah said. She looked at Iris. "Mike hasn't said anything about this?"

"No, dear, nothing at all."

Sarah nodded and told Iris the story. "And he's walked away from us. Just like that." Tears began to spill down her cheeks. "I'm sorry. I don't mean to burden you with this. It's just, it's . . ."

"It's just you're still trying to make sense of it all, and you're feeling helpless," Iris finished for her, handing her a tissue and putting her arm around her.

Sarah nodded. "I told Mike that David and I weren't fit for being company."

"And Michael said nonsense and told you to come home to the McLarens. He was absolutely right. It's perfect for some peace and quiet but not too much. You can sit and think, or you can find plenty to do. And we love having young people around. Michael was always good about bringing friends around; Tommy McFarland was living here most of his school years, in fact. But there's been less of that as he's gotten older. So this is a treat for us."

"Iris, you're very kind. I told Mike he was easy to talk with, and he said he got that from his parents. He was right."

Christmas Eve was a late night. The group returned from Edinburgh, trying to look mysterious but only managing to get more rowdy.

Tommy left before dinner, heading home for his own family celebration. "We're coming back tomorrow night," he said when Michael dropped him off at home. "Tell California we'll have Betsy with us."

Michael woke early the next morning. An empty bed said David was already up.

In the kitchen, Iris was pouring coffee.

"Happy Christmas, Ma," said Michael. He kissed her on the forehead. "Am I the last up?"

"Sarah got up an hour ago. I think she's dressing now. As for David and your father, you need to check the stable." Iris smiled. "Our guest got an education last night. But put your boots on. It's snowed a good six inches, and there's more to come."

Michael walked outside to the stable. It was quiet, with a light on in one of the back stalls.

The mare his father had been watching had foaled during the night. Iain was standing at the stall gate and pointed Michael to the colt.

"Da, he's a beauty."

"That he is," Iain said, "in spite of his mother's best efforts to have him as early as possible. I know one client who'll be pleased with his Christmas present."

"Where's David?"

Iain pointed to the next stall. "And don't wake him up."

Michael peered in and saw David sleeping soundly on a blanket in the hay.

"He heard me get up early this morning," Iain said, "and followed me out here. He'll have a story to tell. He helped me with the mare, and it was a job."

"How'd he do?" Michael asked.

"He did everything I told him to do. He's a steady hand. I'd keep him around permanently if I could. The mare seemed to take to him as well. I finally made him rest a little while ago. He went right out. Of course, we'd barely been in bed before I figured I better check on her, so I guess he's been up all night. He did well."

"You should tell him that. It'll mean a lot."

"Already did, son." Iain turned back to watching the mare. "So you seem a bit gone on the fair Sarah."

"You've been talking to Ma."

"And I've eyes."

"Well, yes, I'm a bit gone, as you say."

"And where's she?"

"She loves me, Da, but there are some issues."

"Being a priest is one of them?"

"Yes. A big one, in fact. David's a believer. But she's not there yet. I keep telling myself she will be. But it's a conversation we've had once or twice, and we don't get to answers."

"So where does that leave you?"

Michael stared at the nursing colt. "It doesn't leave me anywhere. I know this can't work unless we resolve it. And we can't resolve it the way she keeps hoping we will."

"Which is?"

"Do something else. I think she'd be more comfortable with a professional cyclist than a priest."

"It's the way of the world today, son. It's a hard thing. To be a Christian today, at least publicly, is something of a liability. At best, people think of you as odd. Especially if you do more than just say you're one. And you, son, have it all over you; you breathe and live your faith like oxygen. Which pleases God, but it isn't going to please too many of your fellowmen."

Michael nodded.

"You've fallen in love with her, son, and it's a hard thing. Now I can tell you what you should've been doing all along—I've always got free advice—but this seems to be one God has put in your way, and it's for a reason. It may be that she's the one, and maybe she's not."

"She is."

"You're convinced?"

Michael nodded. "As soon as I saw her, I knew. I can't tell you how I knew, but I knew. We were created for each other." He paused. "Da, she makes me want to melt."

Iain smiled at his son. "I know, son; your mother and I both see it."

He looked over to where David was still sleeping. "I better wake my assistant up. It's time for all of us to get some breakfast and do our Christmas." He put his hand on Michael's shoulder. "You're a faithful, loving young man, and God honors that. He has plans for you, Michael, and they may include that fair lass in the house, and they may not. But he knows you love him, and he'll honor that."

Michael hugged his father.

"Happy Christmas, Da."

"Happy Christmas, son."

The McLarens generally made Christmas gifts small but meaningful. This year Iain had a surprise. Iris opened a small box and stared.

"Iain McLaren."

Iain smiled.

"Iain, what is this?"

"It's not a horse blanket, Iris. It is what it is."

Michael, Sarah, and David leaned toward her.

"Wow!" said Michael.

"It's beautiful," said Sarah.

"It" was a ring, an engagement ring, with a rather large diamond in the center.

"Iain McLaren, what have you done?"

"I bought you the engagement ring I couldn't afford thirty-five years ago—that's what I've done. Now, before you give me any guff, it's been a good year, and it was something important to do."

"Oh, Iain," Iris said, "my hands." She tried the ring on. "It's beautiful, but my hands—"

"—are just as beautiful now as they ever were," Iain finished.

She leaned over and kissed him. "Thank you." She beamed.

"I think Da just won the lottery," said Michael. "Or near enough to it."

Michael handed Sarah her gift. She opened it and looked up at him.

It was a single pearl in a pendant on a gold chain. "Mike, this is lovely," she said, unhooking the clasp and fitting it around her neck. "It's beautiful." Sarah's gift for Michael had been a biking jersey and gloves.

"So," said Iris, "it's time to start thinking about dinner."

"Oh, wait," said Sarah, "we have something for you."

David reached around the sofa and pulled out a flat, rectangular package. "Sarah did all the work, but it's from both of us. I helped a bit with the—"

"David!" Sarah said. "Let them open it before you tell them what it is."

Iris looked at Michael, who smiled and shook his head.

Iris slid the wrapping off and stared. "It's Michael," she said finally.

The painting looked like a photograph; the likeness was that close. Michael had seen a few of Sarah's paintings and drawings, but nothing had been like this.

"It's incredible, isn't it?" asked David. "I helped with the frame, but have you ever seen anything so good?"

"Sarah," said Iris, "we don't know how to thank you. This is wonderful. We've never had a painting of Michael, and this is superb."

Sarah blushed.

"It's beautiful, Sarah," Iain said. "You've given us a great thing."

Michael felt tears in his eyes. "How long have you worked on this?" he asked.

"Off and on since MedFest," she said. "You know how it is when something gets hold of you and isn't going to let go until it's ready? This was what I had in my mind, and it wouldn't let go. I tried to set it aside, but I had to keep coming back. Do you like it?"

"I love it," said Michael. "I don't know what to say. It's marvelous. You're marvelous."

"And I'm hungry," said David. "I mean, I know she's marvelous; I grew up with her. But before we all get too carried away, can I help with dinner?"

That night, preparing for bed, Iris stared at the painting, which she had placed on their dresser until she decided where to hang it. Iain came up behind her and put his arms around her.

"She loves him, you know," he said.

Iris stood next to him and nodded. "I know."

Chapter 10

David and Sarah stayed at the McLarens' for a full two weeks, returning to their dorms when Michael resumed training, although Iris and Iain urged them to stay.

The new term started, Michael and Tommy's last before graduation. Life became a blur of papers and projects due, training for Michael, wedding plans for Tommy and Ellen, Michael's deepening relationship with Sarah.

Faith remained the issue for Michael and Sarah, and they dealt with it by avoiding it. Yet they spent every minute they could together, and everyone who knew them assumed they'd one day be married. David asked Sarah once or twice about Terry, and she assured him that the relationship was over.

In early March, at yet another discussion over coffee at ExpressoYourself, Michael mentioned that *The Mikado* was coming to campus in late April.

"And that would be?" asked Sarah.

"Ah," said Tommy, "our fair Shoes reminds us that just because it's English doesn't automatically mean it's known or worthwhile."

"*The Mikado*," said Michael, ignoring Tommy, "is a Gilbert and Sullivan operetta, one of their most famous, in fact."

"Time for Professor Kent's tutorial," said Tommy.

"It was first performed in London at the Savoy in 1885," said Michael. "It's about Japan or actually what Victorian England thought Japan was about. The Japanese themselves hardly recognize anything in it. But it's a comedy and love story and romance, and it's great fun, which even Tomahawk here will acknowledge when he drops the anti-English pretense for what he really thinks."

"So you mislead yourself," Tommy sniffed.

"Anyway," Michael continued, "D'Oyly Carte, the most famous of all the companies to produce G and S, will do two performances in April. It'll be a black-tie event, a bit fancy, but what do you say that we go? I'll even get Tommy a top hat and cane so he'll look the epitome of the Victorian gentleman."

"As much as I hate to admit it," said Tommy, "English here has a good idea, which happens once or twice a year, so treasure the moment. I say let's do it. Term will end two weeks after that. We'll have exams and what not, so let's finish this with some class."

The group agreed, and Michael arranged tickets for the Friday of the last weekend in April.

Evelyn McLin had seen Michael and Sarah together more than she could stomach. She finally decided to do something.

She knew from David and Sarah's argument at the restaurant that an American named Terry in Sarah's past might still think he was in Sarah's future. And she was fairly certain that Michael didn't know anything about Terry. *Why would Sarah tell that story?*

All she had was a first name. The next step would be to get access to Sarah's computer or e-mail account. Evelyn tried chatting up a few staff people from the IT department but got nowhere.

Success, however, turned out to be easier than she imagined. She simply waited around Sarah's dorm enough until she saw her come in one day, barely managing books, her artist's portfolio, and a bag of groceries.

"Here," said Evelyn, "let me help you."

"Oh, thank you," said Sarah. "I was just about ready to drop it all."

They introduced themselves as they walked up the stairs to Sarah's second-floor dorm room.

"I've seen you around, I think," said Evelyn.

"My brother and I are in a UCLA study-abroad program here. Although I think we'll both likely stay on through next year and graduate."

Over my dead body. "It's a great university," Evelyn said. "I'm in education myself."

"Do you know Ellen Grant? She's in education, too," said Sarah. "She's a good friend."

62

Of course I know Ellen Grant, you idiot. I've known her for years. "No, I don't think I've met her. But education is a big college."

Sarah unlocked the door. "You've been so kind. Would you like some tea?"

"I'd love some tea," said Evelyn.

"Just drop the book bag anywhere. I have to go down the hall to make hot water. I'll be just a minute and then make us some tea."

"Take your time," said Ellen.

She had spied the computer on the desk. And it was on. Sarah's e-mail was open.

Evelyn saw all the messages from Michael and nearly choked. She started to open one and then stopped. *Focus, girl, focus. This will be history soon.* She scrolled down and saw the name, tbailey. She opened it and knew she'd hit pay dirt.

> Sarah, I need a straight answer. I can't get anything from your father. As far as he's concerned, you seemed to have fallen off the face of the earth. But I need to talk with you. So call! Call collect! I want to make sure we're still on the same page about our relationship, and all you've been giving me is the runaround. Love, Terry.

When Sarah returned with the hot water, Evelyn was sitting in a chair by the window.

"There's a lovely view from here," she said.

"It *is* nice," Sarah agreed, "but I don't see it much. Do you live in the dorm?"

"No," said Evelyn, "I'm in a flat not too far from here." They continued to chat while Sarah fixed tea.

Later that evening, Evelyn sat down at her computer. She couldn't hit Terry Bailey all at once, and she didn't know if he was likely to contact Sarah at once as soon as he heard from Evelyn. She needed to develop a relationship. She could tell him that she was a friend of Sarah's and that they talked a lot. He'd need to keep this confidential, of course, but she wanted Sarah to be happy and was afraid she was in over her head with an older man here in Edinburgh. *Yes, that's how to develop it, but carefully, not all at once.* She'd give it two or three weeks, then start sounding a mild alarm, then a little louder. *Yes, that's it. Bait the hook before reeling in the American fish.*

For *The Mikado*, Tommy had managed to get hold of a top hat and cane, while David and Michael wore more traditional tuxedos.

"Good thing I've the hat and cane," Tommy said, "or we'd look like waiters."

They had their tickets, and outside the dorm they split up to get the girls.

Michael had more than a tuxedo. He was carrying a corsage for Sarah and something else, something that carried his love and hope with it. He hoped it might be enough to convince Sarah of both his love and the need for faith.

He'd debated long and hard and finally decided to do it. He didn't know what Sarah would say. He knew she was planning to stay on at Edinburgh to graduate. What she didn't know was that David had definitely decided to stay permanently in Scotland, graduate from Edinburgh, and then enter graduate school. Sarah knew he leaned in that direction but not that he'd made the final jump; David was being more open with Michael and Tommy than he was with his own sister. Michael hoped that David's decision, and what Michael was carrying with him tonight, might hold her in Edinburgh as well.

He deliberately ignored what he knew Iris and Iain would likely say.

As he entered the lobby of Sarah's dorm, Evelyn McLin was descending the stairs.

"Michael! What a surprise!" she said.

"Hello, Evelyn. What are you up to?"

"Waiting for a friend for dinner. You must be excited about graduation. And you look wonderful in the tuxedo."

"Thanks. Look, I hate to run, but we've tickets for *The Mikado,* and I can't be late. See you." He dashed up the stairs, thankful to escape so easily.

Voices rising in argument seeped through Sarah's door. Michael frowned. *It's a male voice, but it's not David.* He knocked.

A young man a few years older than Michael flung open the door.

"What?" He looked Michael up and down. "Ah, you must be the Scottish gentleman friend, although I expecting someone older. Glad to meet you. I'm Terry Bailey, the Los Angeles fiancé."

"You're not my fiancé," said Sarah's voice behind him.

"Sarah?" Michael asked.

She was in jeans and a sweatshirt. Michael looked from her to Terry and back again, completely forgetting about *The Mikado.*

"Sarah, I don't understand," Michael said.

"Join the club, boyfriend. She's had both of us on the hook, and apparently you're as surprised as I am."

He's been drinking. "Sarah, are you okay?" Michael asked.

"Mike, I'm fine. I can't talk tonight. I'm sorry about *The Mikado.* Please, I'll call you tomorrow to explain."

"Don't worry, boyfriend, nobody's going to win this one. She's telling me we're both going to end up losers."

"Why don't you just shut up?" Michael said, surprising himself with his tone.

"Whoa! Look, boyfriend, you and I are in the same boat here, and we ought to at least be friends. Obviously she hasn't told you about me, the guy back in LA who thought he was marrying the girl. And believe me, she hasn't said anything about you. I had to find that out on my own. But she tells me tonight there's this theology student she likes, even if she can't deal with his fanatical religion."

Michael felt the verbal slap. Red faced, he stared at Sarah.

"Mike," Sarah said, "I need you to leave. I'll call you tomorrow."

"Fine," Michael said angrily. "Call me. Assuming you can stand the fanaticism. Here." He shoved the corsage box into Terry Bailey's hands and half-ran toward the stairs.

Terry shut the door. "You've got quite a collection, Sarah. He's as clueless as I was, poor devil. Is there anyone else you're stringing along?"

She stared at Terry. As the impact of what she had done to Michael began to sink in, she rushed to the door and the hallway. "Mike!" she cried.

But he was gone.

Michael was already in the lobby. He saw Evelyn.

"Mike, what's wrong? You look upset."

He stared at her. "I suppose your being here right at this moment is a complete coincidence."

"You needed to know!" Evelyn said, her voice rising. "She'd been playing you for the fool."

"Stay away from me, Evelyn," Michael said. "Stay out of my life. You poison everything you touch. You always have. And now you've poisoned this. Get away from me." Stopping, he turned back. "And my name is Michael." He rushed out the door.

"Michael!" she called as she ran after him. "You don't mean this. You'll thank me tomorrow!"

He didn't answer as he ran into the darkness. Reaching the end of the block, he felt his stomach churning. He managed to reach a refuse can before he threw up.

At University Theatre, Tommy and Ellen stood with David and Betsy, waiting for Michael and Sarah.

"Where can they be?" asked Betsy. "They're going to stop seating for the first act."

"Michael loves Gilbert and Sullivan," said Ellen. "Tommy, try his cell phone again."

Tommy dialed Michael's number.

"Michael! Where are you? It's about to start. What?" He looked at Ellen and then David. "Are you all right? Do you need me to come—" Tommy listened as Michael talked. "Okay, okay. But after? Are you still coming home with me and David? We'll see you tomorrow then. Are you sure you're okay? And Sarah, too? Okay, then, we'll talk later. Good-bye."

"What happened?" Ellen asked as they sprinted for their seats. "Are they okay?"

"He won't say much," Tommy answered. "Something came up for Sarah. He said they were fine, but he sounded awful. He insisted we see *The Mikado* without them."

"Do you think we should?" Betsy asked. "Should we check on them?"

"If Michael says it's okay, it's okay. They won't be coming home with us afterward. Sarah wasn't with him. He said she was at the dorm." Tommy looked at David. "Do you know what might've happened?"

"No idea," David said. "I haven't talked to Sarah since this morning."

"Well, we'll see the show. After, we'll make a detour to the dorm to check on him, then we'll see Ellen and Betsy home and go to my house." They were shushed as they entered the theatre.

Michael knew Tommy was likely to stop at the dorm after *The Mikado*, and he didn't want to see anyone. He walked to the dorm and, stripping off the tux, took a long shower. He felt dirty, and he was sweating although the night was cool. Leaning against the shower wall, he began to sob.

After drying off, he put on jeans and a turtleneck, along with his Reeboks. He looked at his watch. Intermission was long over, and the last act would be ending soon. He scribbled a note for Tommy, telling him he was okay but most likely would go to the McLarens' for the night. *That's a fudge, but it's where I wish I was.*

Neither Sarah nor David had said anything about Terry Bailey. Bailey obviously knew Michael, and if he thought he was Sarah's fiancé, then he must know David as well. He felt betrayed by both of them, but he couldn't believe it.

He looked around to see where he was. He'd left campus and ended up closer to the shopping and entertainment district of downtown Edinburgh, although it was virtually impossible to tell where the campus stopped and the city began. His stomach growling, he saw an all-night café. He hoped he could keep down whatever he ate.

The performance ended, and the four bolted from the theatre. Ellen and Betsy waited in the dorm lobby, while Tommy and David went upstairs.

"He's been here," Tommy said. "There's his tux and a towel. He must have showered."

"Here's a note," David said. "It's for you."

"David, call Sarah and see if she knows anything."

Tommy read the note.

> Sorry for the last-minute change in plans. Everything's up
> in the air. Don't worry. I'll probably head home for the
> night. If you need to reach me, leave a message on the cell.
> M.

David reached Sarah. "So what's up? We waited forever, and then Michael called and said you weren't coming. Is everything okay? Oh, Sarah, oh, no. He walked in? Why didn't you just throw him out? I told you to talk to him about it months ago." He looked at Tommy. "Tommy, does the note say where he went?"

"It sounds like he went to the McLarens'," Tommy said. "He says to leave a message on his cell if we need to reach him."

"Sarah, he went to the McLarens'. We'll leave a message on his cell. We'll check on Michael tomorrow. If you need me or if Terry shows back up, call me."

"Who's Terry?" Tommy asked after David ended the call.

"Terry Bailey. He and Sarah dated before we came to Scotland. He thinks they're engaged. He flew in today from the States, and Michael walked in on them during an argument."

"Were they engaged, David?"

"Tommy, I don't know. Maybe. Sarah thought she'd broken it off. He works for my father in Los Angeles. He's been sending her e-mails off and on since she got here."

Tommy stared. "David, I'll hang up his tux. Go down and tell Ellen and Betsy, then let's stick to the original plan and go to my parents'. Michael knows we'll be there if he needs us. Let's just go." David left for the lobby.

Tommy shook his head. *This isn't just a mix-up. This is a big one, maybe* the *big one.* As he picked up Michael's tuxedo jacket, he felt a bulge in the pocket.

It was a small box. He opened it and stared at an engagement ring. *My poor English.*

He put the box in Michael's desk drawer, turned out the lights, and left.

After managing a few bites of what was advertised as grilled chicken, Michael drank his water, paid the bill, and left. He wanted to walk. *Walk until I disappear, walk until every molecule of me has disappeared into the pavement.* He knew he wouldn't make any sense of this, not tonight, not without some explanation from Sarah or David.

As he walked down a side street of mostly pubs, a body crashed into him, propelled through a pub door, and almost took Michael down with the force of impact. "And stay out of here, Yank," a bouncer snarled.

The body belonged to Terry Bailey, a very drunk Terry Bailey.

"This is unbelievable," Michael said. "I can't get away from you."

Terry retched into the gutter. Michael wanted to leave him there.

"So where are you staying?" he asked.

Terry looked up at him from the sidewalk. "I'm not. Not anywhere. She's got my wallet." And he retched again. "Look, boyfriend, just leave me alone. I'm drowning my sorrows. Just go away."

Michael stared at him. "I'd like nothing better. But you've got no money, no place to stay, and you're drunk. It's going near freezing tonight. If I don't do something with you, you'll get pneumonia. Sarah's got your wallet?"

"No." He vomited again in the gutter. "The one who picked me up at the airport. Eve, Eve—"

"Evelyn McLin?"

Terry nodded.

Wonderful. He pulled Terry to his feet. "I hope you can walk. It's at least fifteen blocks to the dorm."

His arm supporting Terry's shoulder, Michael started walking.

Dragging a barely conscious Terry into the dorm room, Michael saw that Tommy had been there. The note was gone, and his tux had been hung on the closet door.

Terry mumbled incoherently.

Michael gently dumped him on his own bed. He took off Terry's shoes and jacket, then found an extra blanket in the closet. He shook his head. *Getting to babysit the unknown rival is a bit over the top.*

Then he saw the cut on Terry's temple. The blood had dried, but the skin was dirty. Michael went to the bath and found the unused first-aid kit Ma had insisted he keep on hand.

Michael cleaned the wound and could see it was small, mostly dried blood. He applied antiseptic and then a small bandage. There was blood on Terry's shirt, but Michael wasn't going to undress him. *Mr. Bailey can clean his own shirt in the morning.*

Terry slept.

Michael stretched out on Tommy's bed but didn't sleep. A little after six, he gave up the fight and decided to go for morning coffee. He threw on jeans and a sweatshirt and jacket, and then quietly slipped out.

Returning from Starbucks with a carryout carton of coffee and some rolls, he saw Terry was still asleep.

Might as well try to get some work done. He flipped on his laptop, poured some coffee, and settled down.

Terry opened his eyes. He turned his head but felt like hammers were pounding it. *Where am I? What's happened?*

He looked over and saw Michael typing on his laptop. *The boyfriend. Great. But how'd I get here, and why here?* He had vague memories of a walk, then a taxi. Then he remembered the nasty bouncer at the nasty pub, but not much else. *I must've put on a major drunk. Oh, man, my head.*

"So you run a rescue mission, too?" Terry croaked out.

Michael looked up from his laptop. "Sleeping Beauty awakes."

"Without a kiss from the prince, I hope."

"Not a chance," said Michael. "Even a frog would've been put off with how you looked last night, not to mention now."

Terry slowly sat up, his head in agony, his stomach not far behind. "How'd I end up here?"

"Coincidence, fate, or God's sense of humor," said Michael. "Take your pick. Personally, I think God had a good laugh."

"I'm glad somebody did."

"I happened to be walking down the street when a pub bouncer literally threw you right into me. You'd no money or ID, no place to stay, and you were in no condition to figure out what to do. You also had a nice cut on your left temple." Terry felt the bandage. "And you'll probably need to change the dressing. Do you want some coffee?"

"I don't think I could keep it down."

"You need to try. It'll help." Michael poured it in a cup and handed it to Terry.

"So why are you doing this? If it had been me, I probably would've left you there. The coffee's good, by the way."

"It's your American Starbucks. I couldn't leave you in the gutter, which is exactly where you were, losing whatever it was you last ate. Your clothes are a mess, I'm afraid. There's dried blood on your shirt, your jacket's ripped, and your pants have seen better days."

"The rest of my things are in her car. I hope she hasn't run off with my stuff."

"Evelyn's many things bad, but I've never heard of her being a thief. It'd be easier to care about her if that's all she was."

"She started sending me e-mails a couple of months ago. At first she was friendly. She was a friend of Sarah's—yada yada—and then she started raising some flags."

"She baited the hook and then hooked her fish."

"For what reason?"

"You were a means to an end. How did she get your e-mail address?"

"I don't know. But she was really friendly, even when she dropped me off at Sarah's dorm."

Michael was quiet. Then: "She needed you to do exactly what you ended up doing. She wrote the play and designed the roles for all of us, only I've changed the ending."

Terry swung around and put his feet on the floor. "Whoa! I think I did that too quickly. I'm dizzy. Is there a bathroom anywhere close by?"

Michael pointed to the bath door. "Through there. If you want to shower—and I strongly suggest you do—there's an extra towel and cloth next to the tub. Can you manage?"

"I think so. If you hear a thud, just let me drown."

After the shower, Terry looked more than a little improved.

"Have a pastry," Michael said. "I avoided the sticky things, so there's a croissant or two and, I think, a blueberry muffin."

Terry picked up a croissant. "So really, why'd you help me?"

"I haven't been drunk before, Terry. I'm not much of a drinker. But I've been in bad spots and got help when I didn't deserve it. Call it grace and accept it."

The door opened, and in came Tommy and David.

"What's this?" asked Tommy, pointing to Terry. "Or should I say, who's this?"

"Hi, David," said Terry.

"Terry," David nodded.

"Now this looks like a story," said Tommy.

"Terry Bailey, recovering drunkard," Terry said, waving his partially eaten croissant.

"You arrived like the proverbial cavalry, Tomahawk," said Michael. "We need your car to help Terry recover his suitcase and, he hopes, his wallet and passport."

"And we're recovering these items from where?" Tommy asked.

"Evelyn McLin," Michael said.

Tommy stared. "This must be a better story than I imagined. You've already tangled with the Wicked Witch of the North, our own Evil McLin."

"I'd reprimand you," said Michael, "but she deserves it."

"By the way," Tommy said to Michael, "I put your box in your desk drawer."

Michael frowned, puzzled, and then, blushing, understood. "Thanks, Tommy."

"Wear garlic around your neck," Tommy called as Terry walked into Evelyn's building. "Or hold a crucifix in front of you. It'll be some protection." Even Michael laughed.

Evelyn handed over his belongings and shut the door in Terry's face.

Back in the car, Terry looked relieved. "That turned out to be easier than I expected."

"You were lucky," said Tommy. "She didn't bite your neck, did she? Did you throw water on her? I saw in some American movie that water melts them."

As they dropped him off at his hotel, Terry spoke to Michael.

"Thanks," he said. "You kept me from making a worse fool out of myself or getting into more trouble."

Michael gave a small shrug. "It's okay."

"Michael, I've lost her for good. But don't hold this against her. I think she genuinely didn't know what to do and didn't even think there was anything she had to do. And the religion thing scares her."

"I love her, Terry, but the religion thing, as you call it, is an issue. And now we have to deal with it. Some good may come of it in the long run, but I'm dreading it. I'm going to lose her, perhaps forever."

"I'd put in a good word except my word isn't worth much right now. Thanks again. If I can ever do anything for you, just let me know. Here's my card. Look me up if you ever get to LA."

74

They shook hands.

"Well," said Tommy as Michael got back into the car. "Not that I'm dying of curiosity or anything, but a few details would more than pay for the taxi service."

"Michael," said David from the back seat, "I'm sorry. I should've said something. I'm sorry. It's a mess, isn't it?"

"David, it's a mess, but remember, God is good. I don't know what'll happen next, but whatever it is, God is good. And you're still my brother. So is this lunkhead here, who wants all the gory details." And he ruffled Tommy's hair.

"Has Sarah called?" asked David.

"I don't know," said Michael. "I haven't checked my messages. I don't think I'm ready to talk with her right now. This is all pretty raw still."

"But you can talk with us," Tommy said as he pulled out into traffic.

Chapter 11

Michael left his cell phone off. That afternoon, he biked to the farm. He needed the distance practice, and he needed to release his turmoil into the pedals.

His arrival set Ham to barking, and he waved as Iris looked out from the kitchen window. He put his bike in the stable before coming into the kitchen.

"Hi, Ma." He kissed her on the cheek.

"Michael, I didn't expect you. This is a nice—" She gasped. "What's wrong?"

"I'm going to have to wear a mask or clown's makeup around you. Am I really that obvious?"

"Yes, but that aside. What's wrong?"

"It's Sarah, Ma." And he told her what had happened.

Iris listened and then hugged him.

"It hurts, Ma. It hurts bad. I've lost her." She held him as he cried.

"I'm sorry, son. My heart wants to break. Your father has a saying that usually drives me right off the cliff whenever he says it, and what's worse is that it's true. If God means it to be, then it'll be. Not the way we think, often enough. But it'll happen if that's the plan. We have to trust him. Although I admit that it's a hard thing to hear when you ache like this. So. Your father is away, down near Birmingham. It's just you and me. Are you staying the night?"

"Yes'm. I thought I'd go to St. Bartolph's tomorrow to see Father Andy."

She smiled. "He'll be a tonic, I imagine. In the meantime, if you've no other plans, you can help me dig in the garden while we get the plans down for the commencement. It's less than a month away, it is. Plus I want to hear everything about Tommy and Ellen's wedding. Which I know won't be much, given your general deafness when it comes to important details, but I'd still like to hear."

Michael smiled. "You're the tonic, Ma."

Early Monday, Michael skipped ExpressoYourself and went to Starbucks. Tommy was in Glasgow for a second job interview with an architectural firm, David had a late class, and Michael doubted that he or Sarah would show up.

It felt good to sit by the window, catching the sun. Michael was finishing some of his final course work; there wasn't much left but a few reports. His thesis had been presented and defended last month, he thought thankfully. *It would've been awful trying to do it right now.*

A tapping on the window caught his attention. Sarah gave a small wave. At first Michael stared, expressionless; his stomach churned and he thought he might lose the latte. Then he nodded.

She came in and sat across from him.

"I called," she said.

"I know. I went out to the farm and didn't turn the phone on until last night."

"You didn't call back."

"I didn't."

"Mike, I—"

"Sarah, let's not. You said what you needed to say. Apology accepted for *The Mikado*. Apology accepted for not saying anything about Terry."

"I officially broke it off. I thought I'd ended it last summer, but I guess I wasn't emphatic enough." She paused. "That's not true. I never broke it off with him. Not really. With you here, I just pretended he didn't exist. The fact is, I led you both on, whether I intended to or not. But now it's broken off with him. For real, this time."

Michael nodded. "And now you're officially breaking it off with me."

"Mike—"

"Sarah, as much as I hate to say this, you're right. I led myself on, thinking it would change, thinking and hoping you'd come to believe. God finally had to knock me down to get my attention." He cleared his throat.

"You've been right all along. We can't take this forward as long as we—as long as there's—well, as long as we don't believe the same. It'd put a terrible burden on you. It's no way to start a life together and no way for me to start my ministry. And what would happen if I get assigned to Malawi? It's a hard life there, especially for women and children. If you didn't have the same commitment, it'd be a disaster. I can't ask you to go through that." *But God knows how much I love you.*

"Mike, I want to believe. I want to believe like you and Tommy and David do, but I can't. It's just not there. It's not real to me."

"Am I real to you, Sarah?"

"Of course you're real to me. You're all I think about. You're what keeps me awake at night."

"If I'm real, then faith is real. It's that simple."

"It's not that simple."

"Then you must think me a total lunatic. I walk around praying. I talk about God like he's in the same room. I talk to God because I believe he *is* in the same room. I'm completing my studies so I can serve him as fully as possible. I think about him and even dream about him." He reddened. "So if it's not real, I must be a lunatic. What other possibility is there? So if you think you love me— and I think you do—then you love a crazy man."

"I can't argue with you, Mike. I love a crazy man. But I can't live with him."

He looked down. "So there it is then."

"There it is," she said.

"So, what's next? Have you decided what you're doing for school?"

"I'll finish up at UCLA. I should be able to graduate in December."

"When do you go?"

"In two weeks."

"Two weeks," he repeated. *Lord, I don't think I can stand this. You're going to have to carry me or just let me collapse right here.*

"You know that David is staying."

"Aye. I expect for a lot of reasons, the major one being Betsy, but also the coursework he wants to take. And I think he's considering graduate school after next year."

"Yes. And to study what he wants to study, he needs to do it here in Scotland," she said.

They were both quiet.

"Can I take you to the airport?"

"You don't need to do that."

"I want to. I expect David will see you off as well?"

"No. He thought I'd be leaving later, so he's doing a short seminar here, something that will help him later on. I told him we can say good-bye here just as easily as at the airport."

"Then I have to see you off. We'll need to do something the night before. Tommy, Ellen, and Betsy will want to say good-bye as well."

She swallowed hard. "Mike, let's not. Leaving will be bad enough."

Michael looked almost defiant. "Sarah, they care for you. You've become part of them, like you've become part of me, but different. Please don't shut them out. Let them say good-bye."

She rubbed her hands together and looked down. "Okay, Mike, we can plan to do something. Let's just do it low-key. Maybe sit around and drink coffee or have a beer at the pub."

"And can I see you to the airport?"

She looked at him. "My first thought is to tell you no. But, yes, Mike, I'd like that very much."

Sarah's last night in Edinburgh was subdued, as far as Tommy was concerned, but not as anyone else would define it. He and Michael had reserved a private dining room, and Tommy kept all of them laughing with jokes, imitations, and charades. David and Betsy announced their engagement, and Sarah hugged her brother. "California may be an American," Tommy observed, "but he has the eminent good sense to select a Scot for his wife." Tommy announced that he'd gotten the job in Glasgow.

The next morning, Michael borrowed Tommy's car to take Sarah to the airport. Most of her things had been sent to California, with only two boxes left for the dorm housemother to ship. As he took her suitcases down to the car, he noticed she was wearing the pearl pendant.

They said little as they drove to the airport. He parked the car and found a cart for her bags.

As they stood in line for her boarding passes, he asked her where she was going first.

"To Gran's in Santa Barbara," she said. "She's meeting me at the airport in LA. And I'll stay with her until summer semester starts at UCLA in about three weeks."

"Have you heard anything from your dad?"

"Nothing. It's as if we never existed."

"Will you see Scott and his family?"

"Gran and I will probably make a trip up to visit. The plan is to get together for Thanksgiving. And David's talking about bringing Betsy to meet the family at Christmas."

"They'll be married by Christmas."

"You think so? He didn't say anything about a date."

"My guess is they'll be married before summer's gone."

They reached the front of the line. Sarah handed over her ticket and passport, while Michael put her bags on the scale.

"That wasn't too bad," she said as they walked away. "You don't have to stay. I'll have to go through security in an hour, and I know you have things to do."

"Do you want me to go?"

"No, Mike, I want you to stay." She looked away. "I'm chattering like an idiot because I'm afraid of the silence. I don't want to think about leaving. Not Edinburgh. Not you."

He smiled. "I don't want you to leave. I can't believe this is happening, but it is, so here we are. Would you like a coffee? There's a Starbucks over there."

"And Mike loves Starbucks."

"Aye. And Mike loves Starbucks." He smiled back. *But nothing like Mike loves Sarah.*

They sat in a waiting area with their coffees. A television was on with the BBC anchor reciting up-to-the-minute news.

"Do you need anything?" he asked. "Bottled water? A snack or a magazine?"

"No. I want to sit here with you."

"I've been practicing my wedding toast for Tommy and Ellen. I'd be giving one as the best man, but Tommy's da isn't big on speeches with crowds, so he and Tommy asked me to take on the main duties. Imagine a relative of Tommy's not having the gift of gab. It's strange. I've known them since we were kids, and here they are, adults and grown up and getting married."

"Well, you can say Ellen is an adult."

Michael laughed. "True. Tomahawk will probably stay a kid. The job's a relief for both of them, I'm sure. He's a good architect, but he'll have to become his own boss one day. He's the only one he could work for and not drive crazy. But it's a good job, and Ellen can now put in her applications for teaching in Glasgow since they know where they're going."

"So what's next for Mike?"

"Well," he said, "commencement is Saturday. Then the wedding next Friday. Then London, and the cycling team will be my life for the next two and a half months. We'll leave for Athens the last week of July, and we'll live in the Olympic Village for three weeks. Then I come back to London for ordination and find out my assignment."

"Are you hoping for Malawi?"

"I think so," he answered. "It's where my heart is, and there are definitely openings. They need ordained priests. Archbishop Johnston hasn't said definitively, but he's hinted that I'm likely to be assigned there. And he's got some influence, too, I imagine. It's not exactly the top pick for candidates, although it should be." *If I can't be with you, Sarah Hughes, I need to be as far away as I can get.*

"So next year at this time you expect to be in Africa."

"Aye."

She was quiet. Then she put her hand on his arm.

"There's so much I want to say," she said. "And I can't. This seems idiotic—to be leaving, I mean. No, that's not it. It seems idiotic to be leaving you."

Michael didn't answer. He put his hand on top of hers.

"You're not saying anything," Sarah said.

"If I say anything, I'll break down, embarrassing you, me, and everyone else around here."

They were both quiet for a few moments.

"I have to go through security soon."

He nodded.

"I sent your mom and dad a note."

"They told me. They really appreciated what you said."

"I don't want them to think badly—"

"They don't. Da says all he has to do is look at the painting, and he knows what kind of hand painted that. He also said to remind you about what you talked about at Christmas, about the act of creation. Do you know what he's talking about?"

She nodded, too choked up to speak.

"Here," she said. She handed him the polka-dot scarf she had tied around her purse. "Hold on to it. Maybe you can give it back one day. Just keep it."

They walked to the security checkpoint.

"Will you write or e-mail?" she asked.

"No," he said, shaking his head. "No."

"No?"

"It'd be too hard," he said softly. "It'd be like letting go of you over and over again, like I'm doing now, and I couldn't stand it. This is the hardest thing I've ever done in my life, Sarah, and you may not want to hear it, but I'm doing it by God's grace alone, because I wouldn't have the courage or the strength to do it by myself."

They reached the point where Michael had to step out of line. She squeezed his arm.

"You're always part of me, Sarah Hughes," he said, "for as long as I live. And longer. And I'm part of you."

She nodded and continued walking, then stopped and ran back to him, throwing her arms around him. He held her while people flowed around them.

She finally let go, wiping his tears and her own. She turned and went in through security.

He stood until he could see her no more. Then he walked back to the car park, her scarf in his hand.

Part II

Athens

Chapter 12

After graduation and Tommy and Ellen's wedding, Michael immersed himself in training to prepare for Athens and, he hoped, to provide a distraction from Sarah. The regimen of training only partially succeeded; the separation from Sarah created a depth of pain that shocked him. Tommy and Ellen had been surprised by Michael's official wedding toast—expecting stories about Tommy's antics growing up; instead they heard a moving tribute to what their friendship had meant to Michael and about the love he felt for both of them, leaving no dry eye in the room. Iain and Iris saw their son's usual optimism and good spirits subside into quietness. Iris prayed that training would help.

The men's team settled in Wimbledon, the women's in Lambeth. They used the same training facilities, including the South London Velodrome. For four of the seven weeks, the mountain bikers and the BMXers were in Wales, using mountain and bike parks. Michael and the road team remained in London, except for ten days in Scotland to practice climbing.

No day was like any other. The cyclists did distance trials, then sprints, a day off for weight training, then short trials, back to sprints, and then a long-distance ride. For two days, the road team practiced in Cambridge and tested a new wind tunnel to help gain speed and better overall control of their rides.

"The Americans started it," Coach White said. "All the European teams head to America during the winter for wind tunnel testing. Cambridge just installed this, so we're trying it out."

Michael's roommate was Roger Pitts. Michael learned that as far as Roger was concerned, they might be teammates, but first they were competitors. Roger hadn't forgotten how easily Michael met his challenge in York. Publicly Roger had smiled; inwardly he had been humiliated and vowed not to let this amateur, this theology student, get past him again.

"Has it occurred to you that without all this constant talk about comparable times, speeds, cranks and watts, you and I might become friends?" Michael asked one night.

"No," said Roger matter-of-factly, "it hasn't. I've never really thought of us as friends. Is that a problem?"

"No," Michael sighed, "but it might make you more sufferable to live with."

Roger shrugged and continued working his calculator. "Look, Kent, I intend to win gold in all of the races we're competing in, and you should at least focus on winning a bronze or placing in the top five."

The fact was that Roger, four years older than Michael, was more experienced—the consummate professional cyclist looking to make his name. He was also obnoxious. Cycling was how he made his living, and he'd raced in some of the spring classics—the Tour of Flanders was one—and he'd seen how the professionals raced; he knew the competitors they would face in Athens. If he was to be one of them and if he was to win, he would be as ruthless as needed and reject any overtures toward friendship from this Scot priest or anyone else on the team.

Friendship just gets in the way, Roger told himself. *This isn't personal; this is business. The Olympics are a springboard to something bigger and better.*

Except there was no doubt that Michael was good, Roger soon saw, and if Michael had had the sense to go into racing full-time, he could be even better, possibly better than Roger himself. *This guy is a university cyclist, an amateur; he doesn't know what it means to ride the cobbles of Belgium and France or try an insane breakaway on a 9 percent grade.* While Roger's own experience was limited, *at least I've an idea of what's in front of me.*

After the York embarrassment, he intended to bring this Scot down to size. He'd heard the coaches talking and watched them as they watched Michael. They were rough on Michael, no doubt about that, rougher than on anyone else, including Roger. But they were pushing Michael harder because they saw "the something" within him. Roger saw it, too; it made him even more determined to keep Kent in his place.

Coach White was old school and defined "the something" as heart; Michael Kent simply had the heart for cycling, although the coach could see that

Michael was troubled, guessing that it had to do with a girl. But the young Scot had the heart for the sport.

Watching the coaches study Michael irritated Roger because it raised self-doubts. For Roger, "the something" was the unrelenting commitment to win. Michael had the heart, the joy of it all, the understanding of himself and the machine he rode to know what could happen when the two became one and to experience the thrill. Roger knew that as well, *but thrills are cheap; they never last.*

The other team members began to see what the coaches saw: Michael, the youngest cyclist on the team and the university amateur, and Roger, the most experienced professional, were emerging as team leaders, representing two philosophies of competitiveness and two paths forward. The others quietly but closely watched the Roger-Michael drama play out because it would guide them in how they competed in Athens. One would be the captain, and while there was general sympathy for a fellow professional like Roger, many were already privately pulling for Michael. Roger was flat-out insufferable, ability and experience notwithstanding.

Roger wondered why the coaches had assigned the two of them to room together. After each day's practice, Michael was ready to relax and talk; Roger poured over his computer printout sheets, checking times, watts, and heart rates. He then mentally compared his statistics with Michael's, sharing the comparisons only if Roger's were better. The only thing worse than Michael's talking, Roger soon realized, was the prayer. *The guy's always praying.* It drove Roger crazy.

The one thing Roger admitted young Kent could do better was encourage. Roger defined leadership as using authority and experience to direct others. Michael talked easily with all, always encouraging the other cyclists. Roger thought defensively that they should encourage themselves.

They heard endless lectures and watched hours of DVDs and old videos about the routes they'd be riding in Greece, previous Olympic races, and the competitors they'd be facing. Outside speakers talked of old races; British cyclists had medaled but always a bronze or a very rare silver. None had ever won a gold; with the advent of a whole flock of Americans and other nationalities inspired by Lance Armstrong, it seemed the British might never win gold. Many of the competitors would be coming to Athens directly from the Tour de France, exhausted but, with a little rest, in top form for the Olympics, which they'd see as anticlimactic after the Tour. They were professionals, after all, and the Olympics still had a strong whiff of amateurism, despite the change in recent years.

Roger watched Michael closely without being obvious. *Kent is clueless as to what he's up against. It'll almost be fun to watch the crash-and-burn that's coming.*

In his e-mails home to his parents and to Tommy and David, Michael said very little about his roommate, other than that he was an excellent cyclist. Feeling the emptiness without Sarah, he eagerly anticipated the responses and news from home. Tommy and Ellen had moved to an apartment in Glasgow; Tommy was settling into his job, and Ellen had found a post teaching preschoolers. David and Betsy were inching closer to marriage, and David said they were now considering early August for a small, private wedding. Ma and Da kept him up to date on the farm and on where in Britain Da might be working. No one mentioned Sarah.

"He doesn't like this Pitts character he's rooming with," Iain said to Iris.

"Now, Iain, how do you know that? He's hardly said anything about him."

"Exactly my point. We hear about the others on the team and the coaches but virtually nothing about the man he's rooming with. I hope it's not some kind of competitive thing for Pitts, making Michael's life miserable."

Michael wasn't feeling miserable. Roger Pitts aside, he enjoyed training, thankful that most of his waking hours were filled with something besides thoughts of Sarah. He'd worked hard with the university cycling team, but this was entirely different. And except for Pitts, Michael liked all his fellow cyclists. They were a dedicated bunch, melding together as a team.

All of them would be involved in the heats for the time trial competitions. Seven would be selected for the final roster for the road team with three alternates, and then there would be a second team, which would not likely make it to Athens. The BMX and mountain bike teams would also have ten each on their first teams. No one knew their ultimate team assignment, but they all faced the prospect of a grueling three weeks at the height of the Greek summer. The unusual summer heat in June and July in Britain made training difficult, but the coaches knew it was good preparation for Athens.

Michael felt himself improving each day. The coach was getting harder on him all the time, and Michael, surprised at first, had realized the purpose and responded, increasing both the coach's and his own expectations. Michael's cycling performance improved and then began to thrive, growing in ways he hadn't expected. He found himself focusing his personal pain into the pedals.

The only part of training that Michael dreaded was after lights-out. Then he was alone with his memories of Sarah. He'd catch himself reliving the tango, the endless cups of coffee at ExpressoYourself, Christmas at the McLarens', the smell of her hair as she leaned against his shoulder, how her hand had touched his calf for her drawing.

The last day of training, Coach White called each of the road cyclists into his office one by one to let them know their team placement. It was a nail-biting day, Michael said to Iain and Iris later, and he was the last to be called in.

"Sit down, Michael," the coach said. "And relax."

"I can sit, coach, but I don't know if I can relax."

"Michael, of course you've made the first team. There's been no question of that from the beginning. The only question was whether I would also have you on the first mountain bike team. We watched you in the Highlands, and you were as good as any." White paused and smiled. "I pushed you and kept pushing you, and you kept pushing back and improving the whole time."

Michael relaxed a fraction. "Thank you, sir."

"So how is it with you and Pitts?"

"Tense but generally manageable."

"Pitts is on the first road team as well," Coach White said, "but barely. He's a fine cyclist, and he should ride well in Athens, but he's too caught up in himself to be exceptional. Unless you work on him a bit."

"Swallow my general inclination to slug him and reach out to him in some way?"

Coach White laughed. "Something like that. I really don't expect you to do anything, Michael. But you've something that just might help our Mr. Pitts see that he's his own worst enemy." He paused. "You've done well. You took everything I threw at you and kept cranking."

"I've seen the improvement, sir. This was completely different from university."

"It'd better been," the coach said. "This is the Olympics. I want to see us do this nation proud. And you, Michael, just might be the one to do it. I've watched you closely these past many weeks. Something's been troubling you—I could see that as soon as you arrived—but you've been working through it. Whatever it was or still is, for all I know, you've focused it in the bike. And it shows. You've got the heart for the sport. So go home and see your family, son, and come back ready to ride."

Chapter 13

They had three days to visit home; they'd meet back in London on the nineteenth with the entire British team, some 250 strong. They'd stay in dormitories at the University of London and after a royal send-off fly to Athens.

"We've a meeting with the king at Buckingham Palace and then dinner with the prime minister and the corporate sponsors," Michael told Iris and Iain when he got home. "And they'll announce the captains for all of the teams."

"Are you in the running for the road team captain?" Iris asked.

"No, Ma, I'm the youngest on the team, and there are a lot more accomplished cyclists than me. Anyway, we actually get to see Buckingham Palace. I know the royal family isn't exactly the best we could do, but seeing the palace should be a treat."

Iris glanced at Ian. They'd never said anything to Michael about his birth family, even though they'd been prepared to do so. But he'd never asked, seemingly content to know what little he did.

"Should we tell him?" Iris asked her husband as they were getting ready for bed.

"No," said Iain. "It wouldn't serve any purpose right now. And I doubt that good King James III is asking where his cousin is. He might have a bit of explaining to do if he did that."

"How do you think he's doing, Iain? He's excited about the Olympics, but I look at him and listen, and I just don't know."

"His heart's broken, Iris," Iain said. "It'll mend in time with God's grace, but the ache is deep."

The day before returning to London, Michael rode his mountain bike in the hills behind the farm. He stopped at what he called his lookout, an outcropping of rock that provided a perfect view of the McLarens' below. He'd always thought of it as his refuge, his castle keep when he needed solitude, where he could sit and think and pray. Here at age sixteen he'd prayed about becoming a priest.

He sat there now, feeling a surprisingly cold wind fighting the warmth of the sun on his face.

He unzipped his jersey pocket and pulled out Sarah's scarf. Placing its softness against his cheek, he closed his eyes and began to pray. *I have faith, Father, but this hurts. More than I could've known. But you knew, and you know my heart. Does it go away after a while? This ache, this emptiness?*

The entire Olympic team met with the king and queen in the palace garden in the early afternoon. A bored King James made perfunctory remarks, and Queen Charlotte kept looking at her watch. Michael was disappointed, but to see Buckingham Palace, even from the garden, was wonderful. *It's huge, much bigger than the photos make you think.* Their buses had drawn crowds as they made their way from the University of London to the palace. People applauded and cheered from the sidewalks, and car horns honked all over.

Dinner was a corker.

They assembled at the Ritz at six for the alcohol-free reception before dinner at eight. At 7:30 p.m., the prime minister arrived with a small entourage. Several businessmen arrived separately.

Peter Bolting had been PM for only three months, elected on a reform platform. In his early forties, he looked young, acted young, and moved quickly. He'd already introduced a number of economic and educational reform measures in Parliament, and his popularity was growing. A dynamic speaker, he continued to support the war in the Middle East and had committed even more British troops. But his popularity, for the present, overrode any opposition.

The excitement among the athletes was palpable. They were ready for something upbeat after the disappointing palace visit.

Bolting introduced the Olympic team sponsors, several corporate executives, including the president of the BBC and the BritRail CEO. One name caught Michael's attention. Henry Kent, one of his teammates said, was one of the wealthiest people in Britain, a cousin of the king, with influence extending to

96

Washington and New York and the financial markets in Europe and the Far East. Seated where he was, Michael couldn't see much on the dais and wished for a closer view.

After dinner came the celebratory speeches. Bolting did not disappoint; soon the athletes were cheering.

The PM asked Lord Darnell, chair of the British Olympic Committee, to come to the podium to announce the team captains.

Darnell explained that the captains had been chosen by their fellow team members as those best exemplifying leadership and the Olympic spirit in their specific sport. And then he began calling out the sport and the chosen captain.

Dazzled by the excitement, Michael was shocked when his name was called out, his team members bursting into cheering applause as they gestured him forward.

"I repeat," Lord Darnell said, "Michael Kent, captain for the British Olympic Cycling Team."

Dazed, honored, and completely flustered, Michael walked to the dais.

Lord Darnell shook his hand and presented him with a certificate. The PM placed the captain's ribbon around his neck, shook his hand, and said congratulations, telling him he hoped that he got a ribbon or two in Athens with something hanging on it. And then Darnell gave Michael a surprised look. *The color of his eyes! It's the royal blue!*

Representing the corporate sponsors was Henry Kent. Michael and Henry looked at each other.

What Michael caught first were the blue eyes, the same color as his own. *That's extraordinary; we've the same color. And my middle name is Henry. I wonder if he's a relation.* Then he caught the look of recognition on Henry Kent's face. It was unmistakable. *He knows me.*

"Well done, Michael," Henry murmured, shaking his hand. And then Michael was walking back to his table, wondering if he'd come face-to-face with a piece of his past.

At the table next to Michael's, Roger Pitts was red faced and furious.

The next morning in their Glasgow apartment, Tommy sat reading the newspaper, shaking his head.

"What is it?" asked Ellen.

"The cycling team chose Michael as captain," he replied. "Every time I think they're totally hopeless, the English do something that implies they've a miniscule chance of redeeming themselves one day."

Ellen laughed as she hugged Tommy around his neck and leaned over to read the story.

Chapter 14

Arriving in Athens at night, they could see the lights of the city from the plane and caught a quick glimpse of the floodlit Parthenon. Buses took them to Olympic Village, quickly named the OV, where they joined thousands of other athletes looking for rooms, searching for roommates, and reporting lost baggage amid typical arrival chaos.

The next morning after breakfast, Michael posted an index card on the bulletin board in their building wing.

> Bible study and prayer tonight for all interested.
> 7 p.m. Suite 233 West Building.
> Michael Kent, UK

"You're serious?" asked Roger Pitts, standing behind him.

Michael jumped. "Sorry, Roger, I didn't know you were there. Yes, I'm serious."

"Kent, this is about athletics and competition. It's the Olympics, not a missionaries' meeting. This isn't about religion."

"Well, I agree with you it's not about religion, Roger, but God's often found in unexpected places, including the Olympics."

Roger shook his head. "Fine. Think like that. We'll all end up losers." He got right in Michael's face. "You're the captain, so act like one. Or maybe you can be content with meeting a few kindred spirits and lose all of your events."

Michael pushed him back. "Roger, I want to win as much as you do. But it's not only about winning."

"It is for me. We'll see who's right. We've four days until the time trial. We'll see who's got the best head to win. And I'll wave at you from the podium." He walked off.

Wednesday was devoted to practice and physical workouts. The road team had been assigned to a workout area at a high school that had a cinder track and decent weight facilities.

After dinner, Michael waited in his four-man room. His roommates were exploring Athens.

By seven thirty, he knew he'd had no takers.

Thursday's training focused on the individual time trial. Coach White called it "shooting out the barrel." All 235 road cyclists would participate in trial heats of ten kilometers on Friday, with the slowest placed first in line and the fastest placed last for the seventy-five kilometer medals event on Saturday. Every two minutes, a cyclist would leave the starting line and ride to be fastest. The record time was 68.74 minutes, set in 1956 and never broken.

After dinner, Michael checked the building's bulletin boards and saw his cards were still posted. *At least Roger's left them alone.* In his room he prayed while he waited, leaving the door open. *Maybe this wasn't a good idea, Father. But I wanted to try it. There must be a few believers here who might want to pray, who might need encouragement. But I'm content. You want us to make the effort, and you take it from there. So I'll keep praying and wait on—*

He heard a throat clear, and he looked up at the tallest, blackest man he'd ever seen.

"I am Moses," the man announced in a booming voice with an African accent. "But I forgot to bring my stone tablets." He dissolved in laughter.

Great, now it's a joke.

The visitor finally stopped laughing, wiping tears from his eyes. "I am sorry," he said. "But it is my little joke. My name is indeed Moses, however. Moses Paul Akimbe. I am your brother in Christ from Kenya."

Moses had been born and raised in western Kenya near the Ugandan border. His parents were small farmers, and he was an only child, born to parents in their early forties. "Almost like Abraham and Sarah," he said. "They are good Christian people and were raised by their parents to be good Christians. So I come from a long line of Christian people."

100

A small child, he had been ideal for bullying. Village children had chased him from their games and hounded him at school. "They liked to catch me and rub my face in cow dung, which fortunately wasn't too often because very few people had cows," he said.

So Moses had learned to run.

His small size continued into his early teens. So did his running. Because of the bullying, Moses found himself running across fields and hills, just to escape. "My good mother prayed that God would use this to make me a Christian man and that good would come from this evil inflicted on me by the other children and even some of the adults." He entered a few local races and shocked himself, his parents, and his village by winning them—and by wide margins. The short boy was finding a way to distinguish himself.

Not long after he turned fifteen, he noticed that his pants were getting shorter. He was growing, as if pent-up physical growth suddenly couldn't be contained. "I grew from five feet two inches to six feet four inches in eighteen months. By the time I turned seventeen, I was the tallest in the village, taller than even the grown men. And no one bullied me anymore."

Moses kept running because he liked it and grew another two inches. He was now twenty-four and a running champion in Kenya. He was also a teacher in his village. "So my mother's prayers were answered."

"So how can I pray for you, Moses?" Michael asked.

"Kenya has sent ten of us to these games," he answered, "because that is all my country can afford. We participate both in our specific sport and others as well. So I am in the one hundred meter and fifteen hundred meter, in addition to my own specialty of the marathon. I also have to do the long jump. My prayer is that I can do my best and not injure myself before the marathon." He paused. "And what can I pray for you, brother in Christ?"

"The heat for the time trial is tomorrow," Michael said. "It determines where I'm placed in the individual time trial lineup on Saturday, although I'm not sure if it really makes much difference. Some think that there's a psychological edge, but I don't know if that's real or not."

The two brothers in Christ prayed.

At the trial heat on Friday, Michael finished 21st out of 235. Roger Pitts was 7th.

"Enjoy watching me on the podium tomorrow, Kent," he sneered as they rode back to the Village. "Maybe spend a little more time in practice and a little less in your ladies' prayer meeting, and who knows what might happen? You could work your way up to eighteenth, or even seventeenth."

Michael said nothing.

At the prayer time, Moses showed up with a recruit in tow. "We have found another brother. This is Lucio Pena; he is a swimmer from Chile. He heard me ask the blessing over my lunch and introduced himself. Maybe I should pray louder so more Christians will hear me." Moses laughed.

Lucio Pena O'Shea had a Chilean mother and an Irish father, a businessman sent to Santiago on foreign assignment with his company. They met at an embassy event—her father was a diplomatic official, and he'd brought his wife and daughter. The young Irishman had been overwhelmed by the beautiful Chilean girl, and they were married a year later. Both were evangelical Christians, which helped her parents accept and bless the marriage.

Lucio was the oldest of five children. He had his mother's dark hair and slightly dark complexion but his father's angular facial features and slender physique. He had started swimming when he was three and was competitive by the time he was seven. By high school, he'd become one of Chile's top swimmers and had won gold in several South American regional games.

As Michael welcomed Lucio, a third person stood at the door, tentatively looking in. "Hello," said Michael. "You're welcome to join us."

"Well, I'm not sure if I should. I mean, I probably don't belong here." He hesitated, obviously uneasy. "But I saw the card on the bulletin board and figured you must be Michael Kent on the British Road Team, and I thought, well, I thought I might see what this is about."

Michael smiled. "And you are?"

"Sorry. I'm Robin Pearce. I go by Robbie. I'm on the cycling team for Canada."

"How'd you do today?" asked Michael.

"So-so, I'm afraid," Robbie said. "I placed twelfth."

"Which is better than the captain of the British team did at twenty-first," said Michael. "Come in and join us. You're free to listen, and if you want to talk, you're welcome to do that, too. And if you get uncomfortable, you can leave at any time. Fair enough?"

"Fair enough."

"So let us do some serious praying here," said Moses. "Robbie and Michael have a big day tomorrow."

Chapter 15

The individual time trial, what the cyclists called the ITT, was laid out on a combination of flats and hills, two of which were steep but not severe. The riders would leave at two-minute intervals, with the lowest-ranked rider going first and the one ranked number one in the trial heat—in this case a Belgian—going last.

Coach White, who hadn't said much about Michael's 21st place in the heat, said more today as he helped Michael get ready. "Kent, you can do this. Easily. It's like that ride you talk about from your parents' house to Edinburgh. Only a few miles farther, in fact. Don't worry about the other riders and don't worry about Pitts. I know he's been on your back. Ignore him." He put his hand on Michael's shoulder. "Race like the wind, son. Race with that huge heart of yours."

Michael watched until it was time to line up behind the other riders. Then he was in place, waiting for the start signal. Sarah's scarf was tied to his handlebars.

"Ride like the wind, Michael," Coach White said. "And whether you eat or drink or ride that bicycle or whatever you do, do it all for the glory of God."

Michael looked at the coach in surprise. "Paul's first epistle to the Corinthians," he said.

The coach nodded. "Chapter ten, I believe."

The flag went down, and Michael was off.

Michael said later that he remembered very little of the ride. He could recall spectators cheering and waving, and going under a railway bridge, where there was a banner in Greek. He remembered trees like green smudges in an Impressionist painting. And he remembered passing rider 22. And 23. And then 24. In all, he would pass five riders that day, the fifth having started ten minutes before he did. And he arrived at the finish line just ten seconds behind rider 27.

Like all the riders, he was taken immediately to the medical tent for a blood sample and a urine specimen to check for doping. This was standard procedure in all major racing events, including the Olympics, since the scandals at the Tour de France in 2007.

Completing the tests, he walked back to the arrival area and looked at the scoreboard. Fellow cyclists were applauding and clapping him on the back. His time was listed first: 66:23:05. The record had been broken.

Final Results of the Individual Time Trial:

Gold—Michael Kent, Great Britain

Silver—Robin Pearce, Canada

Bronze—Roger Pitts, Great Britain

After the podium ceremony, Michael turned to Roger Pitts to congratulate him, but Roger turned away, stepped down from the podium, and walked off. Michael turned to Robbie, shook his hand, then hugged him.

Britain had won two medals in one event. Including the gold. And a world record.

Scotland went wild. A near-riot erupted in Edinburgh, with late Saturday afternoon traffic in downtown brought to a standstill as motorists honked and cheered and stood on the roofs of their cars. Students at the university summer session hung a paper banner across the front of the Student Center: KENT RULES. In Glasgow, Tommy and Ellen McFarland danced in the street with their neighbors in an impromptu get-together that evolved into a huge block party. Both Scotland's first minister and Britain's prime minister called Iain and Iris with congratulations.

"Prayer works," Moses Akimbe announced to the prayer group that night, a prayer group that now included two Olympic medalists. "Prayer works."

"It works even if we lose, Moses," Michael said.

On Monday, the seven Britons lined up in second position for the team time trial, a 165-kilometer trial with more hills than flats and almost as many mountains as hills. The trial started in the western suburbs of Athens and ended at Lamia. The team's official time would be assigned by the member finishing fifth, so at least five members of the team had to finish the course—and as quickly as possible. Flat tires and crashes could claim only two at most; more than that and they would be out of the competition.

Roger still wouldn't speak to Michael, and his attitude was affecting the team. Michael finally pulled him aside.

"If you don't stop this, we'll lose," Michael said fiercely. "You can dislike me all you want, but it's getting out of control. You're adding tension precisely when we don't need it. So, Pitts, follow your own advice and get with the program. We have to ride as a team, not as six team members and a guy with his nose out of joint. You can go back to hating me later."

Roger reddened. "You're the captain," he said. But it helped; he began to respond to Michael, and the rest of the team relaxed.

As they started in their time slot, the British looked like a well-oiled machine—legs pumping, wheels turning, gears clicking. Tourists and locals took pictures of the seven as they rode in a staggered line, wearing their Union Jack jerseys and sky-blue spandex pants. They took turns moving from back to front, giving each other a break at the front position. Riding behind allowed the rider to coast a bit in the draft and actually use up to 30 percent less energy than the rider at the front.

Sixty kilometers from the finish, the seven cyclists were moving in almost perfect synchrony when the sixth cyclist suddenly got a flat tire, pulling down the rider behind who couldn't avoid him. The team slowed enough for the two riders to yell at Michael to keep going and not to lose any time while they furiously tried to fix their bikes.

We're now down to the minimum, Michael thought. *All five of us have to finish, or we're out of it.*

Forty kilometers from the finish, Michael saw Roger beginning to lag. He drifted to the rear, where he could see Roger was struggling.

"What's wrong?" Michael yelled.

Roger shook his head, indicating he was okay.

Michael yelled again. "Pitts, what's wrong?"

"I'm bonking," he gasped. Which meant his body lacked enough nutrients to sustain the pace or that Roger had been skimping on meals to keep his weight down. Or both.

"Okay, get in my draft," Michael shouted. *It must be bad*, he thought, when he saw Roger quickly obey. "Do you have any power gels?" Michael shouted, and Pitts shook his head. Michael yelled up the line to the rider ahead of him. "Power gel to Pitts." The rider raised an eyebrow at Michael but dutifully handed one back to Michael, who tore it open with his teeth and handed it back to Roger. Michael then took one of his own gels and handed it to Roger, who quickly swallowed it.

"I have to stop," Roger panted.

"Stay in line," Michael ordered. "Keep focused. We have less than forty kilometers to go. You can do this. The gels will start working."

Roger kept pedaling.

The team kept moving at a furious pace. They had now moved into the final stretch, a flat of eight kilometers.

Michael called back to Roger. "Can you ramp it up at all?"

Roger nodded. "It's kicking in. I can do it." But the previous thirty-two kilometers had been agony.

"Okay. Let's fly. Stay in my draft." The team surged forward, Roger remaining in Michael's draft.

It wouldn't be a record time, but it would be gold.

> Team Time Trial:
> Gold—Great Britain
> Silver—Australia
> Bronze—Italy

Britain had a new crop of heroes. This time, it wasn't only Scotland that went wild.

Chapter 16

While the British rode to gold in the TTT, Moses placed fifth in the long jump, followed by a sixth place in the one-hundred-meter event the same day. "No," he told Michael, "it's not bad. But I am still in shape for the marathon next Monday." In the fifteen hundred meter, held early Tuesday morning, Moses earned a bronze. "My country will be proud, but they expect a gold in the marathon. I hope not to disappoint them. Now we have to get Lucio to win a medal, and we will call ourselves the brotherhood of the medallions." That afternoon, Lucio won silver in the freestyle swim. No Chilean had ever medaled in swimming at the Olympics before. Michael and Robbie barely had time to congratulate him before boarding the buses for their final event.

Wednesday would mark the first day of a new event in Olympic road cycling, a four-stage road race. The stages were held on consecutive days, and each was approximately 150 kilometers. They would be doing a lot of cycling around Greece, starting at Alexandropoulos near the Turkish border. Michael and Robbie told Moses and Lucio good-bye, and the cyclists were bused to the northeast. The British and Canadian teams rode together, and Michael and Robbie had several hours to talk about Robbie's keen and growing interest in the Christian faith.

He's so close, Father. Keep working on his heart. Keep guiding me in what I say.

The stages were a combination of team and individual events. The teams worked together for the major medals for the entire four-stage event, with individual team members' times averaged for an overall time, while the individual who finished each stage first received a special, if smaller, recognition. While the British team had emerged as a major contender, the Canadians and Italians were also strong, as were the Belgians and the French, and no one was discounting the Germans or the Americans, although the overall US cycling team seemed to be off. The race was expected to be wide open.

But the British dominated, finishing the first three stages almost four minutes ahead of the next team, the Canadians, and six minutes ahead of the third-place German team. Because the stages turned out to be a mass sprint at the end, with individual riders racing for individual glory, an American, Rod Wheeler, had won the first stage; a German cyclist, the second; and Michael himself, the third. But the British won the team, placing in all three, and that was the medal category.

On Friday night, at a small-town school dormitory, where all the teams were staying, Robbie prayed to accept Christ as his Savior. Before he went to sleep, Michael sent a text message to Moses and Lucio and asked both of them to pray for Robbie's protection in his new faith and for safety for all of them in the final stage.

And that stage on Saturday would bring the cyclists into Athens, with a finish in the Olympic Stadium, guaranteeing a highly competitive finale before fifty thousand people in the arena and an expected two hundred million on television.

Stage four, the final stage into the western suburbs of Athens and the Olympic Stadium, was the most grueling. Fully three-fourths was through mountains, the two-lane road snaking its way around, up, and down steep hills and deep valleys. Training as much as they had in the Highlands of Scotland and the mountains of Wales had brought an enormous advantage for the British. Based on the coaches' reconnaissance trip the previous week, Michael knew the road would flatten twenty-seven kilometers from the end. As soon as it did, the sprinters would dash to win the individual positions.

The British were in control, however. Even with most of the Canadians just ahead of them, reeling in the breakaway group of cyclists that had formed and taken off early, and the Germans close behind, no team threatened the overall British position. In fact, by the end of the third stage the day before, riders and news commentators all saw the British as unstoppable. They'd put so much time between themselves and their nearest competitors in the first three stages that only some major disaster could threaten their certainty of the gold medal.

Thirty-five kilometers from the finish, Michael directed the team to accelerate to catch the Canadians, help reel in the last few breakaway riders, and allow Pitts to have the best shot possible at winning the individual stage. He thought Pitts could do it; he'd signaled him ahead and to the left of the peloton, right behind Michael and two others, to put him in the best position for the final sprint into Athens. Roger nodded his understanding.

The scenery was phenomenal, but Michael, sweat stinging his eyes and his calves aching, focused only on the road and the riders around him. Two members of the British team, Roddy Williams and Joe Quentin, were riding forward and just to his right side, doing the yeomen's work with the Canadians of pulling the breakaway riders back into the peloton, the main group of the riders. Michael could easily see Robbie two bike lengths ahead of him; in fact, Robbie had never been more than three bike lengths from Michael during the entire stage. *If Roger can win first, Robbie's in position to take second or maybe even upend Roger and grab first.* Michael would be satisfied either way, the individual first won by a fellow team member or the young Canadian who'd become a good friend in the past two weeks. His national sympathies pulled him toward seeing the individual win go to Britain, while his personal sympathies leaned toward the young Canadian who was now a brother in the faith.

Michael looked at his onboard computer and saw they were approaching the thirty-kilometer mark. All but two of the breakaway riders had been absorbed back into the main group, into the peloton, and those two were flagging. Soon the Canadians and the British would be alone for the sprint into Athens.

They approached and began rounding the sharp curve in the road. At this point, the road sloped downward, aiding acceleration.

Fifteen minutes before, Olympic officials led by the 1980s French cycling champion Marcel Deronde had driven through in the advance automobiles with no problems. Deronde and his fellow officials, some on Vespa scooters, were making sure the mountain road was clear of vehicles and spectators, who often posed a danger to the cyclists. The officials were farther ahead of the peloton than was customary in stage races. Here spectators were not a problem. There was no place to stand, with the sheer rock face on the left and a sheer drop on the right, separated from the cyclists only by a guardrail. So the advance cars and scooters had sped up to get to the lower elevations and deal with more likely problems with the crowds.

Fifteen minutes earlier, the road had been clear. But then everything changed.

Michael heard the first crash right as he rounded the curve. He learned later that it was Fabiano Vesti of Italy, the last of the breakaway riders, smashing into a huge mound of fallen rock blocking the road, the result of earth tremors plaguing the country for several days. Vesti died on impact. The entire group had been riding fast, jockeying for the final stretch position along the flat into Athens. In this high but sloping downward stretch, Michael himself was riding at thirty-nine miles an hour.

Fully around the curve, Michael saw the American, Rod Wheeler, somersault with his bike over the guardrail.

Seeing the fallen rock and most of the Canadians already down and blocking what little open road was left, Michael moved right and braked hard. But a Canadian on his left hit a rock and smashed into Michael, who struggled but failed to stay upright on the bike. As he went down and skidded along the road, he flinched as he felt the skin shred on his leg as it met the pavement. Then he saw Joe and Roddy both go down, entangled together and sliding dangerously close to the guardrail.

Within seconds, as the rest of the peloton sped into the crash site, the earth shook. More rock fell onto the road and the cyclists. Michael would forever have the scene seared in his memory. Bikers were plowing on top of those who had fallen; the falling rock made an almost deafening sound as it crashed down around and on top of them. A German rider hit an obstruction and went airborne, landing with his bike on top of Michael, the pedal gashing Michael's cheek. Michael could taste blood but miraculously escaped serious injury when his bike took the brunt of the impact.

He moved the unconscious German and his bike off and looked for his teammates. Riders were crashing behind, and the entire scene took on the feel of a battlefield, with the sounds of metal hitting asphalt and young men screaming in pain.

Michael stood up dizzily and saw that his leg was a mass of blood. Blood was also dripping from his face to his jersey.

Joe was sitting, conscious but white faced, his right arm dangling uselessly at his side; Roddy was lying where he had finally skidded to a stop, moaning, his hands gripping his leg. A few of the riders were staggering up or sitting in shock. Blood seemed to be everywhere. Falling rock could be heard behind them, engulfing the rest of the peloton.

Still moving in what seemed like slow motion, Michael began to shout.

"Who can get up? Who can get up?" A few "Here's" were heard as riders struggled to their feet.

"The injured! Get to the injured!" he shouted. He looked around and started shouting for anything that might serve as tourniquets and splints. He barely hesitated before breaking off a handful of dangling spokes on his own bike. *Splints*, he said to himself, *think splints*.

The German next to him was unconscious, blood flowing profusely from a gash in his arm, exposing the bone. Remembering his first-aid training for last summer's trip to Africa, Michael looked for something to stop the flow and saw Sarah's scarf. He quickly untied it from the handlebars and wrapped it around the German's arm, tying the tourniquet.

Feeling dizzy, he steadied himself and looked around, getting a better view of the carnage. Injured riders were everywhere. He stripped off his jersey and tied it around the head of an American, who had tumbled and landed beside the German.

"Use your jerseys!" he shouted. "For tourniquets, bandages, anything!" Several riders, including Roddy, who was now sitting up but grimacing in pain, stripped off their jerseys.

Stepping carefully over bikes and around riders, Michael moved toward the front of the crash, instructing unhurt riders on how to help the injured.

Then he saw Robbie.

Robbie's left leg was mangled, and Michael had to force himself not to become physically ill when he saw it protruding at an almost right angle from the knee. Robbie's helmet had cracked cleanly in half. Blood was pouring from his head, the large flow not unusual for a head wound. Michael knelt at Robbie's side and unhooked his helmet strap. He had nothing to use for a bandage. *Lord, what do I do? He's dying in front of me!*

My hand, he thought, *all I have is my hand.*

Michael cradled Robbie's head in his arms, placed the flat of his hand against Robbie's temple, and pressed.

At first Robbie's blood continued to pour through his fingers, then trickled off and finally stopped. Michael kept the pressure on, too frightened to take his hand away. He looked around and continued to direct help to the injured. A television cameraman, riding with officials in a car at the rear of the peloton, had made his way forward and began filming, focusing on Michael, who held Robbie while shouting instructions to cyclists to help the injured.

Then Michael saw Roger and two others, French from their jerseys, carry their bikes over downed riders at the very front of the crash. He shouted at Roger to help, but Roger looked back, flicked Michael off, and climbed over the wreckage after the first two.

Chapter 17

When they began arriving some thirty minutes after the disaster, the Greek emergency personnel were afraid to take Michael's hand from Robbie's head, so the two were lifted together in a gurney basket into a medical helicopter.

An Associated Press photographer had climbed a tree to take pictures of the scene from above and, looking down, saw the blood-soaked Michael and Robbie rising above the wreckage of rock and crashed bicycles. He snapped the photo that would within hours grace the front pages of news websites, newspapers, and magazines all over the world; the photo would eventually earn him a Pulitzer Prize for spot photography. In the US, *Time* magazine used the photo for its cover with the words "Olympic Tragedy." Iris opened the *Scotsman* in Edinburgh on Sunday morning, immediately recognized Michael, and wept.

In Santa Barbara, where she was staying with her grandmother, Sarah saw the first reports on TV and tried to reach David but heard only his voicemail. Then she screwed up her courage and called Iris and Iain, who told her they'd been trying to phone the cycling coach and would call as soon as they knew something. They called back two hours later and told her Michael's injuries were minor. Sarah nearly collapsed from relief.

The emergency room staff at the main Athens hospital assumed Michael, covered in blood, was the seriously injured one. Eventually they separated his hand from Robbie's head and treated the gash on his right cheek (*Amazing that I wasn't hurt more badly; that German came down right on top of me*), the severe road rash on his right leg, and a severely bruised hip. Several hours later, he was discharged to Coach White, who hugged him in the waiting area and wouldn't let go. The coach had no word on Robbie's condition but promised to try to find out from the Canadian coach.

"I've talked to your parents in Edinburgh," the coach said as they left the hospital. "I've told them you're banged up but okay, and you'll need to call them when you get back to the OV."

Michael nodded. "Coach, where's Roger?"

Coach White gritted his teeth. "In a jail cell, along with the two French riders. They were arrested an hour ago. It's a crime to leave the scene of an accident in Greece. And it's probably best for their safety right now because a lot of people, including me, would like to hang all three. You didn't see what happened in the stadium. They rode in, and the crowd starting cheering. Then the cheering died down as everyone kept looking for the rest of the peloton. Then we began to hear ambulance sirens, what sounded like hundreds of them. Within a few minutes, my cell rang, and I got the first report. I couldn't believe it. I couldn't believe Pitts abandoned the team."

"Coach," Michael whispered, "they walked over bodies to keep racing. We called to him to come back."

"And he kept going. That's what the real professionals do. When crashes happen, you just keep going. So what if people die? My God. He got his fifteen minutes of fame, all right, and now he'll get a lifetime of infamy. Seven confirmed dead. Scores seriously injured. And he goes riding around the stadium track, waving his arms in victory."

"Maybe he didn't understand," Michael said.

"Don't defend him, Michael," the coach said, "you of all people."

At the OV, the entire British Olympic team formed volunteer squads to canvas the complex for blood donors. Many athletes were still competing and couldn't give blood, but those who'd finished lined up at three Athens hospitals, joining hundreds of Athenians who were doing the same thing. The story of the young British cyclist who'd taken charge at the crash site was already circulating among those waiting in line. An Athens television station had broadcast the video from the crash site into Olympic Stadium, and the report was broadcast to London and other European capitals and then to the Western Hemisphere.

When Michael arrived at the OV, Moses and Lucio were waiting. "We know it's been terrible," Moses said, "but we want to pray for you and Robbie." Michael nodded, physically exhausted and emotionally spent but glad beyond words to see them, and the three prayed. Later he called Iain and Iris, assuring them he was okay. They told him Sarah had called.

On Sunday, Michael woke with every part of his body hurting. *Even the bottom of my feet hurt.* The hospital doctors had warned him of this, as his body absorbed the shock of the crash. They'd given him pain medication, and he was taking it full strength, a drug likely banned by Olympic rules. But he knew his Olympic races were over and he could relax.

Limping into the OV cafeteria for a late breakfast with Moses and Lucio, Michael saw heads turn his direction and conversation stop. Athletes stood and applauded.

"I don't understand," Michael said to his two friends.

"You are a hero, Michael," Lucio said, "whether you know it or not."

After eating, the three went to the hospital to see Robbie. The information desk attendant said that Robbie's parents had asked that Michael be allowed in if he came. Other athletes and people waiting in the area recognized Michael and stood to applaud.

A security guard escorted him, while Moses and Lucio waited in the lobby. Still limping from the bruised hip, he followed the guard down a corridor to elevators and then through what seemed like a maze of hallways. *I hope he helps me find my way out of here.*

They turned down yet another corridor, and Michael saw a couple seated outside an ICU room. Mrs. Pearce looked up, then stood with Robbie's father.

"You're Michael Kent," she said. He nodded, and the Pearces hugged him.

"We couldn't understand the language, but we saw the news report," Mrs. Pearce said. "It was broadcast on the screens at the stadium."

"They were afraid to move my hand from his head."

Mr. Pearce swallowed. "You saved Robbie's life."

Michael shook his head. "God saved Robbie's life, Mr. Pearce. It was just my hand he put there."

"But you knew what to do."

"Actually, I didn't," Michael said. "But I knew I had to do something. Head wounds bleed a lot. At that moment, my hand was all I had, so I pressed it against his head."

Mrs. Pearce was crying. "Did Robbie say anything?"

Michael shook his head. "He wasn't conscious, Mrs. Pearce. There was so much confusion; I don't know if I'd have heard him if he'd been conscious."

"You'd met him before the accident?" Mr. Pearce asked.

"At the OV, almost two weeks ago. He came for a Bible study we were having."

"We're not religious," Mrs. Pearce said. "I'm not sure why he would have come."

Michael nodded. "Robbie was looking for meaning in his life and asking questions. In fact, the members of our prayer group, Moses Akimbe and Lucio Pena, are down in the lobby. Moses is the marathoner from Kenya and won the gold. Lucio is from Chile and won a silver in freestyle swimming. With Robbie's silver, Moses calls us the brotherhood of the medallions."

"So Robbie was asking about God?" Mr. Pearce said. "He hadn't said anything about this."

"He was asking about a lot of things—about God, about faith, about why we believed what we did. He was looking for answers for himself, I think. And he seemed to have found what he was looking for."

"What do you mean?" asked Mrs. Pearce.

"This past Friday night, he prayed with me at the dormitory where we were staying to accept Christ as his Savior. I'm intruding here because I think he'd want to tell you this. But it was a beautiful thing to share with him. You could see he'd found what he'd been searching for."

The Pearces stared at him.

"Robbie's our youngest," Mr. Pearce said finally. "Our daughter is married with children, as is his brother who's in the air force. Robbie's always been our thinker, something of a rebel, going his own way but eventually coming back. He'd been wrestling with something lately, although what it was I didn't know."

Mrs. Pearce took his hand. "Michael, whether it was you or God or both doesn't matter to me. The fact is that Robbie is alive, and seven other riders aren't. He could have easily been—" She stopped, unable to say more.

"He was riding at the front of the main part of the peloton, helping to reel in the breakaway group," Michael said. "In fact, he'd been no more than two or three bike lengths from me the entire race. The Canadians were going to win silver, and he was leading them."

"He would," Mr. Pearce said softly. "He'd do exactly that. He's my fearless one."

"Is there any update on his condition?" Michael asked.

"It's critical but stable," Mrs. Pearce said. "Doctors are the same, no matter what language they speak. They're encouraging but cautious. The head injury is of more concern than his leg. Last night his condition was critical. This morning it's critical but stable. So it sounds better. But they're concerned about possible brain damage."

"Robbie lost a great deal of blood," Mr. Pearce said, "but they were able to do transfusions. They had his blood type on his Olympic badge, and so many of the athletes donated blood."

Michael nodded. "Putting our blood types on our badges was smart. You won't need it ninety-nine percent of the time, but when you do, it's there." He paused. "If you'd be willing, I'd like to introduce you to Moses and Lucio. They were praying for us yesterday as soon as they heard the first reports, and they prayed in my room through most of the night for Robbie long after I fell asleep. I know how you might feel, but they'd like to pray for you as well." He looked at the Pearces.

"We'd be honored, Michael," Mr. Pearce answered.

The next day, Robbie's eyes were occasionally blinking. By Monday evening, he was awake, not speaking, but his eyes could follow activity in the room, and he made a small smile when Michael visited. On Tuesday he told his mother and father hello when they entered his hospital room. Later tests would show there had been some minor damage to the brain, but it wasn't believed to be permanent; more tests would be needed. But Robbie's right leg was shattered. His cycling career was over; his road to recovery would be long, but in time he would recover.

"Prayer works!" Moses chortled when Michael told him. "It works! God is good!"

On Tuesday evening, the International Olympic Committee announced that, despite the unfinished race, the gold medal for the four-stage cycling event would be awarded to six members of the British team, the silver to Canada, and the bronze to Germany. The next morning, Roger Pitts and the two French cyclists were expelled from Greece.

On Thursday, the BBC interviewed Michael and the British road team live from Athens. The program set a record for viewership in Great Britain, as did the prerecorded broadcast for Western Europe and North and South America two days later.

Chapter 18

Early Friday afternoon, the British Olympic Team members were in dress uniform, walking quietly together. They were to be at the Olympic Stadium at five, receive a box dinner, and then wait to be called for the walk around the stadium field.

At the stadium, Michael and the road cycling team would lead the British group. The entire team had chosen Michael to carry the British flag, with the road cycling team serving as official flag escorts.

That morning, Michael had visited Robbie and found him recovering if quiet.

"I want to be there," Robbie said slowly, working hard to choose each word.

"I want you there, too, brother. It won't be the usual ceremony they do," Michael said, "because of what happened."

Robbie nodded. "Watch on TV."

"Look for me. I'll wave at the camera. And look for Lucio and Moses. Alphabetically, Lucio will come first with Chile. Then Great Britain. Moses will be a bit later with Kenya. But look for us because you'll be there with us. But you have to look for us."

Later, standing in line and waiting, Michael hoped Robbie would see all three of them, but he would have the best opportunity to see Michael with the flag at the front of the British team. And the cameras might focus on Moses because of his height and his gold medal in the marathon.

All three of them had sewn a Canadian flag on both of the upper sleeves of their country uniforms.

The entry of the teams began. Every minute, a team was signaled to begin the walk around the oval track, completely circling and then walking to the designated country place. The line seemed to move slowly.

Finally, the British were waved forward and stopped at the entrance to the arena, while the team from Germany walked forward. Behind the British were the Greeks. They had heard music, applause, and cheers as each team entered the field, the applause continuing like a wave around the stadium. They watched the team processions on large-screen video monitors positioned along the corridor to the arena.

They waited for what seemed like an eternity for Britain's name to be called. *Something must have happened with the schedule*, Michael thought.

Finally, they received the signal; they heard Great Britain's name announced and were waved forward by the gate official. Michael led the team onto the track around the field, with Roddy Williams in a wheelchair by his side pushed by a fellow road team member. Joe Quentin walked next to Michael with his arm in a sling. The flag was cumbersome but surprisingly light. Expecting to hear the same applause he had heard for the other teams, Michael realized the music had stopped; the stadium had become silent. He looked around to see what was wrong.

At the hospital, in spite of their son's protests, the Pearces had given their tickets to the ceremony to a nurse and watched the event with Robbie on the television in his room. As the British team entered the stadium, the camera immediately focused on Michael as he carried the flag.

"Look!" said Robbie. "His arm." They saw their country's flag. "He said," Robbie choked, "he said look for him. And Moses and Lucio. Have the flag. Wanted me to see. He said I'd be there."

"Nobody's applauding," said Mr. Pearce.

"They're standing up," said Mrs. Pearce. "Everybody's standing up. Look, even the band."

Both Mr. and Mrs. Pearce stood by Robbie's bed.

On the elevated VIP dais on the field sat Prime Minister Peter Bolting, the Lord Mayor of London, and Henry Kent, chair of the London games four years hence. There to receive the symbolic flame from their Greek counterparts, they stood up. On the stadium's huge video screens, Henry watched Michael carry the British flag, and he wept.

Britons watching on television stood up in their living rooms, dens, and pubs for their country's team. At the farm, Iris and Iain stood up. In Glasgow, Tommy and Ellen also stood up. "I'm standing for Michael, not the English," Tommy said. The McLarens and the McFarlands would be meeting early in the morning at the Edinburgh airport for the flight to London—to meet David and Betsy and to wait for Michael to arrive from Greece.

Already in their London hotel room from their honeymoon on Skye, David and Betsy Hughes stood as they watched Michael and the British team on the television set.

Canadians from Nova Scotia to Vancouver stood to honor the team from Great Britain.

The French stood. As did the Spanish and the Belgians. The Americans. People all over South America. And those who were awake and watching TV in other parts of the world.

In the stadium in Athens, the British team was overwhelmed. In the great silence, they walked around the stadium, arm in arm, many openly crying. Led by their road cyclists, they proceeded with no announcement yet for the country teams to follow. The British team walked alone in silence.

Michael, tears running down his cheeks, kept hearing the sound of the crashing rock and the cries of the injured cyclists reverberating in his head.

When they reached the path to their assigned place on the field, the stadium erupted. The ovation continued for several minutes, finally calming when the band resumed playing music to welcome the Greeks and other teams, who had watched the procession on the screens inside the stadium.

Michael was on the cover of *Time* magazine for the second week in a row, this time carrying the British flag and flanked by Joe and Roddy in the wheelchair by his side. The headline: "The World Stood Up."

Late that night, the prayer group had one final meeting in Michael's room, using Lucio's cell phone as a speaker phone so Robbie and his parents could listen from the hospital. At the end, they swapped e-mail addresses, Moses noting that they could pray by electronic message board. Michael said his good-byes to the three athletes who'd become loved friends.

The next morning, the British Olympic Team was on its way to London. They were told that at Heathrow they would board buses for Albert Hall, their disembarkation point, not far from where Michael would be meeting his family at a hotel in South Kensington near the Victoria and Albert Museum.

When the British Airways plane landed, the athletes soon realized that the celebration wasn't over. Olympic banners draped the terminal. People stood and cheered as the athletes walked by. Outside, instead of enclosed buses, they found a long line of convertibles. Not a ride into central London but a parade, the British Olympic Team meeting with the British people.

"No one said anything about this," Michael said to Roddy as they maneuvered him into the front seat and his wheelchair into the trunk.

"This explains why they wanted us in our formal travel uniform," Roddy replied.

Escorted by police cars, some fifty black convertibles began to make their way from the airport into London. The six remaining members of the road cycling team rode together at the head of the procession, with Michael and Joe seated above the back seat. All the way into central London, cheering crowds lined the street ten and fifteen deep. Police estimated the turnout at more than five million people.

Michael smiled and waved, wishing they could have brought home medals without the injuries and deaths. He felt overwhelmed by the adulation of the crowd, passing dozens of homemade signs with his name on them.

They traveled east on the Cromwell Road, passing the Victoria and Albert (and his parents' hotel; Michael looked but didn't see them). They passed Harrods, finally reached Westminster and the Houses of Parliament, snaked around Trafalgar Square, filled with cheering thousands, and then headed toward Albert Hall. There they disembarked, collected their luggage, and dispersed— Roddy and Joe to Victoria Station by taxi to catch a train home and Michael just a few blocks to South Kensington. His taxi driver refused to take a fare but asked for an autograph. Then with big eyes he said, "Crikey! You're the Kent boy!"

In the early August evening, his family was waiting.

Part III

London

Chapter 19

On Monday evening, the McFarlands, the McLarens, the Hugheses, and Michael belatedly celebrated David and Betsy's wedding. Tommy, despite being in "enemy territory," was in fact fully enjoying himself.

During the dinner, Iris mentioned that Iain was looking for an assistant to help with the practice. "So if you know anyone, let us know, probably someone single. We're remodeling the stable a bit to add a bedroom, bath, and small kitchen."

"And no previous experience is required," said Iain, "only no fear of hard work."

"I might have a possibility," said Michael.

"Who's that, son?" asked Iain.

"Roger Pitts."

Six faces stared at him.

"I know it's a bit edgy," said Michael.

"A bit," agreed Tommy. "We might be more sympathetic if you'd said a serial killer."

"Just hear me out."

"All right, son, tell us what's on your mind," Iain said.

"He's pretty much destroyed himself with what happened, I know," Michael said. "On Saturday at the Athens airport, we heard that the Olympic committee voted to strip him of the medals he'd won, the bronze and the gold with us in the team trial. This morning's *Times* said the British Cycling Committee has revoked his professional license, so that's the end of his cycling career." He paused. "And the team he rides for here terminated his contract. He's become the leper we love to hate. And if I remember correctly, there was this someone who reached out to lepers."

Silence around the table.

"So, like I said, it's a bit edgy." Heads nodded. "And Da, if you think it's a bad idea, I'll drop it. I haven't talked to him, I really don't know where he is, and I don't even know if he'll speak to me. It was ugly when we spoke last. But I thought, well, God gave him a soul, too, right? His situation must be horrible right now."

The silence continued.

"Okay, it was a bad idea," Michael said.

"No," said Iris, "it was exactly what I'd expect you to suggest."

"Which is often the same thing," said Tommy. Ellen elbowed him.

"Do you know where he lives or where he's staying?" asked David.

"Our team directory lists an address in Euston."

"So it's here in London," said Betsy, whose maternal grandparents lived in London.

Michael nodded. "So I was thinking, Da, I could rent a bike in Trafalgar Square and cycle there tomorrow morning. I haven't been on a bike since the crash, and I need to get some exercise. My leg is healing nicely, and it shouldn't be a problem. What do you think?"

Six heads turned and looked at Iain, who was staring at his son.

"I can think of a hundred arguments why it's a foolhardy thing to do," Iain said at last, "but not one good reason. So go talk to your leper tomorrow and see. He may not even be in London. If he's interested, he'll need to talk with me."

"He should've changed his name and left the country, if he'd any sense," Tommy said. He looked at Michael. "I remember the last time you opened our door to help someone, and we ended up with a crazy American." He dodged as David threw a roll at him.

Early Tuesday morning, Michael first tried to reach Roger by phone but only got a busy signal. So he took the tube to Trafalgar Square, rented a bike and helmet from a kiosk in the square, and studied a map for the best way to Euston, north of the British Museum. With his sunglasses, no one recognized him.

Approaching the neighborhood, he saw a policeman standing in front of Roger's house. Michael moved to open the gate in front of the row house with its neat garden in front, but the policeman stopped him.

"Sorry, no admittance," he said.

"I've come to see Roger Pitts," said Michael.

The policeman sighed. "You and three thousand journalists, thrill seekers, and brick throwers, all of whom will start lining up soon, and I'll have to call for reinforcements. I'm sorry, but you must leave."

Michael took off his sunglasses. "Officer, my name is Michael Kent, and I need to see Roger."

"Why do you want to get mixed up with this lot for?" the officer said. "He as good as left you and your mates for dead."

"I need to talk with him."

"It's your funeral, friend. If you need help, there's an officer at the back gate, too."

"Can I park my bike here?"

"I'm here for the next three hours."

Walking to the door to ring the bell, he noticed a bad smell, then saw broken eggshells in the garden and egg smears on the windows and wall.

A woman answered. "Please go away."

"Mrs. Pitts, I need to talk with Roger."

"Please go away. He's not doing any interviews or seeing anyone. Please just go."

"Mrs. Pitts, I'm Michael Kent. I'd like to speak with Roger."

"I'm sorry. He's not seeing anyone."

Michael heard Roger's voice from inside the house. "Mother, just shut the door. They'll go away."

"Roger," she began, but Roger cut her off in midsentence and flung open the door to pull her back inside. And saw Michael.

"Hello, Roger."

Roger stared. "It's Britain's hero, stopping by to gloat. Or is this some missionary project you cooked up at the ladies' prayer meeting?"

"Roger, I came to see if I could help." *He hasn't shaved in days, and his eyes are bloodshot. He looks awful.*

"Help? By doing what? Going back in time and erasing the bad parts?"

"I came to see if you'd consider the possibility of a job."

Roger laughed. "Oh, sweet. A job. As what? Mr. Hyde to your Dr. Jekyll? An exhibit in a circus sideshow? Poster boy for the ethically challenged?"

"No," said Michael. "It has to do with horses."

"You're a trip, Kent. Why don't you just go play hero for all your adoring fans?"

"Okay, Roger, fine. Wallow in self-pity. You can wallow until you realize that someone might want to help, and by the looks of things, I'm all you've got right now. So do you hear me out, or not?"

Roger glared. He finally looked away and flicked his head, indicating for Michael to come in.

Michael followed Roger down the hall to the kitchen at the back of the house. The home was well cared for, Roger's personal appearance notwithstanding. Standing by the sink, his mother watched both of them.

"You're the one in the photograph," she said. "The one with the helicopter."

Michael nodded.

"Did that boy with you live?"

"Yes, ma'am," Michael answered. "In fact, he was released from the hospital in Athens yesterday. He and his parents are scheduled to leave today for Montreal."

"So talk, Kent," Roger said, motioning Michael to sit at the kitchen table.

"My father is a veterinarian near Edinburgh. He's not old, just fifty-nine, but he's getting on, and he needs help. He treats horses and some small animals, and he's never had an assistant other than me and occasionally my mother."

"I'd be cleaning stables?"

"A service does that. He needs an assistant. Someone to help treat the animals, care for them and feed them, see to clients, do probably a hundred odd jobs around the place, things that he's always done himself. The farm is a beautiful place, and they're remodeling the stable to add a bedroom, bath, and small kitchen, so you'd have your own place to live. It's forty miles from Edinburgh, so it's not at the end of civilization. And he'd pay you a fair wage." Michael paused. "It'd be a good place if you want to be away from people for a time. And there are some great trails for mountain biking up behind the farm."

"He's willing to take me on? He knows it's me?"

Michael nodded as he saw Roger grip the edge of the table. "Although he wants to talk with you first."

"So what do you get out of it?"

"Nothing. Roger, I get ordained on Thursday, and then I'll be assigned to who knows where on Friday. It could be Africa. It could be London. I'm out of the picture here."

"Then why?"

"You need help."

Roger said nothing. He looked down at the kitchen table and then sat, still saying nothing.

Michael waited. Mrs. Pitts's eyes were riveted on Roger with some hope in them for the first time in ten days.

Roger finally spoke. "Everything seemed to come to you effortlessly. In training, all of them looked to you, almost immediately. The team, Coach White, the assistants—you were the one they looked to to lead the team. I had the wins, the experience, the grit to do it, and they ignored me. So I got in your face and laid crap on you at every turn. I challenged you. I wanted us to go head-to-head. I knew I could win if you competed with me.

"When we did the time trial heat, I knew I had you. I knew it. I thought you knew it, too. And I go work out one last time, and you sit around saying your prayers with your friends. And then you win the gold. I'm not even close. Oh, I get the bronze, but I'm not even close." Rogers hands were clasped together in a tight, twisting grip.

"And then the team time trial. I start to bonk, and you tell me to get in your stinking draft. You pull me all the way to the finish line. So we win gold again, and I want to die." Roger looked away but not before Michael saw the tears in Roger's eyes.

"The stage race," Roger said, looking Michael full in the face. "Piece of cake. Crushing everyone and everything in sight. And then comes stage four. Remember? The one where you were going to let me do the final sprint for first place? Remember that one? It'd come down to you throwing crumbs to the dog."

"That's not what I intended," Michael said.

Roger ignored him. "I saw you go down. I laughed. I hated you. And then I saw the two Frenchies climbing over downed riders. No way was I going to let them get ahead and race to the stadium. No way. I heard you yelling at me. You were cute at that BBC interview. You could've shredded me; you saw me flick you off. The Olympic committee told me you saw me pointing at you, but you knew exactly what I did. I stepped over bodies and bikes, and I cranked.

"I heard the cheering in the stadium, and I loved it. I didn't care that the Frenchies beat me. They were nothing. I didn't care that there were dead cyclists behind me. I didn't care. I'd beaten the great Michael Kent, the team captain, our hero.

"Except I didn't, did I? Michael stayed with the dead and dying. Michael was a superhero. And I was worse than crap. It was okay to hate me now. Just once I wanted to hear the crowd cheer for me. Just once. I saw my shot and I took it.

"But instead I get egged, and my mother gets insulted by the neighbors. Thugs shout threats until the police get bored and chase them away. And every time the phone rings, it's obscene.

"The worst part is, I screwed myself. I could've stayed and been celebrated and been on TV and gotten fifty thousand people to stand up for me and cheer.

"And now you show up and want to help me. Because I need help."

"Because you're worth helping, Roger," Michael said softly. "Through no merit of your own. Just because you're worth helping. End of story."

Roger looked down, spent.

"Have you ridden your bike?" Michael asked.

"What?"

"Have you ridden your bike?"

"Are you serious? If I show myself in public, I'll be stoned to death."

"Want to go for a ride? Nobody will know us with the sunglasses. I can call Da and get him to meet us, and then you can talk."

"I haven't been on a bike in two weeks."

"I'm not asking you to race. I'm asking you to ride."

Roger looked at Michael for what seemed an eternity. You're doing this for me?"

"Suit up and let's go. I'll call Da and tell him to meet us in two hours at that museum on Hampton Heath. Maybe shave, too. Da's not picky, but he likes a neat appearance."

Thirty minutes later, they were pedaling less-traveled streets in north London toward Hampton Heath.

Iain was waiting for them at the museum, a small affair focused on the arts and crafts movement.

"Da, this is Roger Pitts. Roger, my father, Iain McLaren." They shook hands, eyeing each other. He saw Roger raise an eyebrow at the different last name. "He's been my guardian since I was a kid. And he only bites when he's mad. Da, I'm going to ride around the heath for a bit. I'll check back in an hour." Iain nodded, and Michael took off.

When he returned, the two were sitting on a bench, deep in conversation.

"Roger's to arrive next Monday," Iain said to Michael. "I've given him the directions and phone number. I offered to pick him up at the train station, but he said he's bringing his bike."

"Great," said Michael. "Roger, you'll love it."

After talking a few minutes more, Roger and Iain shook hands, and Roger and Michael biked across the heath to Euston.

"He seems a good bloke," Roger said as they rode.

"He's the best," said Michael. "And you'll like Ma, too. I came to live with them when I was six after my parents died. I couldn't have asked for better."

They pedaled in silence for a while. "Roger, what you said earlier about me. Do you really believe that?"

Roger nodded. "It was harsh; maybe I could've said it better."

"I ask because it makes me sound like I'm something of a prig."

"I didn't mean it that way. What I meant was, it'd be nice to see you occasionally act like a human being and make a mistake."

Michael laughed. "Once you know me better, you won't have any doubts. I make plenty of mistakes. Take women, for example. I fell head over heels for a girl last year and managed to chase her six thousand miles away. I made plenty of mistakes with her."

"What was the problem?"

Michael was quiet for a moment. "She couldn't handle my faith, and I was too dense to believe it. I thought I could bring her around, but I couldn't. It's still a mess."

"Salvageable?"

"Maybe," Michael answered, "but not for a while yet. And who knows whom she'll meet in the meantime."

"Maybe you need some of that faith you talk about." They were approaching Roger's house. "Cripes, they're here already."

Michael saw a crowd of ten or so men and boys having words with the policeman at the front gate.

"Michael, you turn back. I'll slip around the back. It's only a few more days, then I'm gone."

"No. We'll deal with this together." Michael rode to the crowd, Roger following reluctantly.

"Look, it's him," a boy said. "It's the killer." Hostile faces turned toward them.

"And he's got a friend," a man said.

Michael stopped directly in front of the crowd and eyed the look of panic on the policeman's face. He looked at the crowd and took off his helmet and sunglasses.

"Hi. I'm Michael Kent." He reached over and roughed a boy's hair. "What's your name?"

It was instant recognition. The crowd stepped back.

"I asked you a question," Michael said. "What's your name?"

The boy squirmed but finally answered. "Phillip, sir."

"And who's your friend here?" Michael asked, pointing to another boy. "That's Jack."

"Well, Phillip and Jack, I have a big favor to ask."

The two stepped forward, eyes huge, as the men watched.

"My friend here has a problem. People keep egging his house. Now we all know why, and we know he made a pretty bad mistake a few days ago, but he's trying to figure out how to make things right. He's going away soon. He'll be living up north with his new family. And then this won't matter, right?" The boys nodded.

"Here's where I need your help. Do you think you might keep an eye on the place for the next few days to keep the vandals away? You don't have to do anything yourselves because you've got the policeman here. But do you think you might keep an eye out and tell people to bug off?"

The two nodded.

"That's super. I'm so grateful that I'm inviting you to an event on Thursday. I'm becoming a priest, and the ceremony is at 7:00 p.m. at St. Paul's, the big cathedral down in the city. You know which one I'm talking about?"

"Yes, sir," said Phillip.

"Now you don't have to come, and it might be a bit boring. But there'll be a lot of people and probably the newspapers and all that, and you and your dads can be my guests at the reception after. It'll just be cake and punch, maybe some biscuits, but there might be some others from the Olympic team. Do you think you might come?"

Each boy looked at his father. Michael had guessed that the mob was a sort of father-and-son affair by the looks of it, with the dads out of work and little else to do.

Jack's father spoke. "Why you're hanging round with the likes of him?"

"He needs a friend," Michael replied. "I know what it is to need a friend."

The man grunted. "You're smooth, I'll say that. All right. We'll be there at seven. We just walk into St. Paul's?"

"That's it. The ceremony's open, but I'll need to escort you into the reception next door." He got their names from the fathers. "The attendant will have your names on the list."

The crowd then began dispersing, except for Phillip and Jack. They stood on either side of the gate, Phillip next to the policeman, who smiled at Michael. "He's right. You're a smooth one."

"You didn't have to do this," Roger said.

"Yes, I did. You're family now. We take care of family in Scotland." He extended his hand to Roger, who took it.

"Thanks," Roger said.

"By the way," Michael said as he put his helmet and glasses back on, "you and your mom are invited, too, if you're free. You aren't obligated, but you're more than welcome."

Roger nodded. "Thanks, Michael, but I don't think I'm ready for a public appearance quite yet. But thanks. And thanks for the ride."

Michael smiled and held his thumb up. He rode off.

Chapter 20

On Tuesday afternoon and Wednesday, the whole McLaren group played tourist in London. They toured the Tower and St. Paul's, then wandered around Whitehall to see Parliament and the Abbey. They squeezed in a couple of hours at the National Gallery on Trafalgar Square.

Separating, the women headed for Regent Street and Oxford Street, and the men went to South Kensington to relax.

At a pub near their hotel, Tommy kept up nonstop entertainment, and soon they were all laughing to tears, only stopping when Tommy went to find the WC.

"Da," said Michael, "can you tell me anything about Henry Kent?"

"Is he a relative?" David asked.

"He's a business bigwig," Michael said, "one of the corporate sponsors of the Olympic team. He was at our dinner before Athens and helped hand out the captains' ribbons. He'll chair the games in London in four years. When I shook his hand, he seemed to recognize me. Do you know anything about him?"

"He's your brother, Michael."

Michael and David stared at Iain.

"My brother," Michael said. "I have a brother? I never knew."

Tommy walked up to the table.

"Your half brother, to be precise," Iain said. "Same father, different mothers."

"Have I missed something here?" Tommy asked.

"Michael has a half brother," David said.

Tommy's eyebrows went up as he sat down.

"You never asked much about your family," Iain said. "Iris and I often talked about it, debating whether to say something."

"Why didn't you?" asked Michael.

"Because I would've said too much of the wrong thing," Iain said. "Michael, the day your parents died, Henry and the Pr—I mean, Henry and his

141

cousin—descended upon your house like Huns. He hadn't spoken to his father, your father, for several years because he resented your father remarrying so soon after his first wife had died. And the first thing he and that idiot cousin of his did was tell the family attorney to get rid of you. Iris and I'd been in town that night, and the attorney finally reached us an hour before you arrived with the chauffeur."

"Tony," Michael said, remembering. "His name was Tony. He brought my bike with us."

Iain nodded. "We didn't know the duke had named us your guardians."

"The duke?" Tommy asked. "Are you talking about Henry Kent?"

Iain nodded. "Michael's father. His son has the same name. I met him at the Exeter racecourse and became the vet for his horses. And Michael's brother has the same name."

"But," Tommy stammered, "Henry Kent is first cousin to the king. He's royal family."

Iain nodded again. "As is Michael. First cousin to good King James III."

"How could this not be known?" asked David. "A duke's son doesn't just disappear into Scotland."

"I don't know," said Iain, "except that Duke Henry and Michael's mother, the Duchess Anna, had been socially blacklisted for years. They lived quietly at their home in Kent. They weren't really on anyone's radar scope, and no one apparently thought to ask about a child. Most people probably didn't even know he existed. The servants were sacked or quit and dispersed all over. And I don't think young Henry or James would've talked it up. It wasn't exactly their finest hour."

"It's amazing, Da," Michael said. "I'd no idea."

"Iris and I had many talks about this, Michael. We were going to tell you when you were older, but there never seemed to be a good time. Then it didn't seem to matter. I'm sorry we didn't. There's likely some money involved. I get annual notices from an attorney here in London. We should probably check into it."

"No apology is needed, Da. I'm just dumbfounded. And I don't need the money."

"It's worse than I thought," Tommy said. "You're not just English. You're *royal* English. I've been consorting all these years with the real enemy and didn't even know it. And royal English that doesn't need money. The penultimate non sequitur. My poor head can't comprehend it."

Michael laughed and punched Tommy on the arm. "I don't need the royal family, Da. I have you and Ma and these rascals here, and that's royal enough for me."

Michael arrived at St. Paul's Cathedral at three on Thursday. The ordination wasn't until seven, but he and seventeen fellow ordinands reported early for instructions, prayer, and a meeting with their bishop sponsors. Michael's sponsor was the archbishop of York.

Ordination had once included the presentation of the clerical collars. Now the ceremony had been streamlined, and they'd receive their collars at their assigned parishes.

The Church of England was on life support. Most of its funding came from a restless government, and it wouldn't be long before Parliament turned off the oxygen. Membership was less than 6 percent of the population, and weekly attendance had inched below 2 percent. The church was increasingly seen as irrelevant to British society, its tiny minority of votes making it increasingly expendable to a cash-starved Parliament.

Its influence remained in the Anglican community worldwide. It served as the mother church whose many children were either much stronger and more vibrant, as in Asia, Latin America, and Africa, or were rapidly declining but still with significant endowments, as in North America.

It wasn't all gloom and doom. Scores of North American churches had peeled away from their denominations and affiliated with what was known as the Anglican Communion. These more conservative parishes had aligned with bishops in Africa and South America. Paul Nkane, the archbishop of Nigeria, a close friend of Archbishop Johnston of York, was emerging as the unspoken challenger to the archbishop of Canterbury as the primary Anglican leader. This made Archbishop Johnston, a fellow Nigerian but still within the Church of England, a critical player in the political world of international Anglican politics.

Archbishop Johnston was well aware of Michael's royal connections—he'd had birth and death records checked the first time he met Michael and connected the blue eyes with the last name.

They talked and prayed together. The archbishop was amazed that Michael seemed unaffected by his sudden and enormous fame. He'd considered the role Michael might play in revitalizing the English church, but Michael was needed elsewhere first. And tomorrow at 10:00 a.m. Michael would learn of his first parish posting.

It wouldn't be what he expected.

At 6:30 p.m., Michael waited with his fellow ordinands in a changing room behind the main altar of St. Paul's, wearing a white robe. A large crowd of family and friends of the new priests but also reporters, celebrity seekers, and curious tourists had gathered.

The ceremony went quickly. At its end, each new priest was introduced. A minor roar from Tommy, David, and their wives erupted when Father Michael Kent was announced, followed by serious applause from the crowd.

As people left the church, Michael stood chatting and noted Jack, Phillip, and their fathers waiting nervously. *In their coats and ties they look a wee bit different than the boys with rocks in their hands at Roger's house.* He waved them over and deputized Tommy and Ellen to escort them to the reception. "The attendant has their names," he said, "and I'll be along shortly." Tommy looked at him quizzically, and Michael smiled. "Later."

After politely answering questions from two reporters, Michael turned to leave for the reception. And saw his brother.

144

They walked slowly toward each other. Henry extended his hand. "Congratulations, Michael."

"I didn't know you were coming," he said, shaking Henry's hand.

"I wanted to see this," Henry said. "I was in the stadium for the closing ceremonies, but I hadn't seen you personally since the send-off. I wanted to add my congratulations. You've created quite a stir, Britain's national hero."

"Would you like to come to the reception? There shouldn't be any problem with getting in."

"No, thank you. I've an appointment, and I believe the reception is for family and friends."

Michael nodded. "That's why I asked."

The two brothers stared at each other.

Finally Henry said, "If you're free, I'd like to meet for breakfast tomorrow. I need to talk with you, about a number of things."

"I have to be at the C of E office on Great Smythe Street at ten to learn my parish assignment, but I'm free until then. I'd like to talk as well."

"We can meet at my club, say seven? It's Regent's on St. James Square across from St. James Palace." He pulled a business card from a case in his pocket. "I'll write the address on the back. If a conflict arises, that's my cell number on the front."

"I'll be there," Michael said.

Henry smiled and left.

Chapter 21

The next morning, a club attendant led Michael to Henry's table and seated him.

"You look quite dapper today," Henry said, nodding at Michael's sport coat and bow tie. "I was expecting somber clerical garb."

Michael laughed. "Then you give the C of E more credit than you should. We don't get the outfit until we arrive at our parish—and it'll probably be recycled."

"Any idea of where you'll be posted?"

Michael shook his head. "Not really. I've put in for Malawi, but they could send me anywhere. It might be Malawi or even London."

"What are your hopes? The press reports say Africa."

"My hopes are Malawi. I was there last summer, and it's where my heart is." *Except California.* "And while they won't officially say anything until today, for months I've been receiving reports, health advisories, and general information about Africa. I've an appointment this afternoon to get vaccinations, in fact. So Malawi may be it."

"You're aware of the general state of affairs with the Church of England? That's a stupid question—of course you are. What I'm really asking is, are you troubled by it?"

"Why am I becoming a priest in a church that's disintegrating? Because it's what God has called me to do. Henry, from the outside my decision appears irrational. But I'm at peace with it because whatever happens, I know there's a plan for me."

"I like your confidence."

"I'd call it assurance. If I relied on my confidence, I'd be in serious trouble."

Henry smiled as he poured them coffee from a silver carafe. "So how are you taking to fame?"

"I don't think I am. You can't go anywhere without being recognized. And people come up to you, wanting to be near, almost finding some kind of reality, just by being near you. It's strange. I'm hoping that once I'm assigned, this will calm down some."

"Most likely," Henry agreed.

They were both quiet.

"So you wanted to talk?" Michael said.

Henry nodded. "I did. From your comments last night, I gather you know our relationship."

"At the send-off dinner, when you shook my hand, I saw that you recognized me. I also saw that you've the same blue eyes I've been looking at in the mirror for almost twenty-three years, and Henry is my middle name. I thought we might be related, but once we were off to Athens, I didn't think about it again until this week. I asked Da, and he told me."

"He hadn't said anything before?"

"No. Until I asked. And it was the first time I'd asked. It didn't seem important when I was growing up. I had Ma and Da and didn't really think about where I came from."

"Do you remember much?" Henry asked.

"Not really. Memories are vague. I remember Tony, the chauffeur, and a long ride in the car. Tony had my bike in the boot. And I remember a big house, almost like a museum."

"An apt description."

"And some toy soldiers I played with, lining them up on the windowsill. But not much else, I'm afraid."

"Nothing about the day of the car crash?"

Michael shook his head. "No. Da told me some things on Wednesday but said he didn't want to inject his own reactions and memories."

"He was charitable," Henry said. "What happened was bad, almost evil. An old-fashioned word, *evil*, but that's what it was."

Michael remained silent.

148

"I had a flat in the docklands, one of those trendy condominiums that overlook the Thames. Very modern, lots of glass and contemporary furnishings. I'd been there a year while I finished up at the London School of Economics."

"We stayed there with the Olympic team," Michael said.

"Small and forbidding dormitories, if I recall. But I was a duke's son, even if I'd stopped speaking to the duke and the nephew of the king. So I stayed in my trendy condo. The Prince of Wales was usually around, generally up to no good, but he was my cousin, and we'd been companions since childhood. The king took me in when I walked out on Father, after he . . ."

"After he married my mother," said Michael.

"Right," Henry said. "Please understand. It wasn't your mother. It would've been anyone. I was furious that my mother wasn't even cold in her grave. It took me years to realize I was also angry with myself because I wouldn't see Mother when she was dying."

He sipped his water. "So when the family attorney called me in London, my first reaction, I'm ashamed to say, was gratification. The prince was with me when the call came, and we decided to have some fun. We drank ourselves silly while driving down to Kent and were pretty soused by the time we arrived." He paused. "I'm not proud of this."

Michael nodded.

Henry went on. "James walked around, insulting the staff, saying horrible things about the duke and your mother. And you. I could've stopped him but, to my shame, I didn't. The attorney was growing quite alarmed; I think he concluded that we meant you physical harm. So he had you spirited away. We thought it was funny, Father naming his vet as your guardian. But that bear of a Scot was the best thing Father could've done for you, and he knew it."

Michael smiled. "That's what I thought he was when I was young. A big, friendly bear."

"Our behavior was abominable," Henry said. "Let me rephrase that. *My* behavior was abominable. One of the things I wanted to do today was to apologize. And I hope you can forgive me."

"I don't remember what you're apologizing for. And God turned it into good. Da and Ma loved me more than anyone could've a right to expect. But I accept it, Henry. I accept it gladly."

"There's more."

"More?"

"You're a wealthy young man. Your mother had a sizable fortune from her first husband, and she put it all in a trust for you. Father also provided for you in his will, with instructions to his financial advisors that the funds designated for you and for me were to be invested identically. He named me executor of their wills, and by doing that he gave me a message—he wanted me to know that I had some responsibility for you. Even though we hadn't spoken in several years, he believed he could trust me to provide for you and manage the investments.

"He also made provision for your care by the McLarens and for your education. However, despite the annual instructions for accessing the funds, McLaren never touched the money."

"Never?"

"Not once. When the attorney called him about it, he said that the duke had been his friend and that his friend had asked him to accept this responsibility. So he would, and he'd take care of you."

"It sounds just like him," Michael said quietly.

"Our cousin didn't help. He started pressing friends and acquaintances not to use your father's services."

"Why?"

"James could pretend he was influential, I suppose. Plain viciousness is the more likely reason. Eventually he tired of it and turned to other things. But it hurt your parents financially for a time, as James intended it would."

"They've never said anything about this," Michael said.

"Anyway," said Henry, "each year we've added those funds to a second trust, and between the two trusts, plus what you inherited directly from Father's estate, it all adds up. While it's mostly stocks, bonds, and real estate, your total assets come to about three billion pounds."

Michael stared at him. "Three . . . billion . . . pounds?"

"Give or take." Henry smiled. "So if you don't like your assignment, you can chuck the church and retire."

"Do I have to do anything about this right now?"

Henry shook his head. "No. But the trusts end when you're thirty, and it would be best for tax purposes to start planning now."

"Can I leave this in your hands?"

"If that's what you want."

"I'd like to think on this some," Michael said, "but that's what I would like to do. Maybe have some put in a bank account. Do you think we could take, say ten thousand, and do something?"

"Ten thousand?" Henry looked amused. "What do you have in mind?"

"In Athens, I got to be friends with Moses Akimbe, the chap from Kenya who won the gold in the marathon."

"Yes?"

"He's a schoolteacher in a rural area. And they've nothing. It's a one-room schoolhouse, with Moses and two other teachers with seventy or eighty kids. They don't have enough books or supplies or even a chalkboard, and as far as AV or computer equipment, well, they wouldn't help because there's no electricity for the building. Now I don't think we should just build them a twenty-first century schoolhouse. We have to get the community involved so that everybody owns a piece of that school and wants it to work."

"You've been thinking about this," Henry said.

"Some," said Michael, "but I need to think about it more. But would that work, do you think?"

"Michael, the money is yours to do with as you please."

"Do you think we might do this together?"

"Together?"

"Henry, all this money is wonderful, and it's important, but it's not the most important thing. I was thinking that perhaps we might . . . well . . . I didn't know I had a brother. I don't know what brothers are supposed to do. But I'd like to find out, if you'd be willing. I mean . . ." He shook his head. "I'm saying this badly. I know what it is to have friends. David and Tomahawk and Moses and Lucio are my friends. I've known Tomahawk since we were six, and he's probably the closest thing I've had to a brother. But now . . . well, you and I are probably going to be separated, maybe by thousands of miles and cultures and who knows what else. But we could still talk, we can e-mail, we can try to get together perhaps. I'm saying this all wrong."

"You're saying it fine, Michael." Henry smiled. "I'd like to find out what it means, too. I've never been close to family—not really. Not even to the king when he was the prince. I've never married—never had the time, I suppose. Now I'm forty, and I find myself with a brother, and I'd like to find out what that means."

"Thank you, Henry. This means a lot."

"To me, too, brother. And let me look into the situation of your friend Moses. I've some contacts in Kenya who might help. Then we can talk."

"It's a plan, then. Thank you."

"So tell me, Michael, what happened to your American?"

"My American?" asked Michael.

"I thought there was a girlfriend," Henry said.

"Sarah?"

Henry nodded. "I met her once, you know. In Glasgow."

"You did?" said Michael, surprised. "How'd you meet?"

"At your cycling race at the University of Glasgow. She was with a group from Edinburgh."

Michael nodded. "Yes, she drove with Tomahawk and the others. I'd gone on the bus with the team."

"They sat in front of me. I didn't realize at first who they were until I listened to the conversation for a while, which I suppose was eavesdropping. But it wasn't difficult with the Scot nationalist entertaining the crowd."

"That's Tomahawk." Michael grinned. "Tommy McFarland. Years ago I called him Tommy Mac, and that became Tomahawk at some point. He was Tomahawk, and he's always called me English. You met Sarah?"

"It wasn't a formal introduction; we didn't exchange names or anything. But I'd ask questions, and she was full of answers about the best cyclist in Scotland. She knew what races you'd been in; she knew your statistics and that you were in training for the Olympics. She sounded like your walking biographer and statistician, not to mention publicist."

"I'd no idea. I won that day, if I recall."

"You did, and she explained to me all of the scientific details of why you won. She talked the jargon—cranks and watts and whatnot. When I asked her what she was studying and she said art, I was shocked."

"I thought she just let my bike talk wash over her. Amazing. But what were you doing there?"

"I'd come to see you ride." He hesitated. "I'd a story prepared if I needed one, that I was there on behalf of the British Olympic Committee to observe. The real reason was that I wanted to see you ride. I'd been following your cycling for some time, in fact. I was seeking an excuse to meet you and introduce myself. But it didn't work out. So, what happened?"

Michael told him the story.

When he finished, Henry asked, "Do you see any possibility for getting back together?"

"Not any time soon. The gulf in faith is too wide. Or actually it's not a gulf; it's more like presence and absence." He looked at Henry. "For Sarah and I to plow ahead would be a disaster."

"It sounds wise on both your parts. So what do you do? Give it time? See if something might change?"

Michael nodded. "Yes. But Henry, I believe with all my heart that she's the one God created for me. It was so clear the first time I saw her. It's still clear. It's hard for me to explain, but I believe we'll eventually be together."

"You've a lot of faith, brother."

"Not as much as I need. During training here and in Athens, I'd lie in bed, unable to sleep, plagued by terrible doubts. About Sarah. About my own faith. About being a priest."

"Michael, doubts are common for all of us. Keep straight to your course. I'd like to offer profound advice, but I'm a bit short in the faith department."

Nearby, two men sat talking.

Neither had a particular right to be in the Regent's Club. Josh Gittings was there through the membership of his boss, the prime minister. Stuart Milligan, a journalist, was trying to wrangle information from the man who many said was the second most powerful person in government and who was avoiding saying anything important to this pain of a reporter from the *Telegraph*.

"Gittings," Milligan said, "look over there. That's Michael Kent."

Josh looked and agreed it was the cyclist.

"Who's his breakfast partner?"

"Henry Kent."

"The Duke of Kent? Are they related?"

"I wouldn't think so, Milligan. Michael Kent grew up in Scotland. His father's a veterinarian, I believe. A distant cousin, perhaps? They're probably discussing the Olympics; Henry's chairing the summer games here in London in four years."

"I smell a story." He stood and walked over to Henry and Michael's table.

"Milligan!" Josh said sharply, to no avail.

"Sorry to interrupt," Milligan said to Michael and Henry. "I'm Stu Milligan of the *Telegraph*. I saw you sitting here, and I wanted to congratulate our Olympic hero."

Michael extended his hand. "It's nice to meet you."

Henry said nothing. He detested reporters. He looked and saw Josh Gittings mouthing a silent "sorry." Henry winked.

"So, I've got a question. I never would've thought of it if I hadn't seen the two of you together. Are you related, given the same last name?"

Henry spoke before Michael could. "I suppose we could be, Mr. Milligan, if you looked hard enough. Actually, this is the first real conversation we've ever had, other than a handshake on a stage last month."

"Oh, well, my mistake then. Anyway, I just wanted to introduce myself and say hello." He handed a business card to Michael. "If you ever care to be interviewed, please call."

Michael nodded. Milligan said good-bye and returned to his table.

"Satisfied?" Josh asked.

"Yes. I suppose my story sense led me astray this time."

Wouldn't be the first time, Josh thought.

Milligan turned to look back at the two Kents, once again engrossed in their conversation. *Oh, I'm satisfied, all right, I'm satisfied that there's something there. Michael Kent has the blue eyes—the famous royal blue eyes— just like the man sitting across the table. There's a story here all right.* He smiled and resumed the conversation.

"Vampire," Henry said after Milligan returned to his own table.

"You misled him a bit."

"No, I misled him a lot. He'll eventually ferret it out, but by then you'll be in your new assignment and away from here."

"I don't understand. Is it a problem?"

"He's most likely trying to squeeze Josh Gittings on where the PM stands on the bill in Parliament to rein in the expenses of His Royal Highness. There's considerable public sentiment for it; James isn't exactly known for his frugality, and the royal family's debts are a public embarrassment." He explained Gittings's role in the Bolting government.

"So he's trying to find out if Bolting supports the bill?"

"On the surface, yes. But it's deeper. There's rising public sentiment, Michael, to do away with the monarchy altogether. It's not a fire yet, but it will be within a year or two. The only thing holding the king in place right now is the tourist trade. The royal family still manages to bring in a considerable amount of tourist money. But that's been declining as well. Because of my connection to the royals, I get these fishing expeditions all the time. But you don't need to complicate your life with it. This is one area where I do have vast experience and can offer sound advice. Stay away from the mess with the royals. It's going to get ugly."

Michael looked at his watch. "It's nine thirty, Henry. I should head to the C of E office. I'll need to call a taxi."

"Let me give you a ride."

"Are you sure? Do you have time?"

"Come on."

Michael was expecting to see a chauffeured Mercedes but was surprised when Henry walked him to the car park and his Volvo station wagon. They talked as Henry maneuvered through the thick London traffic.

"This card has my e-mail address," Michael said. "And my cell. For staying in touch."

"I'll use it, brother. In fact, I'd like to check with you at lunchtime to see what your assignment is."

Reaching Great Smythe Street, Henry pulled over to the curb.

"Michael, thank you. I didn't know what to expect, and this has been a great thing for me."

"Me, too, Henry. I couldn't be more pleased. And thanks for the breakfast. We'll stay in touch. I'd like to figure out how we might spend time together. Once I'm settled, wherever it is, can we figure something out?"

"We'll do it." They shook hands. Michael squeezed Henry's arm.

"Thanks, big brother."

Chapter 22

At the receptionist's desk, Michael gave his name.

"Yes, Father Kent," she said, dubiously eyeing his bow tie. "Please be seated. They'll send someone directly."

The waiting area was shabby. The sofas and chairs had seen better days. Coffee tables and end tables bore years of coffee cup rings. The magazines were all old. *No worldly riches here.*

He pulled out his cell phone and sent a text message to Iain and Tommy. *Waiting now at the C of E. Breakfast with Henry was good. Details later.*

At ten thirty, an older man in clerical garb appeared. "Father Michael, please come with me." They walked down a hallway, turned left, and then went down another. Michael could see that the building was constructed around a central courtyard.

The man tapped at a door, and said, "Please go in, Father."

Three people were waiting for him. He recognized only Philip Johnston, his official sponsor.

"Michael, come in, my boy, and welcome," the archbishop of York said. "Let me introduce Father Edward Stanton, bishop of Norfolk, and this year's chair for the parish assignments committee; and Father George Martin, who is a special emissary to his grace Lord Canterbury."

He nodded to both men. Michael had caught the "emissary to" reference. The archbishop didn't say where Martin was an emissary from. *Something's off here.*

"So, Michael," the bishop of Norfolk said, "we could chat, but I suppose you'd like to get down to basics."

"I would, sir," said Michael, "but might we pray first? I'll be glad to lead."

The bishop reddened. "Of course," he said. "You're absolutely correct. It's entirely appropriate to begin with prayer." He motioned for Michael to pray.

"Dear heavenly Father, we come before you with the knowledge of what you've told us in your Word, that whenever two or three gather in your name, there you will be also. We take great encouragement from your presence.

"Dear Father, you know my heart. You know my desire to serve. And my desires and wants may not be yours. So, Father, I ask that your will be done and that our discussion today be a blessing to all of us. And if it's not what I expect, then Father, I pray for your grace to help me understand and accept. My vow is obedience and faithfulness to you, and I need you to help me be obedient and faithful to my vow. Without you I am nothing.

"Thank you, Father, for these men, your servants. Thank you for the time and care they've taken in making decisions. Thank you for the service they render to you and your church.

"Father, we ask and pray all these things in the name of your Son, who died so that each one of us might live. Amen."

Michael looked up. The archbishop of York was smiling thoughtfully at him. Stanton and Martin were looking down at the floor. Finally, Stanton cleared his throat. "Thank you, Father Michael. Your prayer blessed us all, I believe."

He continued. "Father Michael, we've had many long discussions about your assignment. Lord Canterbury has been involved as well and took a very keen interest in your particular situation."

Father, it's not going to be Africa. Please don't let it be a staff job in London.

"We knew of your desire to serve in Africa. To undertake an assignment like that voluntarily is, of course, commendable. Very few of our priests are willing to do that."

Michael gave a slight nod and waited. *No, it's not Africa.*

"Despite that desire, Michael," Stanton said, "we must recognize the needs of our larger church as well as the needs of our larger Anglican community."

It's definitely not Africa, Father, but I don't think it's a staff post.

"And one of those needs is to help heal wounds in the church body itself. You know, Michael, that our broader Anglican community is marked by increasing division over social issues and how to address them, over geographic and geopolitical concerns, and over many other things."

Michael continued to listen. *Where is this heading, Father?*

The archbishop of York had had enough. "What the bishop is trying to say, Michael, is that the assignments committee and the bishops council have decided that you will be assigned to St. Anselm's Anglican Church in San Francisco."

Michael sat, outwardly composed but inwardly reeling. *San Francisco?*

"It is not a Church of England parish," Philip Johnston said. "Nor is it part of the national denomination in the United States. It was at one time. A number of years ago it broke away over doctrinal differences. But it *is* Anglican. And it is obedient to Canterbury, at least for now, although it's closer in spirit and teaching to the Anglican Church of Nigeria and is, in fact, aligned formally with Nigeria," he said.

"St. Anselm's been growing slowly," said Father Martin, "but it has been growing. And it's in an environment and neighborhood where one wouldn't expect growth."

"Which suggests," said Michael, "that God's involved somewhere."

Martin nodded. "St. Anselm's has asked for help. On behalf of the Anglican Communion of North America—"

That's where he's an emissary from.

"—we've asked the Church of England to send us an outstanding young priest to be the assistant pastor. Lord Canterbury consented, and the bishops' council recommended you."

"You can take the time you need to think this over," the bishop of Norfolk said. "We know this is a surprise and not what you and many others"— he glanced at the archbishop of York—"expected. So feel free to consider and pray about this."

"I accept it, Father Stanton."

Stanton was taken aback. "I beg your pardon?"

"I accept," Michael said. "When do you want me to leave for St. Anselm's?"

Michael and the archbishop of York sat on a bench in the courtyard.

"They expected something of a protest, even a small one," the archbishop said. "To be honest, I expected some objection."

"So what was going on?"

"I can tell you some of it, Michael. I don't know everything, although I could speculate."

"And?"

"There were several things at play here. For one, your achievements in Athens did not go unnoticed. The bishops were as awed as any group of young teens at a rock concert. It was like waking up on Christmas morning, expecting a tie or sweater and finding a Maserati. A national hero had fallen into their laps, and they didn't know what to do with him."

"So one reason was Athens. Was that all?"

"No. Because of Athens and other things, the archbishop decided to make you his assistant."

"Other things?"

"Your family."

"Adopted or real?"

The archbishop looked at him. "So you know."

"Just in the past few days. Da told me on Wednesday. I had breakfast with my brother this morning. But why would the archbishop of Canterbury care?"

"Because as dense as he is, or pretends to be, he sees this very clearly. The monarchy is heading for oblivion. And the monarch, as you know, is the official head of the church. And if the official, if largely token, head goes, can the official, if largely token, body be far behind?"

162

"Meaning the king may not be the only one to see his budget cut by Parliament."

"You understand this better than I expected."

"My brother talked about this at breakfast. But how does that affect me? I can't stop Parliament from doing something."

"No, but you might be a conduit to your brother and through him to the government."

"So rather than serve God in Malawi I would serve church politics in Whitehall?"

"Blunt but accurate," the archbishop said.

"But that's not the assignment."

"No," the archbishop sighed. "It wasn't. I think I know your heart, Michael. Assigning you to the archbishop's staff wasn't an option. You'd have quit the church in six months, likely less. I had to find a way to assuage the Canterbury's anxiety over Parliament and seek a post for you that would work. It wasn't easy. Nothing was available in Britain. I've called in more favors than I care to think about. But you did not deserve a bureaucratic post that would stifle your spirit.

"Michael, the future of our church is in grave doubt. If there is a future, then you and others like you are that future. It will be better for you to be on the periphery than at the center because the center is rotting and collapsing. The future of the church is at the edges, and there you'll find a willingness to abandon what's dead, to meet the spiritual need, to fearlessly preach the gospel—that is our way to survival. In Canterbury's place, what would you do about Parliament?"

"I'd tell them to cut us loose from the budget," Michael answered immediately, "and let God fend for us."

The archbishop laughed. "You prove my point. And nothing would frighten Canterbury more because he and his hierarchy cannot imagine that future."

"And San Francisco?"

"It was a compromise between Africa and bureaucracy. It turns out the church there had indeed asked the archbishop of Nigeria for help, and he weighed in with Canterbury. Everything Stanton and Martin said about the assignment is true. It also would serve notice to the denominational establishment in the United States that they can dally all they want with heresy, but the Church of England and the larger Anglican community ultimately won't tolerate it, no matter Canterbury's personal feelings." He paused. "So why'd you accept it immediately?"

"Because, I'm afraid, I was listening less to the bishop of Norfolk—he did go on, you know—and looking beyond his words, knowing God was in control. I was talking to God, and when you finally said what it was, I was surprised, but I knew I could trust in God regardless of where I was sent. I have to trust that if this is what God would have me do, then he will give me what I need to do it. I also had enough faith in my sponsor to know he wouldn't jettison me without working something out."

The archbishop laughed again. "You are a remarkable young man. You will do great things, Michael, not as the world defines them, but great in the way God defines them. So what do you do for two weeks until you leave?"

"I go home tomorrow. I'll likely need to cancel my vaccination appointment this afternoon unless you know of a cholera outbreak in California. I go home with Ma and Da, and I spend some time talking with Father Andrew and ride my mountain bike up in the hills and maybe have a glass of wine or two with family and friends.

"By the way, archbishop, would the people at St. Anselm's mind if I brought my bike?"

Chapter 23

After meeting with the archbishop, Michael met with an administrator about his schedule and travel plans. He'd return in two weeks for final instructions and his green card for working in the United States. The assistant also handed him a thick envelope, containing background information on St. Anselm's and its ministries, living in San Francisco, and US cultural practices.

Once outside, he stood for a moment in front of the C of E building. He turned on his cell phone and left a voicemail for Iain.

"Da, it's Michael. I've been assigned to a parish in San Francisco. I've already canceled my doctor's appointment. I'm headed back to the hotel now."

As he ended the call, a text message came in. From Henry.

"?"

"San Francisco," Michael typed back.

The cell phone rang almost immediately.

"San Francisco?" Henry asked. "What happened?"

"It was some of the politics you told me about. In fact, our conversation at breakfast helped tremendously, Henry. When I walked in the room, I knew something had happened, and what you talked about came to mind. So I prayed my way through the discussion."

"Disappointed?"

"If I said yes, I suppose I'd be saying I was disappointed in God. A wee bit, perhaps. But he's got a plan here, so I need to be content. I could've ended up on the archbishop of Canterbury's staff."

"You've accepted the assignment?"

"Yes."

Henry was quiet for a moment. "Michael, go spend some time in those hills of yours on your bike. I'll call in a few days."

Michael started walking down the street to find a taxi. He stopped abruptly, forcing a couple of pedestrians behind him to narrowly miss a collision.

I know someone in California.

Back at the hotel, the group gathered for a late lunch and peppered Michael with questions about the meeting and his assignment. David quickly assumed critical importance in the conversation and described what he knew about San Francisco.

"Michael, I'll call Scott and Barbara. They'll be glad to help. Scott's a bit older than me and Sarah—he was twelve when we were born." He paused. "Do you want me to tell Sarah?"

The table became silent. Michael looked at his friend, surprised that the question had been a stab of pain. "David, she thinks I'm going to Africa," he said slowly. "And this might be too much to deal with. So, if she asks, then certainly tell her. But if she doesn't ask . . . well . . . maybe it'd be best to say nothing."

"Are you sure, English?" Tommy asked.

Michael nodded. "I don't want her to think she has to do something. She's got school to finish, and she'll likely have her hands full without worrying about whether there's a relationship left or not."

"She may find out anyway," Ellen said.

"Aye," said Michael. "But we'll deal with it if and when it happens."

Back in Scotland, Michael did exactly what Henry suggested. To the extent he could, he set St. Anselm's and church politics, if not Sarah, aside. The first week home, he spent time on his mountain bike and talked with Father Andrew. Friends from the university visited to celebrate his Olympic victories. Roger Pitts arrived on Monday, and Iain let him work gradually into a schedule, giving him time to ride with Michael.

"It's odd," Iain said to Iris one morning.

"What's that, dear?"

"Those two. By the world's lights, they should be bitter enemies. But they're becoming friends."

Michael introduced Roger to Father Andrew and took Roger on a bicycle tour of Edinburgh. A day later, Michael went to Glasgow to stay with the McFarlands, and they ate and drank and laughed together. Parting was hard, however.

"When are you back, English?" Tommy asked.

"It'll be next July, almost a whole year. I don't know if I can stand it."

"Who could stand being away from Mother Scotland for a year?" Tommy replied lightly, then became serious. "I'll miss you badly, you know. We've been together since we were six, and now you're off to the wilds of America."

"San Francisco isn't exactly the end of civilization, Tomahawk," Michael said. He hugged Ellen and Tommy together. "You two are always with me. Always. And there's e-mail and telephones. We'll stay in touch. And will you keep an eye on Ma and Da?"

Two days later, immediate luggage needs identified and bags tagged, and two boxes already shipped to California, Michael was checking his bags and a packed-up road bike for the short flight to London. Iain and Iris drove him to the airport, where David and Betsy met them.

Outside of security check-in, the group sat quietly in a waiting area, a different one from the one Michael had waited in with Sarah more than three months before.

"This isn't a funeral, you know," said Michael. "I'll be back next summer, assuming they can stand me at St. Anselm's."

"Now I know what to pray for," Iain said. "That the Americans find my son so obnoxious they put him on the first plane back to Scotland."

"And you're staying with Henry tonight?" Iris asked for the seventh time.

"Yes, Ma, he's to meet me at the airport, and I'll stay at his place, then he'll get me to Heathrow tomorrow."

She nodded as she patted his hand. *She's not listening. This is harder on them than on me.*

"I think I need to do the security thing about now." He hugged David and Betsy, then turned to his parents.

"I'll call when I get to London and when I get to California. And there's e-mail. David will help set up the video cam on the computer, and we'll be able to talk and see each other at the same time."

His parents embraced him together.

"You've launched me," he said. "You loved me more than I'd any right to expect. I'm going to miss you horribly. But we'll stay in constant touch, okay?"

They nodded.

"Godspeed, son," Iain said. Michael walked to the line for security check-in. The four watched him until he disappeared behind security.

Henry was waiting at Heathrow. Checking the bike crate with the airline, they stowed Michael's bags in the back of the Volvo.

Henry lived in Mayfair in the upper half of a large family mansion converted into a duplex. They ate dinner nearby and walked back to the flat.

Henry had actually done the C of E office one better and had set up a bank account and line of credit. "You may need this, and you can draw up to one hundred thousand pounds with no approval required, and amounts above that with the approval of the trust manager or me."

"I don't know what I'd use that large a sum for," Michael said.

"You'll eventually need a place to live, and housing is expensive there. You'll need more than what's in the account. US real estate continues to be a positive investment, at least for the short term."

He poured them both a glass of wine.

DANCING PRIEST

"I've something for you, Michael. About three years ago, Father's old housekeeper contacted me. James and I had ordered everything of your mother's and yours to be burned or thrown out." Michael nodded. "But the housekeeper— her name is Mrs. Pratt—disobeyed and managed to save a few things. She was cleaning out her home; she's going to live with her daughter because she's rather elderly and needs looking after. She contacted me to see if I knew where you might be. I'm surprised she trusted me with it." He handled Michael a large envelope. "I think you'll find it important."

Michael took the envelope. He didn't immediately open it but looked at the envelope and then back at Henry. Finally, he opened the clasp.

First, he saw a formal photograph of a man and woman. The man looked remarkably like Henry, except older. His blue eyes were arresting. The woman was a knockout.

"It's a photo of Father and your mother," Henry said quietly.

Anna had dark hair pulled back from her face. Her face was slightly oval. Her eyes pulled you into her.

"She's beautiful," Michael whispered.

He looked next at a photograph of the couple and a young boy, perhaps four or five years old, sitting on his father's lap. The boy looked like his mother—same dark hair but with a narrower face and the blue eyes of his father.

Too moved to speak, Michael looked at the other contents. A copy of the marriage license. Michael's birth certificate. And two photographs of Anna and Michael in a setting that looked distinctly unlike England.

"Do you know where these were taken?" Michael asked.

"My guess would be Italy. Anna was from a small town near Assisi, although I don't know which one specifically. Croce was her married name before she met Father. I don't know her maiden name. I'm afraid that information likely burned that night. I can try to find out."

"No," said Michael, "maybe one day. It's enough right now to have these photos."

The next morning, Henry said they had to make a stop before Heathrow, St. Lucia's Catholic Church, not far from Euston and Roger's old home.

They got out and walked through the churchyard to the church cemetery.

"I need to apologize again," Henry said. "Anna wasn't buried with Father in Kent. I wouldn't hear of it. So the attorney made other arrangements, and I never asked. After you were here two weeks ago, I tracked it down." He led Michael to a marble headstone.

> Anna Croce Kent
> Wife of Henry
> Mother of Michael

> She had beauty and beauty of soul.

"Who did the tombstone?" Michael asked. Emotion squeezed his throat, and tears filled his eyes.

"Most likely it was Shanks himself, the family attorney," Henry said. "He might've been a little in love with her himself."

Michael knelt and ran his fingers over her name.

"You can't imagine what this means to me, Henry."

Henry knelt and put his arms around his brother's shoulders. "I needed to do this for me as much as for you, Michael. It helps close a wound of my own making."

They walked slowly back to the car.

Part IV

Los Angeles

DANCING PRIEST

Chapter 24

After leaving Michael in the airport waiting room, Sarah boarded her flight from Edinburgh to New York. It was uneventful, affording her time to think—the last thing she wanted to do. But everything reminded her of Mike—a flight attendant's smile, a joke by the British Airways captain, another flight attendant's accent. Even the in-flight magazine had an article on bicycling. Tears came to her eyes when she heard the man behind say, "It sounds like a plan, then," one of Michael's favorite expressions.

She'd talked with David and Betsy before she left and realized that Mike was right—David and Betsy would be married before the summer was gone. It was hard to imagine her brother married. But seeing him and Betsy together made it obvious. *They just fit together. Their temperaments complement each other. And they look so comfortable together.*

Regardless of their feelings, she knew she and Mike could never work. It was an entirely new situation for her. *You either love someone or you don't. But how do I love someone with as much passion as I feel for Mike and yet know I can't? None of this makes any sense. It's ridiculous. So why do I feel so superficial and shallow? Maybe because I have been?* The one positive from the Terry episode was forcing everything into the open, out of the shadows where they had consigned it to avoid dealing with it. But nothing had been resolved.

The night Terry arrived was the first time, she realized, that she'd seen Mike angry; expecting an enjoyable evening, he'd instead found Terry. And while his anger had focused on Terry, she knew it was really meant for her. *And I deserved it. I should've told him. I should've made both of us deal with the religion thing. But I wanted to avoid it as much as he did. So we pretended it didn't exist, and when Terry stripped away the pretense, it blew up in our faces. My face, that is. Mike was the innocent bystander.*

David was right. I should've said something about Terry. I should've point-blank told Terry to go away and not come back. I should've dealt with all of this honestly, but I didn't.

She was tired and tried to nap, but sleep was fitful and elusive. *Those eyes. Like sky.*

After a four-hour layover in New York and a six-hour cross-country flight, she landed at Los Angeles Airport. She entered the terminal to find Gran waiting for her.

Helen Hughes was seventy-three but looked years younger. She'd led a physically active life, battling age at every step. She played tennis, although not as often as she used to, refusing to admit that she felt her age more after each game. She'd had a face-lift and talked about it; some of her friends whispered it was more like two face-lifts and a tuck here or there. She loved to dance—she'd been the one who convinced Sarah to take ballroom dancing in her sophomore year at UCLA.

Her only obvious concession to aging was the swapping of her beloved Honda CR-V for a Lexus.

"It sat too high," she told Sarah as she pulled out of LAX for the freeway north. "I needed a ladder to get into it. And it was a little noisy, although all I had to do was turn up the volume on the CD player. Do you want it?"

"Want what, Gran?"

"The CR-V. I still have it. I was going to give it to you and David for getting around at UCLA. Is he going to marry that girl he keeps talking about?"

"My guess would be yes. Most of our friends"—*Mike*—"think they'll be married before summer's out. Betsy's a sweetheart. You'll love her. And yes, I'd love the CR-V if you're giving it away."

"You're welcome to it. With Seth still acting like the perfect fool, I can't blame David for staying, although I'd love to see him."

"Have you talked with Dad?"

"Some, when he sees fit to call, which isn't often because he knows to expect a lecture from me on what he's done to his children. I haven't talked with him in at least a month."

"Gran, do you have any idea why Mother would've done this? Why she'd have three children by another man and pass them off as Dad's?"

Helen was quiet for a surprisingly long time, and Sarah thought she'd colossally offended her. Finally Helen spoke.

"Seth was always a dominant personality. He put his stamp on everything. He wasn't physically large for a man, just average height and build, but when he walked into a room, even as a young child, you knew it. He had presence. Much like his father, in fact, which attracted me to Mark Hughes to begin with.

"When he brought Marie home from college to meet us, we were surprised. We expected a quiet, shy type because that was the kind of girl he'd always dated. But there was nothing quiet or shy about Marie. And maybe that's what the attraction was. In many ways, your mother was Seth's true soul mate. He couldn't get anything past her because she'd call him on it. And he relished that. I'm sure they had some famous battles in their marriage—you probably could've sold tickets.

"When Marie got pregnant with Scott, not long after they were married, I was surprised." She hesitated. "It doesn't matter now whether you know this or not. I thought Seth couldn't father children."

"What?" Sarah asked. "Why?"

"When he was fifteen, he caught the mumps. The doctor warned us that it might make him sterile. I wanted Seth to be tested, but Mark wouldn't hear of it, and that was that. Families do stupid things sometimes. Of course, had Mark allowed the test, you and I wouldn't be sitting here right now because Seth would have known and likely adopted children with whomever he married.

"When Marie got pregnant, Mark felt vindicated and told me more than once he'd been right to avoid humiliating Seth. And I accepted that, particularly when I held eight pounds of bouncing baby evidence.

"None of us, Seth included, as far as I know, ever noticed that Scott didn't look like any of us in the family. We were thrilled, of course. He was a beautiful baby, our first grandchild; your grandfather had a grandson to pass the name down to, and so on.

"So we thought Scott would be the first, followed by more. I knew Seth wanted more children, but I wasn't so sure about Marie. She was always uneasy about the subject and often told Seth and us that she might just want to have the one child.

"And that's what happened for many years. I knew your father was disappointed, and I should've known that he was determined to prevail, even if it took twelve years. When Marie became pregnant—I believe she would've been thirty-four—Seth was jubilant. And when it was twins, he was overjoyed.

"We were a little surprised because neither side of the family had twins, and multiple births tend to run in families. As you and David grew out of babyhood, we could all see that David was a spitting image of his brother, and you—well, you, Sarah, my dear—looked like your mother. In fact, seeing you right now is like looking at the young woman Seth brought home from college. You inherited your mother's looks—that's for sure—and she was a great beauty. That's a compliment, by the way."

"Thank you." Sarah smiled.

"None of us, Seth included, ever thought that the three of you were anyone else's but Seth's. There was no reason to think otherwise. Had we been more observant, we might've seen that Scott and David looked like Ty Zimmer—a lot like Ty Zimmer—the business partner. Looking at it now, it's embarrassing we missed it. Of course, Mark and I rarely saw Ty after he and Seth went into business together. Ty never married. In fact, the last time I saw him was at Scott and Barbara's wedding ten years ago. He, Seth, and Marie had been great friends in college, and when they were in college, Ty was at our house as much as Seth was. But not later, once they were partners. Ty had his own life. Seth and Marie had theirs, although I'm sure they remained close."

Helen checked traffic in the rearview mirror. "In a way, I'm glad Mark didn't live to know this. He probably would've been as devastated as Seth.

"That was exactly what Seth was when your mother left you, and then with the note from Ty, he was destroyed. But he knew he still had two children to take care of, even if you were ready for college. So he bore up. And he'd do that. He wasn't one to indulge in self-pity, or for very long. Which surprises me now because that's exactly what he's doing.

"Then came that trip to see Scott and Barb last fall. That was almost the final puzzle piece into what had happened with Marie and Ty. I say *almost* because when he got back to LA, he went to the doctor and had a fertility test done. And he was sterile, just like the doctor warned when he was fifteen.

"So to answer your original question, Sarah, I don't know whether Marie knew he was sterile or not. But I think she knew he wanted children so badly that she turned to Ty. While it might have been a brief affair when she got pregnant with Scott, I suspect it was deliberate when she got pregnant with you and David. I think she wanted to give Seth what he wanted. That's what I think happened." She paused. "There's another thing here, too. Ty Zimmer was a twin. He had a twin brother, and apparently twins ran in his family."

"Do you know where Mother is now?" Sarah asked. "We haven't heard anything in more than three years."

"No, I don't. For a time she and Ty stayed in Denver. And then they left. If your father knows, he's never said."

They rode in silence for a while.

"Sarah, I'm surprised you didn't stay in Scotland as well. Weren't you seeing someone?"

"It didn't work out." Sarah stared out the side window.

"Well, I can't tell you how delighted I am you're staying with me before summer school starts. We have two weeks to play, and I need some clothes. Sarah, I do believe we should burn some plastic in Santa Barbara and points south."

"Gran, you don't mind that we're not your biological grandchildren?"

"Honey, I love the three of you so much, I wouldn't care if your parents were kangaroos."

Sarah laughed and leaned over to squeeze her grandmother's hand. "You're the absolute best, Gran; I don't know what I'd do without you." They were finally entering Helen's neighborhood.

Helen lived in the hills above Santa Barbara with a view of mountains to the east and ocean to the west. Helen and Mark had built the home when Seth was twelve. With a Frank Lloyd Wright-type of upscale design common in southern California at the time, the house used the same kind of stone found in the surrounding mountains. The west terrace was one of Sarah's most favorite places; there she had spent a considerable portion of her growing-up years sleeping, sitting, painting, and just dreaming.

She stood there now, dog tired and jet lagged, looking toward the ocean. She knew what she had to do—erase Michael from her mind. She'd scheduled a heavy load in the summer session and would be in a dorm during the week and at Gran's on weekends. She was going to bury herself in course work and commuting.

Chapter 25

The summer session at UCLA started well enough, but Sarah found herself confronting a problem she'd never faced before. She couldn't paint. Or draw.

She'd scheduled four art classes, only one of which, fortunately, involved actual drawing. The fall semester would be easier, with general electives and her senior project the only requirements remaining. But her summer schedule was heavy, and she needed the credits to graduate in December. She didn't want to wait until spring; she'd have the credits she needed, and she wanted to finish school, even if she was unsure what life after graduation would be.

At first she thought she was experiencing a block because of the full day's worth of classes and evenings of study. But as the semester continued, she found herself beginning to feel anxious, and that, she knew, was making the problem worse.

Her advisor, Nick Epstein, who usually spent summers in Italy, was teaching this summer. Sarah took her problem to him.

"I can't paint. It just won't come. It's always just flowed, and now it's not even a trickle. Dr. Epstein, I can't even do simple drawings. Everything looks awful."

"Sarah, it's not uncommon," Epstein said. "It happens. You've been abroad for a year, adjusting to being back, and you have a massive summer schedule."

"I don't need this right now."

"Worrying about it will only make it worse. Don't sweat it, Sarah. Seriously, what's the worst that can happen? You take an incomplete? You can finish the work in the fall if you have to. Relax."

But she couldn't relax. She sensed a connection between her artist's block and the ended relationship with Michael. She had burst into tears when David called to say he and Betsy were getting married in early August, and there was no need for Sarah to fly back to Scotland for the wedding. It would be a small, private wedding for family and a few friends. He would be bringing Betsy to California in December.

She paid little attention to most of the Olympics, but she followed the cycling events, although the newspaper gave only a brief mention of the time trials. *This isn't going to help me forget Mike.* She found more in-depth stories and videos on the Internet. And she saw the stories on the British Cycling Team. She visited the websites for the *Times* of London, the BBC, and the *Scotsman*, and the stories positively glowed. Mike's name was everywhere.

The summer session ended on Friday. On Saturday, Sarah found herself unable to sleep. Giving up at 4:00 a.m., she fixed coffee and read for a while in Gran's den. She then sat in a chaise lounge on the east terrace to watch the sunrise over the mountains.

Gran shook her awake. "Sarah, dear, you might want to see this. There's been a terrible tragedy at the Olympics."

Gran had the large-screen TV on in the den. Before Sarah could hear the announcer's words, she saw the tangle of bicycles.

"There was a rock slide," Gran said. "The riders in the lead smashed right into it, and others right behind them piled on. They say that at least five are confirmed dead."

Sarah stared at the TV screen, unable to hear much of what Gran was saying or much of the news report. She ran to her bedroom for her cell phone, her hands shaking so badly she could barely punch in David's number in the UK. As she rushed back to the den, she reached only his voice mail.

"David, it's Sarah. Please call me. Please. Do you know anything about Mike? Please, please call me." Her heart was pounding in her chest; she had this terrible feeling that Mike was injured or worse. Then to Gran: "I forgot. He's on the island of Skye with Betsy for their honeymoon. He probably doesn't know anything." She suddenly realized she might have lost Michael forever, and she felt overwhelmed by panic.

Sarah then drew in her breath and called the McLarens in Edinburgh.

"Mrs. McLaren, it's Sarah Hughes in Los Angeles. Have you heard anything from Mike? I'm sorry to be calling like this; I know you must be desperate for information."

"Sarah," Iris said, "we've been frantic to get hold of anyone in Athens. No one knows anything yet but people are trying to find out." She began to cry.

"Oh, Iris, I'm so sorry, and I'm tying up your phone. Please, if you hear anything, please, please call me." She gave Iris her cell number and Helen's home number.

"You know someone who's in the crash," Gran said when Sarah had ended the call.

"Michael Kent," Sarah answered. "David's roommate, the one who took David in after the dorm burned." She looked back at the television.

"Maybe he was near the back," Gran said.

"Oh, Gran," Sarah said, the tears starting, "he'd be near the front. They were ahead in the race. They'd already won three of the four stages, and they were expected to win the fourth and the overall gold medal. He'd be riding near the front of the peloton. He's the team captain."

Gran put her arms around Sarah's shoulders. "You've obviously been following this more closely than I realized. I didn't know you had a friend in the race. Let's hope he's okay."

I wish I had his ability to drop everything and pray. He could do that, just stop and talk to God.

Two hours later, Sarah jumped when the phone rang.

"Mrs. McLaren? Yes. Oh thank God, thank God, he's okay. What did they say?"

"He's banged up pretty badly, but he's okay," Iris said. She gave Sarah the details from Coach White.

"I'm so glad. I'm so glad. Thank you so much for calling me. I know how difficult, well, just thank you. When you talk with him, will you tell him I called?"

This time Sarah cried tears of relief. "He's okay, Gran. The coach called his parents. He has a gash across his cheek and a bad case of road rash on his leg where he skidded on the pavement, but he's okay."

Helen hugged her granddaughter. *This Michael Kent is more than just David's former roommate.*

The next morning, Gran handed the *Los Angeles Times* to Sarah. "Your friend is famous," she said, pointing to the helicopter picture.

Sarah stared at Mike's photo. She could see it was him, even with blood all over him. He was yelling something to someone nearby as the gurney was being lifted. His jersey was off, and Sarah discovered why when she read the story. She looked at Gran. "They used their jerseys for bandages and tourniquets."

"He knew how to do that?" Gran asked.

"He took a first aid and emergency health course before he went to Africa last summer. He'd know what to do. They had no medical help for half an hour after the crash. The doctors say he saved that Canadian cyclist's life. He held his hand to his head to stop the blood."

"It must've been awful," Gran murmured, "like war."

Both Sarah and Gran watched the closing ceremonies. Gran watched Sarah closely as her granddaughter watched the British team proceed around the stadium. *Michael Kent certainly looks better without the blood all over him; in fact, he's drop-dead gorgeous.* Sarah stood as the crowd in Athens stood up. Her eyes glistened with tears.

"This young man was more than just David's roommate, wasn't he?" asked Gran.

Sarah nodded.

"Do you want to talk about it?"

"I love him, Gran. I love him and I can't love him. He has this enormous faith in God. He'll be ordained as a minister when he returns to Britain from Athens, and then he goes to Africa."

"Is it the religion, Sarah?" Gran asked.

Sarah nodded again. "I just don't have it. David does. He became a Christian last fall in Edinburgh. But it just doesn't work for me."

"And it works for Michael Kent?"

"Oh, Gran, it's everything about him. It's not like he preaches on street corners. It's not that. But it's everything about him."

"How was it left with him when you came back home?"

"I ended it. I thought it was over, but it wasn't. Not really."

"Have you heard from him?" Gran asked.

Sarah shook her head. "No. He said he wouldn't write or call or e-mail. He said it would be like letting go of me all over again, and he couldn't stand it."

"Oh, my," Gran said. "This was serious."

"It was. It still is. I don't know what to do. I could have lost him in that crash."

Gran put her arm around Sarah's shoulders and hugged her.

Chapter 26

Back at UCLA for the fall and, she hoped, last semester, Sarah found herself still struggling with her art. She'd taken the incomplete in the summer course and now faced delaying graduation altogether.

She walked and thought when she wished she could be painting. The critical class was the senior project. She had nothing but drawings and minor paintings from Edinburgh. The days began to slide past her.

Three weeks after school started, she walked from her dorm room to the Fine Arts Building. It was unusually cool and looked to turn into one of those stellar, if rare, southern California days—cool, low humidity, and no smog. As she passed the Student Center, she saw a crowd watching several dancers from the drama society as they demonstrated a tango to promote the fall play, *Evita*. She stopped and stared, then burst into tears, surprising several people nearby as she rushed from the plaza. Reaching the Fine Arts Building, she sat on the steps to calm herself.

"Hi, Sarah."

Terry Bailey was standing next to her.

"Terry." She nodded, wary.

"I wasn't sure I'd find you today, but I figured if you showed up anywhere, it might be here. Is something wrong?"

"I'm fine," she said. "What are you doing here?"

"Looking for you, actually, for a couple of reasons," he said. "I'm getting married next month."

"Congratulations. And I mean that. Sincerely."

"I bet you do," he laughed. "Thanks. She's from Kansas; she's been working here with an investment firm. I met her at a luncheon right after I got back from Scotland."

Sarah smiled, waiting for him to continue.

"Like I said, there was another reason." He paused. "I figured if you were back here, then things didn't work out with Michael."

She nodded.

"I don't know whether you knew everything that happened when I went to Scotland."

"Other than our conversation?"

"There's more to the story. David or Michael didn't tell you?"

"No."

"Well, Michael saved my butt. I got dead drunk and was thrown out of a pub, just about into his arms. He picked me up out of the gutter, literally, and he took me to his dorm to let me sleep it off. I was lacking everything—my wallet, cash, passport, everything. I'd left it all in that girl's car."

"Girl?"

"Evelyn McLin. She'd been sending me e-mails about you and Michael. She encouraged me to go to Scotland to get things straightened out with you and even picked me up at the airport. Turns out she was more interested in getting her hooks into Michael." Terry sat on the steps.

"I had no idea," Sarah said. "I'd met her once or twice. She helped me one day get stuff to my room."

"Somehow she got my e-mail address. Anyway, forget her. You saw all the news about the Olympics?"

"Yes."

"Sarah, don't let that guy go. One thing I learned in just a few hours was how much he loved you."

Sarah looked down, saying nothing.

"He loved you far more than I did," Terry said, "and that's not easy for me to say. But it's true."

"Terry, I know," Sarah said. "I know. And I love him just as much, if not more. But this just won't work. The religion thing is too big."

"Sarah, if what we saw in Athens comes from his religion, sign me up. It's funny. Doing what he did after that crash was on a bigger scale, but it was like what he did for me. He could've walked away and let me lie in the street where I was. He owed me nothing, and I'd just come waltzing in and wrecked

188

his life. And yet he took me in and took care of me. Sarah, people don't do that kind of thing anymore, if they ever did."

"Except for Mike," she said softly.

Terry was quiet, then said, "I talked with Seth."

"With Dad?"

Terry nodded. "When I got back from Scotland. I screwed up enough courage to ask him what the heck was going on with your family."

"The father who's not our father?"

"Well, right. I don't defend how he's cut you off. I can understand it, but I think he's wrong. I even told him that, and I thought I was going to get fired. But he just threw me out of his office."

"My brother Scott's trying to hold us together," Sarah said. "David and I are separated by distance but most of all emotionally, and that's because of Mike or maybe because of the Christian thing. David became one, you know. A Christian. Mike and Tommy, the other roommate, helped him make that decision."

"I didn't know that," Terry said. "I met Tommy in Edinburgh. He kept us in hysterics with jokes about Evelyn." He paused. "So you're feeling isolated."

"I have Gran, my grandmother, but I suppose you're right. It's odd, Terry, but it's as if when David and I went to Scotland, the trip ended up changing my entire family. It certainly changed me and David. David's staying there permanently. He's married to a really neat girl, and she's a Scot. He'll finish his undergraduate degree at Edinburgh and do his graduate studies there as well. Scott and his family are in San Francisco, and I don't have a clue as to what I'm going to do with a fine arts degree, assuming I can get over my creative block and graduate."

"Artist's block on top of everything else?"

"I sound like a mess. I'm just trying to get through each day."

"Do you miss him?" Terry asked.

"I miss him so much I can't stand it," she said. "When I got home, I told myself I was going to get on with my life. I thought that time and distance would help, but if anything, it's gotten worse. All the news from Athens made me realize how close I came to losing him forever. I almost died, Terry, when I saw the first reports on television, before we knew he was okay."

"Can you call him or e-mail him?"

She shook her head. "Not when he's in Africa. And I don't know how to resolve the big problem between us. I really don't."

Terry stood. "Sarah, I need to go because otherwise Seth's going to fire me for sure. You don't need any advice, but I'm going to give it anyway. Find a way to hold on to Michael. I don't know how; I'm not religious, so I'm no help in that department. But hold on to that guy. Somehow. And take care of yourself, okay?"

She smiled at him. "Thanks. This conversation went better than our last one."

Terry smiled. "Sarah, you're one of the most intelligent people I've ever known. Don't be stupid about Michael."

She watched him walk away, amazed at the effect Mike could have on people. Including her former boyfriend.

In early October, she knew she'd have to talk with Dr. Epstein. She could complete her electives; they were easy and interesting. But the incomplete in drawing and the senior art project were hopeless right now.

She stopped at the Student Center Starbucks for coffee. *Starbucks. I can't go anywhere without thinking of Mike.* Wandering outside the coffee shop, she sipped her coffee while she read notices on the nearby bulletin board.

"Need ride to Frisco for Thanksgiving." "Roommate needed." "Apartment for Rent, Immediate Occupancy." "Krishna Heals." "Need tickets for Dodgers Playoff."

Then she spotted a card that read, "Maybe God is trying to talk with you. Talk with us. Campus Christian Ministry." *They're here in the Student Center. No. I am not going to do this.*

She started to walk away, then stopped. *Okay, I can always get up and leave if they get too pushy. Nobody's going to kidnap me. It's UCLA, not some cult out in the boonies.*

She wandered the maze of upstairs offices until she found it. She drew a deep breath and opened the door. *I can handle this; these are people just like me.*

The first thing she saw was a framed poster of Michael and the Canadian being lifted in the gurney to the helicopter. It was on a wall behind a student sitting at a desk. She stared, dumbfounded.

He looked up. "Hi, and welcome." He followed her gaze to the poster. "It's from the summer Olympics. That's the captain of the British Cycling Team. He's an incredible guy and a dedicated Christian. A minister now, in fact."

She continued to stare.

"Are you okay?" he asked.

She nodded. "I need to talk to someone," she said. *I am so not going to be able to handle this. The last thing I expected to see. What is going on with me?*

The student at the desk introduced himself as Tim Watson and offered her a seat. "I'm the only one here right now, but I can try to reach our director, Ted Jensen. Let me make a call. Would you like some water or coffee or something? Tea?"

She shook her head. "I just need to talk."

The poster was a blow right between the eyes. *Maybe God is trying to talk with me.*

Chapter 27

Ted Jensen wasn't available, but Tim got Ted's wife, Pam, to come instead. Sarah was in distress. She was sitting on the sofa by his desk, waiting for Pam to arrive, staring at the poster.

Pam came bursting through the door. "I'm so sorry it took me so long," she said as she approached Sarah. "Visitor parking was full, so I hoofed it from student parking." She smiled. "I'm Pam Jensen. My husband, Ted, is staff director for Campus Christian Ministry."

Sarah extended her hand. "I'm Sarah Hughes. I'm really sorry; I didn't mean to cause trouble."

"It's no trouble," Pam said. "Would you like tea?"

"No. I mean yes. Yes, that'd be nice. Thank you. I saw your sign."

"Our sign?"

"On the bulletin board. 'Maybe God is trying to talk with you.'"

Uh, oh, thought Tim, *she's either searching, or she's a wacko. That notice brings in all kinds. I warned Ted to try something else.*

"Let's go into Ted's office and talk. Tim, when the timer goes off, could you let me know? I'll get the tea."

"Sure, Pam. I'll bring it, if you want. I'll knock."

"Thank you, sir. Sarah, this way."

The office was neat but small. A bookshelf lined one wall and contained Bibles, binders, and an array of Christian books. *Knowing God. Surprised by Joy. The Brothers Karamazov* and *Crime and Punishment* in a boxed set.

Sarah sat and told Pam the story behind the poster on the wall.

Pam was quiet after Sarah finished.

"It's an incredible story, Sarah. You care deeply for this young man— that's obvious. You're trying to sort out whether this is about him or about God or maybe both. And in the meantime you've got a creative block that's disrupting your classes and jeopardizing your graduation."

"That's it in a nutshell, yes."

"First, you made absolutely the right decision to return to the United States. While your relationship with Michael hadn't progressed this far, the Bible teaches about being unequally yoked, when one spouse is a believer and the other isn't. Those relationships can work, but they're either much more difficult to maintain or become lifeless quickly. You don't think in the same way, you won't make decisions the same, you won't agree on how to raise the children. Marriage is tough enough without adding more pressures. Where was Michael on this?"

"He agreed it was best." She looked at her hands in her lap. "But he said it broke his heart."

"Where is he now?"

"He's in Africa. In Malawi. Doing church planting. He said that he couldn't ask me to go with him unless I was as committed as he was, because Africa was hard on women and children and especially hard on missionary women and children."

"I don't know from first-hand experience, but from what I've heard at missions conferences, he's absolutely right," Pam said. "It's not an easy place to live, even for a man."

"But it's misery here in Los Angeles."

"And it'd be worse in Africa. So, from what I see, God wanted you here, Sarah, and not with Michael in Africa. Now the question is, why? And follow along for a moment. I know you don't believe in God, but whether you realize it or not, you do believe in something. It may be yourself. It may be your parents. It sounds to me like you at least believe in Michael."

Sarah nodded.

"But regardless, we all believe in something. We have to because we're made that way. We're made to think and ask questions and to challenge everything, but we're really trying to find reasons to believe in something. It's like we can't help it because we're made to believe.

"So let me tell you what I see happening. And I reserve the right to change this because we've known each other less than an hour, and it's terribly presumptuous of me to be saying anything. I can't even tell you why I am because this isn't how these things usually go. Usually there's first a relationship and a lot of conversation. But it sounds to me like you're well beyond that point.

"So the first thing to look at is that you're not really dealing with Michael or your father or anybody in your family. They may be a cause, a conduit, a tool God is using, but I think what's happening is God is trying to reach you, Sarah Hughes. This is about you and what He wants you to know. And He may very well have used your relationship with Michael to start breaking down the walls."

"If you're right—and I'm not saying you are—what does He want me to do?" Sarah asked.

"He wants you to do nothing, Sarah. First, He wants you to *know* something. And that something is that He believes in you even if you don't believe in Him. Whether you believe in Him or not doesn't really matter because if He believes in you, He's eventually going to pull you to Him, even if you fight Him every inch of the way. I'm a case study on this, Sarah. I went to college and loved to party. I ruined my reputation, Sarah; I slept around. I destroyed my health with anorexia, and I got myself into serious trouble with drugs. I was the original prodigal daughter, and I broke my parents' hearts and the hearts of everybody else who cared about me. No one knew what to do with me.

"I had a friend who was a Christian. She was the only one who didn't give up on me. She reached out to me and loved me in spite of myself, in spite of my reputation and the huge mess I'd made out of my life. She helped me understand that I was trying to find God in everything except God. And nothing was going to work because there was no substitute for Him. And I gave up. I stopped fighting. I said, 'Okay, God, You want this mess, You've got it.'

"And He loved me, Sarah. It was as if He took me into His arms, and He cleaned me up, and He put a beautiful white dress on me, and He said, 'You're mine now.' Marriage is a picture of that, I think. I didn't think anyone could want me. But God wanted me first.

"A few years later, God brought Ted into my life. I went head over heels over him, we got engaged, and I was terrified he'd find out about my past. And he did because God helped me understand that I had to tell him. It was the worst and best moment of my life because Ted took me in his arms and he loved me. We have two wonderful kids, he's a wonderful husband, and there's not a day that goes by that I don't wonder why all this good stuff is happening to me when I feel like I should be punished. But I belong to God now. I hold onto that with all my life.

"That's my story. Yours is radically different. You haven't totally screwed up your life. But Sarah, it sounds to me like He's standing there with His arms wide open, and it's like He's saying 'You're mine now. Trust Me.'"

"You're telling me to trust what I don't see," Sarah said.

"Sarah, you see Him. You just don't *realize* that you see Him. He's there. He's in nature, He's in Michael and your brother, He's in the art you're so desperate to create. He's there, all right."

"Mike said something like that. He asked me if I thought he, Michael, was real because if I did, then I would have to accept the fact that he was a total lunatic, praying to God, talking to God, dreaming about God. I couldn't argue with that. I suppose I'm in love with a total lunatic."

Pam stood up. "Are you busy right now?"

Sarah stood as well. "No, not really. Why?"

"Come home with me. The kids will be out of school in a little while. Ryan's nine, and Meg is six, and I need to pick them up. Why don't you take a ride with me, and we can talk, and then I'll bring you back?"

They picked up the children and kept talking. Pam convinced her to stay for dinner, and the conversation continued with Ted when he arrived. *They both must be used to having total strangers at home. And the kids don't miss a beat either.*

Ted dropped her off at the dorm after dinner. The Jensens had given her a Bible, and Ted suggested she start reading the gospel of John. She and Pam would meet in two days and talk more.

Chapter 28

When Sarah and Pam next met, Sarah brought the Bible with her.

"I have questions," she said.

"That's great," Pam said. "I love questions."

"I've never read the Bible before. Or at least I can't remember ever having read it. Who's the one John keeps referring to—'the disciple that Jesus loved'?"

Pam smiled. "That's how John describes himself. He doesn't call himself the disciple who loved Jesus. Why do you think he would choose one way and not the other? Don't they mean the same thing?"

Sarah thought for a moment. "He's saying Jesus loved him first."

"Exactly."

"Oh."

"'Oh' is right," Pam said. "He's saying a lot of other things, too. But you've got it right. Jesus loved him first. He loved John and the others before they even knew He existed. He selected each of the disciples, Sarah, and He loved them before they knew what was happening. John and his brother James, like Peter and Andrew, were fishermen, probably the last people in the world you or I might pick. But they were the ones Jesus chose. And when you read the book of Acts, the story of Paul, you find out what it means when God really goes chasing someone. In Paul's case, God had to blind him temporarily so that Paul could see more clearly."

"What you're saying is that God used Mike and probably David and a lot of other people, not to mention the poster on the wall, to get my attention, maybe even my artist's block."

"I'm saying all of that is possible and even likely, Sarah," Pam said. "But He wants more than your attention. He wants your heart. In a way, it's like He's wooing you. He does this with men and women. He pulls us to Him. And most of us, or a lot of us, fight it like crazy. Because it seems weird—but only at first. At some point, we stop fighting; we begin to realize how natural it is and start to see things, really see things, for the first time. There was a Christian writer named Flannery O'Connor; she died in the 1960s from lupus. She said that you have to shout for the nearly deaf and draw large pictures for the nearly blind. That's one of the best descriptions I've ever heard to describe how God brings us to Himself. He shouts and draws large pictures so we can hear and see what He wants us to know."

"So, Pam, if He pulls me to Him and I become a believer like Mike and David and you, then what happens to me? Does my personality get crushed in God's embrace? Do I cease to exist as an individual?"

"Has that happened to Michael or David?"

Sarah looked at her. "No."

"In fact, from the sound of things, just the opposite's happened. You become more of an individual, more real. I don't know what God will do with you and through you, Sarah. Only God knows that. I can't give you a road map because it's different for each one of us. I can't tell you that you and Michael will get together or that you will paint again or anything else. All I know is that whatever happens, God is right there with you, and because it happens to you, it also happens with Him. He lives it with you, and He plans things for you to grow and develop into the woman He wants you to be. But what those things might be, I'm clueless."

"God is as real to you as He is to Mike," Sarah said.

That evening, Ted Jensen asked his wife how Sarah was doing.

"She's moving, Ted. She's moving closer each day. She's an incredible young woman, and I'm not surprised the Olympic hero fell in love with her. And it's strange."

"Strange?" Ted asked.

"Yes, strange," Pam answered. "The more I talk with her, the more a conviction grows in me, and I can't explain it. Each time we talk, I'm more convinced that God is going to use her in ways none of us can imagine. I'm talking about big ways. It scares me to death. I'm evangelizing or part evangelizing and part discipling because she's that close; she's already asking questions new believers ask. But I'm doing this with someone that God is going to use in extraordinary ways. It's humbling and it's terrifying. Surely there are better people for this than me."

"And what do you tell Sarah? That God chooses His disciples, the people He needs to further His work? Isn't that part of the discussion you're having?"

"Yes, but—"

"Yes, but nothing. Physician, heal thyself. And believe it. God knows what He's doing, Pam. Accept it. He's using exactly the right person for the job."

A week later, Sarah was back at the Jensens' for dinner. The children had finished eating and had scampered off for homework and play.

"I'm over here so much, I think I need to pay for room and board." Sarah smiled as they finished eating. "Meg calls me Aunt Sarah."

Ted laughed. "Well, Aunt Sarah, you're a joy to be around. You can't imagine how God's already blessed Pam and me just by bringing you into our lives."

Sarah looked at them. "He has? I don't understand."

"You've livened us up, Sarah," Pam said. "You ask provoking, intelligent questions that make us think—think hard. You challenge us. You want answers. And, believe it or not, you're fun to be with. So yes, Ted is exactly right. God's blessed us by bringing you into our lives."

"So how do I do this?" Sarah asked.

"Do what?" Ted asked.

"How do I become a believer?"

Ted and Pam looked at each other.

"You pray," Ted said gently. "You tell God that you're His, that you accept His Son as your Savior, that you claim the promise He made to forgive your sins. That's it."

"That's all?" Sarah asked. "I just talk with Him and tell Him that?"

Ted and Pam nodded.

Sarah bowed her head.

Pam held her breath as she watched Sarah.

Sarah looked up. "Am I supposed to hear or feel something? Voices singing? Bells?"

"You prayed?" Pam asked.

Sarah nodded.

"No!" Pam shouted in joy. "You don't hear voices or bells! I'd be worried if you did." She rushed around the table to hug Sarah.

Ted stood up, a broad grin on his face. "Sarah, you won't hear it, but there are voices singing because a soul has joined God's kingdom tonight."

Chapter 29

Pam began discipling Sarah, helping her study the Bible, praying with her, introducing her around the UCLA Christian community. Ted found a church in Santa Barbara that she could attend when she stayed at Gran's. Sarah soon found herself in a Bible study, led by Pam with four other women.

"The odd thing is," she told Pam, "I don't feel any different. I didn't hear any bells or cannons go off, no angelic choirs singing. Are you sure this is real?"

"It's real," Pam laughed. "If you 'feel' anything, it will be a confidence that grows over time. God knows you, Sarah, and He's going to take you at the pace that's right for you. The theologians call it sanctification. Trust Him. Talk to Him. That's really what prayer is, a conversation. But it's like one you've never had before. You don't have to worry about saying the wrong things or maintaining a facade, or worry about what the other person is thinking because God knows. What He cares about is the heart you bring to Him and you being open to hearing Him through His Word, the Bible. And making each day a step in the journey to know Him better."

The next weekend at home with Gran, Sarah said little about her newfound faith, but Gran saw her reading the Bible and decided to wait for Sarah to talk about it.

On the west terrace on Saturday afternoon, Sarah was reading in Exodus, the book her Bible study group was studying. Chapter 14 was about the Israelites fleeing from Pharaoh, and Moses raising his hand to divide the waters of the sea.

She stared at the text. She reread it and then looked toward the ocean. *The outstretched hand. The hand. Mike's hand. The hand pointing to the menu. The hand I fell in love with.* She stood and went to her room, found her drawing pad and pencils, and returned to the terrace. She began to sketch a hand. She finished one sketch, tore the page from the pad, and began another.

She could draw again. For the next three hours she drew hands singly and together, folded and clasped, pointing and fisted. She turned to the mountains and began to sketch them. Gran walked outside to the terrace to watch, and Sarah sketched Gran's profile. Then she focused again on hands.

At school on Monday, she went to the art studio and stood before her easel, unused for the past six weeks. She pulled the cover off and starting mixing colors.

Nick Epstein was walking down the hall in the Fine Arts Building when a student called out to him. "Dr. Epstein! Go look in the studio. It's something else!"

Curious, he went to the studio to see a crowd of fifteen or twenty quietly sitting and watching Sarah Hughes. Seemingly oblivious of the people in the room, Sarah was painting.

Epstein looked at the canvas. His jaw dropped.

Sarah was painting a man's hands, but Epstein had never seen a painting like this before. At first he thought it was a photograph, but then he watched her work the brush. She worked slowly and carefully, and what was emerging from her hand, the brush, and the color was the most realistic and beautiful pair of hands he had ever seen. He had a faculty meeting at three, but he sat with the others, mostly students but a faculty member or two as well, and watched. He missed the meeting.

Two days later, Sarah signed the painting. Looking at it made her want to cry. She was working again but in a way the creative impulse had never flowed before. It had direction, she realized, and purpose. It was richer and fuller than she'd ever experienced before. Looking real enough to be photographic, the

202

painting communicated something far beyond anything she'd previously done. She knew why she was painting now. *It's that creative impulse Mr. McLaren talked about in the barn. The creative impulse that comes from God. He knew it, and he said it just that way to see how I'd respond. And he was right.*

She heard a noise, looked around, and saw more than sixty people in the room, silently watching her.

"Sarah." Dr. Epstein smiled. "Can we display this in the foyer?"

"Yes, Dr. Epstein," she said, flustered. "I didn't know you were here."

"I've been watching for three days now," he said. "Do you have a title for this piece?"

She looked at the painting. "*Hands*. Just call it *Hands*."

"And how does the signature read? I need better glasses."

She smiled. "Shoes."

"Shoes?"

"Yes," she said, "Shoes. It's a nickname. It stands for S. Hughes."

The next day, she began a new painting. The concept had come to her as she painted *Hands*. She began sketching out a circle with spokes radiating from the center and then part of a leg. She had drawn this leg before, and she worked from memory. She could feel her fingers and palm moving over Mike's calf. She remembered the contours of the muscle, the smoothness of the skin, the hardness when she asked him to flex it.

She worked on the painting for a week, surprising herself with how quickly it was done.

"And the name for this one?" asked Epstein, clearly awed by what he had seen her do in just a few short days.

"*Cycle and Leg*," she said and signed it. The leg was mostly the calf and ankle. Her hand was tingling—she thought at first it was from the numbness of holding the brush too long. Then she stared at her own hand, astonished. *I'm feeling his leg again, right here, thousands of miles away.*

Chapter 30

By the time she was into the third painting, enough people had seen the two earlier works in the Fine Arts Building foyer to create a major buzz. The crowd watching Sarah was now more than one hundred strong; they sat on the bleacher seats behind the easel area and on the floor with pillows. Word was spreading about the girl and the paintings.

This one was giving her more trouble than the first two. She finally realized she needed to look at bicycles, not at the motley student collection found in bike racks around campus but at serious racing bikes. She found a bicycle shop in nearby Brentwood and received permission to sketch the bikes. The teenage shop attendants behind the counter were amused but intrigued. She sat and sketched steadily for two hours, close enough to the front windows to draw a crowd and actually a few customers.

When she finished, she thanked the shop attendants and saw a DVD display on the counter.

> Tragedy and Triumph: The Story of the Olympic
> Bicycling Race in Athens. Includes the BBC-TV
> interview with the British Olympic Team and extensive
> coverage of the closing ceremonies and the salute to
> the team in London.

She looked up. "Is this new?"

"Came in yesterday," the young man answered. "Those are the last two. We've already ordered more. People can't get enough of them. One guy bought five."

Sarah bought both remaining DVDs, thanked the attendant, and left, driving straight to the Jensens'. When Pam answered the door, her face lighting up to see Sarah, Sarah said, "I need to use your television and DVD player. Can I watch this on your TV? Can you watch it with me? Do you have time?"

"Of course, Sarah. What is it?"

Pam joined her in front of the television set. They paused only when Ryan and Meg came in from school. Ted came home early, and the three of them watched it all over again.

"So that's your Michael," Ted said thoughtfully.

"Well, he's not *my* Michael—not now anyway. But yes, that's him," Sarah said. "That's Mike. I've been painting him, and I can't seem to stop. I've done his hands and his calf, and now it's his legs with the bicycle."

"Sarah," said Pam, "he's incredible. I'd read the stories and listened to you talk about him, but I wasn't prepared for the reality."

Sarah nodded. "Try being around him. I spent most of my junior year within five feet of him." She paused. "Thank you so much for watching this with me. I need to get back to campus." She paused again. "I haven't seen him in almost six months, but I don't think I could've watched it by myself. Thank you."

After Sarah left, Ted said to Pam, "She really loves this guy, doesn't she?"

Pam nodded. "Enormously. She did before she became a believer, but now the walls around her heart are down, and she's overwhelmed by God's love for her and her love for Michael, and she doesn't know what to do about it."

"Should she call him and tell him she's become a believer and say what's been happening in her life?"

"Maybe," Pam said. "But she'll know when. I think she wants to, but you don't just pick up the phone and call someone in a remote African village. Plus she needs more time. But she'll know when it's right."

The painting of *Bicycle* drew so many people that the School of Fine Arts had to limit the number because of fire code regulations. If the crowds surprised her, Sarah never said. The afternoon she finished the painting and stepped back from it, the room burst into applause.

Pam had brought the other members of the Bible study to see Sarah's work in the foyer, now up to four paintings with the latest one, entitled *McLarens'*. Its subject was different, a farmhouse in the hills, but it had the same unmistakable reality that characterized its predecessors.

Sarah was now working on the fifth and last painting she'd do in the school year. Epstein had already told her that she'd aced the senior project and the drawing class she'd taken the incomplete in. He suggested resting until after graduation, concerned about the intensity of her work.

"No, Dr. Epstein," she said, "I have one more in my head, and I have to get it on canvas. It's my own personal final exam. I just have to do it."

For those who came to watch her, it was clear that she was painting a human figure but not a complete one. This was a close-up with the bottom of the painting cutting off the view of the figure's legs. He—for it soon became obvious it was a he—was turning away from what was behind him, which was mostly a blur of some kind of equipment or structure.

The longest any of the previous four paintings had taken was a week. On this one, however, Sarah worked for three weeks. The last week and a half coincided with finals, and many students brought their books with them. Pam brought Ryan and Meg one day when school was closed for teacher conferences. It was nine-year-old Ryan who said, "It's like church."

When Sarah signed the painting, Epstein asked for its title.

"*Mike, Airport*," she said. "That's Mike comma Airport."

Epstein looked openmouthed at *Mike, Airport* and was astonished. She had surpassed the previous four paintings, and by a wide margin.

"I see his face," Epstein said, "and the turn of his shoulders, and I want to hold him. His pain is so real."

"Yes," said Sarah. "It was." *And I caused it.*

Fall graduation was scheduled for December 20. Scott, Barb, and Scottie drove down from San Francisco and stayed at Gran's. David had intended to bring Betsy home for graduation and Christmas, but Betsy was more than two months into pregnancy and grappling with severe morning sickness. Her doctor finally nixed the trip. They called the night before the ceremony and talked with Sarah for an hour, apologizing again for not coming.

"Don't even think about it," Sarah said. "It's just a ceremony, and my niece or nephew is far more important." She paused. "Do you hear much from Mike?"

David's response was cautious. "Some. He's doing well, working very hard, and ran into more problems than he expected. But he seems to love the work."

"Is he physically okay?" Sarah asked, thinking about Africa and illness.

She caught David's hesitation before he answered. "I think so, Sarah. He hasn't said much. We've only had a few e-mail messages, really."

He's not telling me something. I can hear it in his voice. She started to press him when something—or someone—stopped her. *You have to have faith,* she told herself. *Trust your brother.*

So she bit her tongue.

At the School of Fine Arts reception after the ceremony, Gran and the Hugheses were able to see Sarah's paintings on display.

"Sarah," said Scott, "these are fantastic!"

She smiled, pleased that Scott liked them.

"This one," said Barbara, pointing to *Mike, Airport*, "looks familiar. I know him from somewhere." She puzzled over the painting, trying to place the face.

Gran had seen the DVD, so she knew. During the drive home to San Francisco from Santa Barbara, Barb finally made the connection. "Scott! I know who that painting reminds me of! It's Father Michael at St. Anselm's!"

"Are you sure, Barb? David said Michael knew Sarah, but that was months ago, and this was just painted. There's probably a resemblance, but it's more likely someone she knows at UCLA. Sarah painted someone full of pain, and that doesn't strike me as Michael."

"You're probably right. But still. It's rather haunting, don't you think? It's not obvious, but it reeks of pain. I wanted to reach out and touch his face and tell him it's okay."

"And Father Michael has a scar on his cheek, and the guy in the painting doesn't."

"Fair point, Dr. Scott Precise Hughes. Fair point," she laughed and forgot about it.

Part V

San Francisco

Chapter 31

Scheduled to fly tourist class to San Francisco, Michael found himself unexpectedly upgraded to business class, courtesy of a canceled reservation and a gate agent who recognized the Olympic cyclist.

Waiting to board, he looked through the materials on St. Anselm's. Named for the saint considered the founder of scholasticism, the church had been established in 1885 as a mission for sailors. But as San Francisco grew, the church began to attract wealthy people building homes nearby. Following the fire after the 1906 earthquake, rebuilding began in 1908 and finished in 1919, in the midst of the influenza epidemic. Its first use was as a makeshift hospital for flu victims.

The church grew until the late 1950s, when growth leveled off as people moved to the suburbs. Older members raised in the church remained, tending to be more conservative than the denomination was known for, a divide that grew in the 1970s and 1980s as the denomination moved increasingly to the left. Tired of seeing their tithes supporting revolutionary groups in Africa and the Mideast, and horrified by what they saw as heresy from the national church, the members voted to become independent but affiliated with the Worldwide Anglican Community. In 2006, St. Anselm's established a "special relationship" with the Anglican Church of Nigeria, a move made by many other conservative Anglican and denominational churches in the United States and Canada.

The church operated a school for grades kindergarten through eighth grade; it was highly regarded by both Christians and non-Christians alike. The school's principal was Veronica Meyers. The senior priest was Father John Stevens. He and his wife, Eileen, both fifty-nine, had adult children living elsewhere. Father John, according to the report, had done an outstanding job halting the decline in membership and attendance, and the church was beginning to grow. Though not a gifted speaker, he was well liked and strongly supported by his parishioners. His gift was in worship. He loved music and played both the organ and drums.

Drums? An odd accompaniment for the organ.

Fully supported by the board of elders, Father John had requested a younger priest to help with youth ministry, both for the youth of church families and homeless youth in areas near the church. This was to be Michael's position, although e-mails he'd received from Father John hinted at occasional sermons as well.

Finishing his reading, Michael reopened the envelope of pictures and documents from Henry.

Michael had a window seat, and a woman in her forties smiled as she sat next to him. He thought she looked tired. Perhaps she was returning home from vacation or business. He saw her wedding ring; seeing she was alone, he guessed business.

They were airborne before she spoke. "I'm sorry; I'm going to be rude. Aren't you Michael Kent?"

Michael smiled and nodded.

"I saw you in the waiting area and thought that's who you were. Weren't you going to Africa?"

"That was the plan, but things changed, and now I'm going to San Francisco."

"I'm sorry. I should introduce myself. I'm Abigail Weston, but please call me Abbie. My husband, Frank, coaches a cycling team back home in San Francisco."

"Professional?"

She nodded. "It's more of a regional team. They're called the Frisco Flash, and they race mostly in California and some up in the Pacific Northwest. They're like a feeder team for the national outfits. So my family and especially Frank and my twelve-year-old son, Beau, follow the international racing circuit. Beau's our youngest. We also have two teenage daughters, Emily and Erica."

"Were you in London for business or pleasure?"

"Frank and I are both attorneys. Frank does criminal law—defending nasty people, mostly—and I practice corporate patent law, defending a different kind of nasty people. I've been in London the past two weeks, helping a client prepare for a patent trial in California. So what's with San Francisco?"

"I've been assigned to St. Anselm's Anglican Church near downtown."

She nodded. "I know where it is. The area's undergoing gentrification, housing prices being what they are. You're wedged between the glittering stores of Market Street and—how should I say it?—a less-glittering area. It's edgy but coming back. Warehouses in the area are being turned into loft condos."

"Have you been to the church?"

"No. But I've passed it many times. It's a beautiful building, most likely constructed after the 1906 earthquake. Virtually nothing exists from before 1906; what didn't get knocked down by the earthquake was destroyed by fire afterward."

"Construction started in 1908," Michael said.

"You've been reading your briefs."

"Background information from the church."

"Will you continue your cycling career?"

"I haven't thought about it," Michael said. "I don't know if I'll have the time."

"I ask because members of the Frisco Flash all have day jobs. We have a lawyer or two, a couple of teachers, an accountant and other professionals, mostly in their twenties and early thirties. It's a good group."

The flight attendants started serving lunch.

"Frank and the team would love to meet you. If I'm being pushy, you can tell me to shut up."

"You're not being pushy."

She smiled. "Well, the team would love to meet you, and so would Beau. He has your picture on his . . ."

She stopped, and Michael said, "Yes?"

"He has your picture on his wall. The one from the *Time* cover."

"Ah, the helicopter shot."

"Yes." Abbie paused. "Was it as terrible as they said?"

Michael nodded.

"I know it must've been awful. The news was everywhere, and my family stayed glued to the TV. Beau and Frank were following the Olympic cycling events closely, and they were blown away by this young student from Edinburgh, who captained the British road team. Beau found a hero."

"Who's not quite as heroic in person." Michael blushed.

"So what can I tell you about my hometown? Food? Culture? Where to live?"

"Any and all of those," Michael said, "if you don't mind me monopolizing your time."

"Not a bit. Frank and Beau, not to mention Erica, will be wild with envy to know who I sat next to on the plane."

Chapter 32

When they landed in San Francisco, Abbie gave Michael her business card. "Please call if you need anything. Even a lawyer. And someone's meeting you?"

"Father John from St. Anselm's once I clear customs and immigration."

"Frank and Beau are picking me up, but knowing those two, I'll have to call."

They separated in the lines for customs, and she waved as she made it through first and disappeared. Michael was grateful for her kindness and attention. *I hardly thought about Sarah.*

He thought he might have a bit of trouble, perhaps over his green card or the bicycle packing case, but was pleased to find his processing by the customs officials fairly perfunctory. Exiting into the terminal, he looked around at the crowd. Father John said he would be holding a card with "MK" on it.

Fifteen minutes later, the crowd had thinned considerably, and still no sign of his ride. He was beginning to feel a bit worried; his palms were sweating. *I'm more anxious about this than I realized.* He found the church's phone number and called on his cell phone.

"St. Anselm's Anglican Church."

"Yes, this is Michael Kent. Do you know if Father John is at the airport?"

"Oh, Father Kent, I'm Millie Hensley, the church secretary. Aren't you due in tomorrow?"

"Did I give the wrong date?"

"I have it right here. Here's your e-mail to Father John, and it says quite clearly that you're due in . . . today. Oh no, this is terrible. We confused this on our end. Father John and Mrs. Stevens are doing hospital visits right now. Oh dear."

"It's no trouble. I'll take a taxi."

"Are you sure? I can probably find someone."

"No, no, it's all right, I can get a taxi."

"We'll be looking for you, Father Michael. Father John is so excited to have you. He'll be very disappointed over the confusion about the dates."

"I'll see you soon," Michael said.

Okay, the American taxi system can't be that much different from home. He wiped his hands on his shirt. *You're more nervous that you thought, Michael, so take a deep breath and calm down.*

He stopped first at an ATM machine to get enough dollars for the taxi or what he hoped would be enough. Then he walked out the terminal door, pushing the cart with his bags and bike case, to look for a taxi.

"Michael!" It was Abbie.

"I thought you'd be long gone by now." He smiled, trying not to show how glad he was to see her.

"So did I, but Frank left home later than he should've and got caught in bridge traffic. He and Beau will be here soon. Did your ride show up?"

"Well, they thought I was arriving tomorrow. And they're doing hospital rounds, so I'm looking for a taxi."

"We can drop you off at the church."

"No, I'm sure that's out of your way. I can find a taxi."

"It's no trouble. And my two men will be thrilled."

"Well, if it's not an inconvenience . . ."

"It's no problem," she said. "Look, they're here now."

A silver SUV pulled up. A man and a boy jumped out.

"Abbie, I am so sorry." The man kissed her and grabbed her bag.

"Frank, I've offered your chauffeur services to someone I sat next to on the plane. His ride didn't show, and he was going to take a taxi, but I insisted we'd help. Frank, this is Michael Kent. And Michael, that ruffian there is our son, Beau. Beau, come here right now and kiss your mother."

Frank looked at Michael and extended his hand, recognition dawning in his eyes. "You're Michael—"

"Yes, Frank," said Abbie, "he's *that* Michael Kent. He's been assigned to St. Anselm's Church downtown, and that's where we need to drop him off." She looked at Michael and grinned. "I love this. I have them both speechless."

"I've a bit of baggage with the bike," Michael apologized.

"Not a problem," Frank said. "Bike luggage is normal for us. This is a great thrill."

"Not just for you, Frank," Abbie said, nodding toward Beau.

The twelve-year-old was staring wide eyed. Michael walked over to him and smiled. "It's nice to meet you, Beau."

The boy shook his hand. "Nobody's going to believe this," he said. "Nobody."

Michael laughed. "Then we'll have to take a picture, right? I have a camera, and we'll have your mom take a photo of us, and there you'll have it." Michael found his cell phone in his carry-on, turned it on, and handed it to Abbie. "Just aim and hit the button on top."

With Frank on his left and Beau on his right, Michael put his arm around Beau's shoulders as Abbie snapped several shots. Frank gave Michael an e-mail address for sending the photos.

On the way into the city, Michael sat with Beau, while Frank and Abbie caught up with each other in front.

"What grade are you in school, Beau?"

"I'm starting seventh. Are you going to race here?"

"Well, I don't think so. I don't know if I'll have the time. But I might like to do some riding or at least hang around events some."

"Michael, if you'd like, you can come meet our team next week," Frank said from the front seat. "Has Abbie told you about the Flash?"

"Yes, she has," Michael said.

"We're having a little get-together to celebrate the official end of the season," Frank said. "A ride in the morning and then a lunch at a little place nearby. We take a month off and then start training for next year. Maybe you'd like to come on our practice rides. They're on Saturdays, usually finishing up with lunch somewhere."

"I really might like to do that," Michael said.

When they reached St. Anselm's, Michael thanked the Westons. "You're great ambassadors for America," he said. "You've gone a great deal out of your way to be kind."

"It's our pleasure, Michael," Frank said. "I'm thrilled we could do this."

Michael looked through the window at Beau. "Do you do the practice rides, too?"

Beau nodded. "But I usually have to ride in everybody's draft."

Michael laughed. "Well, that's where I usually am, too. So maybe we can ride in the drafts together."

He thanked the Westons again, and they waved as they drove off.

Chapter 33

Michael turned to look at St. Anselm's. The pictures in the background materials had been accurate but missed the majesty of the church. It was a Spanish-style design with a plaza in front. The grounds were well kept. As he looked around, he could see that Abbie had been right—the area was transitional. Some buildings were boarded up. A pawn shop was on the corner. And yet, across the plaza from the church, a warehouse building that looked like it had gone through rehab displayed a banner advertising condos for sale. He looked back at the church and felt his stomach fluttering. *It's just normal nerves, so stay calm, Michael. Take another deep breath.*

A sign indicated the church office was around the side of the building. He pushed on the door but found it locked. He pressed the buzzer.

"Yes?" said the voice he recognized from the telephone. "Can I help you?"

"Millie, it's Michael Kent."

"Father Michael, welcome to St. Anselm's." A buzzer sounded, indicating the door had been unlocked. *Security's an issue here.* He pushed his bags through.

Millie came hurrying down the hall. "Father Michael, it's so good to have you with us. I'm so sorry about the mix-up at the airport."

"It actually worked out fine," Michael said, shaking her hand. "The lady I sat next to on the plane had her husband give me a lift."

Millie is about Ma's age, midfifties. She was short, maybe five three on her tiptoes, black hair going unimpeded toward gray. *She looks efficient.*

"I'm so glad I was here when you called," Millie said. "I don't normally work on Saturdays, but I had to finish up the bulletins for tomorrow. It's so good to have you here. My, what's in that large crate?"

"My bike," Michael said.

"I should've guessed. Father John expected you to bring one or buy one here."

"Is he due here soon? Do you know?"

"Probably in an hour or so. By four for sure."

"Do you know where I can put my things?"

"Why don't you leave your bags here for now, and I'll show you your rooms." She pulled out a set of keys from her pocket. "This all happened so fast. When they said you were coming, we didn't have time to do things properly. But we've had your rooms cleaned. It's a small apartment above the church office that we've used as a meeting room. One of our elders is a building developer; you might have noticed his condos for sale across the street. He had a crew in here to fix it up. We thought it might be temporary, that maybe you'd find a place to live once you're here. It's small, but it does have a nice kitchenette and a closet for your clothes."

She came to a door and unlocked it with a key from her ring. "I'll give you your own key, of course; we've been keeping it locked so people wouldn't come wandering in to use it for something."

The place is small, but it's clean. A throw rug lay on the freshly waxed hardwood floor. The furniture included a small bookcase, a table and chairs, a slightly used sofa, and a dresser. A door led to what Michael hoped was the bedroom. Behind the table was the kitchen area with a countertop range and a small refrigerator. When he looked through the doorway, he saw a small room with a single bed, pillows, and a comforter. A desk and chair finished off what space was left. Another door near the bed led to a small bathroom with a shower.

He turned to Millie. "It's quite nice. Someone's gone to some trouble."

She looked relieved. "We didn't know what you might want. The only problem is that your chest of drawers and clothes closet are in the living area because the bedroom's so small."

"It's far more than I expected; it's really lovely."

"Oh, and the desk is wired. Paul, Paul Finley—that's the elder I mentioned (he's also the chairman of the board)—he had the connection put there for the phone and wireless for the Internet. There's also a phone in the kitchen."

222

After the miss at the airport, Michael felt reassured. They'd been working hard to welcome him. He noticed a small vase of flowers on the table.

She followed his gaze. "That's from Eileen Stevens, Father John's wife. She brought them this morning, although she worried that they might open too fast for tomorrow. But since you are here today, it's worked out well, hasn't it?"

Millie needs reassurance herself. "It has, indeed. Millie, I'm so grateful. I didn't know what to expect. Three hours ago I'd never set foot in America, and already I've learned how generous Americans can be. I'll get my bags and bring them up."

"I'll get your key. You'll need two—one for your room here and one for the side door. You'll need to be careful around the area in the evenings. It's not bad, but people do come wandering about. Oh, and a third key for your office. It's rather small, too, I'm afraid. It was a storage room, and Paul had it fixed up, too. It's a tight fit, but I think you'll like it. And be sure to use your keys. This neighborhood is coming back, but we have occasional surprises."

"Do Father John and Mrs. Stevens live here?"

"No," said Millie. "They live about thirty minutes away, out in the suburbs." She paused. "Do you mind being alone here? I mean, at night? It's a large building."

"I'm fine," Michael said. "And you can't beat the commute."

She laughed. "We're so glad to have you here."

After depositing his bags in his room, Michael left the bike case in the hallway and started exploring. He found the door connecting to the main part of the church.

He entered from the side of the altar area, and the physical beauty of the sanctuary took his breath away.

It was a traditional stone and timber nave, bisected by a transept, with the altar at one end. The pews could probably seat six hundred, he guessed. Stained-glass windows of various biblical scenes lined the nave with the donor's name and dates at the bottom. Most dated from the 1920s. The building's stone was sand colored, and the timbered arches were darkly polished wood.

Michael sat in a front pew, pulled down the kneeling rack, and began to pray.

"Father, You're so good to me. You've prepared a welcome for me on the plane and at the airport, and a welcome here in my new home. It's not what I'd have planned, but You did it perfectly.

"Father, thank You for this parish. I pray I'd be faithful with what You've entrusted me with. I'm going to make mistakes. I don't know the half of what I'm supposed to do, and I'm scared to death. But You're here. So keep Your hand of grace upon me, and I pray that all would look at me and see You.

"Thank You for these people You've brought me to labor among and the people that You'll bring through the door. And for the young people I'll work with. Thank You for this elder, Paul Finley, who's prepared a place for me to stay.

"Thank You for the Westons, who turned a disconcerting situation into something good. You always put the right people in the right place, just when they're needed.

"Father, keep my heart humble and give me Your grace to serve Your people here."

Michael lost track of time.

Checking his voice mail, Father John Stevens found the urgent message from Millie ("Father John, we had the date wrong. Father Michael's at the church"). He and Eileen hurried to St. Anselm's. The priest almost tripped over Michael's bicycle case.

"What on earth is that?" he said.

Millie hurried down the hall toward them. "It's his bicycle, Father," she said.

"Where is he, Millie?" he asked.

"I believe he's in the sanctuary. He's been in there a long time. I hope he's all right, but I didn't want to disturb him."

224

"Thanks, Millie," Eileen Stevens said, trailing after her husband as he rushed toward the sanctuary.

Months ago, he and the elders had agreed to expand the staff in the areas of youth and missions. As they were required, they'd submitted a request and job description to the Anglican archbishop in Nigeria, who in turn worked through the Worldwide Anglican Community. As it turned out, eighteen young men were approaching ordination in the Church of England, but the church lacked parishes to send them to.

John and the elders, and Eileen and John separately, had prayed long and hard for just the right young man. When they learned that the candidate being offered to St. Anselm's was Michael Kent, the British Olympic hero, John and the elders were stunned. The only caveat was that they would need to accept Michael unseen, although they'd all seen him on the news from Athens. At an emergency meeting called by Paul Finley, they talked long into the night about whether Michael would even be interested in St. Anselm's (they'd heard about Africa), how long they had before some other church tried to ferret him away, and how his fame might affect the church itself. And why couldn't he follow the usual process for candidates?

To that question, Father John provided the most likely answer. "Whenever something doesn't make sense," he said, "it usually means intense politics."

Thirty-four-year-old Paul Finley, both the youngest elder and the board chairman, finally summed up the consensus reached after midnight. "All things considered, we want him."

When the word came back that he'd accepted the assignment on the spot, they were overjoyed.

As John listened to Millie's voice message, he'd become visibly upset. "I screwed up the date. That poor young man finds himself in a strange country with no one to greet him and no ride."

"How did he get to the church, John?" Eileen asked.

"Someone he sat next to on the plane offered him a ride. I feel like a perfect blockhead."

While she knew John was excited to have an assistant priest in general and this assistant priest in particular, she also knew he was anxious. Would Michael Kent take humbly to John's leadership? Would he divide the elder board? Would the church be mesmerized by his gold medals and heroism, not to mention his celebrity?

So she knew her husband's mind when she followed him to the sanctuary.

John stopped, and she was hurrying so fast she almost ran into him. She followed his gaze to their new assistant pastor.

Michael, head bowed and apparently unaware of their presence, was praying. They couldn't hear his prayer, but they heard the murmuring of his voice as he prayed aloud. In that moment, all of John's concerns and all of hers disappeared.

They stood for several minutes, unmoving. Michael finally looked up and smiled.

Chapter 34

Father John and Father Michael liked each other immediately. Each complemented the other. Without saying so, Michael acknowledged his subservience to Father John in all things related to the church. Father John found himself taking a "godly delight" in the young man, who was seven years younger than his own son, Ronnie.

Michael was pressed into service for worship the next day. He met early Sunday morning with Father John, who talked him through the worship service. They prayed and put on their vestments. Father John handed Michael his new collar, still in its packaging.

"Not much time for a ceremony, I'm afraid," he said.

"God's more interested in the service than a collar ceremony, I think." Michael smiled but felt a little apprehensive as they entered the church. *My first worship service with real people sitting in the pews.*

The congregation looked to see who was assisting Father John, thinking their new priest wouldn't be with them until next Sunday.

Father John stood in front of the congregation. Michael could see perhaps 250 people present.

"Before we begin our worship of the Lord today," Father John said with a very serious look on his face, "I need to make a confession." The congregation was moved to silence. "I've misled you—and misled you badly." He paused, then continued. "I told you that our new priest, Father Michael Kent, would be serving in the worship next Sunday." He paused again. "I was wrong."

Heads turned back and forth. Paul Finley looked at Father John from the fourth pew, wondering if something had gone wrong. "I was wrong because"— here he paused again—"I read the date wrong on his e-mail. He actually arrived yesterday, and despite general disorientation and a case of jet lag and time zone shock, and despite your head priest not being there at the airport to meet him, he managed to find his way to St. Anselm's." Michael began grinning. "And he's graciously assisting me this morning in our worship of our Lord."

The congregation burst into applause as necks craned to get a better view of Michael.

"We've scheduled a reception for Father Michael this Wednesday after evensong, to which everyone is invited. With God's grace, I'll not forget that as well." Michael and the congregation laughed out loud. Turning toward the altar, Father John said, "Let us now begin the worship of the Lord our God."

After the service, during which Michael made only two mistakes, which no one kindly brought to his attention, he stood with Father John in the vestibule, greeting people as they left. Everyone stood in line to meet their new priest. When Paul Finley came up, Father John introduced Michael to Paul and his wife Emma.

"Welcome, Father Michael," Paul said. "We're incredibly pleased to have you here."

"In spite of that unusual introduction, Father John," Emma said.

Paul Finley, Michael was surprised to see, was in his midthirties. *A young head elder.*

"I need to thank you for fixing up the apartment," Michael said. "It was a welcome experience to arrive and find I'd a place to put my head."

"We know it's small," Paul said.

"Small perhaps but perfectly fit. And the Internet connection works; I sent several e-mails to friends and family last night. It fits my needs exactly."

"When you've settled in a bit, I'd like to talk with you."

"Just tell me when. As for settling in, I've another box or two being shipped from Scotland, and that's it for settling."

"I'll call."

"It's a plan," Michael said.

After lunch with Father John and Eileen at a nearby restaurant ("Nothing fancy," said Father John, "but the food is good, and it's open on Sundays—that's the main thing"), Michael went looking for a food store. The neighborhood was showing definite signs of revival, and the church was at the center of it. Increasing activity at the church and school was bringing people into the area. A small food shop, next to the pawn shop, was open Sundays.

After stocking up on basics, he returned to the church. *Millie was right. This place is big and really quiet, especially when you're the only one in the building.* But he liked the quiet, and he was tired. The trip and excitement were catching up with him. He stretched out on his bed and fell asleep.

He woke early in the evening. *Great, I've likely wrecked a good night's sleep with that nap.* He looked out the windows at the gathering twilight. Few people were about.

Michael fixed himself a sandwich and a glass of milk and checked his e-mail.

Ma and Da had been praying for him. Roger was turning out to be a great assistant in the veterinary practice. Tomahawk and Ellen had spent the day exploring Glasgow. David and Betsy had wandered around New Town in Edinburgh, looking at antiques they couldn't afford. David had attached a photo of the two of them in front of a shop.

After dropping Michael off at Heathrow, Henry had gone to Kent.

Michael felt the distance. E-mail and the photos helped. He didn't think he'd get homesick this quickly, but he felt the strings tugging. He saw Sarah in everything he read.

Robbie's mom in Montreal wrote a note dictated by her son, who was still having some trouble with small motor skills. "Therapy is okay but a pain. Miss the bike." Michael wrote a note to remember to pray for Robbie.

No responses yet from Moses or Lucio.

Beau had received the pictures and printed off several copies for his friends at school, Frank reported. "And don't forget about practicing with the team. I'll call and check if you're still interested. And tell us to bug off if we're too much in your face." Frank and Abbie were both persistent, but *I might need some friendly persistence right now.*

I need to take driving lessons. I'll have to learn to drive like an American or rather drive on the right like everyone else in the world except the British and a handful of others. And get a driver's license. And a car, and a car means insurance. And a local bank account. And he'd need some basic stuff—a TV, kitchen things, cleaners, and sprays of one sort or another. Maybe Eileen or Millie would take him shopping. He started a list.

Surprised by tiredness at 9:00 p.m., he got ready for bed and was asleep within minutes.

The next several days passed in a blur. On Monday, he met Veronica Meyers, the school principal, and the teachers. Father John was off on Mondays, so Michael spent time sitting in classrooms, meeting students, getting his office organized, walking around the neighborhood, and introducing himself to shop owners and people working in the area.

He had lunch with Millie, and she told him a little of the background of the church and congregation and about Father John and Eileen.

"They met in high school, in Philadelphia I believe it was," Millie said. "They married a month after he graduated from seminary. They have two children, Ronnie, who's a high school speech and drama teacher in Sacramento, and Gloria, who's a buyer for a department store chain in Chicago. Ronnie and his wife are expecting their first child right at Christmas, and Father John is nearly beside himself with excitement."

On Tuesday, he and Father John spent most of the day together, planning out schedules, sermon series, and times for Michael to preach. They decided what days Michael would be off (Thursday afternoons, Saturdays, and Sunday afternoons) and talked at length about the church's plans for the youth ministry.

"We have some teenagers who are members," Father John explained, "but they're few and far between. Most live well away from here, so it's hard to come back to church for activities."

"Unless you make the activities something pretty interesting," Michael said.

"Right. Field trips generally work, as long as it's not a museum. They liked going to Alcatraz though."

Far more numerous were the homeless youth. "These are tragedies," Father John explained. "We're talking teenagers from twelve to nineteen. Some live in communes in abandoned buildings. Paul had to chase some out of the warehouse he's now selling for condos, in fact. But they're all hard cases. Male and female prostitutes, some as young as thirteen. The drug scene. Some gangs. Petty crime and sometimes more than petty. It's not pretty and it's not easy."

"Some in the parish have problems with reaching out to them?" Michael asked.

"It's not the idea of reaching out. It's both a more general and a particular fear. It's easier to pretend these kids don't exist. And the kids prefer it that way. Talk with some of the social workers who work the area. They'll give you a more complete picture. But Michael, the social workers can't and won't talk about God, and God is what these kids need. So we have to figure out how to pull them in so they can find God. But we have to be careful. Some of these kids are violent. Some should be on medication but aren't. Some have HIV and won't get treatment and manage to infect a lot of other kids and adults. Keep in mind that all of them can be quite ruthless and think nothing of stealing from you, hurting you and anybody else."

"It sounds heartbreaking."

"It is. But it's no different here than in LA, New York, Chicago, or any other big city. I'm sure London and Edinburgh have their versions. These are kids from broken homes, pitched out of homes to fend for themselves; runaways; all the human flotsam and jetsam from our crazy culture."

"You care for them."

"God cares for them, Michael, and I want to try to reach some of them. Or what else are we doing here?"

Chapter 35

On Wednesday, Michael signed up for driving lessons and met with social workers. Without a driver's license and a car, he used his bike to get around and quickly discovered San Francisco's hills. Paul Finley called to set up a lunch appointment for Thursday. Wednesday evening, church was unusually crowded for evensong and the reception for Michael afterward. The enthusiasm and warm welcome greatly encouraged him.

When he finished at church for his Thursday afternoon off, he met Paul at a restaurant in the business district.

"You biked here?" Paul asked when they were seated.

"Since I don't have a driver's license yet, it was that or walk." Michael laughed. "I rode all the time in Edinburgh, and the hills are similar, although there are a couple of wild ones here I'll avoid next time."

"How are you settling in? Do you need anything?"

"More hours in the day," Michael answered, "but, no, I'm doing fine. Father John and Eileen have been great, and so has Millie. I've met Mrs. Meyers and the teachers, and I'm finding my way around the school. Everyone's welcomed me with open arms."

Paul smiled. "I'm glad. We were shocked when London called and said you were the priest they'd like to send. Weren't you thinking you'd be sent to Africa?"

Michael nodded and described his mission work in Malawi. "But God apparently had something else in mind. So let me ask you a question. How did someone your age come to chair the elder board?"

"At the last election, no one else stepped forward, so I was elected by default. And it's a problem. You saw the congregation on Sunday. They're wonderful people, but many are elderly, in the rest-and-take-it-easy time of their lives. And I understand that. But we need leadership. We need to grow it and nurture it. But to do that, we have to recruit younger people into the church, people my own age and in their forties as well. It's also a matter of the church surviving. We have to think about how God might want us to grow, and not just in numbers. We also need to grow in our faith. I can't begin to describe how critical Father John has been to stabilizing and growing the church."

"How did he come to St. Anselm's?" Michael asked.

"He had had a solid career," Paul said, "but he had a problem. He was a conservative in the increasingly liberal national denomination. He had been in Sacramento when his bishop decided to make Father John conform or leave, and an ugly diocesan judicial process spilled over into the newspapers. It was an awful thing for Father John and Eileen to go through, and the publicity was mortifying for them and their church. Our pastor here had retired, and we had a search underway, and his principled stand for orthodoxy immediately recommended itself to us.

"He gained a freedom with us that he had never had before, and he just blossomed. He'd be the first to tell you his gift is not preaching, but he is absolutely wonderful with people, and he has a first-rate worship service."

"I saw that Sunday," Michael said.

Paul nodded. "He also helped the school negotiate local building and zoning requirements when we expanded two years ago, and he's convinced more than one retired member to get active in ministry."

Their lunches arrived and Michael prayed the blessing.

"Father John says you're a real estate developer."

Paul nodded. "I followed my dad. He built in the suburbs. My orientation is the city. Emma and I live in a loft I rehabbed downtown, and we love the city. So do our kids. It's a different world than the one I was brought up in."

"How'd you become a believer?"

"In college. I'd set a whole passel of challenging goals for myself—academic, fraternity, athletic, student government. I was pretty ambitious for a college freshman. By my senior year, I'd accomplished all of them. I thought I'd find purpose and fulfillment. What I found instead was that the holes in my life had gotten bigger. And I crashed, big time. I was a mess and getting messier.

234

Right about the time I hit bottom was when a guy with Campus Christian Ministry grabbed me by the scruff of my neck and wouldn't let go."

"What happened?"

"He helped me understand that I had a God-sized hole in the middle of my heart, and nothing was going to fill it except God. So I accepted Christ. My family didn't even do the Christmas-Easter circuit for church, and they were horrified. My dad was more upset by me becoming a Christian than he was by the mess I'd made of my life. Our relationship has been strained for years. It's better now but still a problem. What about you? Where are your parents?"

"My guardians actually, but I think of them as my parents. They brought me up a Christian. It was never an issue at home. Faith was how it was. When I landed with Iris and Iain McLaren, it was like winning the Irish Sweepstakes."

"You're blessed, then, and probably doubly blessed. I have two boys; they're six and four. It makes all the difference in the world when the parents are believers. They're still kids, and we're still human, but to think with one mind, to have the same perspectives, to stand together—it's just a completely different thing. So, is there someone special in your life?"

"No. Not really."

"You hesitated." Paul smiled.

"Well, there is someone, or there was. I haven't seen her or talked with her since May, and I can't even say when I might see her again. I was head over heels in love with her. But we had a problem. She's not a Christian."

"That's tough."

"Especially when you're entering the ministry and thinking you're going to Africa. But anywhere would've been tough. It wouldn't have worked, or worked for long."

"Give yourself some time. And give her some time, too. Do you stay in touch?"

"No, except through her brother. He was one of my roommates. He doesn't say much unless I ask. But he became a believer, so there's some hope.

She did call my parents when Athens happened. So there's some feeling there, I think. I hope."

"Pray and give it time," Paul said. "God's full of surprises. You were one of his surprises for us."

When they finished, Michael cycled back to St. Anselm's but took a roundabout way. He had a good sense of direction, but he had a map of downtown just in case. Seeing San Francisco by bicycle was far more revealing than by car, although he had to focus hard to make sure he stayed on the right side of two-way streets.

In his room, he called Frank Weston at his law firm.

"Frank, Michael Kent."

"Michael! It's great to hear from you. How's the job?"

"It's going better than I could've hoped. The people are wonderful, and I'm starting to acclimate. Frank, does your offer still stand? To do practice rides with the team?"

"Are you kidding? Of course it still stands. We meet this Saturday at seven thirty at my house in Marin. And we'll bike from there and find some place for lunch. I can pick you up."

"No, it's fine. I can get there. If you can give me your address, I'll get the directions online."

After giving the address and the general location, Frank said, "Michael, you have no idea what those photos meant to Beau. He's a hero at school. He's already blown them up and made posters. So don't be surprised to see yourself all over his room."

"I'm glad he liked them. I'll see you on Saturday."

Chapter 36

On Friday, Michael was walking down the school's main hall just as the children were arriving for classes. Some were with their parents. Michael turned a corner and came face-to-face with a replica of David Hughes. He stood with his mouth open.

"David?"

"Close but no cigar." The man smiled. "I'm Scott, David's brother. And you must be Michael Kent. Scott Hughes." He extended his hand, and Michael shook it. Nodding to the boy beside him, Scott said, "This is my son, Scottie. I'm dropping him off on my way to work."

"Sorry about the mistaken identity." Michael could see that Scott was older, but the resemblance to David was extraordinary.

"Everybody does it. I'm the one who looks like David's twin, instead of Sarah. David said you were coming to St. Anselm's. Scottie's starting third grade here. It's a new school for him." A shadow crossed Scott's face, then he brightened. "When David told us about your assignment, we couldn't believe the coincidence."

Michael turned his attention to Scottie. "So how's school so far?"

"It's okay," Scottie replied, looking down.

"Son," said his dad, "Father Michael here was Uncle David's roommate in Edinburgh. Remember the e-mails about the fire in the dormitory?"

Scottie looked up at Michael. "You were in the Olympics."

"I was."

Scottie gave a hint of a smile. *This boy is really serious*, Michael thought, *or really troubled. Or both.*

"You won three gold medals. And you were in that crash."

Michael knelt to meet Scottie at eye level. "Would you like to hear about all that some time? In fact, I could sit with you in the cafeteria today at lunch."

"You could?"

"I'll be there. And I'll tell you stories about your Uncle David that you can embarrass him with the next time you see him."

The bell rang, and Scottie ran into his classroom.

"That was kind of you," Scott said.

"I'll be glad to talk with him."

"Scottie's had problems," Scott said. He hesitated. "It started with Dad, when he cut us off. David told you about that?" Michael nodded. "Scottie adored him, and Dad was crazy about him. It's hard to explain to a child his age."

"It's hard enough to explain to adults," Michael said, thinking of Sarah and David.

"And then the move here to San Francisco was tough on him. He became withdrawn. Barb—that's my wife—Barb wanted him to get counseling. I thought he'd gradually get over it. I should've listened to her."

"It's not too late for counseling, is it?"

"No. Probably not. We'd been looking at schools, and a colleague of mine at the hospital suggested St. Anselm's. It's convenient; the hospital's only eight blocks away. He rides into town with me, and Barb picks him up after school."

"I've been here less than a week," Michael said, "but I can tell you the whole place has a good feel about it. Mrs. Meyers runs a tight but loving ship. And there's a waiting list of teachers who want to work here, and that says something."

"I think you're right. And it's been a good week for Scottie. At least not a bad week. No major problems anyway." He looked at his watch. "I wish I could stay and talk, but I need to run. We want to have you over, so let's plan on it soon."

"That'd be super," Michael said.

At lunchtime, Michael went to the cafeteria, chatting in line with the students. He looked for Scottie and found him at a table alone.

"So you want to hear about the Olympics?" Michael asked as he sat down.

Scottie nodded. "I didn't know if you'd remember about lunch."

"Now how could I forget an opportunity to talk with the nephew of one of my best friends?"

"Have you met Aunt Betsy? I've seen her picture, but we've never met her."

"I've known her for years. You'll love her. She's smart as a whip, she loves to play, and she's full of mischief."

"Is she pretty?"

Michael thought a moment. "I'd say she is, if you don't mind the eye in the back of her head."

Scottie's eyes widened. "Really?"

"No, not really. I made that up. She's actually a very pretty girl, and she has a beautiful way about her. You'll see when you meet her. Didn't David say they might be coming home for Christmas?"

"Yep. So what was it like?"

"The Olympics?"

"And the crash."

As Michael answered Scottie's questions, more and more children crowded around to listen. Michael introduced Scottie as "the nephew of one of my bestest friends." They were all asking questions by the time the bell rang.

Michael walked Scottie back to his classroom. "You know, Scottie, God has you here at St. Anselm's for a reason."

"He does?"

Michael nodded. "I don't know what it is. But He's got one. You'll have to stick around a bit to find out. He's got me here for a reason, too. I thought I was going to Africa, but everything changed."

"Did you get mad?"

"Well, I was disappointed at first. I really thought Africa was the place for me. But God must've known something I didn't because He sent me here instead. So I'm just waiting to see what He's up to, just like you."

"Do you miss your friends?"

They reached Scottie's room.

"All the time, Scottie. E-mail helps. But I really miss them. And God knows that."

"Thanks, Father Michael," Scottie said as he dashed into the room.

E-mail helps, Scottie, but I'm so homesick I could cry. And I'm in love with someone I have to give up.

After school ended for the day, Michael talked with several of the parents who were waiting for their children. When he returned to his office, he had a voice message.

"Michael, this is Barb Hughes, Scottie's mom. I'm calling to thank you. I don't know all of what you talked about with Scottie today, but when I picked him up this afternoon, he was bubbling. He told me all about the Olympics and about you having lunch with him and about the other children standing around. After lunch his teacher asked the class what all the excitement was, and Scottie told them about you and David being roommates." Her voice broke. "It's like my child's coming back. I'd love to meet you, and we want to have you over for dinner. And thank you."

Chapter 37

On Saturday, Michael was up at five. After some breakfast, he gathered his maps and directions, a couple of bottles of sports drink, energy bars, his cell phone, a spare tire, and his portable air pump. He threw them into a backpack and headed out.

According to the online directions, the distance from the church to the Westons' home in Marin County was about thirty-five miles. He was allowing a good two hours to get there, should he get lost or encounter problems along the way. And while the ride generally went as planned, he was surprised by the wind's force as he rode the bike lane over the Golden Gate Bridge. He slowed dramatically, at one point dropping below ten miles an hour as he fought a vicious head wind. As he descended into Marin, the wind dropped off considerably, and he resumed his normal cruising speed.

He only got lost twice but finally found the area where the Westons lived. He arrived right at seven thirty. *Good thing I had the extra time.*

Their house wasn't hard to find. Twelve cyclists in spandex shorts and jerseys stood out front. Michael pedaled up and braked.

Frank greeted him warmly. "Michael! Great to see you. Before you are the members of the Frisco Flash." He introduced each by name, which Michael knew he couldn't possibly keep straight.

"You rode all the way from town?" one asked.

Michael nodded.

He saw a mix of emotions on the different riders' faces. Curiosity, questions, friendliness, a little skepticism, and one that could be read only as overt hostility. *Oh, no, it's like looking at old Roger again. Dear Lord, am I going to have to repeat the same trial again? All I want to do is ride with a group.*

The hostility came from Brian Renner, an attorney at Frank's firm and the team captain. His message was unmistakable: *Stay out of my way, hotshot. I'm the captain here, and you're just along for the ride.*

"Okay, guys," Frank said. "Let's go."

Beau rode along for the first fifteen miles until they stopped at a shopping center, where Abbie was waiting to take him to basketball practice. The boy protested, but a threatening look from Abbie quieted him.

They rode on. Michael could feel his legs working with the team. Something in the sounds of the shifting of gears, the pedaling, and the wind in the ears had to be an experience close to perfection, he believed.

Frank put the team through the paces, but mostly it was a simple, long training ride. They ended up at a pasta shop not far from the Westons' home.

As they ate, Renner looked at Michael. "So, Kent, what's it like riding with lower life forms?"

Conversation stopped.

"Brian," said Frank, his warning tone unmistakable.

"I just thought I'd ask," said Renner. "I mean, after riding with some of the best pros in the world, we've got to seem a little dull."

"I enjoyed the ride with the team today, Brian," Michael said. "This is a great bunch of guys."

"But we're not like the real professionals, right?"

Michael paused. "I wouldn't know. I never rode with professional riders until Athens, and Olympic cycling events tend to erase the differences between the professional riders and riders like me."

"Obviously. How would you win a medal otherwise?"

"Brian," said Michael, standing up, "all I wanted to do was ride. I just wanted to be around cyclists and do a group ride. That's all. I'm not joining your team. I don't want to be captain. I'm not trying to take anything away from anyone. I just wanted to ride. So I'll find another way to do it." He turned to Frank. "Frank, thanks. I need to get back to town. Please tell Beau good-bye for me." Michael walked out of the restaurant, got on his bike, and pedaled away.

242

I didn't handle that very well. I put him in his place, which was not good. But I got angry and made a scene, and that was bad. Why do I keep running into things like this? Maybe I need to ride by myself.

As Michael walked out the door, Frank looked at Renner. "Great leadership, Renner. You embarrassed me, and you embarrassed your team. What the hell do you think he was here to do? He just wanted to ride. He's six thousand miles from his friends and family, and you decide to play the Ugly American."

Renner turned crimson. Frank got up and left in disgust.

Sunday's worship service went well. Michael was learning the rhythm of the place and how much revolved around Sunday worship, the high point of the week when God's church came together.

He saw a few new faces, including Scott, Barb, and Scottie. Scott introduced Michael to his wife.

"We're not major churchgoers, Michael," Scott said, "but Scottie wanted to come. Barb and I were curious as well."

"You can come back next Sunday and see me flub my first official sermon," said Michael. "I've been working on it, but there's a long way to go. Any moral support would be welcome."

"Michael," said Barb, "we want to have you over for dinner. Friday?"

"Given my general lack of social engagements at the moment, plus having to eat my own cooking, I'm most happy to accept."

"Great. Let's plan on about seven? Oh, you don't have a car."

"I can pick him up when I leave the hospital," said Scott.

"I could get a taxi," suggested Michael.

"No. I'll pick you up. It'll probably be near six, but I'll call when we get closer."

Chapter 38

Michael would later be amazed by how a simple question could create a major change in life.

On Monday, Father John was off, and Millie had a dentist's appointment. Michael volunteered to answer phones and watch for visitors.

"No appointments or deliveries are scheduled, so it should be quiet, except for an occasional call," Millie said.

She was right. He sat at her desk to catch the phones while he worked on his sermon. He was revising the printed draft by hand.

The buzzer sounded, announcing a visitor, and Michael looked at the monitor. He saw a teenage girl and a boy.

He leaned toward the speaker box and said, "Hello. Can I help you?"

"Can you tell us about the school here?"

"Surely. I'll be right there."

Michael walked to the door and pushed it open. "I'll take you around to the school. Its main entrance is actually on the other side. I'm Father Michael Kent."

She looked at him closely. "You're kind of young to be a father, aren't you? I'm Jenny Marks. This is my son, Jim."

Michael hoped he didn't betray his shock and moved quickly to cover his surprise. *She can't be the boy's mother; she's far too young.*

Jenny's blondish hair was done up in a leather bow and peg at the back with wisps trying to escape. She was perhaps five foot four. She wore black slacks and a light blue sweater blouse. Michael was drawn to her eyes. She had pretty eyes, but they were hard—eyes that had seen too much and were trying to pinch themselves to keep from seeing any more. *She has a history.*

"You're kind of young to be a father," Jenny repeated. "You're the minister here?"

She's reacted to me the same way I have to her. "Actually," said Michael, "I'm the assistant pastor. I'm in my second week here at St. Anselm's.

Father John Stevens is our head minister, and he probably looks more like a father than I do."

She laughed. "I hope so."

"So, Jim," Michael said, turning to the boy, "how old are you?"

"I'm eight."

Michael looked at Jenny. She had to be in her early twenties at most; more likely she was eighteen or nineteen. "So he'll be going into third grade?"

"Right," she replied.

"Here we are," he said, opening the door. "Sue," he said to the school secretary, "this is Jenny Marks and her son, Jim." Sue's eyebrows shot up. "She's looking for information about the school. Is Veronica in?"

"She is, Father Michael," said Sue, "but she's on the phone right now. She should be off soon. Please be seated. It won't be a moment."

"I'll leave you in Sue's capable hands," said Michael.

Back at Millie's desk, Michael started working again on his sermon notes. After a few minutes, his phone rang with the internal ring.

"Father Michael, this is Veronica. Can I ask you to show Jim Marks around while his mother and I talk? I've looked for Sue, but she's away from her desk right now."

"I'll be right there." *Anything to avoid working on the sermon. This isn't like one for class. I have to give this to real people.*

Michael put the phone on the taped message response and walked through the church to get into the school by the back and shorter way.

Veronica was waiting outside her office with Jim. "Father Michael, thank you so much. If you could show Jim the school and tell him what it's like here, I can talk with Jenny about admission requirements." She gave him a look that said there was a whole lot more here, and she'd fill in the details later.

Michael nodded. "Right. I'll be glad to. Jim, let's take a look at the classrooms and get a peek at the gym and cafeteria, too." Veronica flashed a grateful smile.

As they walked down the hall, Michael pointed out the classrooms and which grade they belonged to. "This one here," he said, "is the third-grade class."

Jimmy peeped through the door window. "It's got a lot of kids."

"About twenty, I think," said Michael.

They walked through the cafeteria, then out on the playground. Michael pointed to a large building nearby. "That's the gym. It's pretty cool. It has two basketball courts and an area for gymnastics."

As they walked back toward the main school building, Jim said, "Do you want to know why she wanted me out of her office?"

"I didn't know she did," Michael said. "All she said was to talk with you about the school."

"She asked my mom what she did for a job. And Mom told her. She's a dancer in a bar."

"Oh."

Jim nodded. "And men give her money, and she sleeps with them."

Michael stopped and looked at Jim. "You're either making this up or you're not. But either way you're trying to shock me."

"I just want you to know. So you don't get mad when you find out later and make me leave."

"This has happened before, I take it." Michael asked.

"Twice. She's a good mom, though. We have an apartment. I hate the other stuff."

"So how did you find out about St. Anselm's School?"

"A guy she knows told her to check it out."

"Jim, do you have other family here?"

"Nope. It's just Mom and me. I never knew my dad, and Mom doesn't talk about it."

"Jim, how old is your mom?"

"She's twenty."

Dear Father in heaven, she was twelve when she had him.

"So do you live here?" Jim asked.

"Yes," Michael answered. "I have a small set of rooms in the church building for now. I'll eventually get my own place."

"Why do they call you Father?"

"It's what they call all the priests. I'm a brand-new one."

"Can you get married? I thought priests couldn't."

"Catholic priests can't marry. But Anglican priests can."

"Maybe you should check out my mom. She's pretty nice."

"She seems to be very nice, but I've only just met her."

"So?"

"So, if you develop a relationship with someone, it takes time. You have to get to know each other and decide if you like the person or not. And if you do, you have to think about spending the rest of your lives together. And that takes more time. Does that make sense?"

"I think so."

Michael saw Veronica waving at them with Jenny Marks at her side.

"So," said Veronica, "I've explained to Jenny that we'll meet tomorrow morning with Father John and see if we have a place for Jim. I have Jenny's cell number and told her I'd call after we meet."

Michael looked at Jenny, whose expression said she'd heard this many times before.

"Jenny, Jim and I had a great talk. He's sharp as a tack."

Jenny looked at Michael and smiled. "He is. He's really smart, smarter than me. Thank you, Mrs. Meyers. I'll be waiting to hear."

"See you, Jim," said Michael.

As Jenny and Jim walked away, she asked her son, "So what do you think?"

"If it's up to Father Michael," Jim said, "I'm in. If it's her, I don't know. You surprised her."

"I'm tired of pretending. It's better to get it out early."

"I told Father Michael."

"Did he faint?"

"No. But he was surprised."

"I bet he was."

Jenny Marks was born in Odessa, Texas. Her father was an oil field worker, her mother a waitress. Life had been middle-class normal for her and her older sister until Jenny's father died in an oil rig explosion when she was nine.

Within a year of her father's funeral, "Uncle" Bob moved in with the family, sleeping in their mother's bedroom. Jenny and her sister hated him. He said nasty things about them and their mother, and talked about "having a little talk with Uncle Bob" out back, which meant him saying nasty things as he tried to touch them. He was disgusting.

Jenny's sister ran away when she turned thirteen. Jenny was crushed—her one confidante had left her. When Jenny turned eleven, she found out why. Uncle Bob began putting his hands on her. She squirmed away and hid outside until her mother came home from work.

One afternoon, he found her before her mother came home.

She felt destroyed. Uncle Bob kept coming after her, threatening to kill her mother if she told on him. When she started throwing up in the morning, her mother took her to a doctor, who confirmed the pregnancy. Her mother slapped her in front of the doctor, demanding to know who the father was. When Jenny told her, her mother slapped her again, calling her a liar and a little slut. Her mother drove her directly from the doctor's office to an abortion clinic. Jenny had never known anything to hurt so much, not even Uncle Bob and his little talks.

A week later, Uncle Bob started again. She fought back and stabbed him in the neck with a pencil. She fled, knowing she wasn't going back. She had exactly eight dollars in her pocket.

She wandered around Odessa for three days. No one was looking for her. A Catholic priest gave her some money and offered to find a family who'd take her in. While he went to make the call, she ran off.

Jenny hitchhiked west. Near Albuquerque, she met a guy named Zach at a truck stop, and she stayed with him for two months. He treated her well and wasn't as ugly as Uncle Bob. When she started throwing up again, he offered to pay for an abortion, but the first one had been too painful. So he said she'd have to go. He gave her $1,000 and a bus ticket to Los Angeles.

Jim was born in Los Angeles six months later. Jenny was not quite thirteen.

That has been eight years ago. A lot had happened since then. Now there was St. Anselm's. She'd seen the kind look in the young priest's really blue eyes, and she allowed herself a little bit of hope that they'd accept Jim for school.

Chapter 39

On Tuesday, Veronica Meyers, Father John, and Michael met in the school's faculty lounge. She explained the interview and the Marks's situation to Father John. They sat in silence.

"A number of people in the parish would be very upset if the boy was admitted and this became known," Father John said.

"I have my own board to think about," Veronica added. "We've all worked so hard to build the school's reputation. This could be a black eye."

"What about the boy?" Michael said. "He's really, really bright."

"But isn't his knowledge base a lot broader than that of most eight-year-olds? Would this be a problem with the other children?" Veronica asked.

"He told me what he did, partially as a defense mechanism and partially to shock me," Michael said. "I don't think he'd be as open with the other children, or even his teacher."

"My young colleague has a big heart." Father John smiled.

"What if I served as his official sponsor at the school?" Michael asked. "What if we were open about this, an opportunity to help a child who might eventually be left to who knows what? I could be his sponsor. I could do that, couldn't I?"

Veronica eyed him warily. "I don't know."

"If we're open about it, at least with key people like Paul Finley and a few others on the school board, no one could say we were hiding anything because we wouldn't be," said Father John.

Veronica sat silently.

"Could we at least try it?" asked Michael.

In the end, that's what they decided to do.

Jim Marks started school at St. Anselm's on Wednesday.

The decision changed Michael's life.

On Sunday, Jenny surprised everyone, including herself, by attending church with Jim. Except for asking for the occasional handout, she hadn't been in a church for at least ten years, much less sat through a church service.

The Hugheses attended as well, lending moral support as Michael had only half-jokingly asked the previous Sunday. They sat with Jenny and Jim; Scottie and Jim had become friends from the minute Jim walked into the classroom.

When it was time for the sermon, Michael stood in the pulpit and looked around the nave, seeing a lot of faces. *I may blow this, Father, so give me and the congregation the grace to endure.*

"Our text today is from the second epistle of Peter, chapter one, beginning in the nineteenth verse: 'And we have the word of the prophets made more certain, and you will do well to pay attention to it, as to a light shining in a dark place, until the day dawns and the morning star rises in your hearts.'"

After struggling with how to structure his sermon, Michael had finally realized that God had structured it for him. He'd organized the sermon around five questions. Why was the word of the prophets made more certain? What was that word? Why should we pay attention to it? Why was it like a light shining in a dark place? And what was the morning star that will rise in our hearts?

As he spoke, he found himself moving to another rhythm, familiar and yet new. It surprised him. Things came to mind that he hadn't prepared or studied. He cited other passages, better and lesser-known ones, where the writers used *word* and *light*. He noted the intended recipients of the letter and why they affected what Peter was saying. He contrasted Peter's letters with Paul's, noting how Paul almost always included personal greetings in his letters, whereas Peter did not.

He read supporting passages and asked the congregation to read them aloud with him "because it honours God to have His word spoken aloud by us, His children." He finished by pointedly asking each person there whether the morning star had risen in his or her heart and what that meant to everyone and to God.

252

Michael finished with a short prayer. Father John led the closing hymn.

Father John knew they'd been in the presence of something sacred. *That boy has the gift of explaining the Word. St. Anselm's may have found its preacher.* Inspired by Michael's words, Father John sat at the church organ to play the postlude, discarding the original choice for Bach's "Ode to Joy."

As Paul Finley said afterward, "Father John cut loose."

It was as if the words of the sermon had been translated into the music. How Father John played was as much worship as it was skill. Eileen stood near the first pew, hand to her throat. The congregation stopped filing out and instead stood almost spellbound. Michael stopped halfway up the aisle and turned to listen. When Father John finished, sustained applause followed as he looked around, bewildered, not realizing the impact of his playing.

As the congregation filed out of the church, Michael was grateful for Father John's music because he had the distinct impression that the sermon hadn't gone well. He felt physically spent, like after fighting the headwind on the Golden Gate Bridge, as well as emotionally spent. Before Father John had begun playing the postlude, the congregation had been quiet and subdued, whereas Michael had hoped they might be joyful. The "Ode to Joy" seemed to have lifted spirits.

Jenny took his hand and said, "Do you always talk like that?"

"It was my first real sermon," Michael answered. "I practiced, but this seems to have fallen flat."

"Flat?" she said. "You spoke like poetry, and the old guy played it like poetry."

Scott and Barb Hughes were next. "I'd like to talk with you about this, Michael," Scott said as he shook his hand.

"I'm sending the tape to my dad, Michael," Paul Finley said. "If that doesn't explain what this is all about, then nothing will. As for Father John, well, all I can say is, wow! You two are unbelievable."

As the last of the congregation filed past, Father John joined Michael and put his hand on Michael's shoulder. "Something miraculous happened in this church today, Father Michael Kent. Don't ever doubt you were called to the ministry. God's hand is on you, son."

Maybe it went better than I realized. "His hand is on you as well, Father John Stevens. That 'Ode to Joy' was played with the joy of heaven."

"So"— Father John smiled—"we have a problem. What do we do for an encore?"

"I don't know. But I'm exhausted, Father John. I feel totally washed out."

Father John nodded. "That's what happens, Michael. You're the vessel God pours through. And it's exhausting."

Chapter 40

Checking his e-mail that night, Michael learned that Moses Akimbe's Internet provider had had connection problems and that he'd received three messages from Michael at the same time. And Henry had visited Moses for three days.

Henry had also sent Michael a message. "Have met with Moses. He's well named. I have some ideas to discuss."

Michael immediately replied to both Moses and Henry. And invited Henry to come to San Francisco for the American Thanksgiving. "I know you're hugely busy. But I'm free that week—I'm off for Thanksgiving holiday, while Father John is off for Christmas. And we could see the sights, do some of the wineries, and I might even get you on a bike. Somebody's bound to invite us for an American turkey dinner, or we'll make our own. No, scratch that. We'll figure it out, but you don't want my cooking. My place here at the church is small, but if you don't mind a single bed, we'd make do. I'd really love to see you."

Frank Weston had also written. "Michael, I feel terrible about Renner's behavior. I'm hoping you'll hear from him directly." Michael responded, telling him not to worry about it but that he wouldn't put Frank and the rest of the team in a difficult spot. "You've enough on your hands, and I'm just looking for a group to ride with."

The next evening, Michael started canvassing the few young people at church, calling them at home as well as talking with some of the eighth graders in the school about what they thought might draw the homeless youth to the church. Flattered to have been asked, the church's kids had both conventional and unconventional ideas. The one that seemed workable was a coffeehouse.

Finding the homeless kids was more difficult than he'd imagined. They'd gather in parks and then evaporate when a police car passed by. The city park a half block from the church was a popular spot, particularly when the weather stayed warm, as it did as September turned into October.

Michael decided the best approach was the direct one. He walked up to small groups of kids and explained about the church coffeehouse. Might they recommend a band or two to play on Friday nights?

Initially, the responses ranged from silence to vulgarity—some quite imaginative. Some of the teens asked Michael if he was looking for a pickup. He smiled and thanked them, then moved on to the next group. After three days of no results, he began to question his "business model," as Father John called it. *This isn't working very well.*

On the fourth morning, when he tried again, one girl spoke up.

"Purple Stash," she said.

"Purple Stash," he repeated. "Can you tell me anything about them? How might I contact them?"

"You're serious about this, aren't you?" said the one boy in the group. "You're really looking for a band. We've been thinking all along you were a perv."

"A perv?" Michael asked.

"A pervert."

"Oh. Well, no, I really am looking for a band," Michael said. "We've got the place worked out, and the acoustics aren't great, so we're limited to small and something that doesn't depend upon speakers blowing out the street lights." He noticed a few smiles. He turned to the girl again. "Who's Purple Stash?"

"My brother's band," she said. "The music's not what I like, but it might work in your coffeehouse."

"So," Michael said, looking around, "if I wanted to let you know when we'd be doing this, how should I do that?"

"Look for us around here," said the boy.

"And your name is?" Michael asked.

The boy hesitated, then answered. "It's Jason."

"Jason, it's nice to meet you," Michael said, extending his hand, which after a short pause the boy took. "I'm Father Michael Kent. I hope to see you at the coffeehouse."

256

DANCING PRIEST

Michael and Father John chose a room next to the fellowship hall. It seemed the right size for a coffeehouse, smaller than the hall but large enough to handle tables and chairs for thirty or so people, with the fire code allowing up to seventy-five. It even had a counter for serving coffee.

During the next few days, Michael contacted Purple Stash, who said they'd charge only $200 for a nonprofit event and set a time to check the room and meet Michael. Michael found a hardware store owner who gave him paint, brushes, and rollers at cost, and a Starbucks did the same for an elaborate coffee machine and kicked in coffee and cups for free. One of the baristas even volunteered to work the first evening.

Now if we can only get some kids here.

His three high school students at church helped him paint the room, and he worked under their direction. One was taking a class in graphic art and created the classy design—soft, muted colors. They found some old tables and chairs in a storage room, and the eighth-grade class at school was pressed into service to paint them.

As the eighth graders worked, Michael came from his office and discovered they were listening to rock music and dancing in place while they painted. One of the girls quickly turned off the boom box, and they all stared at him, worry in their eyes. Unsmiling, he walked over to the boom box and turned it on. And then he began to dance, and the kids joined in. "We've got a dancing priest," one said as they all collapsed in laughter when the song ended. *I haven't danced since Sarah.*

Michael worked the park and surrounding areas, handing out flyers and posting them on telephone poles and bulletin boards, at stores and at a Laundromat.

Coffeehouse
St. Anselm's Church, Friday, Oct. 15, 7 to 11
Free coffee from Starbucks. Music by Purple Stash.

By five thirty that day, the band had positioned the sound equipment, the Starbucks volunteer was setting up the coffee system, and signs had been posted around the church, giving directions to the room.

At ten to seven, disaster struck.

The manager/guitarist/lead singer found Michael and said, "We have a problem. Our drummer's busted. We can't do this without the drummer."

"Busted? For what?" Michael asked.

"Possession. Marijuana."

Michael fought down panic. *Okay, so what do we do? Where do I find a drummer with ten minutes to go? Lord, I need a miracle.*

The miracle stuck his head in the door. "Michael, Eileen and I are taking off now if you don't need us for anything."

Michael stared at Father John and remembered his briefs on St. Anselm's. Father John played the organ—and drums. "Don't move," he said to Father John. He turned to the guitarist. "I've a solution."

The first kids hesitantly walked in at seven fifteen. The band was playing blues. Father John was on drums, wearing a beret Eileen had found in his office. She stationed herself with the barista to help with coffee.

An hour later, the room was packed. Michael recognized several of the kids from the park, including Jason, but many others he'd never seen before. Some were smoking. The two priests had debated about providing ashtrays, finally deciding to have them.

For the kids, the evening's highlight was the old guy in the beret on drums. He did several drum sets, the last one bringing the kids to their feet.

The band played until eleven thirty. St. Anselm's Coffeehouse had launched.

Chapter 41

Michael's driving lessons went well. He took his driving test and became an official American driver.

He looked at the classified ads for cars but didn't have the time to check out so many different possibilities. Internet listings posed the same problem.

Father John introduced him to a church member, who was an accountant for a Honda dealership. The accountant connected him to the sales manager, who turned out to be a biking enthusiast, had followed the Olympics, and knew far more about Michael than Michael knew about cars. Michael got a better deal than he could have hoped for on a red Civic hybrid.

When he picked the car up, he found a two-bike rack installed on the roof. "My welcome-to-America gift," the sales manager said.

Jenny Marks continued to attend Sunday services, and she picked Jim up every day at school, becoming just another mom waiting outside. Michael could see that she was enjoying something totally new in her experience. The other moms included her in their conversations about kids, illnesses, doctors, and teachers.

Jenny started asking Michael questions about God.

At first he didn't know whether she was interested in God or him. And he was wary. He'd heard enough stories from fellow priests and Father John to be aware of potential sexual issues. But Jenny didn't pose a problem that way. He didn't ask but assumed she was continuing her line of work. He knew that, as a single man, he'd ultimately be limited in communicating with her.

So one afternoon, as she waited for Jim, he walked up to her. "Jenny, would you be open to talking with another woman about God?"

"Why?" she asked, almost suspiciously. "You don't know enough to answer my questions?"

"It's not that exactly. I don't know enough to answer the questions you have as a woman. I obviously haven't had the experience of being a woman who believes in God. And while I don't think it's radically different from a man's experience, there are some differences."

She looked at him thoughtfully. "Father Michael, do I threaten you?"

He was surprised and a bit confused. "Threaten me?" He thought a moment. "I don't feel threatened. But there are times when I'm confused. You ask questions in a completely different way from most people. You don't lead up to the subject—you go right to the heart of what you want to know."

"Are you attracted to me? Physically, I mean."

He blushed. "I'd be a liar if I told you I didn't find you to be an attractive woman. But my heart's elsewhere, Jenny. It belongs to a woman I haven't talked to in almost six months, and I don't know if I'll even see her again. But I still love her."

She nodded. "She's lucky, Father Michael, and maybe stupid if she doesn't realize what she has. Yes, if you can find a woman who's willing to talk, I'll do it." She paused. "Jim asked me if you might like to come for dinner." Michael could see she was embarrassed to ask the question, almost as embarrassed as he was in answering it.

He nodded. "Well, yes, that'd be nice, but you shouldn't feel like you have to go out of your way."

"It's not that," she said, clearly blushing. "I mean, we've had a friend or two over from time to time, but we've never . . . we haven't had . . . well, someone from a church, if you know what I mean."

"I'd be pleased to come, Jenny," he said.

"What about this Thursday?" she asked. "I'm off on Thursdays. Say seven?"

"Sounds like a plan." He smiled.

"Great," she said. "We'll see you then."

He walked away, feeling even more confused. *I don't do this female thing well at all. I'm a complete novice.*

260

He called Emma Finley and explained his request. She accepted immediately, so he gave her the option of backing out and told Emma what he knew of Jenny's life.

When he finished, Emma was quiet.

"I don't know how to handle that," she said. "I can't imagine having a baby when you're twelve. It's unreal."

Michael's heart began to sink.

"I mean, how do I connect with her? Perhaps through the kids and the school?"

His heart lifted a notch. "Emma, she asks the questions that anyone asks. She sees Jim doing well and being accepted, and she's asking why we're different from everyone else she's known. She's finding acceptance here, and she doesn't quite believe it. This has never happened to her before."

"Okay," she said, "I'll see her tomorrow after school and introduce myself and tell her we've talked."

"Thank you," Michael said. "Thank you so much, Emma. If you run into a problem, let me know. Don't think you have to keep on doing this either. But I think you can answer the kind of questions women can only really ask each other."

Later that week, as Michael worked on Sunday's sermon, Veronica Meyers knocked at his door.

"Yes, ma'am?" he asked.

"I'm sorry to interrupt, Father, but I want you to hear something." Millie was with her. She took them to the room where the music teacher taught band and voice to the kindergarten through sixth-grade classes once a week and to the seventh- through eighth-grade classes three times a week.

"Just listen," she said.

Two boys were singing a duet, and their voices were beautiful when they sang individually and together.

"Look who it is," Veronica said.

Michael and Millie peered through the glass in the doorway. It was Scottie and Jim.

"I'm astonished," said Michael. "I'd no idea."

"They sound like angels," Millie said.

Veronica nodded. "Mr. Schultz heard their voices when the third-grade class was singing. He worked hard to convince them to sing by themselves."

"You're thinking about the school Christmas program," Michael said.

She nodded. "And a Sunday service."

That night Michael received Henry's e-mail. "Arriving on the Tuesday before Thanksgiving. Airport Executive Hangar. Can you meet me, or do I arrange for a ride? Can't wait."

Michael whooped out loud. His brother was coming.

Chapter 42

Early Thursday evening, Michael got ready for dinner at the Markses'. He wasn't quite sure what to wear; the clerical garb seemed a bit much, but a polo shirt and slacks seemed too casual. He finally decided on a white dress shirt and bow tie with his blue blazer and khaki slacks. It was less formal than the priest's garb but kept some formal distance. *It's just a dinner with people who attend the church.* But he knew he was nervous; he hadn't said anything about the dinner to anyone, including Father John and Millie.

Leaving the church, he stopped at the food shop to pick up a bottle of wine. As he looked at the wines on display, the counter clerk called out to him. "Big date tonight, Father Michael?"

Michael blushed. "No, not exactly. I'm having dinner at a parishioner's house, and I'm looking for a good wine to bring." He finally selected a Merlot, paid for his purchase, and left. *It's not a date; it's not that at all. What's confusing me is the loneliness. I'm not attracted to Jenny romantically. I know I'm not. But it's all confusing. I need to focus on having a good time.*

The Markses' street was quiet. At one time an upper-middle-class neighborhood, it was now divided into duplexes and fourplexes. He eventually found a parking space a few houses down the street.

Jim answered the door of their upstairs flat and stared at Michael's clothes.

"You look like a normal person," he said, surprise all over his face.

"Maybe I *am* a normal person," Michael laughed.

Jenny joined Jim and duplicated his look of surprise. She was dressed in slacks and a simple blue blouse with an oriental collar. Blue was a good color for her. Her hair was down, and it hit Michael with a thud that she was about the same age as Sarah. She was just a little younger, and in normal circumstances she'd be in college.

She quickly regained her composure. "Come in, Father Michael. You look pretty good for a priest."

Michael covered his embarrassment by handing her the wine. "Just a small thank you for saving me from having to eat my own cooking tonight." He smiled.

She laughed. "You can thank Wan Fu Chinese takeout."

The flat was simple, the furnishings plain. Jenny had added a few wall decorations, mostly drawings and artwork by Jim from school. Jim showed Michael his room while Jenny opened the wine.

As they ate and talked, Michael found himself relaxing and enjoying the evening. Jenny watched Jim talk with Michael, and Michael respond to the boy. She realized that her son had found a hero. It pained her to see how hungry Jim was for a father figure. He and Michael talked easily together, and she had to keep reminding herself of their separate and unbridgeable lives. But she indulged herself and let herself believe, for this evening at least, that this was a normal relationship, something she'd never known but only imagined.

As they cleaned up, Jim suggested the ice cream shop for dessert, a two-block walk from the flat. The mid-November evening was cool. Jim embarrassed both Jenny and Michael when he took Michael's hand as they walked, but then the naturalness of the gesture overcame embarrassment.

Returning, they stood in front of their building. Jenny told Jim to get ready for bed since he had school tomorrow.

"Jenny," Michael said, "this was really nice. Thank you for inviting me. It's been a while since I stepped outside my job and was just able to be me."

"Thanks for coming, Father Michael," she said. "And thanks for the wine and ice cream."

"I'd like to return the invitation to you and Jim, but we'll need to avoid my cooking."

She laughed. "Is it really that bad?"

"No," he said, "it's a lot worse than that. So let me figure something out, and we'll talk."

She laughed again. "Just let me know." As she watched him walk to his car, she pretended he'd really call.

The phone rang as she walked into the flat.

"Hello?" she said.

"Are you moonlighting, or maybe he doesn't know what you are?"

Leo.

She fought the immediate sense of fear. "Come on, Leo, for God's sakes, he's the priest from the church where Jim goes to school. He visits all the kids." She hoped he didn't sense her anxiety.

"A priest in a bow tie? And he takes all the kids and their mothers for an ice cream cone?"

"Yes, Leo, a priest in a bow tie. He's not Catholic. He's Anglican. They don't have to wear the priest clothes all the time."

"I'm just making sure, Jenny. I keep an eye on all my best employees. I don't want to see their friends get hurt." He hung up.

She realized that he or someone must have been parked nearby, watching. She heard an engine rev as a car drove down the street.

The Sunday before Thanksgiving, the usual order of service had one change. The offertory included special music by "singers from St. Anselm's School."

That morning, while getting dressed, Jenny could see Jim was excited, but whatever was up, he wasn't saying. "You have to wait." He said he had to sit separately from her, and she'd find out why.

Scottie was the same. Scott and Barb hadn't seen him this excited in a long time.

When the time for the offertory came, several children in choir robes assembled in front of the altar, facing the congregation. A beaming Jim evoked a smile from his mother. *So this was his surprise,* she thought.

Mr. Schultz, the music teacher, directed the children in "Amazing Grace."

Amazing grace! How sweet the sound
That saved a wretch like me!
I once was lost, but now am found;
Was blind, but now I see.

'Twas grace that taught my heart to fear,
And grace my fears relieved;
And precious did that grace appear
The hour I first believed!

And then Scottie and Jim stepped forward and sang their duet a cappella.

Through many dangers, toils and snares,
I have already come;
'Tis grace hath brought me safe thus far,
And grace will lead me home.

The Lord has promised good to me,
His Word my hope secures;
He will my Shield and Portion be,
As long as life endures.

They stepped back, and all the children continued singing.

Yea, when this flesh and heart shall fail,
And mortal life shall cease,
I shall possess, within the veil,
A life of joy and peace.

DANCING PRIEST

The earth shall soon dissolve like snow,
The sun forbear to shine;
But God, who called me here below,
Will be forever mine.

When we've been there ten thousand years,
Bright shining as the sun,
We've no less days to sing God's praise
Than when we'd first begun.

There was silence, and then applause erupted.

Tears streamed down Jenny's face. Her child had sung to the entire congregation, but she knew he had sung to her.

Equally stunned, Scott and Barb had gripped hands as the two boys sang, and Barb saw that Scott was as moved as she was.

God added three believers to His kingdom that day.

When the children left, Michael led the congregation in prayer before the sermon.

"Father God, we come into Your presence today, led by little children. And we are awed. You tell us to have the hearts of children, and we ignore You until You confront us. We are overwhelmed by Your goodness and mercy. We deserve nothing, and You give us everything. We deserve condemnation, and You give us freedom. We wallow in filth, and You clean away the dirt. Your Son died, even for me. And today You gave us these young voices to pierce our souls. We are overwhelmed. Amen."

Chapter 43

When the two priests realized that Jenny, Scott, and Barb had become believers, they talked with Paul and Emma about a discipleship program. Paul and Emma would disciple the Hugheses together, and Emma would continue meeting with Jenny. They would regroup with Father John and Michael after Thanksgiving and decide a path forward.

At lunch on Monday, Michael bought a road bike, gloves, and a helmet for his brother, then added a jersey and pants, guessing Henry's sizes. Henry's plane would arrive at 10:00 a.m. on Tuesday. Monday was Michael's last day in the church office before the holiday.

Millie looked up as he walked in. "You have a visitor, Father Michael; he's waiting in your office." She shrugged slightly to indicate she didn't know who it was.

Brian Renner jumped up as Michael entered his office. The two looked at each other.

"Uh, Michael, I'm—"

"I remember."

"I wanted to stop by."

Michael waited.

"I wanted to apologize," Brian said. "I was an idiot." He paused. "Do you always wear that collar?"

"Only when I'm working. I accept the apology, Brian. But you could help me with one thing. You seemed to take an instant dislike to me, almost as if you'd made your mind up before you even met me. This happened to me once before, and I'd like to understand why."

Brian nodded. "Frank and Abbie told us about meeting you. They went on and on. Frank said he'd invited you to ride with us and said maybe you might join the team." He paused. "I got mad. Or jealous. Then you show up after riding for thirty-five miles. When you stayed at the back with Beau, I thought you were trying to impress Frank by playing to his kid."

Michael shook his head. "No. I just like kids. I was also trying to stay out of your way."

"I was that obvious? Well, I was already mad. Then I watched you ride. I'm going to sound like . . . well, I'm not . . . I mean, I like girls. I'm married, but anyway, I watched you on the bike, and it was beautiful. Don't take that wrong. It was beautiful to watch you on the bike, is what I mean. And you still had the scars on your leg from the crash in Athens, and that made me madder." He paused. "It's jealousy. Envy. Both."

Michael smiled. "Thanks. I'd never faced this problem until it happened with a teammate in Athens. Some good came of it, but it was pretty bad."

Brian cleared his throat. "So I'm here to apologize and ask you to ride with us again."

Michael smiled. "Well, it's been really busy."

"Have you been riding with anyone else."

"No, I haven't. I've looked, but it's mostly group rides sponsored by the bike shops. I was looking for more serious cyclists who don't care if outsiders come along on rides."

Brian nodded. "I don't just mean on rides. I mean ride with us. With the team."

"Frank's idea?"

"Mine. Frank doesn't even know I'm here. I'm sure Frank and the other guys won't have a problem."

"Do you want me to?" asked Michael.

Brian nodded. "Yes, I do."

"Then it's a plan. Let's do it."

Brian smiled. "Thanks, Michael. I'll let Frank know. Training rides are always on Saturdays. I'll send you the schedule. Oh, and no practice this Saturday because of the holiday. Starting in February, we do some minor regional racing, usually on Saturdays but occasionally on a Sunday. Could that be a problem?"

"Sundays would be a problem."

270

"We'll work something out. Our big race is the Tour de Frisco in May, and it's on a Saturday. It's a one-day, 150-mile race, sometimes 175 miles. We'll know the route in January. And we'll do some fairly intense practicing for that, but it's either on Saturdays or after work during the week, checking out the route and stuff."

"I'm looking forward to it."

"Well, I guess I better go. Thanks. And thanks for accepting my apology. I'd like us to be friends if we could."

"I'm looking forward to that, too, Brian. And thanks." They shook hands.

Arriving at the airport earlier than he expected, Michael was waiting when Henry's plane landed. Thanksgiving was the busiest season for flying in the States, and Michael had anticipated traffic backups, and he was still learning the freeways. But traffic, while heavy, kept moving, and the executive jet terminal was well away from the main airport complex.

He watched the plane come to a stop. Henry came down the steps and waved. Homesickness washed over Michael.

The brothers embraced.

"You look great, Michael." Henry grinned, obviously as glad to see him as Michael was to see Henry.

"It's so good to see you again, Henry. I can't believe it."

Stowing Henry's bags in the trunk of the Civic, they started toward the city, catching each other up on news—Michael about St. Anselm's and the bike team, and Henry about Kenya.

"When I met him in Kenya, I couldn't get over how tall he was. He lives in a small town or what passes for a small town in western Kenya. They've got some serious drought issues right now to the north of where they are, and it may become a problem for them as well."

"Where'd you stay?"

"With Moses and his family. His wife, Florence, is a sweetheart. They have a one-year-old and another on the way."

"He hadn't told me she was pregnant. You actually stayed at their house?"

"I did. And went to school with Moses and helped teach the kids. I can't tell you when I've enjoyed myself more."

"Obviously, I'm not the only missionary in the family."

"Well, I didn't convert anybody. I loved the people and the children. They were all over me. I even played soccer and got soundly beaten. I'd live there permanently if I could."

"You were that taken with it?"

"Absolutely. I can help them more from London, but I'm going back in February."

Henry described some of the projects "where we might invest some money." When Michael said it was he, Michael, who was doing the investing, Henry grinned. "Just try to keep me out of it."

Arriving at St. Anselm's, Michael introduced Henry to Millie and Father John, then took him to his rooms.

"You said it was small. I was expecting something smaller than this."

"It's cramped for two. I'm putting your stuff in the bedroom. You're the guest, and you get the bed; I'll take the sofa." Henry protested, but Michael said it wasn't debatable.

"I thought that you might like to rest up a bit today, then we could see some of the city tomorrow. Scott and Barb Hughes invited us out for Thanksgiving dinner on Thursday afternoon."

"He's David's brother?"

"Right. You'll like them. He's a doctor and works at a hospital about eight blocks from here. Their son, Scottie, attends St. Anselm's School. So on Friday, I thought you might like to see some of the wine country around here and maybe bike for a bit."

"I see you have a new bike there."

"No," said Michael, "you have a new bike there. And a helmet and gloves, along with the clothes. I guessed on the sizes, so you'll need to try everything on."

"Well, I'm game; I've jogged some but haven't been on a bike since I was eleven or twelve."

"It'll come back. We'll find some easy roads and avoid the hills. And then on Saturday, we'll just 'goof off,' as my American friends say."

"You're the tour guide."

During the next five days, the brothers thoroughly enjoyed the region and each other. They played tourist—Chinatown, Fisherman's Wharf, the Presidio, Alcatraz, and the winery tours. Biking through part of wine country, Henry did surprisingly well despite his lack of "recent experience." On Thanksgiving morning, they biked Golden Gate State Park and then drove to the Hugheses' house for dinner. Henry loved the family and let Scottie try to teach him how to play baseball, which, while unsuccessful, provided great entertainment for Michael, Scott, and Barb.

On Sunday, Henry attended worship service and got to see his brother at work.

"I thought you were going to do the sermon," Henry said.

"Next week. I couldn't host my brother and prepare a sermon. All you would've seen of San Francisco would've been my rooms here at St. Anselm's."

That afternoon, Michael drove Henry to the airport with the bicycle mounted on the rack. Henry was taking it back to London.

"What time does your plane leave?"

"When I arrived, I told them to plan for 2:00 p.m., so they should have the clearances, or they would've called."

"So the plane should be here?"

Henry smiled. "If it's not, then someone stole it."

Comprehension dawned. "Ah, it's *your* plane," said Michael.

Henry nodded. "It's a lot more convenient that flying commercial. Plus I can impress myself with how important I am."

"How big is it?"

"It seats up to twenty, but it's usually only me. Want to take a look?" He took Michael on the two-minute tour while the bike was stowed away.

"So," Henry said, "do you need anything? You've only tapped a little bit for the car."

"My needs are pretty simple," Michael said. "Although I'll need to start thinking about finding a place to live. Living at the church has been great, but it's only supposed to be temporary. And we're growing, so the space is needed."

"Just let me know," Henry said.

"I will. Thanks for coming, Henry. This has been great for me."

"Michael, you've no idea how much I've enjoyed this and how much I enjoyed being with you. I wouldn't trade that little apartment of yours for a flock of suites at the Ritz. I felt like I·was home. And I love the bike. I may have to take it up."

They hugged, then Michael stepped back down on the tarmac.

"You take care of yourself, little brother, and I'll see you for sure next summer, if not before."

Too choked up to say anything, Michael watched the plane door close.

Chapter 44

On Monday, Michael called the Finleys to talk through the discipleship program for the Hugheses and Jenny. Emma had stayed in touch with Jenny through the holidays and said Jenny was making some major life changes.

"She's quit her job, Michael," Emma said. "And while that's good from a spiritual point of view, it means there's no money coming in and no medical insurance for her and Jim. Paul's scouting for possibilities, and he'd hire her if he could, except that sales of those loft condos by the church just aren't happening, and he's got a lot of money tied up. So pass the word and keep your ears open. Paul's also getting some help for her from the alms fund at church."

"Emma, is she okay? I mean, with quitting her job. I had the impression that the people she worked for wouldn't take kindly to a change."

"She says it's okay," Emma said. "She said they were planning on letting her go anyway. So I think it'll be all right."

Two weeks after Thanksgiving, Jenny was waiting for school to end when Michael walked up.

"How are things?" He smiled.

"Upside down." She smiled back. "My whole world's upside down."

"Is there anything I can do?"

"Find me a job," she said. "I'm finding out that my skills and experience aren't exactly in demand in most places."

"Well, I was wondering. Would you and Jim like to do something on Saturday? I've my bike team practice in the morning, but perhaps we could do lunch somewhere. I haven't forgotten I owe you one."

She looked at him, struggling with a response. *Stay away from me, Father Michael. It'll mean trouble if you don't.* She looked into his incredibly blue eyes, and she wanted to believe that her future could be something different.

Hope finally won out.

"That would be nice," she said. "Lunch would be nice."

"What if I pick you up at eleven thirty?" he asked. "I'll pick you up, and we can decide where to eat."

"Well," she said nervously, "we've moved. I needed to get away from the building; some of the tenants were too noisy. We're staying with friends right now. Why don't we just meet you here at the church?"

"I can pick you up," he said.

"It's no trouble, really. They don't live far from here. We'll be here at eleven thirty on Saturday."

Right at eleven thirty, Michael found Jenny and Jim sitting on the bench near the office entrance.

"So," he said, "what will it be? We could do Chinatown or Fisherman's Wharf if you'd like seafood."

"What if we went someplace out in the country?" Jenny said. "Unless you need to get back here quickly?" *I don't want to be where Leo can find me or see us with you, Father Michael.*

Michael smiled. "My day's wide open. My sermon's done for tomorrow, and a trip to the country sounds perfect. So, what do you think we find ourselves a country restaurant or maybe a winery?"

Jenny smiled. "Great."

She missed Leo's SUV across the street.

They drove for an hour while Jim chatted with them from the backseat. They found a winery restaurant tucked in the hills east of Oakland. Opening the menu, Jenny gulped when she saw the prices.

"It's too expensive," she said. "We can try somewhere else."

"It's okay." He smiled. "It's not a problem."

The food was wonderful; after lunch, they did the winery tour. It ended in an area that provided wine tasting for adults and offered a play area for children. Jim went straight to the swing sets and extensive jungle gym built like a castle. Sipping small glasses of wine, Michael and Jenny sat and watched him.

"His father's name was Zach," Jenny said. "I had run away from home; my stepfather had raped me once, and I wasn't going through that again."

Michael froze, unsure of what to say, or even if he should say anything.

"I got to LA. I lied about my age and finagled my way into a home for unwed mothers. They wanted me to give Jim up for adoption but I couldn't. He was all I had. So one day I took him for a walk and didn't go back. I found some kids living in an abandoned warehouse, and I moved in with them. I was the leader's girl until he got tired of me, and we had to leave."

"Jenny, you don't have to tell me this," Michael said.

She clenched her fists. "I have to. Please listen."

Michael nodded and she continued.

"I found a Mexican woman who watched children, and, and . . ." She hesitated. "And I worked the streets during the day. You could make better money at night, but I had no one to watch Jim. So it was truckers, businessmen on their lunch hours, once even a college professor who didn't have afternoon classes.

"Then the lady who watched Jim got deported as an illegal. I couldn't find anyone else to watch him, and my money was running out. Someone said it was better in San Francisco, so we came here. I found a woman who would babysit at night, and I worked the streets here. One night I met Leo."

"Leo?"

"My pimp. He calls himself a personal services agent. He manages a bunch of girls and even a few boys. Anyway, it simplified my life. And I started making better money. He asked me to be a dancer in one of his bars and had one of his older girls teach me how to dance. And the money got better. Or it got regular. That's where things had been until I quit. That's the story." She paused. "I need to find a bathroom."

As Jenny got up, Jim came running up with a Frisbee, begging Michael to play. Disconcerted by Jenny's story, he nodded and walked with Jim to an open field next to the playground.

As she walked away, Jenny stopped and turned, watching them laugh as they tossed the Frisbee back and forth. *I want to believe things can be different, that my life is going to get better. I had to tell you, Michael, so if you're going to reject me, you can do it now.* She was afraid to hope, but she hoped anyway.

A few minutes later, as she walked out of the bathroom, a hand grabbed her by the wrist and pushed her against the wall.

"So, my favorite employee doesn't like returning my phone calls."

It was Leo; behind him stood one of his "attendants," as he called them.

"Does your priest get it for free, or does he even know what you are?"

"I'm out of the life, Leo. Go away. I don't want to see you anymore."

"So here's the deal, tiny dancer. You come back to work, or your priest's going to get hurt. Seriously hurt. And you will return my phone call tonight."

She broke free. "I'm finished with that. Stay away from me. And if you touch him, I'll go straight to the police." She ran toward the parking lot, where Michael and Jim were waiting.

"Ready?" Michael asked. Then he stopped; he could see she was upset. "Are you all right?" Jim looked at her as well.

"I'm fine. Just some rude person in the bathroom. Let's go."

A week later, Michael was in his church apartment, fixing his dinner, when he realized he was out of milk and had no buns for the hot dog he was warming up in the microwave. He grabbed a jacket for the cool night air and walked quickly down to the food shop before it closed.

"Out late tonight, Father Michael?" the shop attendant called as Michael entered the store.

"Just a few items," he said. He picked up milk, the buns, two packages of frozen vegetables, and a loaf of French bread.

"The church has made a big difference," the attendant said, ringing up his purchases. "We never would have stayed open this late before."

"It's only a little after seven," Michael said.

"I know, but it's dark. You still need to be careful, so keep an eye out."

Michael left the shop and walked back toward the church. As he passed the corner by the loft condos, two figures seemed to materialize from nowhere.

The attack was fast. One man grabbed his arm, knocking him off balance and shoving the plastic grocery bag from his hand. His arms were pinned behind him as the second figure moved in and began to punch him. He took one blow to the face and two to the chest, then another blow to the face. He kicked backward and connected with something; he heard the man behind him grunt in pain. The one in front renewed his blows to his stomach, and Michael felt pain on his left side as the pummeling intensified.

He lost consciousness.

He was dreaming. He was floating in a fog of clouds. He heard voices, but he couldn't see anyone. At one point he turned his head. Jenny was sitting nearby, her hand on his hand. He looked again and saw Father John and Eileen. He smiled and fell back asleep.

The first thing Michael was consciously aware of was pain, pain in his chest and his face.

A nurse walked up and smiled. "Well, you're awake. That's a good sign."

"Where am I?" he asked.

"San Francisco General Hospital. You had a run-in with someone nasty last night." She inserted a thermometer in his ear and wrapped his arm for the blood pressure check. "We've been cautioned by the police not to say too much before they talk to you," the nurse said. "In fact, they'll be here any minute. The doctor will be by in a bit. How's the pain?"

"Everything hurts but especially my face and stomach."

"No surprise," she said, and she made an adjustment on his IV drip. "That should help. You've got a pretty black eye and a fractured rib. Be thankful that it wasn't worse."

A man in a raincoat entered the room. The nurse mouthed "the police" as she nodded at Michael and left.

"Father Kent, I'm Detective Beeson. I'm investigating the attack on you last night."

"Do you know anything?" Michael said.

Beeson shook his head. "The attendant at the food shop saw two men beating you and yelled. You had apparently just left there."

Michael nodded.

"Did you see them at all, anything that might give us a physical description?"

Michael thought a moment. "They were big. One held me from behind. I kicked him at one point. But I didn't see their faces."

"It wasn't a robbery or your typical mugging," Beeson said.

"How do you know?"

"They left your wallet and keys alone. They were only interested in attacking you. If they wanted your wallet, they would have pulled a gun or knife and held you while they searched you, or just shot you outright." He paused. "Do you have any enemies that you're aware of?"

"I'm mystified, detective. There's no one like that. No one at all."

"Well, Father, someone has a different opinion."

Beeson asked Michael a few more questions and then left. An hour later, the doctor stopped by to examine him, gave him instructions for his medications and the admonition of no physical exercise for six weeks to let the rib heal, and then discharged him. The nurse explained that she had called Father John, who would be coming to pick him up.

In the car with Father John, the older priest was visibly upset.

"I feel responsible, Michael. We should have found you an apartment in a safer place."

"Father John, it's okay. I should have been more cautious about running out at night."

"Well, you look terrible. I'll preach the sermon Sunday instead of you."

"You'll do no such thing," Michael said. "I may look awful, but I'll be able to preach."

Chapter 45

The two weeks left before Christmas seemed to fly by. Both the church and school were moving into high gear to celebrate the season. Michael's bruised eye gradually yellowed and faded. Later, looking back, Michael knew he should've seen the warning signs, his attack being one of them.

The school's annual Christmas program, set for December 23, featured all the classes. Scottie and Jim were to sing a duet in the third-grade's program.

A week before Christmas, he found Jenny behind a tree near the school entrance instead of with the other moms.

"Jenny?" he asked.

She jumped, stifling a small scream. "Father Michael, you startled me. I'm fine; I just felt a little cold in the wind." She looked at his face. "Your face looks better. How are you feeling?"

"Much better, thank you. I meant to ask you, during my drug haze in the hospital, I thought I saw you sitting by the bed. Did you come by?"

She hesitated before answering. "No, no I didn't. It must have been someone else."

Two days later, she came to his office and asked if he could drive her and Jim home, to an apartment she'd moved to a few blocks from the church.

"I've been pounding the pavement all day looking for a job, and my feet are killing me. If it's a problem, just say no."

"No," he said, "I'll be glad to." She had Jim sit in the front seat. When they started driving from the church, she dropped an earring on the floor and bent over to find it.

"I can pull over and help," Michael said.

"It's okay," she said. "I'll find it in a minute. These things can be a hassle."

Michael frowned slightly. *It's as if she's hiding from someone.*

The afternoon of the program, Michael saw Jim walking by himself out of the school gate.

"Jim!" he called. "Where's your mom?"

"She's home," Jim called back. "She wasn't feeling well, so she told me to be careful and walk home."

Michael walked over to the boy. "Well, I've got some time. I'll come with you." Michael didn't really have the time, but he couldn't let Jim walk home by himself. *This isn't like Jenny.*

Walking the few blocks to the apartment, Michael was surprised that Jenny would let Jim walk by himself. While nothing was overtly threatening, the neighborhood was run down; they passed a number of boarded-up buildings and encountered the inevitable unfortunates staggering with bottles in paper bags. Jim walked quickly and occasionally looked over his shoulder.

"I didn't see your mom at church on Sunday," said Michael. "Is she feeling okay?"

"I think so," said Jim. "But she's been home a lot."

They finally reached the Marks's apartment house. As Jim went up the steps, Michael said, "Don't forget. Be there at six sharp tonight. Do you need me to come get you?"

"No," the boy said, "Mom said she'd be feeling okay." He darted inside.

Michael wondered if he should check himself. But he turned to go back to St. Anselm's, where there was plenty to do. Father John and Eileen had left at lunch for Sacramento, after Michael reassured them once again that it was okay to go; he'd take care of the opening and closing for the school program (prayers only), the Christmas Eve candlelight service (no sermon, just a short commentary on Luke 2), and the service on Christmas Day (short sermon and lots of carols).

"You haven't had a Christmas with your families in years," he told them, "and you've got a brand-new grandson, so get out of here." He'd already finished what he needed for the two services.

DANCING PRIEST

By five thirty, the school was pulsating with children being dropped off by parents, the tramping of young feet running up and down halls, frantic teachers trying to fix robes, and the usual hubbub of a Christmas program. Michael served as errand boy and was simultaneously trying to find a choir robe collar (eighth grade), missing angel wings (fourth grade), and a plastic baby Jesus (first-grade nativity scene).

Miss Hendricks, the third-grade teacher, grabbed his arm. "Father Michael, have you seen Jim Marks?"

"No, but I saw him home today, and he said he and his mother would be here by six."

"It's ten after, and there's no sign of him. Scottie's looking for him as well. Could you look around?"

"I will, if you first let me bring the baby Jesus to first grade," he said.

After pressing two seventh graders into service to look as well, he checked the church building. Scott and Barb, who'd been in Los Angeles for a few days (Michael thought for Sarah's graduation but hadn't asked), hadn't seen them; neither had the Finleys. At 6:20, he checked back with Miss Hendricks, whose anxiety now had Mr. Schultz frantic as well.

"Okay," said Michael, "I'll keep looking, but what's Plan B?"

The two teachers looked at each other.

"Can Scottie do it solo?" Michael asked. They found Scottie, who was worried about his friend but finally agreed to sing by himself if Jim didn't show.

"So," Michael said to Mr. Schultz, "how long before the third grade performs?"

"They're toward the end, so it will be about seven fifteen."

"I'll keep looking for them, but I have to do the prayer."

The church was crowded with parents, siblings, and grandparents, who quieted as Michael entered and prayed.

He stepped aside as the kindergarten class entered. He waded through wise men, shepherds, and a small flock of human sheep on the way to his office.

The message light was blinking.

285

"Father Michael, it's Jenny. Something's come up, and we can't come tonight. Please tell Miss Hendricks and Mr. Schultz I'm sorry. I'll call later."

She knows this is a big night for Jim. Whatever it is, it must be something really serious to keep them away.

When the program ended, after the applause of family and friends and the sounds of more than one crying baby, and after the punch-and-cookie reception in the fellowship hall, Michael helped with cleanup. Scottie's solo had been superb, but everyone was asking about Jim.

By ten thirty, the last of the trash bags were deposited in the garbage containers behind the school cafeteria. Spilled cups of punch were mopped up, and tables and chairs were folded and put away. Michael was exhausted, but he called Jenny on his cell phone.

When the voice mail instructions came on, he left a short message. Worry finally got the better of him, and he drove to Jenny's apartment. *Walking might be problematic at this time of night.*

He buzzed the Markses' apartment but heard only silence. He could see lights in some of the windows, but he wasn't sure which apartment was theirs.

I'll check tomorrow.

Chapter 46

On Christmas Eve, he called the Finleys, then remembered they'd left for Portland to spend Christmas with Emma's family. He tried Jenny's phone several times during the day, leaving his name and both his cell number and the church office number. But he heard nothing.

The Christmas Eve candlelight service started at six, and Michael was surprised at the filled pews. He was pleased to see Jason and some of the kids from the coffeehouse. He looked for Jenny and Jim but didn't see them anywhere.

He read the second chapter of Luke and delivered a short commentary, focusing on the angels appearing to the shepherds, announcing the birth of the Messiah. He pointed out that the shepherds weren't the most exalted group in Judea, picturing this as a harbinger of Jesus's ministry to come—the ministry to the poor and outcast, the blind and the lame, the people who didn't count in society.

They sang and prayed, then the service was over. Michael stood in the foyer to greet the congregation.

The kids from the coffeehouse had made some attempt to clean themselves up. They didn't say anything as they filed past, although Jason nodded. *This is a major victory for Jason and the rest of them just being here. Thank You, Lord.* The greetings from others were warm with holiday spirit. Millie hugged him as she walked past with her husband.

He then saw Detective Beeson standing with a uniformed police officer. He hadn't seen them at the service.

"Father Kent, is there someplace we could talk?"

"Let me lock the front door here, and we can go to the office."

"I'm investigating a homicide. We have an unidentified victim, but an officer apprehended one of the suspects at the scene. We've had several witnesses tell us that two men dumped the victim's body from the trunk of a car."

"You don't know who it is?"

Beeson shook his head. "No. The body was found about twenty blocks from here, on a street off Market. Our problem is that the witnesses are mostly homeless people."

"Why are you here?" Michael asked. "I don't understand."

"You're not a suspect, Father," Beeson said. "The body was dumped at nine last night. You were here at the church. We checked."

"Then why would you check on me?" Michael asked, perplexed.

"The church's phone number was written on her hand. We need to see if you can identify her."

Michael rode in the back of the police car, noticing the lack of inside handles on the doors. The uniformed officer, who'd yet to say a word, drove.

"You're not American?" asked Detective Beeson.

"No, I'm English by way of Scotland." Michael felt a growing sense of dread. He didn't know what he was going to see, but whatever it was would likely be an awful sight. And why would someone write the church's phone number on her hand?

"How long have you been here in San Francisco?"

"Since the end of August. I was assigned here by the bishops council."

"He's the bicycle guy," the uniformed officer said, at last breaking his silence.

"The bicycle guy?" asked Beeson.

The policeman nodded. "The Olympics this summer. Three gold medals. And the crash." He looked at Michael through the rearview mirror. "I recognized you at the church." Then to Beeson: "He was on the cover of *Time*. Twice."

"My fifteen minutes of fame," Michael said.

"No kidding. Three gold medals?" said Beeson. "I didn't follow the Olympics; I'm a baseball-only guy. But that's something."

They pulled up at a modern if nondescript building.

The uniformed officer stayed with the car, while Michael accompanied Beeson inside. *I'm going to see the body of someone who likely didn't expect to be spending Christmas Eve in a morgue. Last Christmas Eve I was with Sarah. It seems so long ago.*

A strong chemical smell assaulted his nose. "What's that smell?" he asked.

"I don't even notice it anymore," Beeson replied. "It's chemicals in the autopsy lab."

Michael shivered.

They descended a flight of stairs; the smell grew stronger.

"If you haven't done this before—and I assume you haven't—it's not easy for most people. Some people get physically ill, depending upon the condition of the body."

"And this one?"

"She was raped, at least once and probably twice. We'll know by tomorrow. And she was severely beaten and finally strangled."

"Dear Lord," Michael said. And then he began trembling; he feared he knew who he was going to see.

"It's not as bad as some, Father," Beeson said. He pushed the swinging door and signaled to the attendant. "The one from Viejo Street."

Michael watched the attendant open a drawer, pulling out the body shelf on rollers. The body was in a plastic bag. *Dear Lord, prepare me for this. I don't know what I'm going to see. Help me through this with your grace.*

The attendant motioned Michael forward. He looked.

It was Jenny.

"Oh, Father God!" he cried out, his voice breaking in a sob.

Her face was heavily swollen and bruised, her lower lip cut, and yet she looked strangely peaceful, as if she had come to terms with whatever had happened and was at rest. Her neck was badly cut. She'd been strangled with wire.

"You know the victim?" Beeson asked.

Michael nodded, feeling weak and almost stumbling when Beeson grabbed him. He walked Michael outside the room and had him sit on a bench.

"Her name is Jenny Marks," Michael said in tears. "She has an apartment on Gilbert Street. She's been attending our church since mid-September."

"Any idea why this might have happened?"

"She'd quit her job," Michael said, the tears streaming down his face.

"Quit her job?"

Michael nodded. "She was an exotic dancer"—he hesitated—"and she'd been a prostitute. She'd been attending the church and had become a believer about a month ago. She quit her job—" Michael broke down again.

"How well did you know her, Father?"

"What do you mean?" Michael asked.

"I mean what I said. How well did you know her? Enough to have a couple of thugs beat you up on a dark street corner?"

Michael put his head in his hands.

"It's okay, Father, it's all right. Just take it easy." He opened his cell phone and made a call. "It's Beeson. Positive ID on Viejo. The victim's name is Jenny Marks." He repeated the address Michael had given him. "Yeah, the priest from St. Anselm's knew her."

Michael interrupted him. "Detective?"

"Yes?"

"She has an eight-year-old son. He goes to our school."

Beeson stared at Michael. "Crap, I hate it when it's kids I have to look for. Okay, Father, if you're up to it, let's go see if we can find the boy."

Chapter 47

When they arrived at the apartment building, three police cars were parked in front, lights flashing. A small crowd had gathered, watching two police officers as they held a black woman with her hands cuffed behind her.

"We caught her going into the apartment," an officer said.

"I told you that I'm just trying to find the boy," she said.

"Why were you looking for the boy in the first place?" Beeson asked.

She didn't answer.

"Since you're so cooperative, I'll need to book you as an accessory to murder."

She glared but was clearly frightened. "Murder?" Then she saw Michael.

"You're Father Michael," she said. Michael nodded. "Jenny's talked about you."

"Do you know where Jim might be?" Michael asked.

"I think so," she said. "Maybe."

The day before, Jenny was terrified until Jim came through the door. She had put off Leo as long as she could, and now he'd be coming for her. She locked and bolted the door. She peeked out the window and saw Father Michael stare at the front door of the building, then turn and walk down the street.

Jim saw their two suitcases by the door.

"We're leaving?" he asked.

"We have to, honey," she said. "I'll explain later. At the bus station." *I can't go back to the life. I just can't. And if I don't leave, he'll kill me or Father Michael or both of us.*

"But I'm supposed to sing tonight. It's the Christmas program."

"Oh, Jimmy, I'm sorry. I truly am. I wanted to hear you. But we have to leave. Some bad people are looking for me, and we can't stay. I need you to pack what you need, and then we'll eat something and go."

Jim stared at her for a moment, then went to his room, which was more a small alcove than a bedroom. He took his schoolbooks from his backpack and started putting his treasures in their place. A photo of him and Scottie. A rather ratty-looking stuffed dog that he had had since he was a baby. A baseball from a Giants game Father Michael had taken him to.

Jenny called him to the kitchen. "It's just sandwiches, and I have some fruit, too. We'll eat the sandwiches now and bring the fruit with us."

"I don't want to leave. I like my school."

"Jimmy, don't make this harder. I know you like your school. I do, too. And we both like Father Michael. But we have to—"

A pounding at the door interrupted her.

"Quick," she whispered, "the closet."

"No. I won't leave you."

"Jim, get in the closet. You know the drill." The pounding continued. They heard a male voice say, "Come on, Jen Jen, open up the door." Another man laughed.

She pushed Jim toward the bedroom closet. "Get in there," she whispered fiercely. "And don't make a sound. There's food and water, a flashlight, and a can to pee in. We've been through this a hundred times. Now what do you do? Tell me!" The pounding was so hard she knew the door wouldn't last. Where were the neighbors? *Hiding, like I would be.*

"I sit quiet until I hear someone I know, who gives me the code word."

"And what is it?" Jenny asked. "Hurry!"

He whispered in her ear.

"Right. Now go. No matter what you hear or think you hear, you stay in there, do you understand me? Don't make a sound. Stay there!"

He slipped in the closet and pulled a panel of the closet out as she dashed and placed a doll in the bedroom window. They'd discovered the closet space when they moved in three weeks ago, and Jenny had incorporated it into an escape plan for Jim. *Now if Tammy only remembers to come by and sees the doll.* She closed the closet door and rushed to the living room, opening the curtain and the small window. *Please let them think he got away.*

The apartment door splintered and gave way.

Inside the closet, Jim could hear only muffled sounds. He heard something fall. At one point the closet door was yanked open. But the panel was a close match with the closet wall. The space he was in was small, but if he worked his legs right, he could stretch out. He stayed perfectly still.

He could hear things being thrown around the apartment and glass breaking. Something turned over.

And then, silence. He didn't hear his mom once.

He didn't move. His mom had told him to wait. He eventually fell asleep.

Chapter 48

Detective Beeson was about ready to commit his own homicide as he glared at Tammy Williams.

Michael raised his hand to hold Beeson off as he spoke to Tammy. "Jenny's dead. I have to find Jim. Anything you know could help us. Please."

"I saw the doll in the window. That was the signal to look for Jim."

"Do you know where he is?" Michael asked.

"She said the apartment. I'm supposed to use the code word."

"This is ridiculous," Beeson said.

"Can we try it?" Michael asked Beeson.

"Nobody's in there," an officer said. "We looked."

"All right," Beeson said. "Let her do her thing."

"What's the code word?" Michael asked.

"Bicycle," Tammy said.

The apartment was in shambles. Someone had been looking for something. Or for Jim.

Beeson pointed to the open suitcases. "She was leaving. Okay, people, here's the deal. Don't touch anything. This is a crime scene, although we're fairly sure the murder happened somewhere else."

Tammy moved quietly through the apartment. "Jim? Jimmy boy? It's Tammy. I'm here with Father Michael from church. Jim, the word is 'bicycle.'" She went to the kitchen, repeating her words.

Michael went into the bedroom. "Jim? It's Father Michael. I need you to come with me. Jim, the word is 'bicycle.'"

He heard a small noise from the closet. He flung open the door just as Jim pushed the panel down, shielding his eyes from the light.

An hour later, they were at a police station. Tammy was being questioned in another room. Jim clung to Michael, having told the detective what little he knew.

"I have to call the juvenile authorities, Father Kent," Detective Beeson said.

"What happens then?"

"Given the hour, they'll ask us to put him in protective custody."

"That means what?"

"He'll spend the night in a cell. He'll be watched and cared for. He'll be fine."

"No. He's coming home with me."

"Against regulations. I can't do it," Beeson said.

"Then who can?"

Beeson hesitated. "My captain."

"Call him." Michael could barely control his anger.

"He's off duty. He's celebrating Christmas with his family, Father. And it's midnight."

"Happy Christmas, detective, to you and your captain. Call him now, or you're going to have to shoot me when I walk out with Jim. I'm leaving in two minutes, and he's coming with me."

Beeson called the captain at home, who wasn't happy with the call but listened to Beeson. The detective ended the call.

"You have to keep him through Christmas and be down here at 10:00 a.m. on the twenty-sixth."

"It's a plan." Michael got up, carrying Jim and his backpack in his arms, and walked to the door.

"Father, wait," said Beeson. "I'll get a car."

Michael and Jim sat on Michael's sofa, Michael's arm around Jim's shoulders. It was raining; they watched the patterns made by the streetlights across from the apartment's wet windows.

With Jim's clothes still at the Marks's apartment, Michael found an oversized T-shirt to serve as pajamas, one he'd received at the Olympics but never worn because it was too big. Jim was wearing it now; it hung well below his knees.

There's problem number one—clothes. All he has is his school uniform, which he's been wearing for two days, in that closet. Michael was already washing the shirt and slacks so Jim would have something to wear tomorrow. *Problem number two. It's Christmas, and I don't have anything I could give him as a gift. I didn't even put up a tree. I didn't see anything at their apartment, but she might've hidden some things. Well, I'll see if I can find something tomorrow. What a happy Christmas this will be.*

"What's going to happen to me?" Jim asked suddenly, startling Michael out of his thoughts.

"The truth is, Jim, I don't know," Michael said. "If I told you anything else, I'd be lying. What we have to do is get through tonight and then tomorrow, and then we'll see. But I'll be there, okay? I don't know what we'll have to do, but I'll be there."

"Did they hurt her?"

Michael hesitated before answering. *I won't lie to him.* "Yes. They hurt her."

"Was it bad?"

"It was bad, Jim. It was really bad."

"You saw her?"

"Yes. The police had me identify her."

"Father Michael, could God have saved my mom?"

Michael paused for a long time. *Do this one right, Father Michael.* "The easy answer would be to say, yes, He could've saved her, but for His own reasons He had another plan. But if all we do is wonder why He didn't save her, we'll miss the most important thing."

"What's that?"

"The look on her face. She knew God was with her the whole time. He went through it with her. When those men hurt her, they hurt Him, too. He died with her. I don't mean He died Himself, but He knew her death. And because He was with her, she knew she was going to a better place. And Jim, I believe with all my heart she's with God right now."

"I think so, too." And then the tears started. Michael held him while he cried.

"I need to get you to bed," Michael said. "We've a church service at nine, and it's so beyond your bedtime I can't believe you're still awake."

"Can we sit here for a while?"

"Okay."

Within a few minutes, Michael heard Jim's deep breathing. Michael picked him up and carried him to bed, covering him with the sheet and blanket. He stood looking down at him, then returned to the sofa, stretched out, and fell into a deep sleep.

Chapter 49

Jim woke in the morning and padded into the kitchen.

"I see you're up, Young Jim," said Michael.

"What time is it?"

"It's about seven thirty, and we have church at nine. I'm afraid you'll have to wear your school uniform—it's all we have—but I've cleaned it so you'll be presentable. The eggs are almost ready."

"Are you a good cook?" Jim asked.

"Now there's a question. There are days when I think I'm not half bad, and there are days I wouldn't feed it to a dog. But I'm usually okay with eggs and microwave bacon."

"Mom's a lousy cook, too."

"Hey! I didn't say lousy. I just have my good moments in the kitchen and my bad. Although the bad far outweigh the good. Drink your juice there. I'm great with pouring juice out of the carton, and we'll eat in just a moment."

"So what do we do after church?" Jim asked after they'd said grace and were eating.

"We'll have to figure that out. We'll have to find ourselves a Christmas dinner somewhere, although most of the restaurants are closed today. Maybe a hotel—hotels have to be open."

Michael paused. "Jim, the story about your mom is going to be in the newspapers. So I need to say something this morning at the church service. I'll keep it short, all right? Is that okay?"

Jim nodded. "It's okay."

"What I'd like you to do this morning is sit toward the front. Maybe if the Hugheses are there, you could sit with Scottie. I just need to keep my eyes on you, so I know you're okay. It'll make me feel a whole lot better."

"Scottie said they were coming."

"Great. I have to shave and shower. Your shirt and slacks are on the hangers there, and I've got an extra toothbrush."

The rain had stopped; the sun was peeking through the clouds by the time the Christmas service started. The Hugheses did indeed arrive, and Jim ran to join Scottie and his parents. Scottie was overjoyed to see his friend.

As they sang the first carol, Barb whispered to Scott, "Michael looks terrible. He looks like he hasn't slept for days." Scott nodded.

Michael did look haggard with circles under his eyes, and he seemed subdued, his usual smile missing. Millie and her husband and Veronica Meyers also noticed.

He stood to give the sermon. *Lord, I hope I don't ruin everyone's Christmas. I need You right now, like always. Give me compassion and wisdom. Let them hear what You would say. Let them hear Your heart, not mine. Mine's a mess.*

"I had a Christmas sermon planned," Michael began, "but I need to set it aside and instead tell you about how God lives in us and how we live and die in Him.

"Some of you knew Jenny Marks." In the fourth-row pew, the three Hugheses looked at Jim, who was totally focused on Michael.

"She started coming to St. Anselm's in September, when she enrolled her son in school." He paused. "She had a story, like all of us have a story, but her story is not what's important. What's important is that she'd accepted Christ as her Savior and had been washed clean of all her sins.

"Jenny was killed on Tuesday evening." Gasps were heard from the congregation. Shocked, Barb looked across Scottie at Jim, who was still staring at Michael.

"It was ugly and it was brutal. You ask why God would allow such a thing to happen. And now there's an eight-year-old boy with no mother.

"So why? I would mislead you if I said that God works in mysterious ways and that all things happen for the good of those who believe in Him. That's true, but not the answer to the question.

"The fact that Jenny died is also true, but it's the wrong answer as well.

"So my answer to that question—did God let Jenny die?—is yes, He did. We don't know why; we may never know. But I know that He was with her, and He suffered with her, and He was there the moment physical life left her to welcome her home, where there's no more pain, no more ugliness, no more brutality.

"This is why there's Christmas. This is why we celebrate it. Because God loved us so much that He gave His Son to be born as one of us, to live as one of us, to teach us, and to suffer and die for us, to suffer and die worse than Jenny did, and to be raised from the dead, to conquer death once and for all.

"Jesus died an ugly, brutal death. He was beaten and whipped. He was mocked and ridiculed. He was spat upon. He had nails driven into Him to hold Him to the cross.

"Jesus was with Jenny when she died her ugly, brutal death. And He loved her, and He loves her still, as much as He loves each of us. He's welcomed her home, just as He'll welcome each one of us home one day.

"Amen."

Michael prayed. The choir and congregation sang. The service ended.

Afterward, Michael stayed near the front, keeping an eye on Jim, who was sitting with Scottie and Barb with Veronica next to them. Millie had come up to Michael and squeezed his hand; others hugged him. Scott had been waiting, then spoke.

"Jim says he's staying with you."

Michael nodded. "At least until tomorrow. Because it was a holiday, they wanted to keep him in a jail cell, and I said no. So he's with me."

"You're coming home with us."

"Really, Scott—"

"You're coming home with us," Scott insisted. "What were you going to do for Christmas dinner—sandwiches or go to a hotel?"

"Well, we'd thought about a hotel restaurant."

"Michael, you look terrible. Both of you must be devastated. Jim said you identified her body."

Michael nodded again. "Scott, I don't think either one of us is fit to be around man or beast right now."

"I know, and you don't have to be. If you want to sit in a corner, that's okay. But it may help Jim to be around Scottie, and it may help you to be around—well, people who care for you deeply."

Michael looked at his friend's brother. "Thank you. And you're right." He paused. "I'll need to call Ma and Da."

"You can use our phone," Scott said. "And you can ride with us, and I'll bring you back, or you can stay with us."

"I have to be at the police station at ten tomorrow, so we need to get back tonight."

At the Hugheses', Michael sat in Scott's office and called home.

"Michael!" said Iris. "Happy Christmas! Iain! It's Michael! Pick up the phone."

"It's so good to hear your voices," Michael said. "I wish I could be there."

"What's wrong?" asked Iris. "Are you all right? Are you sick?"

"Ma, I'm okay. I'm being taught things I never dreamed of learning."

"Son," said Iain, "we hear it in your voice. Tell us what's happening."

So Michael told them. When he finished, they prayed with him.

In Santa Barbara, Helen Hughes finished her Christmas call with Scott. Sarah wandered in from a break in packing—she and Gran were shortly leaving for a week in Hawaii, Sarah's graduation present from Gran.

"What's wrong?" Sarah asked, seeing Gran's face.

"It makes you realize just how fortunate we all are. That was Scott, calling to say merry Christmas. They have one of their pastors at home right now. It's a terrible story."

"What happened?"

"A woman in the congregation was brutally killed two days ago, and the pastor identified the body. Then they had to find her little boy. He was okay but hiding in a closet. He's staying with the pastor right now. It's terrible."

"Oh, Gran, that's awful. What's going to happen to the little boy? Is there no other family?"

"Apparently not. Scott said they have to go back to the police tomorrow. And to happen at Christmas. Although any time would be just as bad, I suppose."

Sarah made herself a note to pray for the pastor and the little boy. "Gran, what are their names?"

"The boy's name is Jim."

"And the pastor's?"

"I'm sorry, Sarah. I didn't ask."

After they had eaten, Barb and Michael sorted through bags of clothes marked for charity.

"Scottie's a little bit bigger than Jim, but some of the clothes from last year should fit him," she said. She held up a pair of jeans. "This'll work. There are a couple of other pairs here as well. And these clothes are almost brand new. Scottie grew a lot last year, and it seemed like I was buying clothes every time I turned around." She looked at Michael. "Underwear's a problem. But K-Mart's open today. I never thought I'd be thankful for that. I'll get Scott to drive you over."

At the store, Michael was able to get boys' underwear and T-shirts, a toothbrush, and a pair of pajamas.

"I'll need to get him some shoes, but he'll need to try them on," Michael said. "His tennis shoes should be okay for a few days anyway."

"What do you do tomorrow, Michael?" Scott asked. "What if they want to put him in a foster home?"

"We're putting one foot ahead of the other right now," Michael said. "I need to pray. If you and Barb could pray, too, I'd be grateful. I don't know what'll happen."

Chapter 50

The next morning, Michael and Jim walked into the police station promptly at ten. Michael had Jim leave his backpack and clothes at Michael's so they'd have to return no matter what happened. Michael had talked with Jim about the different possibilities—a foster family until the authorities figured out what to do, or they might let him stay with Michael.

"But the short of it, Young Jim, is we won't know until they tell us."

Detective Kennett was handling the case at the moment. They waited for thirty minutes, then Kennett came into the waiting area. He introduced himself and gave Michael a piece of paper.

"His mother's attorney called us this morning when she saw the story in the *Chronicle*. She said to bring the boy to family court at eleven. She's filed an emergency notice, and the judge agreed to a hearing." *This is going faster than I would have expected. What's going on?*

"Where's family court?" Michael asked.

"Not far. I'll draw you a map."

Thanking the officer, Michael drove Jim downtown.

"Did you know your mom had a lawyer?"

Jim shook his head.

"Does the name Gwen Patterson mean anything?"

Jim thought a moment. "She called once when Mom was out."

"Well, we need to meet her to see what's what."

They found the court building and parked nearby. Inside, after passing through security, Michael asked a guard for Judge Pamela Wingate's courtroom, and he directed them to the second floor. Outside the courtroom, a woman sitting in a chair saw them and jumped up.

"Father Michael?" she said, shaking his hand vigorously. "I'm Gwen Patterson, Jenny Marks's attorney. This must be Jim." She shook Jim's hand.

"Jim, I'm so sorry about your mom. I'd only known her a few weeks, but I know how much she loved you."

She turned to Michael. "I saw the story when I got up this morning. The detective said one arrest has been made, and two more are imminent."

"He didn't say anything about it," Michael said. Jim sat on a small bench across from them.

She nodded and lowered her voice. "Let me explain what happens now. I filed an emergency motion with the court, and Judge Wingate agreed to a short hearing. I've explained the situation, and there shouldn't be any problem with Jim staying with you. Usually, social workers get involved first, and there's an investigation, and there will likely be one still, but it will be in a few weeks. The judge seemed agreeable to you taking custody immediately, once I explained Jenny's will."

"Her will?"

"The estate isn't big, about thirty-five thousand dollars. It's virtually all in a savings account for Jim, but she needed to provide for a guardian."

"Did she say why she was doing this?"

"No, but she wanted it done quickly. She asked me to be the executor, and she left a small bequest to a Tamara Williams. Do you know her?"

"I met a Tammy Williams Wednesday night. She's a friend of Jenny's."

"Jenny left her fifteen hundred dollars that she hoped she'd use to leave San Francisco. Everything else is left to Jim. And of course she named you the guardian."

"She named me what?" Michael was suddenly reeling.

"She named you Jim's guardian. Didn't she tell you?"

Michael shook his head. "No. It's the first I've heard of it." *Dear Father, what do I do?*

"Oh dear," the lawyer said, "then we have a problem. Since you'd taken him home, I thought you knew. The judge'll ask you a number of questions, but she's ready to grant temporary custody, given that you have permanent custody according to the will." She frowned. "Jenny should've told you."

Michael turned and looked at Jim, who seemed out of earshot of the conversation and more interested in a couple arguing down the hallway. *What do I know about raising an eight-year-old? And this particular boy—he needs a mother, surely. Lord, what are You thinking here?*

He turned back to Gwen Patterson. "I'll do it."

"Are you sure? Everybody will understand if you haven't agreed previously to do this."

"I'm sure."

Judge Wingate first talked with the attorney from the bench, then asked Michael to stand before her.

"How old are you, Father Kent?"

"I'm twenty-three, Your Honor. I'll be twenty-four in August."

"And you're single?"

"Yes, ma'am."

"You may refer to me as 'Your Honor.'"

"Yes, ma—Your Honor."

"And you agree to provide for this boy and to accept responsibility for raising him, essentially becoming his father?"

"Yes, Your Honor."

"Do you know anything about raising children?"

"No, Your Honor, except I was one myself once."

He saw the glimmer of a smile. "You're confident you could raise this child, alone if need be?"

Michael thought a moment. "No, Your Honor, I don't feel confident. In fact, I'm terrified. But with God's grace, I hope I wouldn't make too bad a botch of it. And there are friends at church who could provide me with good counsel. And my own Ma and Da would help, too, although they live in Scotland."

The judge openly smiled. "I see no reason why I shouldn't grant temporary custody to you for sixty days. I'm ordering social services to

307

undertake a full investigation, which will include a home visit, a background check, and a physical examination of both you and the child by a physician. Do you have any problem with any of that?"

"No, Your Honor."

"If the investigation demonstrates that you are likely to be a suitable parent for the child, then I'll grant permanent custody, according to the terms of the will. I'd now like Jim Marks to come before the bench."

Jim made his way to the front of the courtroom. Michael lifted him on the witness chair.

"Jim," the judge said gently, "do you understand what's going on here?"

"You're saying it's okay for me to live with Father Michael."

"That's exactly what I'm saying, if the social worker agrees. But I think that's likely. So, how do you feel about living with Father Michael? Can you tell me much about him?"

Jim looked at Michael, then turned to the judge. "I'd like it. He gave me his bed, and he slept on the sofa. And he makes pretty good eggs and bacon, but I'm not sure about other food. He lives right next to my school. And he could teach me to ride a bike."

"You don't know how to ride a bike?"

"No ma—Your Honor. I never learned. My mom didn't know how, so she couldn't teach me."

She smiled. "So if I said it was okay for you to live with him, you'd have no problem?"

"No, ma'am—I mean, Your Honor."

"Since this is what your mother also provided for, I hereby grant temporary custody of James Zachary Marks to Michael Kent effective immediately, with a hearing to be scheduled in sixty days for the purpose of granting permanent custody, pending investigation by the appropriate representatives from the Department of Social Services." She pounded her gavel.

"And Father Michael?"

"Yes, Your Honor?"

"Congratulations on your Olympic medals. And your overall performance in Athens. All of us were proud for you."

Michael looked at her, surprised. "Thank you, Your Honor."

"And teach this boy how to ride a bike."

Gwen Patterson laughed. "She's a bicycle fanatic. Every day, she commutes twenty miles each way by bike, rain or shine. She sponsors races. And she takes vacation every July to see the entire Tour de France."

He thanked the attorney and asked her to continue to represent them. She gave him her card and said she'd be in touch about Jim's trust.

"So I get to live with you?" Jim asked.

"Well, Young Jim," said Michael, "it looks like you're stuck with me for life."

Jim put his hand in Michael's. "Do I still call you Father Michael?"

"We'll have to figure that out."

Chapter 51

The Finleys returned from Portland, Father John and Eileen from Sacramento, and by telephone Michael explained what had happened. He also asked Paul if they could meet in the next few days.

"Sure, Michael. I have to look over some work at the loft condos on Monday, so why don't you meet there, or I can come by the church. Say 10:00 a.m.?"

"That'll work."

"Anything in particular?"

"Yes," said Michael, "but it'll keep until Monday."

On Monday, Michael walked to the loft condos across the plaza from the church.

"Where's Jim?" Paul asked, meeting him in the front lobby. Paint, tarpaulins, piles of brick, and boxes were everywhere.

"Millie's keeping an eye on him for me."

"How are things working out?"

"They're good, Paul. It's early stages of getting to know each other, but things so far are good."

"Emma's broken up about Jenny. I keep telling her she's not responsible."

"She's not to blame," Michael said. "If anyone was responsible, it was me. There were signs. But no one could've expected this."

"She understands this in her head," Paul said, "but in her heart, well, she's being tough on herself. I wish I could spend more time with her right now, but I have to keep working on this building and try to figure out how to make a sale."

"That's what I wanted to talk to you about. Can you tell me about your lofts here?"

311

"You mean the ones I'm having trouble selling. I've still got sixteen units, the same number I had four months ago."

"You really know how to sell someone, don't you?" Michael grinned.

"You're interested?"

"I am. I'd been thinking about finding a place of my own, and now with Jim, it's taken on some urgency. We need more space."

"Well, maybe we can figure something out. I have a less-expensive development, but it's out a ways from here."

"And you're wondering how an assistant pastor in his first position could even think of affording a loft in a development"—he picked up one of the brochures—"that starts in the four hundred fifties."

"I guess that's what comes to mind."

"Why don't you show me a unit?"

Paul smiled. "Okay. This way. The model unit's on this floor."

Paul unlocked a door. The unit was large, probably three thousand square feet, decorated and furnished in high-tech style. Michael wandered around, asking questions about kitchen appliances and utilities. The hardwood floors were original to the building but repaired, cleaned, stained, and buffed to a high gloss. The overall feeling of the loft was airy and light.

"Could I see one on the fourth floor, even if it's not finished?"

Paul was amused and more than a little curious. "Sure. By the way, the parking garage is behind the structure. Each loft gets two spaces."

The loft unit Paul took him to looked completely different—larger and unfinished. Workers were still painting, and the floors had been repaired but not yet stained.

Michael loved the brick walls, although he wondered about earthquakes. "It's actually brick veneer," Paul said, guessing his thoughts. "The entire building exceeds state requirements for earthquakes. It was built in the 1920s, and we had to gut it to bring it up to code. It's one reason the price is what it is."

Michael nodded. The master bedroom was large with its own bathroom and sitting area; two smaller but still sizable bedrooms shared another bathroom.

But Michael's eyes were drawn to a partially enclosed space near the windows, adjacent to the main living area. The model unit didn't have this.

"We put this in on the upper floors because the units catch the light. It's ideal if you're an artist."

"I thought of an artist's studio as soon as I saw it," Michael said. "What does this one go for?"

"Five hundred and ten thousand dollars."

"It's really nice. I'll take it."

"What?"

"I'd like to buy it." Michael said.

"Are you sure?" asked Paul. "I mean . . ."

"I know what you mean, and yes, I'm sure. I can't beat the location for church. I love how the space feels. It's plenty of room for me and Jim, and it's obviously close to school." He paused. "And who knows, maybe one day I'll marry an artist."

"So do you want to discuss financing and mortgage?"

"No. It's cash. When do you need to have it?"

Paul frowned in puzzlement.

"Paul, I couldn't afford this on my church salary. But I've got some family money."

"You could have bargained me down twenty thousand dollars."

Michael smiled. "Which my good friend Tommy McFarland in Scotland would say proves I'm English and not a Scot because a Scot would've bargained it down by thirty thousand dollars."

"I'll sell it to you for four hundred and ninety thousand dollars."

"Let's do this. Could we leave it for now at five hundred and ten thousand dollars? And then you help me figure out what additional features might be good. Could you help with appliances?"

"I'll throw them in with the price." Paul hesitated. "Michael, given the area, this is a risk. Don't forget what happened to you right at the corner here."

"I know. But I have faith in my church and my builder. So what do I need for a down payment? I assume there's a contract."

"I have it in my car. Wait here." He stopped and looked at Michael. "You're full of surprises. But I can't tell you how grateful I am."

The first sale was the critical one that encouraged other potential buyers to see what the lofts were like. In the next three weeks, six more units sold. By the end of February, the project had sold out.

In mid-February, Michael and Jim moved in.

Chapter 52

A few days later, Michael took Jim to buy a belated Christmas present, a bicycle. At a bike shop in the Marina District, they tried various models before deciding on an Electra.

"We'll start here," Michael said, "and we'll see how you like it. Don't feel bad if you don't. We'll find another sport for you. But even if you don't want to cycle as a sport, you probably need a bike, right? Every kid needs a bike."

Michael had the store add a training wheel to one side of the back wheel, which mortified Jim but prompted him to find his balance within a couple of days. Then Michael removed it and watched Jim go. They practiced in the park near the church.

One evening in late January, Jim wandered in while Michael was sitting at the desk in the bedroom. He found Michael staring at the computer screen, tears falling down his cheeks.

"What's wrong?" he asked, climbing into Michael's lap. Michael had learned almost immediately that Jim often needed the reassurance of physical touch.

Michael shook his head. "Nothing's wrong, Young Jim. Everything's right. God is so good."

"You're crying."

Michael nodded. "Someone I care very deeply for has become a believer. Her brother sent me an e-mail. It happened a couple of months ago, but he waited until now to tell me."

"Is it the girl in the picture?" Jim asked, referring to one of the several photos of friends and family on a wall in the living area.

"How would you know that?" Michael asked, surprised.

"I've seen you looking at it. And my mom said there was someone you were in love with. I figured that might be the one."

"Yes, Young Jim, that's the one who's become a believer. And that's the one I'm in love with."

"What's her name?"

"It's Sarah."

"Does she live in Scotland?"

"No, actually she lives near Los Angeles." *And it's better not to say whose aunt she is. Not yet.*

"Can you call her?"

"I don't know, Jim. I don't know what she still feels for me. I haven't seen her since last May. I think she needs to get to know God first." He hugged Jim tightly to him. *I need the reassurance as much as Jim does.*

The Flash began to increase its practice rides, both in duration and intensity. Jim stayed with Abbie and Beau while Michael cycled with the team. He'd been careful at first to defer to Brian, but they soon began training together, both on rides separate from the team and at the gym to work on overall body strength.

Frank Weston watched his team's progress. *Brian's coming into his own as a competitive cyclist, and Michael is sparking the team to a higher level of performance.*

They began going to practice races and small-town competitions. Their first race was a disaster; the entire team was off. "Not to mention lousy," Frank said. But the team went back to Frank's house and talked the race through—what had happened, what they should've done, and how they might better position sprinters.

Michael had to miss a few Sunday morning races, but there were enough on Saturdays around northern California to help him and the team get their heads around the idea of winning.

316

They won a criterium in Fairfield and placed second in a race in Sonoma County. And then a first in Palo Alto and a third in San Jose. By the middle of April, the Flash was emerging as one of the top teams.

The Tour de Frisco was in three weeks.

Part VI

San Francisco

Chapter 53

After Hawaii, Sarah permanently moved in with her Gran, Helen. Nick Epstein, her professor, had contacted a special effects company in Santa Barbara that worked for film companies, and after several interviews Sarah was hired as a graphic artist. She devoted evenings and weekends to painting; often asked out by coworkers and acquaintances, Sarah always politely declined, knowing her heart was in Africa but not knowing what to do about it. She followed what little news there was about Malawi on the Internet, but she found nothing on the Anglican mission or Michael's work.

Helen loved watching her granddaughter work. She knew little of the "how" of art, but she loved watching Sarah become physically involved with the canvas. She'd sit in a comfortable chair and watch, sometimes for hours.

In late February, with some apprehension, Sarah took two paintings to Swenson's Gallery in downtown Santa Barbara. *The worst that can happen is they say no.* To her surprise, the owner, Moira Swenson, accepted both for display. They agreed on a price and didn't hear anything until Helen called her at work several days later.

"Sarah! The gallery called. Both paintings sold, and they want to know if you have any more." That night she went through her portfolio and decided on four others. She wasn't willing to sell the Michael paintings, which Helen playfully referred to as the "Michael Cycle." But she thought others were good—a landscape, a cityscape of Edinburgh, and two anonymous portraits— and she brought those to Moira during her lunch hour the next day.

On Saturday, Moira Swenson came to Gran's house, visibly excited.

"I have the manager from Barry's in San Francisco in the car," she said. "This morning, he saw the landscape in the window and came in. He bought the three paintings I had left, and he wants to meet you."

Barely containing herself, Sarah welcomed Richard Rendell inside. She took him and Moira to her studio, a room near the western terrace, which Helen had emptied except for her sitting chair and Sarah's painting materials. Fourteen paintings leaned against the walls or occupied an easel. Number fifteen, partially finished, sat on its own easel. Rendell walked slowly around the room, closely observing each painting. He said nothing; he simply studied the paintings. After almost an hour, Sarah thought she was going to die. Helen finally sat in her chair; Moira was so nervous she smoked four cigarettes in rapid succession on the terrace. Sarah watched Rendell.

He finally turned to her. "Are any not for sale?"

"Well, there are four."

He smiled. "And I'll show you which four they are." Walking around the room, he picked out the four comprising the "Michael Cycle," scattered among all the paintings.

Sarah was amazed. "How did you know?"

"All of these reflect a great deal of feeling, physical and emotional, an intensely personal passion, held within the almost rigid structure of the composition. Those four break out of the composition, as if you couldn't stop them. There is a tremendous depth of passion in those four, but everything in this room is superb." He pointed to *Cycle and Leg*. "That one," he said, "is almost sensual. It's as if you reached out and touched the muscles on the leg, to feel them as you painted them."

Sarah turned slightly toward the painting so Rendell wouldn't see her blush. *That's exactly what I did.*

"I'll need to confirm with Barry's," Rendell said, "but we'd like to do a show. I'll work with Moira to see if the owners who bought the others will loan them. That would round it up to about twenty or so works, a decent number to exhibit. We'll worry about what is or isn't for sale later." He and Moira packaged two of the paintings for him to take with the three he'd bought.

A week later, during which Helen and Sarah both jumped every time a phone rang, Rendell called. Barry's would do the show in early May for three weeks. Anything else she painted would also be considered.

Moira threw a party at the gallery. This was as good for her as it was for Sarah, helping establish Swenson's as a feeder to larger cities.

"I just need to find one or two more Sarah Hugheses, or they need to walk in off the street and find me," she laughed.

Helen called Scott and Barb, and they insisted that she and Sarah stay with them. "We'll take you to church," Scott said. "You'll love it. We really want you to see what's happening there."

As May approached, Barry's sent a curator to pack the remaining paintings. Sarah experienced a fleeting moment of panic as she watched her entire portfolio, especially the Michael Cycle, leave the house.

Chapter 54

The Saturday before the show, Sarah and Helen flew early from Santa Barbara and were in a taxi to downtown by ten thirty. "We may get delayed a bit," the driver said. "It's the Tour de Frisco. The cyclists will ride right in front of this place you're going to, probably right after lunch."

"You're a cycling fan?" Sarah asked.

"You're my last fare until it's over. I wouldn't miss it. Thousands of people will be lining the streets."

The cab driver was right. The streets were still open but would close by eleven thirty for the race. The sidewalks were already thronged with race fans and the curious.

Inside Barry's, the receptionist took charge of their bags as Bruno Barry himself came with Rendell to meet them. He took them to the exhibit room, and even though setup continued, the exhibit was stunning.

Twenty-two paintings comprised the show. One owner in Santa Barbara had declined to loan his, a side profile of an anonymous man (but loosely based on Tommy McFarland). Positioned among the paintings were road bikes—shiny, gleaming, and, as far as Sarah could tell, expensive.

"Bruno's marketing," Rendell explained when the owner left the room to take a call. "Because the tour is today, he's been distributing brochures to the crowds outside."

"These bikes cost more than the paintings," Sarah said.

Rendell nodded. "Bruno borrowed them from a friend at a bike shop." Sales tags were on all the paintings except the Michael Cycle. Those had a small card reading, "Artist's Personal Collection."

Finished at the galley, Sarah and Helen walked outside to find that they wouldn't be leaving anytime soon. The street was closed, and the sidewalks were crowded.

"We passed a Starbucks in the cab," Sarah said, immediately reminding herself of Mike. *As if a bike race wasn't enough.* "It's around the corner. My treat?"

"Look," said Helen. "Here come the riders."

Sarah felt like she was back in Britain again. She'd watched many of Mike's races, and while they looked the same, he'd explained how each was different with its own challenges and opportunities. *Every race, no matter how much it looks like the others, has its own story.* She smiled as the first of the sprinters flew past.

The main part of the peloton was right behind, almost caught up to the sprinting group. They were moving fast.

Sarah froze.

"Sarah, what is it?" asked Helen.

"That cyclist. In the green jersey."

She looked around and saw a man with a program. "Can you tell me who the team in green is?"

"The Frisco Flash," he replied. "They've been tearing up races all over. Here. Look at their page in the program."

Sarah looked at the team photo. Faces were too small to distinguish, but all cyclists were wearing the green uniform. She looked at the team roster.

M. Kent.

She stood there, trembling. *But it can't be Mike. He's in Africa.*

She pointed the man to the name. "Who's that?"

"Their newest member. Michael Kent. The guy who won the gold medals at the Olympics last year. He's a minister at some church here."

She handed the program back to the man, thanked him, and turned to Helen.

"It's Mike," she said. "They went by so fast I thought at first I'd made a mistake."

"You recognized him?" Helen asked. "They all look alike with the helmets and sunglasses."

326

Sarah shook her head. "I didn't recognize Mike. I recognized the scarf on his bike."

The crowds thinned. Sarah and Gran retrieved their bags and hailed a taxi.

Sarah said little during the thirty-minute ride. Images of Michael, MedFest, Christmas, and the scene with Terry Bailey kept crowding into her head.

Then came the second shock. *Scott and Barb's church. The new pastor came last August. The one who identified the woman's body. But they never said it was Mike. Surely they would've said something. What happened to Africa? Wouldn't David have said something?* Then she realized that all Scott and Barb's conversations about their church had been with Helen on the phone. With Sarah at graduation, they'd only talked about becoming believers and the couple discipling them. *But wouldn't they have thought I knew him?*

As the taxi pulled up in front of the Hughes home, Scottie came running down the walk, Scott and Barb right behind him. They greeted and hugged, and as Scott carried the bags to the house, Sarah stopped her brother.

"Scott, is Michael Kent the pastor at your church?"

He nodded. "Assistant pastor. Father John Stevens is the pastor. Didn't you know Michael in Edinburgh? He was David's roommate."

"I thought he'd gone to Africa."

"There was some switch at the last minute. He ended up here at St. Anselm's."

As they talked, Scott and Barb found Sarah totally preoccupied but attributed this to the upcoming gallery opening. At dinner, the conversation about Michael and St. Anselm's continued.

"His brother was here at Thanksgiving," Barb said, "and we had them out for dinner."

"He had a half brother, who was older," Sarah said. *The one who ordered the six-year-old out of the house, Iris said.*

Scott nodded. "That's him. His name is Henry. Same father as Michael but different mothers. Henry bunked with Michael at the church apartment, and they spent several days together. Really nice guy, too. Scottie tried to teach him how to play baseball, but he was hopeless. Michael seemed thrilled to have him here."

"Is there a boy who lives with Mike?"

"It's a terrible story, Sarah," Barb said. "His name is Jim Marks; he's Scottie's best friend at school. You should hear them sing together—they're wonderful. He and his mother started attending St. Anselm's; she became a believer the same time we did. But right at Christmas she was killed."

"What happened?" Sarah asked. *The boy and assistant pastor I prayed for.*

Scott glanced at Scottie as he played in the next room, making sure he was out of earshot. "She'd been a prostitute but was turning her life around. Her former employer didn't like the idea. The story was all over the media for several days." He explained what had happened to Jenny and Jim.

"It was awful, Sarah," Scott said. "I can't even imagine what Jenny went through. She was raped, horribly beaten, and strangled with a wire. Then there was Jim in that closet. Who knows what must've gone through Michael's mind. Michael was the one who identified her body and helped the police find Jim."

Sarah shuddered.

"Did they get the people who did this?" Helen asked.

Scott nodded. "Two men confessed and then implicated the guy who owned the club where she worked. He was convicted, but his lawyers are appealing."

"How did Jim end up with Michael?" Sarah asked.

"Jenny must've had an idea of what might happen. Her will named Michael as Jim's guardian. He didn't know about it until he found out in court. But he plunged ahead into fatherhood."

328

Sarah smiled. "It sounds like something he'd do."

"They're really good together, Sarah," Barb said. "Michael bought a loft condo from one of the church elders; it's right by the church. It's a beautiful place, although we all wonder how Michael could afford it on his salary. The brother may have helped, or Paul Finley—that's the elder—gave him a great deal. But Michael and Jim together are really something." She laughed. "Back in January, while they were still in the church apartment, Jim came down with a fever, scaring Michael to death. He called here at two in the morning, asking what to do. And this was the guy covered in blood in Athens."

"You'll see him tomorrow," Scott said, "And he's preaching. You're in for a treat."

After they cleaned up, Sarah sat on the back porch, staring into the darkness. Helen came out with a shawl and put it around her shoulders. "I thought you might need this." She smiled. "It's a little chilly at night here in the north."

"Thanks, Gran. I've just been trying to understand all of this. I think Michael's in Africa, and he's actually in San Francisco. He pastors a church, races with a cycling team, and has a child."

"He sounds like a young man who shows up, and things happen. So what do you think, dear?"

"I'm terrified about tomorrow. His life's completely different than when I knew him. I don't even know if he still cares. I don't know if I'm still a part of his life, or if he would even want me to be part of his life. Maybe I was just a college romance. I hurt him badly. He could be seeing someone now."

"Scott and Barb said nothing about there being anyone else except the boy," Helen said. "And there's the scarf."

She looked at her grandmother.

"Now, I know it may signify nothing," Helen said, "but he had the scarf on that video from the Olympics, and he had it—or one just like it—in his race today. Surely that means something."

"Maybe."

"Well, dear," Helen said as she stood, "optimism like that didn't settle the West. Tomorrow you'll know, and once you know, then you'll know what to do. Or not do. And now I'm off to bed. It's been a long day. And you think about bed as well. You don't want to show up at church tomorrow looking like something the cat dragged in." She kissed the top of Sarah's head, and Sarah squeezed her hand.

Twenty minutes later, she followed.

Chapter 55

Getting everyone ready at the Hughes household proved more difficult than expected, and they were late for the worship service. Scott and Scottie high-fived each other when they read in the paper that the Flash had won the Tour de Frisco, with Michael placing second in the individual time category, only three seconds behind his team captain, Brian Renner. Scott showed Sarah the picture of the two in the sports section.

They arrived midway through the opening hymn and found a partially empty pew about two-thirds of the way back.

An older woman wearing a large hat blocked Sarah's view of the front. But she was thankful. Although Mike probably couldn't see her from where he was, she was still apprehensive.

As Michael stood in the pulpit to begin the sermon, he looked at the congregation and frowned. It was the familiar scene before him, but something was profoundly different today, as if the air itself had changed. *What is this? What is happening here?*

When he began to speak, Sarah heard his voice for the first time in almost exactly a year. It was the same voice she remembered from Edinburgh but with something new. *It's a voice beginning to speak from experience.* It washed over her like a soft rain.

"Our text today is from chapter three of Paul's epistle to the Philippians, beginning in the thirteenth verse: 'Forgetting what is behind and straining toward what is ahead, I press on toward the goal to win the prize for which God has called me heavenward in Christ Jesus.'"

The sermon was what the congregation expected from Father Michael—a deep dive into context, how a metaphor about "the race" would have been understood by people in Philippi, why Paul might have used it, and what the goal was that Paul was pressing toward. He compared it to his own experience in cycling and discussed how a cyclist forgets the course he's just covered and focuses on what's ahead. And then he talked about how that applied to the Christian's life.

So, Mike, have you forgotten what's behind us? Are you only pressing forward? Do we have only a wonderful year at college in our memories and nothing in our future? Yet Sarah doubted her own doubts. Something was still there. Something was going to happen.

Michael prayed at the end of the sermon, a hymn was sung, and Sarah listened as the older priest pronounced the benediction. She watched Mike walk to the back as Father John began playing the postlude on the organ.

Scott and Barb chatted for a moment with the people in front of them and introduced Helen and Sarah. Sarah smiled and nodded politely, but her head was buzzing. She knew they'd soon join the line of people greeting Mike, and she was terrified.

Michael was talking with the worshippers as they left, sharing jokes and comments about yesterday's race, the weather, school ending soon, and an occasional insight about something from the sermon that had stimulated a listener's thinking.

Only a few people were left to greet. Out of the corner of his eye, he saw Jim and Scottie running around the plaza in front of the church. Last in line were Scott and Barb with an older woman.

"Michael," Scott said when they finally reached him, "congratulations on the race. What a thrill!"

"It was a great race, Scott." Michael smiled.

"Michael, we have two special guests with us this weekend. This is my grandmother, Helen Hughes, who's visiting from Santa Barbara."

Michael shook her hand and greeted her warmly. "We love Scott and Barb, Mrs. Hughes. They've become good friends. And while Scott's the doctor, Barb serves as my official children's medical consultant."

Helen laughed. "I've heard about that, and I've heard a lot about you. I'm so pleased to meet you, Michael."

"And this," Scott said, pulling Sarah from where she'd been standing behind him, "is my sister, Sarah. You probably remember her from school last year."

There they were, face-to-face.

Michael stared wordlessly at Sarah. Sarah stared back, equally silent.

Scott and Barb continued to chat but realized no one was listening. They looked from Sarah to Michael and back again.

Gran slipped her arms through theirs and said, "The three of us need to find something to do for a while. Why don't we go look for Scottie?" She guided them away as they kept glancing back at Sarah and Michael as they lingered on the church steps.

"Hi, Mike," Sarah finally said.

"Hi, Shoes."

"You look good. But a little thin."

"It's the cycling. And having to eat my own cooking."

"Your hair is longer," she said. "It looks good."

He nodded. "You look wonderful."

She smiled. "I didn't know you were here until yesterday."

He nodded.

"Gran and I came out of the gallery downtown, and I saw the peloton go by."

"You recognized me?"

She shook her head. "Not you. The scarf."

"The scarf," he said. "The one you gave me at the airport."

She nodded.

"I tie it to the bike for races," he said.

She nodded.

"To remind me of what's really important."

She nodded again.

"And it's not the race."

They stared at each other.

"I can't tell you how good it is to see you," Michael said. "I didn't know when I'd see you again."

"What happened to Africa?"

He shrugged. "Things changed. I was as surprised as anybody."

She touched his cheek. "You have a scar."

"Athens," he said.

"I saw the BBC interview on a DVD a few months after."

He nodded. "I'll give you a nickel if you touch my cheek again."

She smiled curiously at him and touched the scar again.

His hand covered hers, and he held it to his chest.

"I've missed you badly," he said. "When you got on that plane, part of my own self was torn off."

"We have to talk."

He nodded and looked at his hand atop hers. "I'm afraid to let go of it."

"Then don't," she said.

Jim and Scottie came bounding up and stopped, staring.

"He's holding her hand," Scottie whispered to Jim, who nodded.

"And what are you two rascals up to?" Michael laughed. "Jim, this is Sarah, Scottie's aunt and Scott's sister. She's visiting for a few days. We knew each other in Edinburgh last year. Sarah, this is Jim. Jim is . . . he's my son."

Sarah let go of Michael's hand to shake Jim's, who looked at her very seriously. "You're the one in the picture," Jim said.

"The picture?" she asked.

Jim nodded. "On the wall at our house." He looked at Michael.

"I've some photos of family and friends on a wall at home," Michael said. "Ma and Da, Tommy and Ellen, David and Betsy, some of the Flash, and there's one of you."

"I hope it's a good one," she said, smiling at Jim.

Scott and Barb walked up with Helen. "Michael," said Scott, looking from him to Sarah and back again, "would you and Jim like to come home for lunch? We have plenty of food, and you and Sarah can catch up on what's been going on."

Michael looked questioningly at Sarah.

"I'd like that, too, Mike."

"Then it's a plan." Michael smiled. "I have to change; we have the Flash party later. But I'd love to come." He paused and looked at Sarah. "You could ride with us, and you can look around the loft while I get this collar off." He turned to Scott. "Scottie can ride with us, too."

The Hugheses left with Helen, while Michael and Sarah walked with the two boys to the loft.

As Michael changed, Jim slipped into his room.

"You're supposed to be entertaining our guests," Michael said.

"You were holding her hand," Jim said.

"I was."

"Are you going to marry her?"

Michael looked at him. "Yes, if she'll have me."

"Will I have to leave?"

"Now where did that come from?"

Jim shrugged but kept his eyes on Michael.

"Do you remember what I said when we were in court that day?" Michael asked.

"I was stuck with you for life."

"And did I make any exceptions to that? Did I say, 'You're stuck with me for life unless I get married'? Or, 'You're stuck with me unless I grow a purple foot'?"

Jim grinned. "No."

"So that's the deal, then."

"What if she doesn't like me?"

Michael put his hands on Jim's shoulders. "How could she not like you? Jim, I'm not giving you up. Period. End of discussion. And she's going to love you."

Jim nodded, smiled, and darted out of the room.

Scottie was in Jim's room while Sarah wandered around the living areas. Michael had mounted three bicycles on the wall—his road bike, a mountain bike, and a smaller one that was obviously Jim's. *Keeps them out of the way, and they actually look attractive there.* The scarf was still tied to the road bike's handlebar. Looking closely, she could see it was clean but worn with old stains on it. *Athens.*

She liked the kitchen. She saw a few cookbooks. *He's learning to cook.* She walked through the living room and saw the photographs. There was one of her and Mike. Betsy had taken it at ExpressoYourself, she remembered. *We were laughing at something Tommy said.* Then she noticed an L-shaped divider separating something from the living area, large enough to be a separate room.

Which it was. And it was mostly empty. *He still has some decorating to do.* She looked at the space more carefully. At one end, floor-to-ceiling windows flooded the space with light. A wet bar was set into a waist-high cabinet. *Ideal for mixing colors and cleaning up.*

"It's an artist's studio," Michael said from behind, startling her. "The loft was a lot bigger than what we needed. I'd seen the model downstairs, and when Paul—that's the developer, he's our head elder at church—when he showed me this one, he pointed out how the light played through the windows and said it'd be a great space for an artist. I agreed, although both Jim and I are artistically challenged. But we love the feel of this space."

Sarah nodded. "The light here is incredible," she said. "An artist could just start painting." *He bought this place for the three of us.*

"Exactly," Michael said, smiling.

She was quiet as they drove to Scott's house. The boys in the backseat, however, managed to keep the conversation going.

After eating and cleaning up, Michael and Sarah sat in the backyard swing.

"I didn't know what to think when I learned you were here," she said. "The first thing I wanted to do was shoot Scott and David for not telling me. But Scott thought I knew; he looked so surprised when I asked. But David—"

"David was likely trying to protect us both," said Michael. "Don't be angry with him."

"But you knew I was in Santa Barbara?"

"I knew you were in Los Angeles, and then Barb said something not too long ago about you living with your grandmother."

"You could've called."

"I could have. And the thought occurred at least forty times a day."

"But you didn't."

"I didn't. I didn't know where you were spiritually, Sarah. I knew you'd become a believer, and I had to restrain myself from calling or just showing up to carry you off. Because you needed time to start getting to know God."

"That's what Pam said."

"Pam?"

"Pam Jensen. Her husband, Ted, is director of Campus Christian Ministry at UCLA. She talked with me about faith. She said almost that exact same thing—that while it was you I couldn't get out of my head, it was actually God chasing me down, and it was God I needed to know."

"I thank God for Pam Jensen," Michael said. "I'd love to meet her. But you didn't need me forcing myself into your life. You had plenty of that in

Edinburgh. I would've complicated and confused things. But I almost couldn't stand it. Knowing you were this close has been unbearable." He paused. "And I was afraid."

She smiled. "I couldn't get you out of my head, no matter how hard I tried. And then I got blocked—like writer's block—except I couldn't draw or paint anything for months. I found myself in the Campus Christian Ministry office. I walk in the door, and the first thing I see is this huge poster of you and the Canadian being lifted by the helicopter. It was like getting whacked with a two-by-four." She stopped. "Was it as bad in Athens as we saw on TV?"

He nodded. "It was terrible, Sarah. The only thing I can compare it to is war, and I've never been to war. But it's what you imagine a battlefield to be."

"You saved his life."

"Robbie?" Michael shook his head. "God saved his life. My hand just happened to be convenient."

"You've been dealing with a lot of tragedy," she said. "Athens. And Jim's mother."

"Jenny, yes."

"Scott said you identified her body."

"I did. And I would've rather been in the middle of the crash in Athens again. That was an accident. What happened to Jenny was evil."

"Jim calls you Dad."

"And I call him Son. We went round and round about what to call each other. He didn't feel right calling me Michael, and I'd become something more than Father Michael of St. Anselm's. I still call him Young Jim at times. But we decided to try Dad and Son, and it works. Although it's odd to be called Dad when I'm shy of twenty-four and my son is eight, which makes me not quite sixteen when he was born. And there's no mom around."

"Did you know his mother well?"

"Well enough."

"What was she like?"

"She was young, only twenty, but far older in experience. She was not quite thirteen when Jim was born. She didn't say much about her life, Sarah. Jim only knows that she was from Texas and he was born in Los Angeles. His birth certificate lists just her name. She was surprised we accepted Jim at St. Anselm's School because both of them were used to rejection. She'd become a believer and was turning her life around. She had told me a bit more, but not much."

"Did you care for her?"

He paused before answering. "Yes."

There was an embarrassed silence.

"I'm asking too many questions," Sarah said finally.

"And I'm saying everything wrong," Michael said. "I'm saying too much too fast."

"It's okay."

Jim came running up and whispered in Michael's ear.

"You ask her," Michael said.

Smiling, Jim shyly shook his head.

"It's your idea, and it's a great one, but you should ask." Michael grinned.

"Ask me what?" said Sarah to Jim.

"If you'd like to be our date for the team party today," Jim blurted out.

She looked at Michael.

"It's a get-together for the team after winning the Tour de Frisco," Michael said. "It's at the coach's house, Frank Weston; they live out in Marin. I second Jim's invitation."

"It's okay?" asked Sarah. "It's not just for the team and their families?"

"Well, technically it is, but some bring their girlfriends."

She looked at him. "So how do I dress?"

"It's casual, like what I have on."

She looked at his linen slacks, white open-necked shirt, and sandals. "Give me ten minutes."

Michael talked with the Hugheses while he and Jim waited.

339

Scott grinned. "Should I ask what your intentions are here, Father Michael?"

Michael smiled. "My intentions are simple, Scott. I intend to ask Sarah to be my wife. And if she'll have me—and I think she will—I'll be coming back to you as head of the family—probably this week, in fact—to ask you for her hand in marriage."

Scott and Barb stared at Michael. Helen Hughes grinned.

Sarah came down the stairs, looked at the assembled group, and said, "Is everything all right?"

"Everything's perfect," Michael said. He thanked Scott and Barb and guided her toward the door.

The three watched as they got into Michael's car and drove off.

"That young man really gets the blood going, doesn't he?" Helen said. "If Sarah doesn't say yes, I will."

Chapter 56

As they crossed the Golden Gate Bridge, Jim spoke from the backseat.

"She's going to cause a ruckus."

"What?" asked Michael as he and Sarah glanced at each other.

"I said she's going to cause a ruckus."

"And why is that?"

"Because you're showing up with a date," Jim said.

Sarah tried and failed to stifle a laugh.

"Explain yourself back there," Michael said, eyeing Sarah next to him.

"Well, you never have a date for team things. You never have a date at all. They all worry about it."

"They do? And how do you know this?"

"Because grown-ups think kids don't hear anything. First, they thought you were a Catholic priest and maybe couldn't have a date. Frank and Abbie said no. You were Anglican, and Anglican priests could marry if they wanted to. So they thought you might be gay. Brian told them no; that wasn't it. A cousin or relative of somebody on the team checked you out, and he said you weren't."

"Thanks for keeping me up to speed here, son," Michael said.

"Then," Jim said, "they thought something might be wrong with you, that maybe you did something that made girls want to run away."

Sarah was nearly convulsed with laughter at this point.

"I'm getting great support here in the front seat," Michael said.

Jim continued. "They finally decided there must be someone in Scotland you were being faithful to."

Michael rolled his eyes and shook his head.

"So they asked me. I said there wasn't anybody in Scotland, but there was somebody here in California."

"Enough," Michael said. "Mercifully, we've arrived at Frank and Abbie's." They parked the car and got out.

"They're gonna be surprised," said Jim. "You watch." And he ran to the door and rang the bell.

"Jim, as you can see, has a vivid imagination," Michael said. "I suspect most of this is invented."

"I wish I had it on tape," Sarah laughed. "Tommy would love it. So, Mike, is there someone in California?"

He hesitated before answering. "Yes," he said. "There is."

Jim rang the bell again; Abbie opened the door as she was calling, "There's more dip in the fridge" to someone behind her. She turned and saw them.

"Michael!" And then she stopped and stared at Sarah.

"I told you," Jim said as he slipped past Abbie and darted inside to look for Beau.

"Abbie, this is Sarah Hughes, a friend of mine from university," Michael said, blushing.

"Oh," Abbie said, obviously surprised. "Sarah, it's so nice to meet you. Please come in."

As Abbie closed the front door, Frank came up, opening a bottle of wine. "Michael!" And then, seeing Sarah, he stopped as if thunderstruck. Abbie introduced them.

"It looks like Jim was on to something," Sarah murmured to Michael as they followed Frank and Abbie to the kitchen and dining area at the back. The party was going full speed on the deck.

They stepped outside, and all conversation stopped.

"All right," said Michael. "It's a sign of the apocalypse. Yes, I have a date. This is Sarah Hughes. She lives in Santa Barbara, and she's in town this week. She's a friend of mine from university. She's an artist. Everyone has my permission to close their mouths."

No one said a word. Then a grinning Brian Renner walked up and introduced himself and his wife, May, to Sarah. He grinned at Michael and turned to face the group. "See, I told you he wasn't gay," he said, sparking general laughter. Turning to Sarah, he said, "I'd heard about you, but I thought you might be a figment of Michael's imagination. May was starting to worry about me because Michael and I train so much together." Michael swung a soft punch, which Brian dodged, laughing.

"I'm glad Jim warned us." Sarah smiled.

Jim fell asleep in the backseat on the way home.

"You and Brian are good friends," Sarah said.

"We are," Michael said. "It started out a bit rough, but we've gotten really close. He and May are the best. Like he said, we train together a bit."

"You're the same age?"

"He's twenty-seven. He and May have been married for five years— right out of college, in fact. They're keen to have kids but no sign yet. He's an attorney with Frank's firm, and May's a civil engineer. She works for a big engineering firm in town that does roads, bridges, big projects like that."

"He seemed to know a lot about me."

"We talk," he said. "And he saw your picture at the loft."

Sarah looked out at the lights of the city.

"I have to work tomorrow," Michael said, "but I'd like to see you again if you're free."

"I have to be at the gallery most of the day," Sarah said. "Dinner?"

"Dinner will work. I'll meet you at the gallery."

"You need to see the paintings."

"I'm inviting myself to the opening," he said.

"No, before the opening. I need you to see them."

"Tell me when and I'll be there."

"The gallery is closed on Mondays, but there shouldn't be a problem if you see them when you pick me up."

They were both quiet as Michael drove into Scott and Barb's neighborhood.

"Sarah, am I rushing you? If I am, just tell me to back off."

She smiled and touched his hand on the steering wheel. "You *are* rushing me, Mike, but I'm rushing me, too. I *want* to be rushed. And I want to rush you as well."

Michael parked the car in the driveway and looked in the backseat at a sleeping Jim before walking her to the Hugheses' door.

"So tomorrow at six then?" he asked.

"Six," she said.

He took her hand in his and folded his other hand over it.

"I can't tell you the joy I'm feeling right now," he said. *Joy.*

"Today when we got to church," she said, "I didn't know what to expect. I was mostly scared. When I heard you speak, I knew that no matter what happened next, just to hear your voice again . . ." Her voice trailed off.

He touched her forehead with his own.

She touched his cheek. He pulled her to him and softly kissed her.

When she came in the door, she saw the light in the family room. Scott was reading.

"Is my big brother waiting up for me?" She smiled.

"Well, actually I was reading. At least I thought it'd be a good excuse. Guilty as charged. Did you have a good time?"

She sat next to him on the sofa. "I'm going to marry him, Scott, when he asks me. Or I may ask him first."

He put his arm around her. "I had no idea you two had been . . . or were . . . or are . . . well, you know what I mean. Michael never said a word. And we never heard anything about this from you or David."

She nodded. "We were close. But I couldn't deal with his faith in God, and I walked away. David knows all of this, and Mike says he's been protecting both of us. What we've discovered today is that we're even closer than we were, if that's possible. I've never felt so certain. We're both on the same wavelength now, and it's unbelievable. He's changed, but he hasn't. And I've changed a lot."

"How has he changed?"

"He's been through tragedy, Scott. First, it was Athens, then Jim's mother. He's seen more in a year than many people see in ten. And his faith is intact; if anything, it's grown even deeper. His faith is one of the most attractive things about him. There's strength there, more than I could see a year ago."

"You'll be walking into a lot—marriage, motherhood, a minister's wife. It's a lot to deal with at once."

"I know. And it won't be easy. But I'm going to be with him, Scott, no matter what, even if it's eventually in Africa. Because I have more than Mike now. I have God. I think God used Mike to chase me down, and God got me, and now He's putting us in each other's hands. And that's exactly where I want to be."

He kissed her on the forehead. "You need some sleep. You've got a busy couple of days ahead. But Sarah?"

"Yes?"

"I couldn't be happier for you. And for Michael."

Chapter 57

At lunch on Monday, normally Father John's day off, the two priests met with Paul Finley and two other elders on the planning committee.

"Generally speaking," Paul said, "the church's in the best shape financially than it's been for a long time. Attendance is up thirty percent over last year, membership's up ten percent, and giving's up thirty-two percent. But that's only part of the picture."

"That's right, Paul," Father John said. "There's a spiritual renewal going on as well, and the financial side of things reflects the spiritual. Michael's coffeehouse, for example, has not only pulled in young people for music, but fifteen of them are actually attending church every Sunday."

"I attribute that to the fantastic drummer in the beret," Michael said. The men laughed.

"Seriously, it's affecting the local area," Father John said. "The merchants report a decline in shoplifting, and the serious problems, like confrontations or breaking into cars, have disappeared."

"The two adult Sunday school classes are going well?" Paul asked.

Father John nodded. "It was a real blessing to find members who wanted to teach. And in the high school class, we're averaging nineteen each Sunday," he said, nodding toward Michael.

"If this continues with the worship service," Paul said, "we may have to start thinking about a second service, and sooner rather than later."

"It's a wonderful problem to have," Father John said. "Michael and I've been talking about the possibility already. His preaching is pulling people in."

"There, Father John," Michael said, "we have something of a disagreement. It's not just the preaching. The music is spectacular. We've an expanded choir, people are stepping forward to play instruments, and we have a phenomenal organist."

"All right," said Paul, "before our mutual admiration society here gets too carried away, let's put a discussion about growth on the agenda at the next

347

board meeting. If it continues, we may also have to consider expanding staff. And we've got a number of ideas for ministry expansion as well. There's a lot to talk about."

After the meeting, Paul stood, talking with Father John. "So tell me," Paul said. "Everything says you and Michael work like hand in glove."

Father John nodded. "Paul, he's a blessing to the church body and a personal blessing to me. He questions but never complains. He's always positive. He's full of ideas, but he listens and pays heed. He's deferential to the older members of the congregation and has a way about him that endears him to people. I should be jealous, I suppose, but I'm not. I feel blessed. He's freed me to focus on worship and music, and I feel my own ministry is thriving. My only concern is that someone will try to snatch him away."

"That's my worry, too, Father John, but God may have other plans. In fact, I'd be surprised if God didn't have big plans for Father Michael. In the meantime, we're all glad he's here."

"Paul, have you noticed something different about him today? He's positively radiant."

Paul nodded. "It's almost like he's fallen in love."

The fifth-grade teacher and her husband lived in the loft building, and she readily agreed to watch Jim while Michael and Sarah went out. "On the condition, Father Michael," she said, "that you give me all the details."

At four, Michael got Jim squared away for the evening and then changed clothes, deciding on a navy sport coat and khaki slacks with one of the bow ties he liked to wear when he wasn't "in collar" or biking.

At the gallery, Sarah introduced him to Richard Rendell and Bruno Barry. It was still chaotic, with last-minute changes in the exhibit, decisions on where to put refreshment tables, and an idea for streamers that Richard was trying to talk Bruno out of.

"Mike, it's this way," said Sarah. She led him to the exhibit room.

In the exhibit room, Michael stared. His eyes were drawn to the Michael Cycle, which Richard had positioned with the bicycles. He moved closer and looked to see their titles. Sarah stood and watched.

Hands.

Cycle and Leg.

Bicycle.

Mike, Airport.

The painting entitled *McLarens'* was grouped with two other landscapes, which he hadn't seen yet.

Michael stared at the four, not speaking. Sarah began to feel a small wave of apprehension. *What if it's too personal? Will he feel betrayed or violated? What if he hates them?*

He turned and looked at her. His expression was unreadable. He turned back to the paintings. She felt her anxiety ratcheting upward. *Oh, no, he's not saying anything. This isn't good. Please say something, anything.*

He looked at the other paintings, stopping in front of *McLarens'*. When he looked at her, she could see tears in his eyes.

"It's unbelievable how much I miss Scotland," he said. "This is like being home." He continued walking around, looking at the entire exhibit, then returned to the Michael Cycle.

"Can I tell you what I see here?" he asked.

She nodded. "Please."

"I see us. I see the love and the pain, and hope and bewilderment, too. I see two people trying to reach out to each other, but a wall stops them. And then the wall comes down. And I see God." He gestured to the four paintings. "You painted *Mike, Airport,* the last of these four?"

"It was actually the fifth one. *McLarens'* came after the first three and before *Mike, Airport*."

"I told you yesterday that when you left, it was as if part of me had been torn off."

"Yes."

"You painted it here," he said.

She watched him.

"It's as if you knew that when you painted it, maybe not before but certainly when you painted this, you knew it."

She nodded.

He turned back to the painting.

"I painted *Hands* first," she said. "I think I know why. I fell in love with your hands first."

"My hands?"

"At the faculty club, the dinner where I died of embarrassment. You pointed to the menu, and I fell in love with your hands. They were beautiful, delicate, yet so strong. I thought right there that I could feel safe in those hands, and I had no idea where that thought came from."

He looked at her.

"Then," she said, "I painted *Cycle and Leg*."

"I know where that came from," Michael said.

"You remember?"

"I'll never forget it. I'd finished a training ride, we were in the gym, and you needed to draw a part of a human body for an assignment. I felt like I was shattering into pieces when you touched my leg. You were totally focused on the drawing, and you needed to feel my calf to draw it true, I think. Good thing you didn't see my face because it would've told you that it was the most intimate thing that'd ever happened to me."

"When Richard saw it in Santa Barbara, he called it almost sensual."

"He was right," Michael said. "It took me hours to recover. Thinking about it even now is unsettling."

350

"I had no idea," she said, blushing.

"And I wasn't going to enlighten you."

"*Bicycle* was the hardest of the first three," she said. "I don't know why."

"I see Athens," said Michael.

"I did it after watching the program from the BBC. I found the DVD in a bike shop near campus."

"I don't know why I think Athens, but I do." He paused. "You have a great gift, Sarah Hughes. God's blessed you with something more than the ability to draw and paint. Lots of people have that. Hardly anyone has this. I'm overwhelmed and a bit awed."

"You like them, then?"

"I love them. It's like I'm looking at a glimmer of creation. I'm glad I saw them before tomorrow night." He looked at the title cards. "The four here say they're part of the artist's private collection, so you're not selling them?"

"I couldn't," she said. "And I can hardly bear to think of selling *McLarens'*."

"Well, that's not a problem because I'm buying it. Ma and Da will love it. So tell Mr. Barry to put a sold sign on it." He paused. "I'm starving. I never knew you could get hungry looking at art."

They found a restaurant nearby. Sitting side by side in a curved booth, they examined the menu. When they'd ordered and were sipping their wine, Michael spoke.

"So," he said, "here we are. And I keep trying to think how to say this."

"Say what?"

"How do I say I love you, that I've loved you from the first moment I saw you in Fitzhugh's class? That I want to be at your side for always. I want you painting in that artist space in the loft and then coming into my arms and making love with me. I suppose I just said it, didn't I?"

She nodded.

"So, Sarah Hughes, if you'll have me, I'm asking you to marry me, to join with me in whatever God has in store for us." He placed the ring box in front of her.

She opened it and looked up at him. "Oh, Mike," she whispered. "Oh yes, I will marry you." He put the ring on her finger. "It's beautiful," she said. "You're beautiful. I'm going to cry." He kissed her just as the waiter walked up with their salads.

"I can come back," the waiter said, appearing confused and embarrassed.

"Serve them, sir," Michael said, laughing.

When the waiter was gone, Sarah looked at the ring box.

"Mike, it's from Forrester's."

"Yes."

"In Edinburgh."

"The very same."

"When did you get it?"

"A little over a year ago."

She looked at him. "A year ago?"

He nodded. "Right before *The Mikado*."

"You were planning to propose the night of *The Mikado*?"

He nodded.

"Oh, Mike." She looked at him. "Why didn't you return it?"

"It wasn't the plan." He put his hand on hers. "And you were worth waiting for."

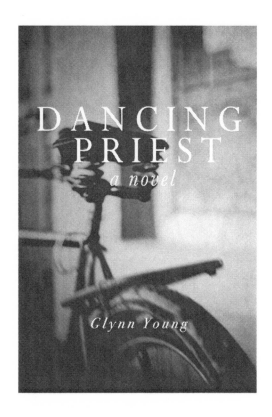

Dancing Priest is also available on Kindle, NOOK and iBook.

And look for the next book in the *Dancing Priest* series in Summer 2012.

About the Author

Glynn Young is an award-winning speechwriter and public relations professional. His speeches have appeared numerous times in *Vital Speeches of the Day* and other national publications, and he's published numerous articles on communications in journals and magazines.

He received two Gold Quill Awards for speechwriting from the International Association of Business Communicators; seven other national speechwriting awards; and two Silver Anvil Awards from the Public Relations Society of America for community relations and employee communications.

Glynn has given hundreds of presentations and speeches on crisis communications, environmental communications, employee communications and speechwriting.

He was named a Fellow of the Public Relations Society of America in 2005 and to the St. Louis Media Hall of Fame in 2009.

A native of New Orleans, Glynn received his B.A. in Journalism degree from Louisiana State University and his Masters of Liberal Arts degree from Washington University in St. Louis.

He is a contributing editor for The High Calling (http://www.thehighcalling.org) and a contributing writer to The Master's Artist (http://aratus.typepad.com/tma/). He blogs at Faith, Fiction, Friends (http://faithfictionfriends.blogspot.com).

He and his wife Janet have two grown sons, Travis and Andrew; a daughter-in-law, Stephanie; and a grandson, Cameron. They live in suburban St. Louis, and are members of Central Presbyterian Church.

Dancing Priest is his first novel.

CPSIA information can be obtained at www.ICGtesting.com
Printed in the USA
BVOW061136040412

286822BV00002B/200/P